ATTILA

THE ATTILA TRILOGY BY WILLIAM NAPIER

Attila

Attila: The Gathering of the Storm*

Attila: Judgment*

*Forthcoming

ATTILA

WILLIAM NAPIER

ST. MARTIN'S GRIFFIN

NEW YORK

ATTILA. Copyright © 2005 by William Napier. All rights reserved. Printed in the United States of America. For information, address St. Martin's Press, 175 Fifth Avenue, New York, N.Y. 10010.

www.stmartins.com

ISBN 978-0-312-59898-3

First published in Great Britain by Orion Books Ltd

First U.S. Edition: February 2010

10 9 8 7 6 5 4 3 2 1

IN MEMORY OF STEVEN THORN

1965–2003

BEST OF FLATMATES, BEST OF FRIENDS

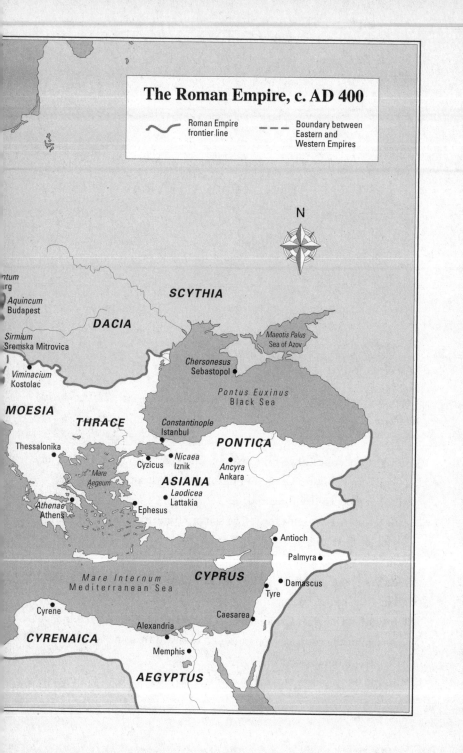

The Roman Empire, c. AD 400

Roman Empire frontier line

Boundary between Eastern and Western Empires

N

SCYTHIA

ntum
rg

Aquincum
Budapest

DACIA

Sirmium
Sremska Mitrovica

Maeotis Palus
Sea of Azov

Viminacium
Kostolac

Chersonesus
Sebastopol

Pontus Euxinus
Black Sea

MOESIA

THRACE

Constantinople
Istanbul

Thessalonika

PONTICA

*Mare
Aegeum*

Cyzicus

Nicaea
Iznik

Ancyra
Ankara

ASIANA

Laodicea
Lattakia

Athenae
Athens

Ephesus

Antioch

Palmyra

Mare Internum
Mediterranean Sea

CYPRUS

Damascus

Tyre

Cyrene

Caesarea

CYRENAICA

Alexandria

Memphis

AEGYPTUS

LIST OF PRINCIPAL CHARACTERS

Characters marked with an asterisk were real historical figures. The rest might have been.

Aëtius* (pronounced Eye-EE-shuss)—born 15 August, 398. The son of Gaudentius, Master General of Cavalry, in the frontier town of Silestria, in modern-day Bulgaria

Attila*—born 15 August, 398. The son of Mundzuk, the son of Uldin, King of the Huns

Beric*—a Vandal prince

Bleda* (pronounced BLAY-da)—the older brother of Attila

Cadoc—the son of Lucius

Claudian*—Claudius Claudianus, an Egyptian, born in Alexandria. A favorite in the court of Honorius, and regarded by some as the last of the great Roman poets

Eumolpus*—a palace eunuch

Galla Placidia* (pronounced Galla Pla-SID-ia)—born 388. The daughter of the Emperor Theodosius, sister of the Emperor Honorius, and mother of the Emperor Valentinian

Gamaliel—wanderer, wise man, holy fool

Genseric*—a Vandal prince

Heraclian*—Master General of the Roman Army in the West after the death of Stilicho

Honorius*—born 390. The son of the Emperor Theodosius, and himself Emperor of Rome 395–423

Little Bird—a Hun shaman

Lucius—an ordinary Roman officer, British by birth

Marco—a Roman centurion

Mundzuk*—the elder son of Uldin, and briefly King of the Huns

Olympian*—a palace eunuch

Orestes*—a Greek by birth, and the lifelong companion of Attila

Priscus of Panium*—a humble and unremarked scribe

Ruga*—the younger son of Uldin, and King of the Huns from 408–441

Serena*—wife of Stilicho

Stilicho* (pronounced STIL-i-ko)—half barbarian by birth, and Master General of the Roman Army in the West until his murder in 408

Uldin*—King of the Huns until 408

PROLOGUE

The Monastery of St. Severinus,

near Neapolis, AD 488

My father always told me that there are two things you need to be a great historian. "You need to be able to write," he said, "and you need to have things to write about." His words sound ironic to me now. Yes, father: I have things to write about. Things you would hardly believe.

I have the greatest and most terrible of stories to tell. And in these dark ages, when the skills of the historian are rare to find, I may very well be the last man on earth who can tell it.

My name is Priscus of Panium, and I am nearly ninety years old. I have lived through some of the most calamitous times in the history of Rome, and now that story is ended, and Rome is done. Titus Livy wrote about the Founders of Rome. It falls to me to write of the Last Defenders; and of the Destroyers. It is a story for bitter winter nights; it is a story of horror and atrocity, shot through with saving gleams of courage and nobility. It is in many ways an appalling story, but it is not, I think, a dull one. And although I am very old, and my palsied hand shakes as it holds the pen over these vellum pages, nevertheless I believe I have the strength remaining in me to tell the final chapters of the tale. Strange as it may seem, I know that when I have written the last word of my tale my time on earth will be done. Like St. Severinus, I know the day of my own death.

St. Severinus? He is being buried, even as I write, in the chapel of this monastery where I scratch out my last days. He lived as a missionary, a holy man and a servant of the poor, in the province of Noricum, beyond the Alps, and he played an unexpected role in the last days of Rome. He died some six years ago, but only now have his devoted followers been able to bring his body back over the high Alpine passes, and down through Italy, miracles attending his progress every step of the way. Who am I to question such miracles? We live in mysterious times.

This monastery where I now live, on the sun-warmed coast near Neapolis, cared for so kindly by monks whose faith, I confess, I hardly share, this monastery itself, now dedicated to St. Severinus and to the religion of Christ, has a strange and instructive history. Once it was the luxurious seaside villa of Lucullus, one of the great heroes of republican Rome, in the first century before Christ; in the time of Cicero, Caesar, Pompey, and the rest. (There were giants on the earth in those days.) Lucullus was celebrated above all else for his brilliant victory over Mithridates, King of Pontus; although epicures have always joked that, as achievements go, they much more admire his introduction into Italy of the cherry.

After Lucullus's death, the villa passed through various hands, until finally, by one of the many strange ironies that so delight Clio, the muse of history, it became, after his forced abdication, the residence of the last Emperor of Rome: little, golden-haired, six-year-old Romulus Augustulus.

Today it is home to over a hundred monks, who are now standing round the coffin containing the mortal remains of their beloved St. Severinus, their voices rising to heaven in their sad, melodious chanting, amid the smoke of incense and the glitter of sacred gold. It was Severinus who told Odoacer the Ostrogoth that his destiny lay in the sunlit lands to the south. It was Odoacer who deposed the last emperor, Romulus Augustulus, disbanded the Senate, and declared himself the first barbarian King of Italy.

There is little else you need to know about me. I live a simple life in my quiet cell, or hunched in the chill scriptorium, with only my vellum and my pen and my near ninety years of memories for company. I am but a recorder, a scribe. A storyteller. When people are gathered round the fire on a cold winter's evening, they listen to the storyteller's words, but they do not mark his face. They do not look at him as they listen. They look into the fire. They do not see him; they see what he tells them. He, as it were, does not exist. Only his words exist.

Plato said there are three types of people in life, as at the games. There are the heroes, who take part, and enjoy the glories of victory. There are the spectators, who stand and observe. And there are the pickpockets. I am no hero, it is true. But I am no pickpocket, either.

The sun is going down, far out over the tired Tyrrhenian Sea, where the great grain ships used to ply their way through the salt furrows from North Africa to Ostia, to feed the million mouths of Rome. Now they sail no more. North Africa is a hostile Vandal kingdom, the grain fields are lost, and the Vandals have looted and taken back with them to Africa any treasures the Goths had not already taken—even the priceless treasures of the temple in Jerusalem, which Titus brought to Rome in triumph four centuries ago. What has become of those treasures? The golden Ark of the Covenant, which contained the commandments of God Himself, they say? Melted down into Vandal coin long since. Likewise, the Column of Trajan today stands bare of the great bronze statue of the soldier-emperor that once stood atop its height, and the bronze itself is melted down in the smoking backstreet smithies, and turned into belt buckles and bracelets and barbarous shield bosses.

Rome is a shadow of the city she once was, and not immortal after all. No more immortal than the men who built her, though we once believed it when we cried, *"Ave, Roma immortalis!"* at the triumphs and the games.

No, not an immortal goddess, only a city like any other; like an old and tired woman, ravaged and abused and cast aside, deserted by her lovers and weeping sore in the night, like Jerusalem before her, and Troy, and timeless Thebes. Sacked by the Goths, ransacked by the Vandals, captured by the Ostrogoths—but the most damage was done by a people more terrible and yet more invisible than any of these: a people called the Huns.

In the ghostly shell of Rome today, the stray, half-starved cats scratch about in the ruins of the Forum, and weeds grow from the cracks in the once golden buildings. Starlings and kites make their nests in the eaves of palaces and villas where generals and emperors once talked.

The sun has set and it is cold in my chamber, and I am very old. My supper is a little white bread and a mouthful or two of thin, watered wine. The Christian monks with whom I live, in this high and lonely monastery, teach that sometimes this bread and this wine are the flesh and blood of God. It is true that wonders are many, and even this may be so. But to me it is only bread and wine; and it will suffice.

I am an historian with a great and terrible story to tell. I am nothing, but it seems I have known everything. I have read every letter, every scrap of chronicle and history that survives from the times I have lived through. I have known and spoken with every principal player upon the stage of history during those tumultuous and world-shaking years. I have been a scribe in the courts of both Ravenna and Constantinopole, and I have served both General Aëtius and Emperor Theodosius II. I have always been a man in whom people have confided, while remaining discreet myself; although when intimate gossip and rumor have come my way I have not closed my ears, but have listened as attentively as I would to the most solemn and objective accounts of mighty deeds and battles, believing with the playwright Terence that *"Homo sum; humani nil a me alienum puto."* They are fine words, and stand for my motto, as they might for any writer whose subject is human nature itself. "I am human; and nothing human is alien to me."

I have known the Eternal City on the Seven Hills, I have known the scented court of Ravenna, I have known the golden, heavenly City of Constantine. I have traveled up the mighty Danube river, and through the Iron Gates and down into the heartland of the Huns, and heard from his own lips of the extraordinary early years of their dread king himself; and survived to tell the tale. And I have stood on the wide champaign country of the Catalaunian Fields, and seen where two of the greatest armies of all time came so bloodily together, in a clash of arms and a cloud of fury such as no other age has ever known, and where the fate of the world was decided: a fate so strange that it was unforeseen by any of the combatants. But some wise men knew. The singers and the seers and the Last of the Hidden Kings: they knew.

I have known slaves and soldiers, harlots and thieves, saints and sorcerers, emperors and kings. I have known a woman who ruled the Roman world, first in place of her idiot brother, and then for her idiot son. I have known an emperor's beautiful daughter, who offered herself in marriage to a barbarian king. I have known the last and noblest Roman of them all, who saved an empire which was already lost, and died for his pains at the point of an emperor's dagger. And I have known the small, fierce friend he played with in his careless boyhood, on the wide and windy plains of Scythia—the boyhood friend who in adulthood became his deadliest enemy; who rode at the head of half a million horsemen, darkening the sky with their storms of arrows, and destroying all in their path like a forest fire. At the last the two boyhood friends faced each other as old and tired men, across the battle lines upon the Catalaunian Fields. And though neither could see it, it was a battle they both must lose. Our noblest Roman lost all that he loved, but so, too, did his barbarian enemy: Romulus's dark brother, the shadow of Aeneas, whom men called Attila, King of the Huns, but who also rejoiced in the name his terrified victims gave him: the Scourge of God.

Yet, out of that fury of battle and destruction at the end of the world, a new world was born; is still being slowly and miraculously born, out of the ashes, like hope itself. For as a wise man used to say to me, with his old and care-worn smile, "Hopes may be false; but nothing deceives like Despair."

And all these things are God. So says the wisest of all poets, grave Sophocles. Unfathomably he describes to us all things both light and dark: nobility and courage, love and sacrifice, cruelty, cowardice, atrocity, and terror. Then he calmly tells us:

And all these things are God. . . .

PART I

THE WOLF IN THE PALACE

1

STORM FROM THE EAST

Tuscany, early August 408

A bright dawn was breaking over the sun-baked plains beside the River Arno. Around the walls of the grim frontier town of Florentia, the exhausted remnants of Rhadagastus's barbarian army were awakening, to find themselves no longer surrounded by the implacable legionaries of Rome. Slowly, uncertainly, and with a defeated air, they began to break camp and make for the hills to the north.

On another hill to the south, commanding a fine view of the retreat, and surveying the scene with some satisfaction, sat two Roman officers on horseback, resplendent in breastplates of bronze and plumes of scarlet.

"Shall I give the order, sir?" said the younger of the two.

General Stilicho kept his gaze on the unfolding scene below. "Thank you, Tribune, but I shall do it myself when good and ready." Impertinent puppy, he thought, with your bought commission and your unscarred limbs.

From far below arose clouds of dust, partially obscuring the sight of the barbarians' great wooden wagons as they creaked and rolled out of the camp and made their way northward. The two Roman officers on the hill could hear the crack of bullwhips and the cries of men as this motley and vagabond army of Vandals and Sueves, renegade Goths, Lombards, and Franks, began its long retreat back beyond the Alpine passes to their tribal homelands.

Rome would survive their attentions a little longer yet.

Rhadagastus's ferocious horde of Germanic warriors had been united only in their lust for gold, and their fierce delight in destruction. They had cut a crimson swathe across half of Europe, from their homelands on the cold Baltic shores, or out on the vast Scythian steppes, to the vineyards of Provence and the golden hills of Tuscany, until they eventually came to a halt at the city of Florentia. Once there, they besieged that sternly fortified colony of Rome on the banks of the Arno. But the great General Stilicho, as imperturbable as ever, rode north from Rome to meet them, with an army perhaps only a fifth the size of Rhadagastus's— but an army trained in the arts of siege craft as well as war.

As is so often said, for every day that a Roman soldier wields a sword, he spends a hundred days wielding a shovel. No one digs a trench like a Roman soldier. And soon the besiegers of the city found themselves in turn besieged. The surrounding army, though fewer in number, had access to vital supplies from the nearby country, to food and water, fresh horses, and even new weaponry. The surrounded army, however, forcibly enclosed in its camp under the heat of the Tuscan August sun, was in no better circumstances than Florentia itself. The trapped barbarians had no resources they could draw on, and slowly began to expire.

In desperation, the frustrated and stricken Germans threw themselves against the barriers that surrounded them, but to no avail. Their horses shied and whinnied, hooves cruelly pierced by the iron caltrops the Romans had scattered across the hard-baked ground, throwing their furious riders beneath the unyielding entrenchments and ramparts, where they were soon despatched by archers up on the embankment. Those who tried to attack their besiegers on foot found themselves having to descend into a ditch six feet in depth, and then struggle out the far side, an equal climb, and up against three lines of wicked sharpened staves. Behind them were lined the Roman spearmen with their long, thrusting javelins. It was an impossible barrier. Those barbarians not slain on the barricades returned to their tents and lay down in exhaustion and despair.

When Stilicho reckoned Rhadagastus had lost as much as a third of his forces, he gave the order for the Romans to break camp in the night and withdraw into the surrounding hills. And so now, as dawn broke, the baffled and exhausted northern tribes found themselves free to move off as well—homeward.

Nevertheless, once they were rolling and in thorough disorder, it would be good to send in the new auxiliaries and see what they could do. Stilicho took no fine pleasure in seeing men cut down on a battlefield—unlike some generals he could mention. But the vast and undisciplined rabble below, which that troublesome warlord Rhadagastus had pulled together for the summer campaigning season, remained a threat to Rome's northern borders, even in defeat. A final harrying attack from these new mounted troops, however lightweight, would certainly do no harm.

At last, with the barbarian army chaotically strung out across the plain, and its vanguard nudging into the foothills to the north, General Stilicho gave the nod.

"Send them in," he said.

His tribune relayed the signal down the line, and only moments later Stilicho saw with some surprise that the auxiliaries had already started their gallop.

Not that he expected much from them. They were small men, these new warriors from the east, and lightly armed. They favored their neat bows and arrows over all other weapons, and even rode into battle with lassos—as if about to ride down a bunch of sleepy-eyed heifers! Who ever won a battle with mere rope? And Rhadagastus's warriors, even in defeat, were no sleepy-eyed heifers.

As well as being small and lightly armed, these horsemen fought without armor, naked to the waist, with only a fine coating of dust over their coppery, leathery skins for protection. They would do little damage to the retreating army, it was clear, but it would be interesting to see them in action, all the same. No Roman had yet seen them fight, although many had heard vainglorious and unlikely reports of their prowess at arms. They were said to move fast on their shaggy little steppe ponies, so perhaps some use could be found for them in future in the imperial courier service . . . With luck, they might even manage to ride down Rhadagastus himself, and bring him in as a captive. It was a long bow shot, but worth a try.

Well, reports of their impressive turn of speed, at any rate, had not been exaggerated.

The horsemen came thundering out from a shallow valley to the east, and made straight for the stricken column of retreating barbarians. Good enough tactics: the sun behind them, and straight in their enemies' eyes. Stilicho was too far away to see the expressions on the faces of Rhadagastus's men, of course, but the way the column slowed, and jostled, and the air filled with panicked cries, and then the heavy wagons lurched desperately forward again, trying to make for the safety of the rough ground and the hills before the furious charge of the eastern horsemen could hit them—such things told him Rhadagastus's warriors weren't smiling.

The horsemen's thunderous charge drummed up a fine dust from the sun-baked late-summer plains, and Stilicho and his tribune strained to see. Then something darkened the air between them. At first they could barely comprehend.

"Is that . . . Is that what I think it is, sir?"

Stilicho was dumbfounded. It was indeed what it seemed. The very air was dark with them. An unimaginable storm of arrows.

He had heard that these people were good on horseback; and he had heard good things of their unprepossessing little bows. But nothing had prepared him for this.

The arrows fell in an endless rain, like murderous stinging insects, upon Rhadagastus's outflanked column, and the stricken Germans began to grind to a halt, their path blocked by the piled-up corpses of their own men. Then the horsemen, the fury of their charge undiminished even after covering a mile or more of hard, sunbaked ground—long after a troop of Roman cavalry would have begun to slacken and tire— scythed into the aghast and petrified column.

Both Stilicho and his tribune had their fists bunched up on the pommels of their saddles, pushing themselves up and straining to see.

"In the Name of Light," murmured the general.

"Have you ever seen anything like it, sir?" said the tribune.

The horsemen cut through the column in seconds, then, with unbelievable dexterity, wheeled round and cut in again from the other side. Rhadagastus's warriors, even after their weeks of starvation and sickness under the walls of Florentia, were now trying to establish some kind of formation and repel the attack. These tall, blond spearmen, these fierce and skilful swordsmen, fought back with the ferocity of the doomed. But the ferocity of their attackers was greater. Nearer to where they sat their horses, the two Roman officers could see breakaway groups of mounted auxiliaries wheeling and turning about as if with pure delight, effortlessly slaughtering the helpless, milling Germans. And they also saw the deadly effect of the easterners' lassos. Any barbarian who tried to mount up and ride was instantly brought down again by the whistle and lash of the cruel noose, cast with terrible, casual accuracy. The victim fell in a tangle of reins and limbs, and was quickly despatched where he lay.

Stilicho watched with amazement as the horsemen, even up close, long after Roman cavalry would have drawn their longswords, continued to use their short bows and arrows. He could now see, as the fighting spread out in disorder below them, why their fighting skill was so renowned. He watched a single horseman notch an arrow to his bow, fire it into the back of a fleeing German, and snatch another arrow from his quiver as he swung round on his horse's bare back. He notched it, leaned down at an incredible angle to take cover alongside the body of his mount, holding on with his thigh muscles alone, then sprang back up and loosed another arrow almost into the face of a German running at him with ax swinging. The arrow punched straight through and came out of the back of the axman's head in a spew of blood and brain. The horseman had notched another arrow to his bow and galloped on before the warrior hit the ground.

Galloped! The entire encounter had been executed, before Stilicho's disbelieving eyes, at full gallop. And there was no sign of its ferocity abating.

"Name of Light," he breathed again.

Within minutes, the plain was strewn with barbarian dead and dying. The eastern horsemen at last slowed their mounts to a walk as they patrolled the bloody field, despatching the last of the fallen with occasional arrows or spear thrusts. None of them dismounted. The dust began to settle. The sun still slanted in low from the east and illuminated the scene in a gentle golden glow. Only minutes had passed since dawn broke.

The general and his tribune at last turned and looked at each other. Neither said a word. Neither could think of a word to say. They spurred their horses forward and rode on down the hill to salute their new auxiliaries.

Under a hastily erected awning at the edge of the battlefield, Stilicho settled his powerful frame awkwardly on a tottering camp stool and prepared to receive the warlord of the auxiliary horsemen. Uldin, he was called. "King Uldin," he styled himself.

Before long he appeared, as small and unprepossessing as his people's horses or bows. But within that odd, short, bow-legged frame, the same wiry, inexhaustible strength.

Stilicho did not rise, but nodded courteously. "It was good work that you did today."

"It is good work that we do every day."

Stilicho smiled. "But you have not brought in Rhadagastus?"

Now Uldin smiled. His curious, slanted eyes glittered, but not with mirth. He clicked his fingers, and one of his men stepped up close behind him.

"Here," said Uldin. "Here he is."

The warrior moved forward and dropped a dark, sodden sack at Stilicho's feet.

The general grunted and plucked open the sack. He had seen enough of the raw realities of battle in his thirty years of soldiering to be undismayed by the sight of severed heads and limbs. All the same, the dismembered remains of Rhadagastus—his hands trailing purple sinews from their ragged wrists, his blood-spattered face and splayed eyes staring back up at him out of the gloom of the sack—slowed his heart for a moment or two.

So this was the great Germanic warlord who had promised to slaughter two million Roman citizens and hang every senator from the eaves of the Senate House. Who had said he'd leave the senators' corpses hanging there from the Senate House to be picked clean by the crows, then the bare skeletons would clang together like bone bells in the wind—the man had been a poet.

A little less wordy now, old friend? thought Stilicho.

When he looked up, he said, "My orders were for Rhadagastus to be taken alive."

Uldin remained expressionless. "That is not our way."

"No, it is the Roman way."

"Do you give King Uldin orders, soldier?"

Stilicho hesitated. He knew diplomacy was not his strong point. Soldiers said what they thought. Diplomats said what others wanted to hear. But for now he must try to . . . Besides, you should always tread warily with a man who refers to himself in the third person.

Uldin took advantage of the general's hesitancy. "Remember," he said softly, stroking the thin, gray wisp of beard that barely covered his chin, "the Huns are your allies, not your slaves. And alliances, like bread, can be broken."

Stilicho nodded. He would also remember, for the rest of his life, the way the Huns fought. God help us, he thought, if they should ever . . .

"When we ride into Rome in triumph, later this month," he said, "you and your warriors will ride with us."

Uldin relaxed a little. "So we will," he said.

With that, he turned on his heel and walked out into the sunshine.

2

THE EYE OF THE EMPEROR

Rome, late August 408

The Imperial Palace lay in silence under the starlit summer sky.

The boy was sweating under his thin bedsheet, his brow furrowed with furious concentration and his hand clutching the handle of his squat little knife. Tonight he would creep out of his chamber into the shadows of the palace courtyard, he would slip past the night guards unseen, and he would gouge out the eyes of the Emperor of Rome.

He heard the night guards go past his door, talking in low, lugubrious voices. He knew what they were talking about: the recent defeat of the ragtag barbarian armies of Rhadagastus. The Roman army had defeated them, sure enough, but only with the help of their new allies: that ferocious, despised tribe from the east. Without the help of such allies, the Roman army was too weak and demoralized to take the field against so much as a phalanx of perfumed Greeks.

When the guards had gone, and the tremulous orange flicker of their torches had died away, the boy slipped out from under his sheet, swiped the sweat from his face with a cupped hand, and crept to the door. It opened easily, for he had taken the precaution of dripping olive oil over the hinges during the day. Then he was out into the courtyard. The heat of the Italian summer night was oppressive. Not a dog barked from the alleyways, not a cat screeched from the rooftops. The distant hubbub of the great city could not be heard tonight.

He heard the footsteps coming closer again. There were two of them: battered old soldiers, retired from the frontier guard. The boy pressed himself into the shadows.

The two guards paused for a moment and one stretched back his hunched shoulders. They were only a few feet away from the boy, standing between two columns against the moonlight, silhouettes as black as doors into a tomb. As black and sightless as a blinded emperor's eyes.

"And then, Rhadagastus said, he'd fill the Senate House with straw and set a torch to it, and leave it nothing but a field of blackened rubble."

The other guard, tough old soldier that he was, fell into a pensive silence for a moment or two. Even if the Senate was nowadays only an emasculated shadow of its former self—even if, as everyone knew, the empire was really run by the imperial court and its few plutocratic cronies, regardless of what the Senate might or might not want—nevertheless, the Senate House represented all that was proudest and most venerable in Rome. For a barbarian force to sweep in and destroy it . . . that would have been a shame unspeakable.

But the barbarians had been defeated. For now. With the help of other barbarians.

In the shadows behind the two old soldiers crouched the boy with his knife.

Every night, he had to pass down that long, lonely corridor in this remote, silent courtyard of the palace on the Palatine Hill, followed by the blood-chilling gaze of the first and greatest emperor. At the far end lay his miserable little chamber—no lavish suite for him—with its single guttering cheap clay lamp, as if he were no more than a *slave*. Such was his accommodation: a bare wooden bed in a windowless cell at the back of the palace, immediately adjacent to the kitchen quarters. The indignity of it all was not lost on the boy, Rome's supposedly most valued hostage. In other chambers around the palace lived other young hostages of other barbarian peoples: Sueves and Vandals, Burgundians and Gepids, Saxons and Alemans and Franks; but even they looked down upon him as the lowest of the low, and refused to admit him to their conversations or games. And their contempt kindled further his always fierce heart.

Tonight he would have his revenge on those unforgiving imperial eyes, and on all those months of slaps and sneers and scornful Roman laughter. The Romans were terrified of omens, as riven with superstitious dread as any people he knew. They feared the garbled prophecies of every toothless old hag in the marketplace, every misbegotten birth of ewe or mare, every portent that their wide eyes saw in the wind or the stars.

The boy believed in Astur, the god of his people, and in his knife; but the Romans, like all weak people, believed in everything. When they saw that great first emperor of theirs suddenly blinded . . . then the boy would see what happened to that scornful Roman laughter. It would freeze in their lily-white throats.

In the tumult of tomorrow's celebrations and games, he would escape. He would soon be far, far away from this corrupt and festering city, heading north into the mountains. After many weeks' or months' hard journeying, he would descend from them again with the sun behind him, and he would be back on the wide and windy plains of his beloved steppe country before the first snows fell. Here, he was nothing but a hostage: a barbarian hostage, caged in a windowless chamber in this decrepit Imperial Palace, in this crabbed, cobwebbed, anxious, doomed old city. But there, among his fierce, free people, he was a prince of the royal blood, the son of Mundzuk, the son of King Uldin himself. Uldin was the son of Torda, the son of Berend, the son of Sulthan, the son of Bulchü, the son of Bölüg, the son of Zambour, the son of Rael, the son of Levanghë. . . .

The names of all those ancient generations were graven on his heart; for the Huns, like the Celts, committed nothing of value to paper or stone, for fear that strangers and unbelievers might discover their holiest mysteries. Among which was this secret genealogy, these links in the divine chain of kingship that led back to the great hero Tarkan, the son of Kaer, the son of Nembroth, the son of Cham, the son of Astur, the King of All that Flies: he who wears the Crown of the Mountains upon his head, and tears the clouds asunder with his terrible talons, in his kingdom of the blue sky over the Altai Mountains and the snowbound Tien Shan. He who devours his enemies before him like the storm; who among the Eastern People is also called Schongar, the head of the ancestral tree of all the wide-wandering Hun nation.

What did the Romans know of this? All men beyond the frontier were mere barbarians to them, and Roman curiosity stopped at their own frontier walls.

Here in Rome, this son of the Sons of Astur was deemed little better than a slave or a spoil of war. He thought of the wide plains of Scythia and his heart ached with longing for his homeland, for a sight of the black tents of his people, and for the great herds of horses moving slowly through the thigh-deep feather grass. Among them was his beloved white pony, Chagëlghan—well named, for she was indeed as fast as lightning: *chagëlghan* in the language of the Huns. When he was back on the plains, he would mount her barebacked and unbridled, with only his legs' strength and his fists in her thick white mane to hold him, and they would ride for unbounded miles over the steppes with the feather grass whipping past his knees and her haunches, the wind in her mane and his hair. Here, in this bitter and withering empire, everything was stifled and bounded, every parcel of land was owned, every horse branded, every straight, unblinking road paved and named, every field and vineyard fenced off—and these Romans had the stupidity to think themselves free! They no longer knew what freedom was.

But he would have his freedom again. His parting gift to Rome would be the blinded eyes of that great emperor; and then he would escape. They would send out soldiers to search for him, he knew. He knew his own value. They would send out whole armies to prevent his escape. But they would never find him once he was out in the mountains and the wilds, no more to human eyes than a ghost or a shadow.

The boy didn't breathe. He pressed farther back into the darkness and made himself invisible. One of the elders of his tribe, a solitary and often silent elder called Cadicha, had taught him how. Cadicha had traveled for many long years in the endless wildernesses of Central Asia, and seen many strange things, and knew how, so it was said in the tribe, to make himself appear like a gust of sand in the wind, or a single solitary tree. Cadicha taught the boy what to do. He pressed as far back as he could into the shadows of the niche. Against his bare shoulder he could feel the cold marble of the pediment, surmounted by yet another pompous marble statue of some defunct hero of Rome. His fingers were sweaty round the coarse rope handle of his dagger. He could smell the salt-sea smell of the rope, damp with his sweat.

He was small for his age, more like a boy of seven or eight than one on the verge of adolescence; his people had always been scorned for their small stature. But what did they know, those enfeebled Romans with their cold sneers of superiority, or those long-limbed, flaxen-haired Goths? Look at his people's horses: smaller than any other breed in Europe, but hardier by far. They could carry a man for an hour at full gallop and not tire.

He still didn't breathe, and he closed his slanted eyes, lest they should glitter like a cat's from the darkness.

The guards talked on, within a few paces of him.

Some guards *they* were. Old and tired and half deaf and ready to fall. Very like the city they guarded. They were talking now of his people, and of how Rome had defeated the barbarian army of Rhadagastus only with the aid of barbarians. How Stilicho, master general of the Roman forces, had joined forces with another barbarian tribe to win his victory: this tribe called the Huns.

One of the guards snorted. "Half animal, they are. Eat nothing but raw meat, wear only animal skins, and their victory rites after a battle . . . you think the arena looks a mess after a triumph, but you don't want to be one of *their* war captives, I can tell you."

"No greater power in this world than to be so feared," said the other guard.

"Well, aren't you the philosopher tonight."

The second guard stared out over the moonlit palace courtyard, and then said softly, "Well, we shall see them for ourselves tomorrow, at General Stilicho's triumph."

"Emperor Honorius's triumph."

"I do beg your pardon," came the mocking reply. "Yes, of course, the *emperor's* triumph."

There was silence for awhile, and then one of them said, "Do you remember that night on the Rhine?"

"Of course I do," said the other. "How could I ever forget it? You saved my poxy life, didn't you?"

"Don't start thanking me for that again."

"Wasn't going to."

"Anyway, you'd have done the same for me."

"Don't be so sure."

The two old soldiers grinned at each other, but their grins soon faded.

Yes, they remembered that night on the Rhine. In the last days of December, when the river froze solid, and the barbarian hordes came galloping across the moonlit ice as if they were coming into their kingdom: Vandals and Sueves, Alans, Lombards, Goths, Burgundians. Yes, they remembered that night, and all the nights and the weeks and the months that came after.

The first guard bowed his head at the remembrance. "I thought I saw Rome go down in flames that night."

They brooded.

"Is the story of Rome finished?"

The other shrugged. "It's been a long story," he said. "And it could yet have one almighty firestorm of a final chapter. The fall of Rome would outshine the fall of Troy as the sun outshines a candle."

"We'll have a place there, too," said the other, "and die deaths as glorious and heroic as the death of Hector himself!"

They snorted with derisive, self-mocking laughter.

Then one said, "Come on then, old Trojan." And wearily the two comrades in arms, now relegated to the status of lowly palace guards, with their stiff old joints and their scars that still ached on frosty nights, moved slowly on down the corridor, their sandals slapping softly on the marble tiles.

The boy relaxed, eased himself away from the cold marble and breathed again. The moment the guards had turned the corner out of sight, he crept out of the niche and scuttled along in the shadows toward the other end of the corridor.

There in the pale, washed light of the moon stood an imposing bronze statue of Caesar Augustus himself, a great brawny arm commandingly outstretched, wearing the plate-armor uniform of a general of four hundred years ago. His eyes shone in the moonlight, his painted black eyes with their unearthly gleaming whites. Round the base of the statue were carved the words PIUS AENEAS. For were not the Caesars direct descendants of the legendary Founder of Rome himself?

By dawn tomorrow, Augustus would look very different: with his knife the boy would turn that cold gaze blind.

He scrambled swiftly onto the pediment, and then, feeling as if he was in some strange dream, began to climb up the bronze figure. He clenched the knife between his teeth and, reaching up, managed to grab hold of one of Augustus's larger-than-life-sized hands. He braced his bare feet against the statue's legs and hauled, stretched up again, and hooked his left arm round the emperor's neck.

He froze. The guards were coming past again.

They couldn't be. They had done their dozen circuits of the courtyard, as regular as the wheeling stars, in true Roman fashion, and now they should be moving on to another of the palace's countless courtyards. In his urgency he must have miscounted.

He kept as still as the statue itself while the guards passed beneath him, both looking somberly down. They didn't see him, hunched there on the imperial giant like a malignant incubus. And then they were gone.

He leaned back and, gripping the statue with both thighs and one arm, took the dagger in his right hand and eased the blade under Augustus' alabaster right eyeball. A little scraping and levering, and it popped out cleanly. He caught it deftly with his knife hand as it fell, the size of a duck egg, and dropped it inside his tunic. Then he turned his attention to the left eyeball, again slipping the thin blade in and easing it—

"And *what* do you think you are doing?"

The voice was colder than any statue of marble or bronze.

He looked down. At the foot of the statue stood a young woman of twenty years or so, in an emerald-green stola, belted at the waist, her hair worn in a severe style, tightly plaited and bound round her head. It had an almost reddish tinge, and her skin was very pale. She was tall and bony, with a fine nose, a thin and sharply defined mouth, and cool green, unblinking, catlike eyes. Her physical presence was one of both brittleness and sinewy tenacity. Now she arched a cool eyebrow inquiringly, as if merely curious, or even amused at what the boy might be doing. But there was no amusement or mere curiosity in her eyes. Her eyes made the boy think of fire seen burning through a wall of ice.

"Princess Galla Placidia," he whispered. "I—"

She wasn't interested in explanations. "Get down," she snapped.

He got down.

She looked up at the mutilated face of Caesar Augustus. "He found Rome brick and left it marble," she said softly. "But you, you found him bronze, and left him . . . mutilated. How very characteristic." She looked sourly down at the boy again. "It is *so* important to know one's enemies, don't you think?"

The boy looked smaller than ever.

She held out her hand. "The other eye," she said.

He could feel it, still nestling there in the folds of his tunic.

"I . . ." He swallowed. "When I came by, one eye was already gone. I was just trying to make sure the other one wouldn't fall out as well."

He didn't understand what had happened when he slammed against the wall behind him. Only when he groggily pulled himself to his feet again did he feel the side of his face stinging with pain. The livid welts of the blue tattooed scars that stood out from his cheek, the mark of his people, cut into his flesh by his mother when he was still in his cradle, tingled with increasing intensity. He touched his fingertips to his mouth, and found that the odd tickling sensation over his numbed lips was the trickle of blood.

He clutched the knife hard in his right hand and took a step forward. His teeth were furiously clenched.

Galla didn't flinch. "Put it away."

The boy stopped. He continued to clutch the knife, but he couldn't take another step.

The princess's eyes, both cool and burning, ice on fire, never left him. "You have been nothing but a plague since the day you arrived here," she said, her voice as cutting as Toletum steel. "You have had the finest Gallic tutors in Rome, to teach you rhetoric, logic, grammar, mathematics, and astronomy . . . they have even tried to teach you Greek!" She laughed. "What touching optimism! You have, of course, learned nothing. Your table manners are a continuing disgrace, you do nothing but scowl and sneer at the other hostages, your barbarian . . . equals. And now you are growing destructive as well."

"Rhadagastus would have done much worse," blurted the boy.

For a fleeting instant, Galla hesitated. "Rhadagastus is finished," she said. "As the triumphal Arch of Honorius will demonstrate when it is unveiled at the ceremony next week. Which you will attend."

He looked up at her wide eyed. "Strange it's not called the Arch of Stilicho, really, isn't it? In my country, when a battle is fought and won—"

"I am not interested in what goes on in your country. Just so long as it does not go on here."

"But we're allies now, aren't we? If it hadn't been for the help of my people, Rome would probably be overrun with barbarians by now."

"Hold your tongue."

"And they'd do far more damage than this." He waved at the muti-lated statue that towered over them. "If Rhadagastus and his warriors had got into the city, apparently they were going stuff the Senate House full of straw and set fire—"

"I order you to *hold your tongue!*" said Galla furiously, advancing toward him again.

"—to it, and leave it and all of Rome nothing but a field of blackened rubble. As the Goths might next, they say, now that Alaric is their leader, and a just *brilliant* general, who—"

The princess's cold and bony hand was raised to strike the little wretch a second time, and his slanted, malevolent Asiatic eyes glittered as he taunted her, when another voice rang out from the far corner of the courtyard.

"Galla!"

They heard the swish of a stola over the paved floor, and there was Serena, the wife of Master General Stilicho, advancing toward them.

Galla turned to her, hand still raised. "Serena?" she said.

Serena contrived a curtsey to the princess as she hurried forward, but the look in her eyes was anything but humble or obedient. "Lower your hand."

"I beg your pardon?"

"And you, boy, go to your room."

He backed up against the wall and waited.

"Do you presume to order me?"

Serena faced Galla Placidia and her eyes did not flinch. She was shorter than the princess, and perhaps twice her age, but there was no denying her beauty. Her hair was simply coiffed, and her stola of white silk left her neck and shoulders bare but for a slim necklace of Indian pearls. Her eyes, edged with fine laughter lines, were dark and lustrous, and few men in the court were strong enough to refuse her wishes when she expressed them in her low and gentle voice, turning her gaze and her wide smile full upon them. But when angered, those beautiful eyes could flash fire. They flashed fire now.

"Do you think it wise, Princess Galla, to maltreat the grandson of our most valued ally?"

"Maltreat, Serena? And what would you have me do when I catch him outraging one of the most precious statues in the palace?" Galla moved almost imperceptibly nearer to her. "Sometimes, I wonder if you really mind about such things. One would sometimes think your sympathies were as much barbarian as Roman! Ridiculous, I know. But of course, I understand that your husband—"

"That's enough!" flared Serena.

"On the contrary, it is not nearly enough. Since your husband was of unbaptized and barbarian birth himself, I—and indeed many others in court circles, though you may be comfortably unaware of it—*many* of us have begun to suspect that you have difficulty in distinguishing between what is truly Roman and what is not."

Serena smiled scornfully. "It has been a long time since even the emperors themselves were Roman born and bred. Hadrian was Spanish, as was Trajan. Septimius Severus was Libyan. P—"

"I know my history, thank you," cut in the princess. "What is your point?"

"My point is that you seem to be suggesting that my husband is not truly Roman on account of his birth. *Romanitas* no longer has anything to do with birth."

"You willfully misunderstand me. I am rather suggesting that you and your husband's party—"

"We have no 'party.'"

"—are in grave danger of forgetting the very principles of Roman civilization."

"When I see a grown woman striking a small boy, I do not see civilization, Princess," Serena said acidly. "Nor do I see subtle diplomacy in evidence, when that boy is the grandson of our most valuable ally."

"Of course, some would argue that, since you are merely the wife of a soldier, however peculiarly . . . *elevated* that soldier may have become, your views are of no consequence. But I would not like to be so uncharitable. Or so"—Galla Placidia smiled—"complacent."

"You see ghosts, Princess," said Serena. "You see things that are not." She turned aside and laid her hand on the waiting boy's shoulder. "Away to your room," she murmured. "Come now."

Together they went down to the corridor to the boy's chamber.

Galla Placidia stood clenching and unclenching her white, bony fists for some time. Eventually she turned on her heel and strode away, sightless with fury, her silk stola sweeping the ground before her as she went. In her darting mind's eye she saw suspicions, plots, and jealousies scuttling away like malign and chattering sprites into the dark shadows of the imperial courtyards; her haunted green eyes cast restlessly from left to right as she walked, and found nothing worth their constancy.

Serena halted at the door to the boy's chamber and turned him gently but firmly to face her.

"The knife," she said.

"I—I dropped it somewhere."

"Look at me. *Look* at me."

He glanced up into those penetrating dark eyes and then looked down again. "I need it," he said miserably.

"No you don't. Give it to me."

With great reluctance, he handed it over.

"And promise me you will do no more damage in the palace."

He thought about it and said nothing.

She continued to fix him with her dark eyes. "Swear it."

Very slowly, he swore it.

"I am trusting you," said Serena. "Remember that. Now go to bed." She pushed him gently into his chamber, pulled the door shut behind him, and turned away. "Little wolf cub," she murmured to herself with the trace of a smile as she went.

One of the palace eunuchs came to Galla's door and knocked. She nodded for him to be admitted.

It was the sharp-witted, sardonic Eutropius. His vital intelligence was that Serena and Attila had been seen outside the boy's chamber, making what appeared to be a mutual promise or pact.

When he was gone, the princess rose and strode restlessly around the room, imagining conspiracies and secret conversations everywhere. She pictured the Huns in secret negotiation with Stilicho, of the boy somehow passing messages from Stilicho and Serena to his own murderous people encamped far out on the wild Scythian plains. Or even to his grandfather, Uldin, who, mistakenly in her opinion, would take part in the imperial triumph tomorrow, alongside Stilicho—as if the equal of a Roman general!

She saw, too, her brother, Emperor Honorius, ruler of the Western Empire, back in his palace in Mediolanum, or hiding away in his new palace at Ravenna, safe behind the mosquito-ridden marshes, giggling to himself as he fed grains of the finest wheat to his pet poultry. Honorius, her idiot brother, two years her junior: the eighteen-year-old Ruler of the World. "The Emperor of Chickens," malicious tongues at court had christened him. Galla Placidia knew it all, both from her network of informants and from her own piercing green eyes, which saw through everything and everyone.

Let Honorius stay in his new palace: it was better, perhaps, that he was kept out of the way. Ravenna, that strange dream city, connected symbolically to the rest of Italy only by a narrow stone causeway across the marshes. Ravenna, with its night air filled with the croaking of frogs; where, they said, wine was more plentiful than drinking water. Let the emperor stay there. He would be safe and quiet, alone with his chickens.

She stood late into the night looking out onto the Great Courtyard, listening to the peaceful splashing of the Dolphin Fountain, and knew that sleep would not come. If she laid down her humming head now, she would only dream of ten thousand thunderous hooves, of painted barbarian faces, blue and scarred with the scars and burns that those terrible people gave their children in infancy. She would dream of a black, unending rain of arrows, of fleeing multitudes weeping and stumbling over a parched and desolate country, or running to hide, in the mountains, from the wrath and the judgment to come. She would cry out in her tormented sleep, and dream of churches and forts and palaces aflame in the fallen night, like the burning towers of tragic Ilium. Her thin, bony shoulders sagged with the weight of the empire of a hundred million souls. She clutched the heavy silver cross round her neck and prayed to Christ and all His saints, and knew that sleep would not come.

She would have been even more troubled if she had seen the strange ritual that took place in the boy's bare cell before he at last crawled into bed and slept.

He squatted on the floor, retrieved the alabaster eye from the folds of his tunic, and set it carefully down in the intersection of four floor tiles, so that it wouldn't roll. After a few moments' consideration, during which he and the unsocketed eye stared grimly at each other, he reached under his bed and pulled out a rough stone. He lifted it above his head, then slammed it down as hard as he could on the eye, flattening it instantly into powder.

He set down the stone, reached out, took a pinch of the alabaster powder between forefinger and thumb, and raised it to his mouth.

And he ate it.

3

THE HUNS RIDE INTO ROME

He awoke from whimpering dreams of childish vengeance.

The little cell was in darkness, but when he opened the shutters onto the courtyard the Italian summer sun blazed down and his spirits lifted. Slaves were bustling about, carrying pitchers of water, and wooden boards bearing cheeses in damp muslin, salted meat, and fresh loaves of bread.

He skipped out of the cell and grabbed one of the loaves as it passed. "Here, you little . . ."

But he knew it was all right. The slave was one of his favorites, Bucco, a fat and jolly Sicilian who heaped the most terrible curses on his head and didn't mean any of them.

"May you choke to death on it, you damned thief!" Bucco growled. "May you choke to death, and then your liver be devoured by a hundred scrofulous pigeons!"

The boy laughed and was gone.

Bucco looked after him and grinned.

The little barbarian. The rest of the palace might regard him with haughty disdain, but among the slaves, at least, he had friends. Only one Roman couple in court circles treated him with anything like kindness.

Some mornings he went over to the water butt in the courtyard to splash his face, and some mornings he didn't. This morning he didn't.

Which was why, when later that morning Serena saw him by daylight, she was aghast. "What on earth have you done to your face?" she cried.

The boy stopped and looked puzzled and uncertain. He tried to smile but it hurt too much.

"For heaven's sake," she sighed, and taking his hand she led him off to another corner of the palace. There she took him into one of the antechambers of her own suite, and sat him at a delicate little table covered in bristle brushes and bone combs, pots of unguent, and vials of perfume, and she showed him his reflection in a polished brass mirror.

He did not, he had to admit, look good. His lip was more deeply cut from Galla Placidia's blow than he had realized; perhaps she had caught him with one of her heavy gold signet rings. In the night the cut must have opened and bled again, then dried and crusted over, so that half his chin was an unsightly reddish-brown smear. The whole of his right cheek had a smooth, swollen purple sheen to it, rendering his blue tribal scars almost invisible; while his right eye, which he had sensed might be not quite right, was almost closed with swelling, ringed with myriad shades of blue and black.

"Well?" she said.

The boy shrugged. "I think I must have hit my head in the night. . . ."

She held his gaze for a moment. "Did Galla Placidia slap you—before I arrived?"

"No," he said sullenly.

She turned away and reached for a little pot among the many on the table. She removed the lid, and took up a pad of linen cloth. "Now, this is going to hurt," she said.

Afterward, she insisted that he should wear a linen bandage soaked in vinegar over his bruised and swollen eye. "At least for the rest of the day." She looked at him and sighed again. Maybe the faintest smile was on her lips. "What are we going to do with you?"

"Send me home?" he mumbled.

She shook her head, not unkindly. "It is the way of the world," she said. "At your grandfather's camp there is a Roman boy your age, who longs to be home likewise."

"Idiot," said the boy. "He can ride the best horses in the world there. *And* he doesn't have to eat fish."

"No one makes you eat fish."

He pulled a face. "Galla Placidia—" he began.

"Now, now," she said. She tapped him on the arm, and changed the subject. She touched his bandaged face with a feather-light finger. "And what are you going to look like on the steps of the palace, for the emperor's triumph?" She pursed her lips. "You'll just have to stand well back. Don't, for once, attract attention to yourself."

He nodded, jumped down from the stool, knocking the delicate little table violently as he did so, and sending all Serena's priceless pots and vials flying. He muttered his apologies, knelt clumsily down to try and help her pick them up again, and then got to his feet and sheepishly slunk from the room at Serena's exasperated bidding.

She began to pick up the wreckage herself. She shook her head, trying not to smile. That little barbarian. It was true, she had to admit: he did not belong in a palace, that little whirlwind, that fierce force of nature in the making.

The boy paused outside, and touched the bandage over his eye. Sometimes he liked to pretend that she was really his mother: his mother, whom he hardly remembered, who on the night of a full moon had carved those ritual deep blue scars into his cheeks with a curved bronze knife, only a week after he was born, proud of her infant son when he cried so little at the pain. But his mother was dead long since. He could no longer recall what she looked like. When he thought of his mother, he thought of a woman with dark, lustrous eyes and a gentle smile.

Eunuchs went to Galla again and told her Attila had been seen emerging from Serena's private chambers, wearing a bandage of sorts over his face.

Galla clenched her teeth.

It was the day of the emperor's triumph.

Outside the cool and formal courtyards of the palace, the teeming city of Rome was in uproar. It was one vast expression of gratitude, one collective sigh of relief. And perhaps, mixed with that relief, there was some perturbation. For the Huns were marching into Rome.

Trumpets blared, banners fluttered, and crowds roared all the way from the Porta Triumphalis to the Campus Martius. White oxen were led through the streets, festooned with garlands of late summer flowers, their great heads nodding sleepily as they walked all unawares to their sacrificial doom. Everywhere there were promiscuous swarms of people, drinking and cheering and singing. Among them an experienced eye could pick out the hucksters and fraudsters, the blind beggars huddled against the walls, no more than rag-bound frames of brittle bone, twitching and muttering at passersby, and the pretend-blind beggars, their hands outstretched, revealing forearms just a little too plump. Here was the veteran soldier with his wooden leg, and there the pretend-soldier hopping along with the aid of a battered crutch, his other (perfectly good) leg strapped up to his buttocks beneath his ragged cloak. And over there the harlots in their high-laced sandals, their soles studded with carefully patterned little hobnails that spelled out *Follow Me* in the dust behind them as they sashayed along. They were all doing excellent business on this day of rejoicing and animal spirits. Their large, seductive eyes were lined with black kohl and shadowed with green malachite, and they were startlingly blonde in their elaborate flaxen wigs imported from Germany. Some of them even took off their wigs and twirled them gaily in the air.

For although it was a solemn as well as a festive occasion, celebrating no less than the salvation of Rome itself, the usual cheating and thieving and whoring went on this day as on any other day in the great city. Little had changed in the four hundred years since Juvenal's time, or in the century since Constantine the Great had declared the empire a Christian empire; since little ever changes in human nature.

Here was the fishmonger selling his "spicy fish balls"—hotly spicy indeed, to disguise the fact that the fish had been netted at Ostia at least two weeks ago. *Caveat emptor.* Here were the fruit sellers, with their apricots, figs, and pomegranates. Here were the fraudsters and the soothsayers, the "Chaldean astrologers" from the backstreets of Rome, wearing ludicrous cloaks embroidered with moon and stars. Here was the sly-eyed young Syrian with his deft hands and his smile and his loaded dice; and here was another, older man, rheumy eyed and crooked with age, Greek, so he said, and an unconvincing advert for his own "miracle panacea," an unctuous green liquid sold in grubby glass bottles, which he offered to passersby—for a fee, of course.

In Rome, anything could be bought for the right amount of money: health, happiness, love, length of days, the favor of God or the gods, according to your taste.

Money could even buy, so it was sometimes scandalously whispered, the imperial purple itself.

On the steps of the Imperial Palace were gathered as many of the royal household as could be accommodated. From every doorway and every upper window, people cheered and shouted and waved banners and cloths, as they did from the meanest houses in the city, leaning precariously from their fifth- or sixth-floor apartments in high-rising *insulae*.

First in the triumphal procession came the aged senators, as always preceding the emperor on foot as a mark of their subservience. The crowd's applause was distinctly lackluster for this superfluous millionaires' club in old-fashioned togas edged with purple. Then, to thunderous acclaim, the long parade of Stilicho's finest troops, his First Legion, the venerable Legio I "Italica," originally raised under Nero and stationed at Bononia. Like other legions, it no longer numbered the full complement of five thousand men, more like two thousand; and they were spending more and more time attached to Stilicho's mobile field army, fighting to defend the Rhine and Danube frontiers. But at Florentia they had shown they were still the world's finest troops. Other legionaries had to stand five feet ten inches, but to join the Legio I "Italica," you had to be a six-footer.

They marched proudly by in immaculate order under raised standards fluttering with eagles, or embroidered dragons or writhing serpents, roused to angry life by the wind that ruffled them. They carried only wooden staves rather than swords, as was the custom during a triumph, but they looked hard, fierce men nevertheless. At the back marched their centurions, thick vine sticks in their fists, grim faced as ever. Then came Count Heraclian, Stilicho's second in command, his eyes darting and uncertain, always jealous, so it was said, of his brilliant commander. And then, on a dignified white stallion, Stilicho himself. The striking, long, and rather lugubrious face, the intelligent eyes, the manner at once mild and disciplined.

With him was an extraordinary figure. And immediately behind him a further fifty or so extraordinary figures. Indeed, so extraordinary that, as they passed, the crowd that lined the street fell silent and seemed almost to lose its voice.

For beside Stilicho, on a small and skittish bay pony, its fierce eyes rolling to the whites, rode a man such as the Romans had never seen before. He

was in his fifties, perhaps, but looked as tough as bullhide. He had curious slanting eyes, and a thin, wispy gray beard which barely covered his
chin. His helmet was pointed, and he wore a rough and battered leather
jerkin, and over that a broad, dusty cloak of beaten horse skin. He bristled with weapons: a sword at one side, a dagger at the other, a beautifully crafted bow slung one way across his back, and the other way a
quiver packed with arrows. His dark, impenetrable gaze was fixed straight
ahead, and although he was of small build he radiated strength.

His name was Uldin, and he called himself King of the Huns.

Close behind him rode more of his kind, his personal bodyguard; they,
too, were clad in dusty and unkempt animal furs, bristled with weaponry, and rode small, fierce-eyed ponies. The neat, prancing hooves
kicked up plumes of dust as they rode, and the open-mouthed bystanders
could smell leather and horses and sweat as they passed: something alien
and animal, something vast and untamed, from far beyond the orderly
frontiers of Rome.

Some of Uldin's horsemen looked to left and right as they rode past,
meeting the challenge of the Roman citizens' gaze with equal curiosity.
Uldin himself kept his gaze steadfastly ahead, but his men could not
help but stare around, and upward, at the monumental buildings of the
city; buildings of a size and grandeur their imaginations could barely
grasp. Even the humblest buildings, the blocks of flats inhabited by the
poorest in Rome, towered higher than anything the horsemen had ever
seen built by the hand of man before. Then there were the palaces of
patricians and emperors, the grand and triumphal basilicas, their windows filled with stuff called *glass,* which let in the light and heat but not
the cold. Opaque sheets of blue or green ice which didn't melt in the sun,
utterly mysterious to them.

The fantastical, overwrought Baths of Diocletian and of Caracalla,
decorated with marble of every conceivable color and shade: yellow and
orange from Libya, pink from Euboea, blood red and brilliant green
from Egypt, along with the precious onyx and porphyry of the east. Then

the Pantheon, the Colosseum, the Forum of Trajan, and the Arch of Titus, and the great temples to the Roman gods, whose treasuries contained, so it was rumored, the gold of half the world. . . .

Nevertheless, the people of Rome resumed their cheering readily enough as the barbarian horsemen passed on, acknowledging, however uneasily, that it was only thanks to the alliance with these strangers that Rome had been saved.

Only the most dandyish of the aristocrats turned their delicate noses up, and covered their mouths in little white cloths impregnated with oil of lavender. Some of them carried silk parasols seamed with golden thread, to protect their fair skins from the sun, and, pointing toward the Hun horsemen, joked that, after all, one didn't want to look as sunburned as *that*. Such dandies wore light silken robes embroidered with extravagant scenes of hunting or wild animals; or, if they wanted to display their piety, perhaps the martyrdom of a favorite saint. What the stern old Roman heroes would have said, how Cato the Censor would have raged, one could only speculate. These epigones, these degenerates . . .

What the Huns themselves must have judged of them, and of Rome herself therefore, one can only imagine.

Many a member of the patrician classes, it was said, had not remained in Rome to see the triumph. With an airy and languid gesture, they had drawled that the city would be too *hot* and too *crowded* with plebs and, still worse, *barbarian horsemen,* to be bearable. The smell would be simply *ghastly.* And they had taken their leave and gone down with their friends to the Lucrine Lake, on the Gulf of Puteoli, to lie exhausted in their painted galleys and sip their goblets of Falernian wine chilled with handfuls of snow brought down in jars by slaves from the heights of Vesuvius. And reclining in their galleys, with other slaves softly playing stringed instruments, perhaps, they would trail their delicate hands in the cooling waters and gaze toward the island of Ischia and sigh for the days of their youth. Or of Rome's youth. Or of any days but these, and anywhere but here. Anything but these hard days and these demanding times.

From the steps of the palace, the imperial household looked on. At their head stood the poised, expressionless figure of Princess Galla, her robe today a brilliant saffron yellow. The rest of the household seemed to stretch away from her on either side; and in the far corner, near Serena, stood a small, hunched and fiercely scowling boy.

"Hey, half ass! Oi!"

The boy looked left and his scowl deepened further. It was a couple of the other hostages, the Frankish children, calling across to him through the throng.

"You want to push through to the front! You won't see anything but people's ankles where you are!" And the tall, fair children laughed.

He was about to advance toward them, teeth clenched, when he felt Serena's hand on his shoulder, turning him gently but firmly back toward the spectacle parading before them.

As General Stilicho passed by, grave on his fine white horse, he turned and bowed to Princess Galla, and managed also to catch the eye of his wife: the slightest smile passed between them.

Stilicho was interrupted by Uldin's voice at his side, asking in jagged and broken Latin who was the boy on the steps with the bandaged eye. Stilicho glanced over his shoulder and caught sight of him, just as he vanished from view. He turned back and smiled broadly.

"That is Attila, son of Mundzuk, son of—"

"The son of my son. I knew him." Uldin, too, grinned broadly. Then he asked, "What hostages do we have in return?"

"A lad called Aëtius—the same age as Attila, and the oldest son of one Gaudentius, master general of the cavalry."

The King of the Huns glanced sideways at Stilicho. "The same Gaudentius who . . . ?"

"So rumor has it," said Stilicho. "But you know about rumor."

Uldin nodded. "Why is his eye bandaged? The son of Mundzuk?"

Stilicho didn't know. "He is always getting himself into scrapes," he shrugged. "My young wolf cub," he added softly, more to himself than

Uldin. Then he wiped the affectionate smile from his face, and reassumed the expression of soldierly gravity that befitted the dignity of a general at a Roman triumph.

Somewhere among the triumph rode the emperor himself, on an immaculate, plumed white mare: young Honorius in his robes of purple and gold. But few people noticed. He made little impression.

From the Palatine steps, Princess Galla gazed out over the triumph.

After the procession, and the interminable speeches and eulogies, and the solemn service of thanksgiving to God in the Church of St. Peter, there were triumphal games in the Colosseum.

As with the closing of the pagan temples by Emperor Theodosius a generation or two earlier, and the banning of blood sacrifices, the Christians had on many occasions tried to bring the games to an end. This was not on account of the cruelty so much as because the crowd derived too much base pleasure from the spectacle; and also because, on the days when the games were held, so many rouged and painted whores congregated beneath the arches of the Colosseum, pouting their lips and baring their wanton breasts and thighs at passersby, that a Christian man hardly knew where to look. And as for a Christian lady . . .

Only four years before, in the year of Our Lord 404, a certain eastern monk called Telemachus, with all the glittering-eyed fanaticism of his kind, had thrown himself into the arena from the steps above, in protest at the disgusting spectacle taking place. The rabble, true to form, promptly stoned him to death where he knelt. For they did love their sports and games, the common people. But later, with that fickleness of mind and heart which is typical of the unwashed and unlettered multitude, they cried out their sorrow and repentance for what they had done. And the youthful and impressionable Emperor Honorius promptly issued a decree that all games were henceforth abolished.

Unfortunately, like so many of his decrees, this one was widely ignored. Soon enough the games had crept back into the arena, and the crowd's appetite for blood and spectacle was renewed. And on this day in August, only four years later, it was Emperor Honorius himself who declared the triumphal games open.

Some criminals were made to dress up as peasants, and kill each other with pitchforks. A man who had raped his young daughter was tied to a stake and Caledonian hunting dogs were set on him, to devour his genitals while he was still alive—the crowd especially appreciated that one. There was a long and bloody fight between a huge forest bison and a Spanish bear. The bison was killed eventually, but the bear had to be dragged from the arena on a travois and was no doubt despatched in the cells below. There were no longer gladiatorial combats, however, since they had been abolished for good, as unbefitting to a Christian empire. Nor were there elephants to be slaughtered, for Africa had been ransacked over four long centuries by Rome, and the vast herds that had once roamed Libya and Mauritania could be found no more. It was said that if you wanted elephants now, you had to travel south many thousands of miles over the Great Desert, and into the unknown heart of Africa; but everyone knew that that was impossible. And there were no fierce tigers left in the mountains of Armenia, no lions or leopards in the mountains of Greece, where Alexander the Great had hunted them as a boy, seven centuries before. They, too, had been trapped, caged, and shipped to Rome for the games, and all were gone.

4

CICERO AND FREEDOM

That night, after the Huns had departed to their temporary camp beyond the walls of the city, a great feast was held for Emperor Honorius and his glorious victory over the armies of Rhadagastus.

The vast colonnaded dining hall of the palace was filled with couches arranged round a long central spread of tables, with as many as three hundred guests in proud and self-congratulatory attendance.

The hostage children were all commanded to attend: Hegemond and Beremond, the two plump Burgundian boys; the tall, fair, quick-witted, laughing Franks; the two slothful Vandal princes, Beric and Genseric, and all the rest. Attila sat scowling in their midst, none of them daring to come too near him. Even the fierce way he handled a fruit knife frightened them.

Nearby, to the boy's solace, were Serena and Stilicho. But it was Count Heraclian—flatterer, charmer, true-born Roman of ancient descent, and outstanding military incompetent—who found the highest favor with the emperor, sitting much nearer to the head of the room than Stilicho.

At the end of the hall, on a raised dais of rich green Egyptian marble, were two huge couches of dazzling white and gold, upholstered in purple; and on them reclined the imperial brother and sister, Galla and Honorius. Honorius ate a great deal, his sister little. Their drinking patterns exhibited much the same difference in temperament.

The food and wine were magnificent. There were oysters brought all the way from fog-bound Britain, kept cool in iced seawater during transit, and now laid out in little osier panniers still fronded with glossy green seaweed. There were the finest *garum* sauces imported from Bithynia and Gades; and exquisite offerings such as honey-roast peacock, boiled thrush, camels' trotters, and a ragout of nightingales' brains. Many of the guests cooed with delight over these fabulous delicacies, as did the other hostage children, feeling greatly privileged to be sampling such fare. The Hun boy however, ill mannered to the core, took one taste of the Spanish flamingoes' brain pâté on a little sliver of soft wheaten bread, and spat it out again in disgust. Even Stilicho heard the noise of his revolted hawking from where he sat, and, turning round, saw what had happened. He turned back quickly, stifling a grin.

There were dolphin fish balls, boar boiled in seawater, squid sausages, and those greatest of culinary rarities, deer's-milk cheese, hare's-milk cheese, and even rabbit's-milk cheese; which, no doubt in the interest of several guests later that night, was said to be beneficial in counteracting diarrhea.

There were red-mullet roes on beds of nasturtium leaves, and rams' testicles, and moray eels in fermented anchovy sauce; there was ewe's-placenta-and-simnel cake, jellyfish omelettes, and slivers of smoked crane, from birds which had been blinded early in life so that they would grow all the fatter. There were sows' nipples in tuna brine, and auroch's penis in a pepper and mulberry sauce. There were roast geese that had been force-fed figs for the last three months of their lives, and there was a rich pâté made from the liver of a pig that had been drowned in red wine. And the wines themselves! There was Pucinum, from the Tergestine

Gulf, and sweet Marino, from the Alban Hills. There was a rich ruby Chian (dangerously heady), a twelve-year-old Numentian, and even a Falernian, of the world-renowned Opimian vintage, as the label on the neck testified: almost one hundred years old, and, to everyone's agreement, only now reaching its best.

"Sir?" asked a slave, extending a bottle toward Stilicho.

The general shook his head. "Water."

The imperial cooks, all one thousand of them, had excelled themselves in hard work and ingenuity. True to the Roman fashion, they had taken immense pains to disguise one kind of food amusingly as another. How the guests' laughter tinkled to the gilt-and-painted ceiling, when they realized that what they had taken to be a pigeon, roasted and glazed with honey, was in fact made entirely out of sugar. And what exquisite imagination had gone into creating that boiled hare, which had then had its fur sewn back on, and kestrels' wings attached to its back, so that it looked like some kind of strange miniature Pegasus!

The whole thing was an absolute triumph of Roman taste and creativity, and the magnificence of the banquet was greeted with almost universal acclamation. The guests ate and drank with gusto, and retired frequently to void their bladders, their stomachs, or both.

There was the usual dinner-party conversation: about the dreadful hot weather they'd been having recently, and how they longed to get out to their little place in the country, just as soon as the triumph was over. The quality of life was *so* much better in the hills of Campania this time of year, and *so* much nicer for the children, too. And the impoverished country people could be quite *charming,* in their funny, uneducated attitudes and opinions.

The guests paused to take another frog's leg or two from the silver dish before them, to crease up their faces and break wind, or to cleanse their fingers in golden bowls scented with rose petals, and dry them on the hair of a passing slave.

One could still pick up a very nice little villa, with a few acres of vines and olive trees, for really very little. They had heard good things about the area around Beneventum, for instance, that lovely old colonial town on the Via Appia, beyond Capua. A little remote and primitive, it was true, and not as easy to get to as Capua; but nevertheless *charming*, simply *charming*. Capua had been rather "discovered" nowadays, and was suffering from what they called "Neapolitan overspill," whereas farther up into the hills, around Caudium and Beneventum, one still felt one was in the *real* Italy. The Via Appia was not as well maintained as in the past, of course—they lowered their voices a little here—and one tended to arrive rather travel sore. And one couldn't get fresh oysters for one's dinner parties in the local shops there for love nor money. One rather had to "make do" with what local produce was on offer, which could some-times be somewhat rough and ready: barley bread, horsemeat sausages, figs, that sort of thing. But all the same, a few weeks in the hills of Cam-pania, at one's little villa, could be *such* a relief from Rome. One did *need* it, really.

Then they talked about the ridiculous property prices in the city: now even apartments on the Aventine were sought after. Soon people would be claiming that it was fashionable to live west of the river! And there were grumbles about economic migrants from the north, especially Ger-mans, and how they had no manners, no sense of law and order, and lowered the tone of an entire neighborhood when they moved in. They wore ridiculous *trousers,* had too many children, and smelt funny.

At last, with wine jugs and dishes nearly empty, the court chamber-lain arose, banged his golden staff on the ground, and prayed silence.

"Your Divine Majesty," he said, bowing so low to the emperor that it looked as if he might slip a disc. "The most beauteous Princess Galla, senators, masters general, prefects praetorian, magistrates, bishops, legates, quaestors, lictors, ladies, and gentlemen assembled, I give you our most esteemed poet, the equal of Lucretius, nay, Virgil, nay of great Homer himself—ladies and gentlemen: pray silence for Claudius Claudianus."

To a rather thin scattering of applause, a fat, sweaty, dark-complexioned man got to his feet and looked anxiously around at the three hundred guests. One or two smiled politely back. They knew what was coming.

The poet craved their pardon, begged their indulgence, and nodded and bobbed repeatedly toward the imperial dais, although he never quite managed to raise his eyes directly to it, for fear, no doubt, that he might be dazzled and blinded for life by His Imperial Majesty's effulgence. Then, producing an ominously thick scroll from the folds of his toga, he declared, in a surprisingly strong and sonorous voice, that he would like to read to the assembled company a brief panegyric he had dashed off that morning, in praise of the emperor's magnificent victory over the barbarian hordes; and he asked his listeners' forbearance, since he had only had so brief a time to work on it.

In fact, it was well known that Claudian had literally dozens of panegyrics already written and stashed away in the library of his handsome villa on the Esquiline, designed to cover every conceivable occasion, and to be brought out as and when required. But everyone was too polite to say so. Besides, for all the snide comments made behind his back, Claudian was very popular with the emperor.

He coughed once and began:

> *O beloved Prince, fairer by far than the day star,*
> *Who shootest thine arrows with an aim more sure than the Parthians,*
> *What stumbling praise of mine shall match thy lofty mind?*
> *What encomia thy brilliance and thy beauty?*

> *On a couch of gold midst Tyrian purples didst thy mother give thee birth,*
> *And then what presages were there for good fortune!*
> *Horned Ammon and Delphi, so long dumb, now broke their silence,*
> *And the rock of Cumae, shrine of the raging Sibyl, spoke again!*

The burly legate beside Stilicho shifted on his elbow and muttered sourly, "Don't remember that myself."

"I think I'm going to puke," mumbled the general in return. "And it's not those dodgy British oysters, either."

The two men bowed their heads and stifled their chuckles.

On the dais, Galla turned her head.

There was more:

> *When in the heat of the chase, thou guidest thy coursing steed*
> *Amid the towering holm oaks, thy tossing locks streaming out in the wind,*
> *Surely the beasts of their own accord fall before thine arrows,*
> *And the lion, right gladly wounded by a prince's sacred hand,*
> *Welcomes thy spear and is proud so to die!*

> *When after thy toils of venery thou seekest the shade of the woods,*
> *And freest thy weary limbs in dreaming sleep,*
> *What a passion of love inflames the Dryads' hearts,*
> *How many a Naiad steals up with trembling foot to snatch an unmarked kiss!*

Many guests chuckled appreciatively at this delightful image. Even the emperor himself giggled into his goblet. Claudian paused generously to allow him to do so, before resuming again.

For there was yet more:

> *Who, though he be more uncivilized than the wild Scythian,*
> *And more cruel than the beasts, but will,*
> *On seeing near at hand thy transcendent loveliness,*
> *Not readily seize the chains of slavery,*
> *And offer thee a ready servitude?*

Attila tested the little fruit knife against his thumb pad.

> *Then shall all the world bow to thee, O most noble Prince!*
> *E'en now I foresee the sack of distant Babylon,*

Bactria subjected to the Law, the fearful pallor of the Ganges' banks before thy
  name!
For to you all the world shall bend the knee;
The Red Sea give you precious shells, India her ivory,
Panchaia perfumes, and China bolts of yellow silk.
And all the world confess your name, your empery
That is without limit, without age or boundary!

The applause lasted almost as long as the poem.

A little later on in the banquet, Galla was passing behind the couches, on her way to speak to one of her chamberlains, when she happened to overhear a drunken and indiscreet guest asking his neighbor absent-mindedly if the emperor himself had even *been* at the triumph that day?

"Because if he was, I certainly didn't notice him," slurred the guest. "Like everyone else, I was all eyes on the divine Stilicho!"

Galla paused.

Unaware that they were being listened to, the other guest said sotto voce, "Our Sacred Majesty was probably too busy feeding his pet chickens."

They chuckled furtively into their goblets of wine. Then one of them glanced up and caught sight of the princess standing right behind them. The warm wine he was swallowing came painfully back up his throat.

Galla leaned forward and plucked a fried lark from the silver dish beside them.

"Pray continue," she said, smiling sweetly, as she snapped the little bird's leg bones in two.

She arranged further business with her head chamberlain, who nodded and departed soon after. Returning to the imperial dais, she noticed that, amid the hubbub of the hostage children, the Hun brat was nowhere to be seen.

She summoned another attendant, who told her that he had been excused.

"How long ago?"

"Well," stammered the attendant, a runnel of sweat coursing down his brow, "some while ago now."

"Go and get him."

The attendant searched the lavatories high and low. There was no sign of Attila. He made his way back to his cell in the slave quarters, knowing his time at the palace was ended, and prepared for the worst.

The Hun boy was by now moving stealthily around the Great Court, in the cool green shadows of the Dolphin Fountain.

The palace was no easier to break out of than to break into. But Attila had planned his escape with meticulous care, patiently observing every movement of the palace guards over this past year of his captivity, every locking and unlocking of the gates, and picking up every whispered password. Despite his native ferocity, he could be patient when need be. His father, Mundzuk, had always told him that patience was one of the great virtues of all nomad peoples. "Nothing can hurry the sun," he would say. The wide-wandering Huns were certainly good at waiting, and the boy himself had all the patience and rhythm of the nomad. Useless to struggle against the sandstorm—but the moment the sandstorm ceased you could take your chance. Seize it in your fierce hands for it might not come again. The Romans were like men trying to move the sands of the desert, like the sands of the Takla Makan when the east wind blew—and in the night the wind came and blew the sand back again. Their work would never be done.

The boy had also worked out the rules governing the frequency with which the palace password was changed, and felt nothing but scorn at how easy it was. From the kalends to the ides of each month, the password was changed at noon; and from the ides back to the next kalends, it was changed at midnight. In other words, eavesdrop on the password used just after midnight in the second half of any month, and it would get you through any gate in the palace until the following midnight.

He had even worked out the encryption system commonly used around the palace, and, again, was scornful at its laziness and complacency: like a Greek merchant overconfident of the safety of his ships at sea, even in the stormy, Dog Star month of October.

It was based on the encryption system that Julius Caesar himself had devised for his military communications. Perhaps those hours and tedious days at the hands of his wretched pedagogue, Demetrius of Tarsus, during which Attila was instilled with the rudiments of Roman history and culture, and therefore, supposedly, with an appropriate respect and reverence for the empire—perhaps those lessons hadn't been wasted after all.

During August, A, U, G, S, and T were used to represent A, B, C, D, and E—and then the rest of the alphabet was shifted five letters down against the code alphabet accordingly. In August, "Caesar" was written "Gatpao." The following month, the first seven letters would change to S, E, P, T, M, B and R, and "Caesar" would be written "Psmosn."

The boy worked all this out in secret, by listening from shadowy corners, by picking up scraps of paper, by brooding in his loneliness and solitude, like a wolf, or a spider. Like the slow-moving Iron River of Scythia for which, some said, he was named.

And all the while that he was breaking the palace code system in secret, his irascible Greek pedagogue was beating him regularly for being slow witted over his books.

As well as these more intellectual preparations for his escape, Attila had amassed practical aids, such as the sharp little fruit knife from the banquet, a store of low-denomination copper coins, a bag of oatmeal he'd stolen from the kitchens, and some corks.

Soon after nightfall on that night of victory celebrations over the barbarians, Attila quit his place at the lower tables of the banqueting hall, and made swiftly for his chamber, where he collected his treasures. Then he slunk through the near-deserted courts of the palace, praying to his father Astur to guide and shield him, until he approached the guards in the main gatehouse, trembling so badly with fear that he could barely trust himself to speak.

"Halt! Who goes there?"

He said nothing, went nearer.

"I said, *halt!*"

Attila halted.

The moonlight shone on the Palatine guard's black cuirass and his plumed black helmet. He was a *tesserarius*—a password officer. He glared down at the boy. "Give me your name."

Attila hesitated, then said softly, "Cicero."

The guard reacted with some surprise. "Who gave you the password?" he growled.

"None of your business," said the boy. "Nor do I have to tell you my name. The correct password is 'Cicero.' So let me pass."

The guard hesitated a little longer, his meaty fist clenched round his spear haft. Then reluctantly he lowered it and nodded to the boy to pass. His fellow guardsmen began to draw back the heavy ironbound gates. Already the *tesserarius* could imagine, with uncomfortable vividness, the feeling of his centurion's vine-wood whip descending on his back. But what could he do? A password was a password.

The boy slipped past him and vanished into the street. The guard looked out after him, but already he was lost to view.

5

THE STREETS OF ROME

Attila breathed free air for the first time in a year. Although the air was that of a great and populous city rather than the wild air of Scythia, nevertheless it was free. And nothing but a few hundred miles now lay between him and his beloved homeland.

He turned left out of the palace, and hurried down the street to the corner, with the great extension to the Palatine complex built by Septimius Severus to his left. He rounded the corner and headed for the shadowy arches of the great Aqueduct of Nero below, and the darkened streets beyond. He had it all mapped out in his mind.

Down to the foot of the Palatine Hill, another left round the Arch of Constantine, with the great, looming mass of the Colosseum to his right. Then, slipping into the alleyway behind the ancient Temple of Venus and Roma, and then the Temple of Pacis—a very small and insignificant temple, by Roman standards—he hurried onward, making for the nameless and dangerous backstreets of the Suburra, with the three hills of the Quirinal, the Viminal, and the Esquiline rising up behind.

After the day of triumph and the games, the midnight streets of the poorer parts of the city were filled with drunken, jeering people. They swayed and staggered about arm in arm, emerging from the *pervigiles popinae,* the city's numerous keep-awake bars, or else disappearing into one of the many brothels in the district, whose line of trade was signaled by a statue of herm outside, with his erect and outsized penis painted in eye-catching scarlet.

The populace chanted songs about the greatness of Rome—or their emperor:

> *The Emperor Honorius*
> *Was sitting in the bathhouse,*
> *His ass was out the window*
> *But his cock was in the hall!*
> *His hair, oh! it was glorious,*
> *All dressed with art laborious,*
> *But his balls were like a chicken's*
> *When his sister came to call!*

Sometimes, for the sake of variety, they broke into songs about the superiority of their favorite chariot team, the Blues or the Greens. Their tuneless roaring was interrupted only by the need to pause from time to time and vomit forth bellyfuls of sour new wine into the flowing gutters. The moment a mob of Blues supporters ran into some Greens, of course, all pandemonium broke out. But, as history so powerfully tells us, people enjoy fighting each other, and need little excuse to begin. A rival chariot team is certainly sufficient reason for bloodshed.

Indeed, in that glittering, God-crazed other capital to the east, Constantinople, didn't the crowds run riot and kill each other over the choice of its priests, as had happened recently with the election of Bishop Eusta-chius? Or even over changes to the liturgy? But they were a mad, excit-able, Asiatic lot over there. At least in Rome the people had the good sense to confine their violence to matters of sport.

For the most part, Attila deftly avoided these scenes of debauchery and tumult. Only occasionally did he pause to gaze in wordless contempt at the squalor and vice that made up the underbelly of this great city. As always, he could not help but compare the Roman plebeians' behavior with that of his own quiet people, back on the great plains, their solemn feasts, their simple dignity, their self-reliance and absolute self-control. Drunkenness they regarded with disgust: an adult trying to make himself like a child again—or even a madman. And as for the idea of the daily dole given out in Rome gratis to this scrounging, unwashed rabble. . . .

For it had been with disbelief that the boy had first learned that, every day, the Roman state gave out food, for free, to anyone who came to queue up for it. Originally it had been a magnanimous gift of bread handed out only to the poor or the terminally idle; but then that free bread had be-come a right. More recently, in the reign of Emperor Aurelian, the daily dole had grown into a lavish, seductive handout not only of bread but also of pork, oil, and wine, to hundreds of thousands of the shameless mob. But of course nothing in this world was free. The dole was given to the rabble in exchange for their quiescence. In exchange for their very hearts and minds.

The boy knew that his people, the nation of the Huns, would never be softly seduced and Romanized like other barbarian peoples. To the Huns, as to the boy himself—a Hun, indefatigably, to his soul—such a surren-der of oneself as this daily dole, such a pitiful abdication of one's own pride and self-reliance, would be a source of dishonor and shame unspeakable. Among the Huns, most proud and warlike of peoples, for a man not to be able to provide meat for his family, with the art and labor of his own hand and eye, would have been a humiliation scarcely endurable.

The boy slipped into a still narrower, darker alleyway, where the second or third stories of the houses seemed almost to meet above his head. He blackened his face a little with mud, and messed up his hair, never exactly coiffed at the best of times. Then, looking much like one of the thousands of ordinary urchins in the slums of Rome, he reappeared on the main street. He glanced skyward again, and found that great constellation which the Romans called Ursa Major, the Great Bear, but which to his people was known as the Wings of Astur, King of All that Flies. From there his eye moved up to the North Star. He allowed himself a small smile, and he turned right and followed it, heading north.

Behind him a drunken old man, sprawled in the gutter and holding a flagon of cheap wine aloft, cried, "*Vivite! ait Mors. Venio!* Live! says Death. I am coming!"

In the banqueting hall, Galla sensed that all was not right when the attendant did not return. She snapped her fingers from the imperial dais, and gave orders for slaves to be sent immediately to check the troublesome hostage's cell. She despatched two court clerks to question the guards on the eastern gate. When they returned, she asked them a single brief question, and only halfway through the clerk's stumbling reply her hand flew out and struck him stingingly across the cheek. Some of the guests saw what happened and snickered.

Then she turned and ordered an attendant officer to send out a search party at once. She wanted the Hun boy found within the hour. For as a hostage, she knew, Attila was one of Rome's strongest guarantees that the Huns would not turn against Rome.

The whey-faced adolescent reclining beside her, in his gold-embroidered robe of Tyrian purple, and with a silver diadem upon his brow, albeit slightly askew, paused in between slurps of wine, and stammered at her with eyes agog, "Wh—what is the matter? You look angry with me."

Galla forced a pleasant smile. "Not with you, dear heart. Just with some of the incompetents whom I have entrusted with some important business."

"Wh–what business? Is it dangerous?"

"No, not at all. Slave!" She clicked her fingers and another slave came running. "His Sacred Majesty's cup needs refilling."

"I, I . . ." said His Sacred Majesty, holding out his cup. The slave filled it to the brim.

Galla smiled at him.

Honorius hiccupped and smiled uncertainly back.

A hoarse and manic voice reached the boy's ears, and rounding a corner he saw a preacher standing on the steps of a church, railing against the sins of the people as they swept past in their mocking laughter: men with wine stains down their front, linked arm in arm with tripping, painted harlots.

But not all who passed by laughed. Not the blind and the mute and the lame; not the leprous outcasts of mankind, hauling themselves forward on their knees and their knobbled and fingerless fists; no laughter from the child pickpockets and the bare, ragged orphans, prostituting themselves for a crust of bread. All the friendless and the many nameless and unloved, whose pitiful, lonely cries moved the heart of God Himself, they say, when He walked as a man on earth.

The preacher was an extraordinary figure, his bare and bony arms reaching out from a cloak which was no more than a tangle of rags, his hair wild and elf knotted, his lips cracked and dry, his eyes bloodshot, and his nails grown long and filthy as the claws of a bear. His voice croaked harshly and he gestured jerkily, and some who passed by, even in their licentious drunkenness, felt themselves commanded by his voice to halt and listen to his terrible and apocalyptic words. The boy stopped and listened, too.

"Woe unto you, O great Babylon!" cried the preacher. "For you that were proudest among the nations, and mightiest among the empires of the world, how you are laid low! Hearken unto my words, all ye that pass by, steeped as you are in the stink and stew of your own wickedness! For as the Lord said unto the prophet Ezekiel, 'I will bring the worst of the heathen, and they will possess your houses, and your holy places shall be defiled. For the land is full of bloody crimes, and the city is full of violence. Destruction cometh, and you shall seek peace, and there shall be none. And you shall hide your faces in the mountains like the doves of the valleys, and your children shall be clothed with desolation, and your princes themselves shall hunger like beggars in the streets.'

"For you have escaped the armies of the Christless barbarians that encompassed you about, O proud Rome—but not forever shall your impunity endure! No, not forever, nor for a year, nor even for the waxing and waning of one moon; for I say unto you, that before one moon is waxed and waned the armies of the north shall sweep down upon you, and your infants shall be dashed in pieces at the head of the streets, and ten thousand Roman nights shall be nights of horror!"

"Tell us something we don't know!" cried a wag from the crowd, hooting with laughter.

The blazing, irresistible eyes of the scarecrow preacher turned upon the wag, and he said softly, "Aye, and Rome went laughing to her death."

Such was the power and mystery of the preacher's eyes and voice that the wag was silenced and the laughter froze upon his lips.

The scarecrow preacher said, "In after years, and in the last years of Rome and in the last age of the world, when God shall raze all clean and Christ shall come again in His glory, in those latter days, which shall come to pass before one of you here has passed away, so that you shall see it all with your own eyes—then a prince of terror shall come from the east, and he shall be called the Scourge of God. And his armies shall raze your proud temples and your palaces to the earth, and his horsemen shall trample your children into the dust, and everywhere your pride shall be laid low, and your haughtiness be made a laughingstock.

"For mighty princes there have been before you on the earth, and proudly stood Sidon and Babylon, Nineveh, and Tire. And now all, all are gone and have left not a wrack behind. They are blown away like grains of sand on the wind by the wrath of the Lord God of Israel, and their proud palaces, and their cloud-capped towers, and their demoniac temples with their altars of Moloch, stained red with innocent blood— they are all laid low.

"For nothing that is of man alone endureth, but only that which is of God. And the blood of the innocent, and the weeping of the widow, and the tears of the orphan cry to heaven for justice! And even as I speak these words unto you, Holy Jerome sits in his skylit cell in Bethlehem, beating his breast with a stone for the sins of the world! And his heart cries out that though our walls shine with gold, and our ceilings, and the carven capitals of our proud pillars, yet Christ dies daily at our doors, naked and hungry in the person of His poor. For man is cruel in his heart from his infancy upward, and scorns the teaching of Christ Jesus. But God sickens to see the wrong that is wrought on the earth. And He will gather His children unto Him: the meek, the gentle; the sowers of peace and the lovers of concord, and all those that hate injustice, and are righteous in their hearts. But the proud empires of the world shall be swept into the fiery abyss, whence cometh no sound but the wailing of the wicked for all eternity!"

The preacher preached on. He would preach until daybreak and beyond, until his voice cracked and dried in his throat. But the boy turned away with head bowed and made his way into the darkened streets beyond.

There he began to run. He couldn't have said why, but suddenly terror or disgust seized him, and he sprang forward and broke into a pell-mell run, and felt as if he must run all night and all the next day before he would be safe.

Racing through the jostling, drunken crowds, he ran hard, headfirst, into a huge, round-shouldered ox of a man coming the other way. He could smell the wine on his breath even as he detached himself and made to run on again.

"Oi, watch your step you little heathen!" the man bellowed down at him.

"Watch yours."

The man stopped moving on, swayed, and looked back blearily at the boy. "What did you say?"

Attila stopped likewise and looked back. His eyes never wavered. "I said, watch yours." Under his tunic, his fingers touched the handle of his stolen knife. "You're drunk," he added. "I'm not."

The man turned round properly and planted his feet wide apart. Now he didn't seem so drunk, as if the promise of a brawl, even with a little gutter-born puppy such as this, had instantly sobered him up.

In the flickering torchlight of the street a goat was being slaughtered under a canvas awning, ready to be skewered from end to end and roasted on a spit. People gathered around, fumbling for coins and tottering where they stood. It wasn't every day that Rome could celebrate a triumph over the barbarians these days, and the rabble were clearly determined to continue eating and drinking, singing and fornicating until dawn.

The goat's resigned and pitiful bleats filled the air for a few moments. Then it was silent, and its lifeblood flowed over the dark dust between the two antagonists. A small crowd had already gathered to watch the fight.

"Take him out, Borus!" called one of his companions.

Borus took a step forward, his sandalled foot splashing in the pooling goat's blood, and he looked down and then up again furiously, as if this too was the little heathen's fault.

"Now look what you've made me do," he said, softly this time, his voice filled with menace.

Attila looked on, unimpressed. "You'd have done it anyway," he said, "you great oaf."

"Right, that's it!" roared the man, advancing on the boy with great lumbering strides. "You're going to get a—"

"Don't you dare touch me. Do you know who I am?"

The man was so astonished and the crowd so amused by this haughty reprimand, coming from this slight, scowling ragamuffin with the mud-caked face, that they paused as one body and waited for the explanation.

The man folded his arms and rocked back on his heels. "Oh, I am so sorry. May the Lord have mercy 'pon my sinful soul. And who might you be, pray?"

The boy knew he should keep silent, that he should say nothing, be nothing; that he should slip away into the shadows, no more than a street urchin like the thousands of nameless others who lived in this city's alleyways like rats. But his pride overwhelmed him.

"I am Attila, son of Mundzuk," he said, "the son of Uldin, the son of Torda, the son of Beren—"

The crowd started laughing, and their laughter drowned his small, proud, steady voice. He continued to list his genealogy, but he could not be heard. The crowd whooped and hollered with inebriated glee, and clapped their hands, and more were joining them all the time. Meanwhile Attila's antagonist only encouraged them all the more, walking slowly round the still boy, as if viewing this strange, stunted specimen from all possible angles. He folded his brawny arms across his chest, furrowed his brow in puzzlement, and then grinned around at his audience with complicit mockery.

"—the son of Astur, the King of all that Flies," finished the boy, his voice never faltering, but trembling now with rage.

The crowd gradually fell silent.

"And who might they be, Attila, son of Mud-Suck?" asked Borus, sweeping his arm across his chest and bowing very low. The crowd began to laugh again. "They sound to me like names it'd be unkind to give a horse."

The crowd erupted with fresh laughter.

"You aren't descended from a horse, are you?" he inquired. "You don't *look* like—although as a matter of fact, now I consider, you do *smell* a little ripe and horse-like."

The boy's trembling hand was clenched firmly round the handle of his knife. His feet did not stir, though an urgent voice in his head was telling him, *Flee now! Drive your way through this mocking crowd and run like the wind, and never, ever look back. Or they will find you. They will come after you and they will find you.*

But his feet did not move, and his pride and anger boiled like lava within him.

The crowd fell silent again, in expectation of further entertainment.

"I am of royal blood," said Attila softly. "And I am bound for my homeland beyond the mountains. Now let me pass."

"The lad's drunk!" shouted an onlooker.

"Mad, more like," said an old woman. "Mad as a sunstruck badger. Set the dogs on him, I say."

"Put him in the Circus," slurred another, before turning aside to vomit on someone else's feet. A scuffle broke out, but most people's attention remained on the strange, mad boy who thought he was a king.

It was only because a fistful of mud hit Attila in the face that his ox-like antagonist got near him. One of the crowd had thrown it, and Attila turned his head in a fury to see who it was, wiping the mud from his face and his still-tender eye where Galla had slapped him only last night. Immediately, and with surprising swiftness, the torchlit shadow of his huge opponent fell across him. Before he could move, Borus had picked him up in a single sweeping bear hug, and raised him high above his head. The crowd bayed in delight as the man shook the boy violently.

"Your Majesty!" he cried. "Oh, your Sacred Majesty, oh, Attila, son of Mud-Suck, son of Udder, son of Turda, son of Ass Lick—let me raise you high up above the level of the common herd, so that you may loftily survey your mighty kingdom! And then let me—but alas, alas, I have dropped Your Majesty in a horrible great puddle of blood! Oh woe is me, oh forgive me!"

Attila lay stunned for a moment in the small quagmire of dust and goat's blood while the crowd, growing in size all the time, jeered and laughed with the contagion of raucous herdlike delight. More onlookers spilled from the taverns round about, and the air was thick with dust and wine fumes and scornful, jeering laughter.

The boy looked up and around at their creased and wine-flushed faces with a black, scowling hatred. In his heart he cursed all Rome.

Borus paraded around the natural ring of spectators like a Cypriot wrestler, flexing his biceps and smiling broadly. He didn't notice the boy getting to his feet again, his hair matted with blood, his face streaked and his once-white tunic half torn from his back and thickly dyed a darkening red. He didn't notice the boy reaching into his bloodstained tunic and producing a sharp fruit knife. He didn't notice the boy stepping up behind him.

But he did notice a sharp and agonizing pain in the small of his back, and reeled round to see the boy standing facing him, knife held out in his right hand, his left hand splayed for balance and deflection.

The laughter and smile froze on every watching face. Everything had suddenly changed. This wasn't supposed to happen.

The man stared at the boy, in pain and astonishment more than anger. The very night was silent and watchful with fear.

"Why, you . . ." he said shakily. He pressed his hand against the wound. It was in his kidneys. He reeled again. "You . . ."

He staggered toward the boy, but it was hopeless. The boy skipped out of his way with ease. Borus turned and reached a bloody hand toward him, more as if he were pleading than threatening.

Attila stopped again and stared back at him. Then he turned and said to the crowd, softly, his voice never raised, his eyes scanning each of their horror-stricken faces, "If you do not let me go now, I will kill every one of you."

This time, they heard his words.

The crowd—as many as fifty or a hundred people—seemed to be in collective shock. Absurd though the boy's threat was, something about the way his alien, slanted eyes glittered in that barbaric, blue-scarred face, allied to the steadiness of his arm, which extended the short blade of the fruit knife toward each of them turn, slowly revolving, silenced them all. There was something about him, as they said later. . . .

As the quiet, implacable force of his threat sank in, the crowd actually began to part before him, like the sea parting before the God-driven command of Moses. And there is no doubt that, incredible as it would seem, the boy would indeed have walked away from them at that moment, leaving his huge opponent kneeling in the dust, looking like a man who has just wrestled with an angel; like Jacob at the brook Jabbok, wrestling with his unknown antagonist blindly in the night, never knowing that his opponent was of God.

But the uproar had by now come to the notice of the city guard, and as the sullen, bewildered crowd began to make way for the boy, a voice of a different stamp altogether rang out in the midnight air.

"Clear the way there, clear the way! Come on, you drunken scum, get out of my way."

Sensing a different danger, the boy turned on his heel and held his dagger out again.

The crowd parted, and there stood no drunken street bully. There stood a tall, gray-eyed lieutenant in the chain mail uniform of one of the frontier legions, with a ragged scar across his chin and a scornful smile playing on his lips. Behind him stood a dozen of his men.

The lieutenant was surprised to find that the cause of all this ruckus was this one small, dusty, bloodstained boy.

For a moment, the boy extended his knife hand toward the soldiers themselves—all twelve of them.

The lieutenant glanced at the crop-headed, tough-looking man by his side. "What do you reckon, Centurion?"

The centurion grinned. "The lad's got spirit, you've got to admit, sir."

The lieutenant looked back at the boy, his right hand resting easily on the pommel of his sword. He didn't trouble to draw it, and when he smiled his eyes were as cold as ice.

"Drop it, son," he said quietly.

Attila returned his gaze for a moment. Then he sighed, straightened, and dropped the knife at his feet.

The lieutenant turned to his men. "You, Ops, Crates, tie him up, arms behind his back."

Still kneeling in the dust, Borus saw the boy being tied, and he relaxed, and felt his legs trembling, and then he stretched out his arms and fell, and lay in the dirt. His head was throbbing. He rolled half over. His mouth felt bitter, metallic, and his back felt strangely cold. He was bewildered. His eyelids kept drooping, he didn't know why, and his limbs ached and tingled. He prayed. He could feel his heart hammering beneath his ribs—or fluttering, rather, like a bird trapped and panicking in a bone cage. He gazed into the stars above and prayed to every god he could name. His eyesight blurred, and it seemed to him as if every star was growing into a radiant circle of light. He prayed to Mithras and to Jupiter and to Isis and to Christ and to the very stars themselves.

The stars looked silently down.

"And you," the lieutenant called to Borus, "get home to your wife. That wound needs seeing to."

Borus didn't stir.

One of the soldiers went over and knelt beside the fallen man and touched his fingertips to his neck. Then he stood up again. "He's dead, sir."

"Why, you little—" roared a man in the crowd, "I'll—"

Two soldiers blocked his way with crossed spears, and one knocked him sharply back with a kick to his midriff.

But the crowd's mood had turned ugly and belligerent.

"You murdering swine!" screamed an old woman.

"Slit his dirty neck!"

"String him up! Look at him, the little demon, look at that look in his eye! He'll kill us all, give him half a chance!"

Several women in the crowd crossed themselves. A man clutched the bluestone he wore round his neck to ward off the evil eye.

The lieutenant regarded his captive. "You're popular," he murmured.

The boy glared up at him with such unabated ferocity that even the lieutenant was momentarily nonplussed. Then he demanded his name.

The boy ignored him.

"I asked you," repeated the lieutenant, leaning down, *"What is your name?"*

Still the boy ignored him.

From the angry crowd, a voice cried, "He said his name was Attalus or some such."

"Attalus, son of Turda, son of Ass Lick," cried another.

For the first time, the lieutenant noticed the blue scars on the boy's cheeks, eerily visible in the sidelong torchlight.

"Not . . . ?" he wondered softly. He turned to his men. "Lads," he said, "I think we could be in for a little donative." He turned back to the boy. "Strip."

The boy didn't stir.

The lieutenant nodded, and one of his men stepped forward, gripped what remained of the boy's tattered tunic at the neck, and ripped it down to the waist.

The crowd gasped. They had never seen anything like it.

The boy's back was decorated with the most fantastic swirls and curlicues, weals and welts, some made by needles and blue ink, some more cruelly cut in with a knife and then sewn up with a horsehair in the wound to ensure that the scar remained bold and prominent. It was the way of the Huns.

Not Attalus. Attila. The fugitive.

Princess Galla Placidia would be grimly pleased at his recapture. She seemed to have a strange obsession with the boy.

"Well done, lads," said the lieutenant. "And the rest of you," he said, raising his voice again, "disperse. Or we'll make you—which will hurt."

The crowd sullenly and reluctantly began to move away. One of them walked over to Borus and covered his face with a cloth.

The lieutenant asked him if he knew the dead man. He nodded.

"Then you'll see to his corpse," he said.

He turned back to his troop. "Right," he barked, "back to the Palatine. On the double."

"Word of advice," said the lieutenant affably as they marched back up the hill, the boy's arms trussed tightly behind him like spatchcock chicken. "Next time you're on the run, try not to attract so much attention to yourself by killing someone."

The boy said nothing.

"Lucky for you we came along when we did, anyhow. They'd have torn you limb from limb."

At last the boy spoke. "They wouldn't have got close."

The lieutenant grinned. After awhile he said, "And the man you put down?"

"Self-defense."

The lieutenant nodded. It was clear enough.

"I didn't mean to kill him," the boy blurted out.

The lieutenant saw in some surprise that the boy's eyes were bright with tears—not such a tough nut as he made out.

The lieutenant nodded again. "It's okay, son. It happens. You did well to defend yourself."

The boy tried to rub his nose with his bound arm, but couldn't reach. If he sniffed the lieutenant would hear him, and he didn't want that.

They marched left into the Vicus Longus and began the long ascent toward the Palatine. At one point they passed the scarecrow preacher again, and the boy glanced at him with consternation and almost with fear.

"Nut," said the lieutenant.

"Are you a Christian?" asked the boy.

The lieutenant grinned. "We're all Christians now, son. Much good may it do us."

At last the drunken mob were beginning to thin out for the night. They made way when they saw a squadron of frontier troops approaching, looking on curiously from the doorways and the alleys at the strange, small, spiky, half-naked captive bound with rope.

"I'd untie you if I thought you wouldn't try to escape again," said the lieutenant, a little more gently.

"But I would."

"I know you would."

"And I'd succeed, too."

"It's possible."

The boy looked up at the lieutenant, and for a moment something like a fleeting smile passed between them.

"So . . . you were trying to get home?"

The boy didn't answer. Instead, surprisingly, he asked a question. "Where are you from?"

"Well," he said, "my dad was a soldier before me, from Gaul originally. But I served in the Legio II 'Augusta,' in Britain, at Caerleon. You won't have heard of it."

"I've heard of it," said the boy. "It's in the west of the province, a frontier fortress to keep down the Silurian tribes."

The lieutenant laughed with astonishment. "How in the Name of Light do you know that?"

The boy ignored the question. "What were you doing in Britain?"

The lieutenant began to wonder if he should be talking quite so much. There was something about the lad that was . . . unusual.

"Well, my mother was a Celt. My father married her over there. So I guess I'm half and half. But we're all Celts under our Roman skins, or so we like to think. We—me and the lads here—served over there until just recently. Then—"

"Then the emperor called the British legions home? Because Rome was in such trouble?"

"Hold your horses," said the lieutenant easily. "Rome's no home of mine. My home's Britain. And anyway Rome's not done yet. We've dealt with worse than Goths before. Remember Brennus and his Gauls? They sacked Rome itself. And Hannibal? And the Cimbri?"

"But what's wrong with the Palatine guard defending Rome? There's thirty thousand of them out at the camp."

"Jove's balls, you really do know it all, don't you? Well, you know what we frontier troops think of the Palatine guard back in Rome. A little . . . soft, shall we say. Too many hot baths and too little real fighting."

"Is there still fighting in Britain?"

"More and more these days," said the lieutenant somberly. "The Picts are always raiding in the north, and now we have the Saxon pirates to contend with, all along the eastern and southern coasts. And our Count of the Saxon Shore is about as much use as a paper bucket. So yes, Britain has its problems, too. But from now on"—he spoke with uncharacteristic hesitancy—"they'll . . . they'll just have to fend for themselves."

The boy pondered for awhile. Then, "What else is Britain like? Your country?"

"My country?" The lieutenant's voice softened again. "My country is beautiful."

"Mine, too," said the boy.

"Tell me about it."

So they passed the time on the return march describing to each other in loving detail their respective countries.

The boy liked the sound of Britain: plenty of space, good hunting, and no fancy cooking.

"Well," said the lieutenant as he watched his men untie the boy and hand him over to the Palace Guard. "Just remember, next time: keep your pride and your anger to yourself. Patience is a great military virtue."

The boy gave a wan smile.

"Shake," said the lieutenant.

They shook hands. Then the lieutenant barked an order, and his men fell into line. "Well, lads, our nightwatch is just about over. In two days' time we march to Pavia, under the command of General Stilicho. So make the most of Rome's glorious whores while you can."

At that glorious news, all the men raised their fists in the air and roared their hurrahs. Then they wheeled and marched away into the night. The boy looked down the street after them for a long time.

He was taken and bathed, and escorted to his cell, and a guard was posted permanently outside his room. He drifted into a light, twitching sleep.

THE SWORD AND
THE PROPHECY

In the hot morning he lay in an uneasy doze when he was woken by low voices by his bedside. He opened his eyes.

Beside his bed stood Serena and, behind her, General Stilicho himself.

"Well, my young wolf cub," said the general, smiling. "And what headaches have you been causing the empire this time?"

Attila said nothing. He didn't smile.

Serena reached down and laid a cool hand across Attila's forehead. "Foolish boy," she said.

He wanted to glare at her but couldn't. Her eyes were so gentle.

"Here," said Stilicho, tossing something onto the bed. "This is for you. But only if you promise me never to try to escape again." Now he was stern, soldierly. "Do you promise, lad?"

Attila stared down at the package by his side, and looked up again and met the general's eye. He nodded.

Stilicho believed him. "Open it when we've gone."

Serena bent and kissed him, nodded to her husband, and departed.

Stilicho hesitated for a moment, then sat down on a small wooden stool, a little awkwardly for a man of his soldierly frame. He rested his elbows on his knees, rested his chin on his clenched fists, and scrutinized the boy long and hard. The boy waited expectantly.

"I'm riding north for Pavia tomorrow," said Stilicho. "Serena will remain here in the palace." He fell silent a while, then said, "The Gothic armies are regrouping under Alaric. You have heard of him?"

Attila nodded. "He's a Christian, too, though."

"He is. If he sacks Rome, he has promised to touch not a stone or a tile of any Christian building." Stilicho smiled. "Some chance. The Gothic armies won't be sacking anywhere soon, least of all Rome. But. . . ." The great general sighed. "We live in difficult times."

Attila looked down. He felt obscurely guilty.

Stilicho was searching for the right words. He felt somehow that it mattered, deeply, what he said to the boy at this moment. Almost as if . . . almost as if he'd not be seeing him again. As those ancient Sybilline Books had said. . . . He put all thought of those haunting Books from his mind, and said, speaking as slowly and carefully as he would to Galla at her most predatory, "Difficult times. Strange times." He looked hard at the boy, and said simply, "Do what is right, Attila."

The boy started. The words surprised him.

Stilicho went on, holding the boy's eye. "I have always served Rome, though I am of barbarian blood. But then, we were all barbarians once. What was great Rome herself, in the days before Numa and Romulus and the Ancient Kings? A village on a hillside."

The boy smiled uncertainly. He was unaccustomed to hearing the general speak in this way.

"What else is there but Rome, to hold back the blood-dimmed tide? To continue . . . history itself? Without Rome, the world would be again a place of dark forests and witchcraft, legends and ghosts, horned warriors, human sacrifice, those terrible Saxon pirates. . . . Without Rome, the world would fall back again into the world before history. Do you see what I am saying, boy?"

Attila nodded hesitantly. The two stared at each other and then the boy's gaze dropped.

"Someone said to me," he said hesitantly, "someone said that the Romans are all hypocrites, and no better than anyone else. They go on about barbarians doing human sacrifices, and how disgusting it all is, and how they need Roman law and civilization and all that—but what is the Roman arena but one huge human sacrifice?"

"Who told you that?" asked the general, frowning.

Attila shook his head.

Stilicho knew better than to try and wring it out of the little mule. He sighed and said, "We have lived through centuries of struggle, we Romans. We are not a soft people. No society is perfect; but judge it by its ideals. We have made laws, we have set limits. There are no more gladiators, you know that. The Christian faith has introduced us to guilt—and no bad thing, perhaps. Only criminals and prisoners of war are now executed in the arena, which they fully deserve. Likewise, a master no longer has the power of life and death over his slaves. He can even be tried in court for their murder. Over centuries of struggle, things do *get better.* Can you say that of life and law in the barbarian lands?"

Attila said nothing.

Perhaps it was fruitless. Stilicho brooded for awhile, and then he started again, in a vein the boy barely understood.

"Prophecies fulfill themselves." He spoke softly, with deep sadness. "And in our time, the twelve hundred prophesied years of Rome will come to an end. We might destroy all evidence of the prophecies themselves— we might indeed burn the Sibylline Books, as has been commanded by the powers that be. But the prophecies would remain. They are not confined by a single scroll of vellum, nor ended by its burning. Prophecies are things of power. Beliefs are things of power, of real power, in the world.

An army that believes in something will always destroy an army that believes in nothing—no matter how great the odds against it. But what do we still believe in? Do we still believe in Rome? Or do we believe in those ancient and implacable Books, which tell only of Rome's allotted twelve hundred years?" He shook his head. "I should have burned them all and had done with them."

There was a silence.

"But that cannot be the end of everything. It cannot all have been for nothing. It cannot!" Stilicho's voice was raised almost to a cry of anguish, his fists tightly clenched. "Those twelve long centuries of suffering and sacrifice cannot all just be lost in time, like dead leaves in the wind. The gods could not be so cruel. Something must survive of them."

He lowered his voice. "I am sorry, I—I am making little sense." He compressed his lips, and then started again. "The believers, those who defend what they know in their hearts to be right, will always triumph. I have seen a small, weary group of bloodied and battle-weary soldiers, surrounded by ten, twenty times as many of their enemy. But those out-numbered men were loyal to each other. They trusted in themselves, and in each other, and in their god. I have seen a band of no more than sixty men, infantry only, protected only with light mail and leather, armed with only shield and spear and sword—no javelins, no missiles, no artil-lery, no cavalry back-up or reconnaissance, no archers or slingers, nor even the time to set staves and put out caltrops. But still I have seen them lock shield to shield, clutch their spears in defensive undergrip, and I have seen them hold themselves proudly against as many as a thousand mounted warriors—and walk from that field bloodied but unbowed. Undefeated." Stilicho nodded. "I know, because I was one of them.

"An army that believes in its cause will always defeat an army of un-believing savages, who believe only in the flame and the sword. Remember that, Attila."

The general stood and resumed his usual aloof demeanor. "You have to believe in something. So believe what is right."

He stepped toward the door of the boy's chamber, and threw a last glance back. He nodded at the package on the bed. "You can open it now," he said.

The door closed behind him.

The boy unwrapped the package and found inside the wrappings of fine oiled linen a most beautiful sword, as long as his arm, with gold scrollwork in the handle and a honed double blade that was sharp even to the lightest touch. It was of finest carburised steel, and rather old-fashioned type, the *gladius hispaniensis* or Spanish sword, a beautifully sinuous and dangerous shape with a swelling then tapering blade and an exceptionally long point. No shield or armor known to man could withstand a straight under-arm thrust from a sword such as this. He wrapped it in its protective oiled cloth again and laid it under his pillow, and daydreamed.

When he finally arose and went out into the courts of the palace, he found that the other hostage children had heard of his escape. They were fascinated. Hegemond, the fat Burgundian boy with the sleepy eyes, waddled up to him in the palace gardens, where they were playing beneath the mulberry trees, and asked if it was true.

Attila was wary. He had heard enough questions from these lumbering, slow-witted German children before. Is it true that the Huns coat themselves in animal fat and never take baths? Is it true that the Huns eat only meat and drink only fermented mare's milk? Is it true that the Huns are the offspring of witches, who were driven out of Christian lands and coupled with the demons of the wind and the desert? "Yes," he used to nod solemnly. "It's all true."

Hegemond made it clear to Attila that he was invited now to join their gang. "Even if you are a Hun."

But the boy kept his distance and his proud aloofness, as he always did. He watched the German children shout and play at soldiers for a

while, amid the Paestum roses in the hot Italian sun. Then he turned
away.

That evening, he had a visitor very different from the morning's. He was
drifting off to sleep when there came a knock on his door. The knock
was clearly a formality, however, as the door then promptly opened and a
tall, lean figure stepped inside. It was Eumolpus, one of the head palace
eunuchs.

He stood at the end of the boy's bed. "A message from Serena," he said
coldly. "You are to have no more converse with her. Neither with General
Stilicho, should you ever meet again."

Attila stared at the eunuch. "What do you mean?"

Eumolpus smiled thinly. "I am so sorry, perhaps your Latin is still not
good enough for you to understand even so simple a command as that. I
repeat: you are to have no more converse with Serena. Ever again."

"By whose order?" said the boy, pushing himself up on his elbow.

"By the order of Serena herself," shrugged Eumolpus. He added, for
his own personal amusement, "She says she finds your company . . .
distasteful."

He had gone too far.

There was a split second of deafening silence in the little room, and
then Attila, screaming "You lie!" sprang from his low bed and hurled
himself at the startled eunuch with his teeth bared and his fists flying.

The guard heard the eunuch's screams and rushed in, tore the raging
boy away from the wailing Eumolpus and knocked him smartly to the
floor. Then he turned back to the eunuch, who was lying speechless across
the bed, and gave a low whistle.

"Jupiter's brazen balls," he gasped.

The eunuch looked as if he'd been savaged by a Caledonian hunting
dog.

"Well, don't just stand there swearing," blubbered Eumolpus through the blood that spilled from his battered mouth, and with a shaky hand held to his throat where the boy had bitten deeply into it. "Get a physician."

That night, for the first time, Attila was locked and bolted inside his chamber, and a guard of three was posted on his door.

He couldn't sleep anyway. His heart thumped with a black rage that would keep him awake for years.

Stilicho was abruptly summoned the following morning to the Chamber of the Imperial Audience before his departure for Pavia.

When he got there he found not the emperor seated upon the throne, but Princess Galla Placidia. Honorius had already departed for the safety of his palace amid the marshlands of Ravenna.

Galla sat resplendent in robes of gold and—most shockingly of all—imperial purple. Flanking her overdecorated marble throne of purest Carrara marble were two of her most-trusted palace eunuchs, Eumolpus himself and Olympian. Stilicho tried not to stare but he could see, even from the lowly and distant place where he stood, a humble suppliant at the bottom of the steps up to the dais, that Eumolpus had several stitches across his cheek, and an unusual kind of linen swaddling round his throat. In addition, both he and Olympian were wearing . . . makeup. Their eyes were rimmed with kohl like those of whores from the backstreets of the Suburra, or of Oriental despots, or Egyptian pharaohs of old, whose downtrodden people believed their ruler to be a god.

As we hold our emperors to be now, thought Stilicho.

When the men in power start wearing makeup, it's time to start worrying. And Galla's eunuchs were very much in power. He bowed and waited.

At last, Galla addressed him. "You have been to the temple building and destroyed the last of the Books?"

"I have, Your Majesty."

"Pagan superstitions such as that can have no place in a Christian empire such as ours. Do you not agree?"

Stilicho gave a tilt of his head.

"We will have an audience with the Bishop of Rome and all his principal deacons," Galla continued. "We will make it clear to them that they must preach an end to such pessimistic superstitions of the past. Rome is a Christian empire now, and under the protection of God. Those ancient scrolls are nothing but the raving of a harridan in a cave."

There followed an awkward silence. Galla enjoyed awkward silences. They affirmed her power. In the Chamber of the Imperial Audience, no one could speak until they were addressed by the Imperial Throne.

What would Cicero have said? thought Stilicho sourly. That great orator. For all his pomposity and his self-regard, the last great voice of Free Rome. Who died for his oratorical pains, his severed head and hands delivered in a sack to Mark Antony, that sozzled lecher and braggard. His wife, Fulvia—now on her third marriage—had snatched Cicero's head from the sack, spat on it, then yanked out its tongue and stabbed it with one of her hairpins. A fine example of Roman womanhood all round.

Stilicho waited, nursing his thoughts.

At last Galla said, "Remind me, Stilicho, what was the name of the barbarian chieftain who destroyed Publius Quintilius Varus's three legions in the Teutoburg Forest, in the otherwise glorious reign of the Emperor Augustus?"

"Glorious indeed," replied the general, "for in the reign of Augustus Christ was born."

Galla closed her eyes slowly and then opened them again.

Stilicho regarded her warily. "He was called Arminius, Your Majesty, which is the Latin version of his real name, Herman, meaning 'Man of War.' 'Herman the German,' the troops called him."

"Arminius," Galla nodded. Of course, she knew it already. "As many as twenty thousand soldiers, along with their families and attendants, cut down in the dark forests of Germany, over the course of two or three days. It must have been terrible. The worst disaster ever to befall Roman arms."

Stilicho hesitated, still trying to work out what she was up to. But it was impossible: you might as well try to guess the next strike of a snake. "The worst," he admitted, "at least since Hannibal and Cannae. When sixty thousand men were lost in a single—"

Galla was not interested in Stilicho's military-historical musings. "And Arminius was raised—raised and educated—in Rome itself, was he not?"

"He was, Your Majesty."

"As was that other great enemy of Rome, King Jugurtha of Numidia?"

"I believe so, Your Majesty."

"And do you think it possible that, like Jugurtha, Arminius's early years in Rome, watching the exercises of the troops on the Campus Martius, might have given him a keen sense of his future enemy, and how they operated? So that when he came to turn upon them in that dreadful, sunless forest in the dark heart of Germany, he was very well advantaged? Thanks to what he had learned in the heart of his enemies' capital as a boy?"

Now Stilicho understood her game, and he feared in his heart for the wolf cub.

He spoke slowly. "I think that is unlikely, Your Majesty. After all—"

Galla held her hand up. Her point had been made. "You may go."

Stilicho held Galla's hard gaze without blinking, and for far longer than was polite. And then, contrary to all Palatine protocol, he turned his back on the Imperial presence and departed without a bow.

Galla's hands clutched the arms of her throne, tense with fury, and as cold and white as purest Carrara marble.

7

CONVERSATIONS WITH
A BRITISH LIEUTENANT

That evening, General Stilicho sat brooding in his white canvas tent on the edge of the army encampment outside the town of Falerii, beside the River Tiber. A long day's march from Rome, but he always drove his men hard.

He was listing the priorities that faced him. First and foremost, he must face Alaric's army in the field and defeat it. As palace whisperers said he should have done more thoroughly to the armies of Rhadagastus.

Alaric would not be easy. The barbarians no longer fought like barbarians. They fought like Romans. In the good old days, barbarian tactics on the battlefield, whether Gothic, Vandal, Pictish, Frankish, or Marcomman, had been pretty much the same wherever you went. They were as follows: 1. Group together on the battlefield any old how. Put the wives and kids in the chariots behind you to watch the show. 2. Bang your weapons and shields together, and shout insults at the enemy. Especially insult the size of his genitals. 3. And then . . . Chaaaaarge!

The barbarian horde of twenty or thirty thousand vainglorious indi-
viduals would rush in on the tight-packed ranks of the bristling Roman
legion, numbering six thousand at the most but working together as a
single ruthless unit, and the horde would be cut to pieces. All males captured or wounded were beheaded on the battlefield. Wives and kids were
sold into slavery. End of story.

But now . . . now they fought on command, in rank and file. They
turned and wheeled and switched fronts with the ease of a drilled Roman
legion. And they were bloody good horsemen, too. It would not be easy.
But that was what must be done first, nevertheless. Alaric's power must
be destroyed. If Uldin and his Huns could be called upon again, all well
and good. If not, the Romans would have to stand alone.

Then he must return to Rome, to that nest of vipers, and, and . . .
and what? In his mind, he could hear the soft, pleading voices of his
closest friends urging him to seize the throne for himself. "For Rome,"
they said, "and for the sake of good government. Raise your legions and
come down to Rome. The people will acclaim you."

And then there was the heavy burden of the slim scroll that he still carried in his pouch. The knowledge that if it fell into the wrong hands. . . .

He glanced up. It was a lieutenant of the Palatine guard who attended
him now, a high-born palace soldier in his shiny black leather breastplates. The only blood on his blade the blood of those he'd executed down
in the palace cells, after a good few hours of torture. Stilicho looked sourly
at him.

"Sir?" said the lieutenant ingratiatingly.

"You're dismissed," said the general. "Send me a lieutenant from one
of the frontier detachments."

The lieutenant blanched. "With respect, sir, I hardly think a frontier
soldier will have the necessary manners or the knowledge of court eti-
quette to satisf—"

The Palatine officer felt the general's wrath blast him full in the chest
like a blow from a ballista. He staggered backward out of the tent and

hurried off to fulfill his orders, the general's parade-ground language ringing vividly in his ears.

A few minutes later there came a rapping at the bar over the door of the tent, and the general ordered him in. He continued to read a while. Despatches from Gaul. They did not make good reading.

When he finally looked up, he saw a tall, gray-eyed lieutenant standing in front of him, with a ragged scar across his chin.

He gave him his fiercest glare. "How d'you get the scar, soldier?"

The lieutenant didn't flinch. "Tripped over a dog, sir."

Stilicho looked down and then up again, his eyebrows quizzically raised. "Repeat."

"Tripped over a dog, sir. In a backstreet in Isca Dumnoniorum. Drunk as a skunk on British mead, sir. Bashed my head on a stone water trough as I went down."

Stilicho suppressed the urge to smile. He pushed back his camp stool and stood and walked over to the lieutenant. The lieutenant continued to stare straight ahead without a flicker of the eyes. Stilicho stood as tall as him, and he adopted that most unnerving of positions, to the side of his man, but just out of his field of vision. Every drill decurion's favorite bullying point.

"A little clumsy, eh, soldier?"

"Damnably clumsy, sir."

The general leaned close so that he needed only whisper in the soldier's ear. "Some soldiers might have had the wit to make up something a bit more . . . soldierly? Such as, it was an ax stroke from a giant Rhinelander that nearly took your head off? Or a bloody great two-handed Frankish sword—but you ducked out of the way just in time, so it only nicked you on the chin? Have you no imagination, soldier?"

"None whatsoever, sir." He raised his scarred chin even higher. "Useless memory, too, sir. Which is why I always have to tell the truth."

Stilicho stood back and grinned. He liked what he saw and heard. He returned to his desk and waved at the canvas stool before it.

"Sit down, soldier."

"Thank you, sir."

"Cup of wine?"

"No, thank you, sir. Keeps me awake at my age."

"What is your age?"

"Twenty-five, sir."

"Hm. Wish I was twenty-five again. At my age, wine only puts me to sleep." The general poured himself a glass of watery wine anyhow, and sat down likewise. "So, how many men in your command?"

"Just eighty, sir."

"A lieutenant, commanding eighty? Where's your centurion?"

The lieutenant grinned as he thought of his centurion. "Still alive, sir. More scars on him than a butcher's chopping board, but still very much alive. But I know, sir, it's fucked up. Pardon my language, but there's just not . . . not enough. . . ." He trailed off, feeling that what he was about to say was tantamount to treachery.

But Stilicho was ahead of him. "I know, I know," he said wearily. "Not enough men to go round. I've heard it all before." He leaned forward and ran his hands over his face and brooded. Then he resumed. "And you're a Brit?"

"Sir."

"Married?"

"Yes, sir."

"So when you marched out of—where were you stationed?"

"Isca, sir. Dumnonia."

Stilicho nodded gravely. "I know it. Pretty, dark-eyed girls, they say."

"Dead right, sir. I married one of 'em."

"And so when you marched out of Isca, on imperial orders to return to Italy, to defend Rome at all costs, you left a wife behind?"

"Yes, sir. And two children."

"And two children," Stilicho repeated. "Tough order. Miss them?"

"Like Hell, sir. I . . ." He hesitated. "I hope one day to go back there, sir. When all this is done."

"Britain is now beyond the frontier, soldier. You do understand that?"

"I do, sir. But it's not yet finished."

"Hm." Stilicho stroked the thinning gray stubble on the top of his head. "But your lot had plenty of desertions?"

The lieutenant looked shamefaced. "Yes, sir."

"Hm. So you joined at—eighteen?"

"Yes, sir."

"And you've got another thirteen years to serve before you get pensioned off. That's a long time to go without seeing your wife and kids. And a long time for a wife to go without seeing her husband. If you know what I mean."

"I'm not complacent, sir."

"Remember Emperor Claudius. He only had to go down to the port of Ostia for a few days, and his wife went and married Gaius Silvus."

"My wife is no Messalina, sir."

"No, no," said the general with some haste. "And you're no Claudius, I'm sure, but only a mere mortal like the rest of us." He grinned. "You know what the Divine Claudius's last words were, according to Seneca?"

The lieutenant shook his head.

" 'Oh dear, I think I've shat myself!' "

The lieutenant smiled. Then Stilicho resumed more seriously, "And when you get pensioned off, you won't get a farm in Britain for your service, not anymore. You'll maybe get something in Gaul. And maybe not."

The lieutenant said nothing.

The general sighed and felt a great weight on his shoulders. It was the weight of responsibility, plus the weight of this good lieutenant's tragic loyalty. And there were thousands more like him, who would not desert their last post.

"Okay, soldier. Now give me a game of drafts before you go. You play backgammon?"

"Badly, sir."

"Me, too. Excellent. Means the game won't last long and we can soon go to bed."

The game lasted, as the general had predicted, only a few minutes. The lieutenant won.

"Badly indeed," said Stilicho grudgingly. He sat back and stretched. "Okay, soldier, you can go. Reveille at first light."

"Sir."

Stilicho sat for a long time on his own, gazing at the scattered backgammon men before him by the light of the guttering candle. He heard the howl of the wolves at the river's edge, eerily nearby, come down from the hills above to drink, or to lie in wait for their prey, when they came to drink likewise. And he heard the answering howl of the camp dogs calling to their cousins beyond, in the wilderness. Like men, penned in the safety of their cities, longing for the ungoverned wilderness in their turn. Bored with civilization and its heavy demands, its frustrating interdictions, and longing for the old forest ways, and the new dark age.

Stilicho reached out for more wine, and then stopped himself. Freedom comes when you learn to say no. He slept at his desk.

Over the next few days of the march to Pavia, the general came to like his new aide-de-camp, the British lieutenant, more and more as they rode alongside each other. Lucius was his name.

"And my horse," said the lieutenant, leaning forward and patting the long, gray, powerful neck, "is called Tugha Bàn."

The general eyed him a little sardonically. "You have a name for your *horse?*"

Lucius nodded. "The finest gray mare from the stock of the wide horse country of the Iceni. And where I go, she goes."

The general shook his head. Horse lovers.

"What do you think of the Palatine guard, soldier?" he asked. "As a frontier guard yourself?"

"Begging your pardon, sir, but in all honesty I'd rather not say."

"Hm," murmured Stilicho. "I think they're a bunch of posturing girly boys myself."

The lieutenant grinned and said nothing.

"You'll dine with me tonight, soldier. Just the two of us. I've things I want to discuss with you."

"Sir?"

"Tonight, soldier. At the twelfth hour."

They dined well, and Stilicho insisted the lieutenant took at least a cup of wine.

"I'm no wine expert," he said, "but this Opimian is pretty good, don't you think? The vines grow overlooking the bay, and it's supposed to have the taste of the salt sea in it." The general took a glug, rolled it round his mouth and swallowed. "Actually, I can't taste anything of the sort, it's just what the wine snobs back in Rome claim."

The lieutenant liked this Stilicho.

They talked of the army, the barbarian invasions, the state of Rome. The vulnerability of Africa, and its vast grain fields; and the inscrutable nature of the Huns.

"They could yet be our salvation," said Stilicho.

"Or . . ." said Lucius, and left it hanging in the air.

"Hm," said the general. "It'll pay to keep cozy with them, certainly. And take care of our Hun hostages, too."

He poured them each a fresh cup of wine, Lucius not refusing. A moment later, he said, "You believe in prophecies, lieutenant?"

"Well," said the lieutenant slowly, "I'm no philosopher, but I *think* I do. Like most people, I suppose."

"Exactly!" The general banged his fist on the table and his eyes gleamed.

"In my part of Britain, sir . . . I don't know if I should say, as we're all Christian now, I know, and they weren't exactly popular with Julius Caesar. . . ."

Stilicho frowned. "Who, the Christians?"

"No, sir, the *druithynn* and the *bandruithynn*—the holy men and women of Britain, the priests of our native religion."

"Ah yes, the druids. Caesar detested them, and the power they wielded. Which was why he pretty much wiped them out, I thought, on the Isle of Môn?"

"He killed a lot of them, sir. But some escaped, to their cousins, over the water in Hibernia."

"Ah yes, Hibernia. Never could get the hang of Hibernia. They're all mad there, aren't they?"

Lucius smiled, and then said enigmatically, "Well, they don't build straight roads over there, let's say. But after the massacre on Môn, it was the home of the *druithynn* for the next four hundred years."

"And now . . . ?"

"Now they're returning to Britain. Even though we're all Christians now, even in Hibernia, the *druithynn* are returning. And many of the people, especially the country people, are still faithful to the old religion."

Stilicho nodded. "Don't tell me. The things that still go on in the hills and the villages—even in civilized Italy. I tell you, soldier, your average village Saturnalia still makes a night in a Suburran brothel look like dinner with the Vestal Virgins."

"In Dumnonia, sir, in my village, the marriage bond is held as sacred as it is among the strictest Christians of the East. But that's not the case everywhere in Britain, especially on the great feast days of our Celtic year—like with your Saturnalia. In Dumnonia we still have the midwinter festival of Samhain, and then Beltane—"

"And that's when men really have to watch their wives, huh?"

Lucius grimaced. "And as for the young people not yet married . . ."

The two men brooded for awhile on the thought of young Celtic girls with no clothes on, and then harrumphed simultaneously and came back to reality.

"How did we get onto this subject?" growled the general.

"Prophecy, sir."

"Ah yes." He poured more wine.

"And I meant to say," said Lucius, "that prophecy is very strong among the *druithynn*—except that nothing is ever written down. Prophecies are considered to possess too much *mana*—that is, sacred power. Once they're written down, anyone can read them."

Stilicho nodded, his burning brown eyes in his long, lugubrious face fixed on the lieutenant. And then, without changing his gaze, he reached down and picked up a scroll from the table, upended it and shook. Another tattered scrap of a scroll fell out, and Stilicho unrolled it and pressed it out flat upon the table. It was brown with age, and blackened with burns round its edges.

"Only two weeks ago," said the general, very slowly and softly, "on the orders of the Princess Galla Placidia, I went to the Temple of Capitoline Jove, which is now a Christian place of worship, of course. And I took up the Sibylline Books, and I burned them. I scattered the ashes off the Tarpeian Rock like dead leaves. And when I looked back, this one scrap had fallen from the brazier and survived. One of the priests emerged—not a man I had ever respected for his spiritual fervor or intelligence. A fat old senator called Majoricus. In earlier days he was actually one of the *quindecemviri*—the Fifteen Men—who guarded the Sibylline Books with their lives. But once Theodosius shut the pagan temples for good, Majoricus knew pretty quickly which side his bread was buttered and became the most vociferous and fervent of Christians overnight. So he never had to leave the temple at all, it was said. A kind of holy sitting tenant, whom the new landlord—the God of the Christians—couldn't have got rid of even if He'd wanted to."

The two men chuckled.

"So there I was, burning the last of the Books, when Majoricus came waddling over and retrieved this scrap of parchment from the floor. He looked it over and then he pressed it into my hand, saying that this was the very last Sibylline prophecy of all and that I must keep it. He didn't know why, but he said it must be meant. He said, mysteriously, that 'God has a thousand and one names.'

"Now I had only reluctantly burned the Books in the first place. Galla had said they were a wicked pagan superstition anyway, and they would sap the morale of the Roman people, with their endless foretelling of doom and destruction. But, with some surprise—at myself, you understand, for I am not a man who is generally much influenced by what fat old senators tell me to do—"

"I imagine not, sir."

"All the same, at this moment, I did as that fat old priest commanded me, and I kept this last scrap of parchment. But it troubles me what I should do with it now. I do not know if my time will last much longer."

"Sir, you seem to me a very fit man."

Stilicho hadn't meant that at all. But he said nothing. Instead, he pushed the scroll across to the lieutenant. "I want you to have this. Guard it with your life."

Lucius frowned. "Why? Why me?"

"Call it a hunch. I've lived all my life listening to my hunches. My wife says it's a female gift, but it's one I've always received with gratitude. I usually get it right. Hunches tell us things that nothing else can. Here. It's yours."

Lucius gazed down at the scroll. There were two columns of verses, written in ancient temple hand, in ink now yellowish-brown with age. Some lines were in long, bombastic hexameters, and others were brief, even vulgarly rhyming riddles, like the rhymes of barbarian peoples, which surprised him.

"Read one," said Stilicho.

By the light of the candles beside him, Lucius read out in his deep, clear voice:

One with an empire,
One with a sword,
One with a son,
And one with a word.

The general nodded. "And read those last hexameters."

The lieutenant read,

When Romulus climbed to the rock,
Brother Remus stumbled below.
The dead man saw six, the king twelve,
And the book of Rome is closed.

He looked up again. "This is . . . this is the prophecy that gives Rome twelve centuries to stand?"

"And in our time . . ." said Stilicho. He opened his great hands wide. "In your hands is the very last prophecy of the Cumaean Sibyl, before she vanished forever from our history. These are the verses regarding the end of Rome. They are difficult and obscure, like all the Sibylline verses; and they say that whoever seeks to interpret them will do so only to misunderstand them. Nevertheless, I pass them on to you."

"To me? Why?"

"I feel somehow—I do not know why—that these last and most terrible verses must not be destroyed after all, but must be taken far, far away from Rome, beyond the frontier. For in some strange way, as yet unforeseen, they may yet save Rome. Or the spirit of Rome, if not the monuments and the temples and the palaces."

The general leaned forward passionately, his dark eyes blazing afresh. "Do your duty, man: take them back to Britain with you."

"But I have thirteen years yet to serve, sir, unless I get leave."

"You go when you go," said Stilicho vaguely. "A burden they are, but remember them. Galla fears them, and the Church fears them, and yet I think it need not. For they are things of power if rightly used, and may yet save Rome in some way I cannot foresee. The Books have never been wrong—only wrongly interpreted." He sat back and looked suddenly like a weary old man. He passed his big hand across his brow. "I could not destroy that last Book. It seems to me that those who start out by burning books end up by burning men."

The two men sat in eerie silence for awhile. The camp outside was all but silent. An owl hooted, the sound carrying through the still, airless night. But within the tent, the two troubled soldiers seemed to feel the wind of the centuries pass by, brushing their very skins like a ghost. They felt both small, and burdened with something far greater than they could comprehend. The end was coming, they knew, but it was not an end whose shape they or any mortal man could see clearly. And it was all the more terrifying for that.

The lieutenant saw in his mind's eye a woman in a long white robe walking sightlessly through a thick sea fog toward a cliff edge like the green and windswept headland of Pen Glas, above the beloved Dumnonian valley he called home. He wanted to cry out, but was dumb and helpless, and he saw the woman walking on with a stately dreaminess toward that teetering edge and the black-fanged rocks far below. And he thought that the woman was Clio, the Muse of History herself.

"You see things." It was the general's voice cutting in sharply.

The lieutenant came back from his reverie with an effort. "I . . ."

"Unusual for a soldier."

"My . . . my people in Britain have often been *fili, barda*—poets and seers and such—as often as they've been soldiers." Lucius tried to laugh it off. "You know what a reputation we Celts have."

Stilicho made no comment. Instead he said, "There's another thing I want from you."

"Sir?"

"I'm sending you back to Rome tomorrow."

"But, sir, the Palatine guard have requested no frontier guards within the city precincts. That was why me and my lads were packed off with you to Pavia, sir, if you don't mind me saying so. And we're up for it, too—crack at the Goths and all that. But I don't think—"

"And the whores of Rome beginning to wear your men out, too, eh, soldier?"

Lucius grinned. "Lads were beginning to say they were a bit exhausted, yes, sir. Said that, after Rome, going back to the Pictish frontier would be a holiday."

"Well, the Pictish frontier is abandoned for good," said Stilicho grimly. "But there are plenty more frontiers still to fight for. The Rhine and the Danube must be held."

"Sir."

"Anyhow, I am well aware of the tensions between the Palatine guard and frontier troops who get stationed back in Rome. But those are my orders, and I am, as the Palatine guard might need to be reminded from time to time, master general of *all* Rome's armed forces. So never mind those girly boys. You and your century will return to Rome tomorrow. I want you to look out for someone for me."

"Sir?"

"Among the hostages there's one who really matters—for obvious reasons just now. The Hun lad, name of Attila."

The lieutenant grinned. "I've met him."

The general was startled. "You have?"

"It was my squad who brought him in, that night he escaped from the Palatine after cracking the codeword."

Stilicho stared hard at the lieutenant. "That is no coincidence, I feel sure," he said quietly. "Well, as you may have gathered, there's something special about the lad. I don't know what."

"Eagle sitting on his shoulder," joked the lieutenant. An old proverb.

"Something like that," said the general, almost to himself. "The eagle, the storm bringer." Then, more briskly, he said, "Anyway, I want you to look out for him. No more escape attempts, of course. But look out for him in other ways, too. We really don't want to piss off his grandfather, Uldin, at this stage."

The lieutenant nodded.

"The boy longs to be home, I know, but I don't want him running off into the streets again. Far too dangerous, especially given his appetite for a fight. But if ever things changed—circumstances—and you felt he was in more danger in Rome than running free. . . . Do you follow my meaning?"

"I believe so, sir."

"The Huns—the Huns are not our enemies. They are not empire builders, so they have no reason to be empire destroyers. They neither fear the destruction of their own homeland nor desire that of another, a philosopher once said of them. After all, how could their homeland be destroyed? It is not a city or a country. It is the earth itself. How can you destroy the forests and the plains of Scythia? They don't want to capture Rome. They want freedom, the wide open plains, pastureland for their horses and their cattle, good hunting. They don't envy what the Romans have. They don't want to take up residence in the Palatine, or recline in the Baths of Caracalla with lots of pretty Greek catamites around to oil them and whatnot. And they will never, ever turn Christian. They will keep to their own religion, and their own kind."

"And they're pretty good warriors, too."

"Pretty good?" echoed the general. "I saw them tear into Rhadagastus's army—who were no schoolboys—and demolish them as if they were slaughtering a flock of sheep. God help us if they should ever turn against . . ."

There was a heavy silence.

"It would be like a beast fight in the arena," said the lieutenant, "between a bear and a buffalo."

"Exactly." The general took another glug of wine. "It would get messy.

But, as I say, I don't see that it'll ever happen. As long as we keep on friendly terms with them, there's no reason to see the Huns as a threat."

"I take your meaning, sir."

"And the hostage lad is a part of that. So guard him well, and see that no harm comes to him. I'm fond of the lad."

The lieutenant nodded. "You have my word."

8

O CASSANDRA

The following afternoon, when Attila had finally been released from his lessons for the day—Livy, always Livy, and the Glorious Founders of Rome—he ran to the kitchens at the rear of the palace, and took his place at the big, scruffy table where the hostage children usually had their supper. He was the first to arrive. But unusually, as soon as he had taken his seat, Bucco, the big fat Sicilian slave, brought him a bowl of soup and some bread on a wooden trencher.

Attila devoured it: Livy always made him hungry. As soon as it was gone, Bucco was back to refill his bowl. The boy was mystified as to what he might have done to be so royally treated. But when he looked up at Bucco, the slave was looking down at him sadly. Almost . . . with pity.

"Bucco?"

"Little master?"

Attila waved his hand around. "Where are the others? Hegemond and Beremond and the rest of them?"

Bucco shifted uneasily and let his eyes drop. At last he said, in a voice that was no more than a whisper, "Gone, sir."

The boy's blood ran cold. "Gone? You mean . . . ?"

"Released, sir, under the general amnesty with Alaric and his allies."

Attila dropped the hunk of bread he was holding. "Then why wasn't I let go, too? How were the Gothic armies beaten, if not with the help of my people? Under the command of my own grandfather?"

Bucco looked miserable.

The boy was already scrambling up from his bench and making for the door. "This is what we get from Rome!" he yelled.

He snatched open the door, and stopped dead. A burly palace guard was standing immediately outside, his spear held firmly across the doorway, and a broad grin on his face.

He turned and took his place on the bench again. Something was going terribly wrong. He longed to talk to Serena and Stilicho, his only friends in Rome.

"Eat your bread," said Bucco.

"Eat it yourself, you fat Sicilian turd!" screamed Attila, seizing the hunk of bread before him and hurling it at Bucco. It was a good shot, and hit Bucco on a pudgy jowl. But he simply stooped, a little awkwardly given his ample girth, retrieved the bread from the floor, waddled over and set it before the boy again.

"Not your soup," he said. "Your *bread*."

Attila stared up at the slave. There was something in Bucco's eyes . . . an urgency.

He gingerly tore the bread open. There was a slip of paper inside it.

Bucco waddled round and returned, whistling with false joviality, to the cooking range.

Attila eased the paper out. It read: *"Wait in the kitchens until after the twelfth hour. When the guard outside the door has changed, come to my room immediately. The second guard will permit it. Do not be seen. Make haste. S."*

Attila did as he was told. For once.

After the bells had struck in the great court, he waited a few minutes and then emerged from the doorway of the kitchens. There was the new guard standing beside the door clutching his spear. He did not stir, as if the boy were invisible.

Attila ran back and found Bucco clearing his plate and bowl away. On impulse he hugged the fat slave round his huge waist. Bucco looked down in astonishment.

And then the boy was gone.

There was another guard outside the door into Serena's chambers. He, too, behaved as if the boy were invisible.

Attila went in.

Serena was seated on a low couch with her back to him. When she heard him she turned, and he saw to his dismay that her face was streaked with tears. Serena, always so composed and dignified. Her large, liquid eyes filled with fresh tears at the sight of him.

"Attila," she said, holding out her hand.

"What is it?" he said, hearing fear trembling in his voice.

She held him for a moment and then pushed him away. "There is danger," she said. "You must go. Tonight, if you can." She hesitated.

"Tell me what," he said.

She shook her head. She looked anxious, bewildered, uncertain. She searched for the right words.

"Where is Stilicho?" asked the boy.

"In Pavia." She spoke abruptly.

"They said," he blurted, "they said—Eumolpus said—you'd ordered me never to speak to you again. He said that was what you wanted."

"He lied."

"I know he did. I . . . I bit him."

Despite her tears, Serena smiled. "I know you did," she said. "The whole palace knows. And much of the palace rejoices." She took a deep breath. "Come and sit beside me. There is little time."

He sat.

She sighed and pondered and then spoke. "Have you heard of the Sibylline Books?"

"The books of prophecy?" He nodded. "Among my people, prophecies and sacred verses and suchlike are never written down. They're too precious, and they're only ever committed to memory by the holy men."

"Ah," said Serena. "It is the same among the Celts, I believe. If only it were the same in Rome." She scrutinized his face, and then she said, "Among the last and greatest of the Sibylline Books is a prophecy that Rome will endure for twelve centuries. When Romulus founded the city, he looked into the sky and saw twelve vultures circling above the seven hills, and he knew they symbolized the twelve centuries during which the gods would permit Rome to reign triumphant over all the world. But the city was founded by Romulus in—you know your Livy?"

"Yes," said the boy a little wearily. "Seven hundred and fifty-three years before the birth of Christ." He frowned. Then he began counting on his fingers. Then he looked up at Serena in shock.

"Yes," she said sadly. "It is coming. It is coming soon—if one believes it. Or: if one believes it, it is coming soon." She drew breath. "I know, I know, everyone talks in riddles these days. Forgive me. Prin—that is to say, the imperial powers that be ordered General Stilicho to destroy the Books, and leave no trace behind. 'That the people might continue to believe,' they said. But . . . there is a storm coming. And much which was precious and beautiful, and which seemed sheer miracle to the multitude, will be torn down and washed away forever."

The boy did not understand all she said. But he understood it when she told him he must go, and now. Rome was no longer safe for him.

"Where am I to go?"

She smiled and touched her hand to his cheek. "Where you have always wanted to go, little wolf cub. Home." She stood. "The sword that General Stilicho gave you. . . ."

"I still have it," said the boy. "It is safely hidden."

"Of course it is," said Serena. "And Stilicho had one other gift to bestow. God send he bestow it wisely. The last, most direful prophecy of all. O Cassandra, why did we sons and daughters of Troy not listen?"

She seemed to be speaking almost to herself, and as if in Sibylline riddles again, distracted with anxiety and murmuring softly as her eyes searched the ground before her. "The prophecy told of the end of the world, we thought, but we misread it. We misread it always, we sons and daughters of Troy. It foretold not the end of the world, but only the end of Rome."

She seized his hand one last time, fixing his eyes with her own troubled, dark, searching eyes, as if trying to communicate to him something that was beyond communication and older than all the ages of the world.

"All will be destroyed, and all will come again," she said. "A holy man taught me that long ago, and I was loth to believe him. But I believe him now. Gamaliel he was called—Sun singer, Fire bringer, last of the Hidden Kings. Where is his voice and his wisdom now?" She let his hand drop and her eyes grew distant.

At last the bewildered boy asked, "How am I to escape?"

"It will be done tonight," she said.

Violent shouting suddenly arose in a distant part of the palace. Serena started, and Attila saw to his dismay that she was shaking with fear. She turned back to him.

"Now go," she said. "The guard at your door is loyal. Stay within your chamber. At the appointed hour of the night, he will unlock the door and will guide you to a—a way out of the palace. It will lead you to the Chapel of the Magdalen, and from thence you will be guided out of the city by a monk called Eustachius, and you will be given your freedom—and perhaps even a pony."

"A pony!"

She smiled and reached out and touched him again. "Ride like the wind, little wolf cub."

"Like the autumn wind on the steppe when Aldebaran is rising in the Eastern sky will I ride," he murmured. "And like the pale birch leaves of the mountains will I ride, when they are driven like multitudes before the autumn wind."

"And they tell us that barbarians have no poetry." She smiled. Then her smile vanished. "Steal what you must. Speak to no one. Give no one your name."

She turned away so that he would not see her tears. "Now go," she said.

He took a step toward her, his hands held out as if in supplication. "But . . . but I . . ."

She did not look back. "I said *go!*" she cried.

He flinched and took a step backward, and then turned and ran, his eyes blurred with tears.

He returned to his room by flickering torchlight, to find that a couple of guards had overturned his bed, ransacked his linen chest, and were searching through his every possession. When he came running in, they barely spared him a glance.

"Outside," they growled.

Attila stepped back outside, and slipped down the corridor toward the statue of Augustus—its mysteriously missing eye now replaced. He felt behind the statue and it was still there: his sword, the gift of Stilicho, in the last place the guards would think of looking.

He heard footsteps behind him.

It was Eumolpus. He raised one finely plucked eyebrow. "And what fresh destruction are you wreaking now, rat boy?"

Without a word, his blood beating, Attila pulled the bundle out from behind the statue, drew the sword from its oiled cloth and turned it round and about in front of the eunuch's eyes.

"Isn't it fine?" he said.

"Give that here."

The boy smiled and shook his head.

The eunuch suddenly looked dangerous. "I said, give it here."

Attila looked up, and then raised the blade to the level of his shoulder, arm crooked ready to strike, the long and lethal point aiming straight at his tormentor's chest.

"If you want it so much," he said, "take it."

Eumolpus stared at him long and hard. Then he moved suddenly, stepping sideways and grabbing at the boy's side. But the boy was faster, ducking under the eunuch's outstretched arm and turning on the ball of his foot and holding out the sword toward him again.

"Well, well," said Eumolpus in a low voice. "And what sort of person—what traitor—would give a little urchin such as yourself a gift as fine as that?"

Contrary to all expectations, Attila suddenly lunged forward, and the startled Eumolpus stepped backward, stumbled against the pediment of the statue of Augustus, and fell. Scrambling to his feet again, all composure lost, he cursed the boy furiously. He paused to brush his resplendent golden dalmatic clean of the barbarian touch, hissed some unintelligible Greek at the boy like a peevish viper, and departed.

"Nasty cut you've got there, by the way," the boy called after him. "Round your throat."

He rewrapped the sword in its oiled cloth and hid it in the folds of his tunic.

When Eumolpus fell, he had dropped a scrap of paper. Once he had vanished round the corner, the boy retrieved it. It was in code. He took it back to his room. The guards let him in, and then locked and bolted the door behind him. He settled down on the low bed to crack the code. He liked codes, but this one was hard. Soon his tired eyes began to close, and he fell asleep.

In his dreams, he continued to work on the code. He knew that it mattered somehow. He saw himself as if from a distance, in the dusk, straining his eyes by the guttering oil lamp. From one of the distant courtyards came a strange, high-pitched cry, like a bird in lamentation.

He dreamed that he leaped from his bed and ran to the Chamber of the Imperial Audience, to find Princess Galla Placidia seated on a painted wooden throne and surrounded by children, which was strange since she had none. And who, as they said in the backrooms of the palace, would want to marry her anyway? "Galla and husband," they quipped. "Virgin and martyr."

Her brother, Honorius, sat at her feet, playing with a child's spinning top. The princess stroked the goat kid in her lap and smiled. The kid smiled, too.

Stilicho was standing beside her. He wore an expression of puzzlement. He reached behind his back, and gave a low groan. Attila saw to his horror that the general had a big knife sticking out of his back, with gold scrollwork on the handle.

"I must go home to my wife," said Stilicho.

The princess stroked the kid and looked at Attila and smiled.

He woke up numb with sorrow, and to the sound of screaming.

He lay wide awake and in a cold sweat, straining to hear again. Perhaps it hadn't been a scream. Perhaps it had been the friendly guard knocking on the door, or even the monk Eustachius himself.

But then another scream came ringing through the night to his chamber, like the cry of one of the exotic birds in the imperial aviary, and he knew that things had begun to go terribly wrong. He knew in his heart that now there would be no friendly guard, and no kindly monk called Eustachius. He was alone.

He heard violent shouting in the corridor outside, and then a sound like scuffling, and a man bellowing as if in raw pain. There were running footsteps, and doors slamming, and then the sound of wood being smashed and splintering. He gripped the edges of his bed with fear, as a man adrift on the ocean in the black night might grip a plank of wood. He was unable to move. Any moment, a couple of armed guards would burst in through his door with drawn swords, and drive those thick steel blades straight through him and into the straw pallet below.

But no one came. He forced himself to loosen his grip on the bed. He shook his head as if to clear it of the fog of nightmare.

He got up and wrapped his light woolen cloak round him for protection, though the night was warm. Then he took his sword and went over to the door. He gripped the hilt in both hands, raised the sword high above his head, and drove it deep into the heavy oak. He was determined to dig a hole through it, no matter how long it took. But at the first blow the door swung eerily open. The guards outside were gone.

He wrenched the blade back and it came free of the wood with a squeak. In a daze he smelt, even tasted, the unmistakable coppery tang of blood in the air. And he sensed with the very hairs on his head that all the palace was under a cloud of fear. The night was in silent, horror-struck uproar.

He started to run. He passed a man slumped in the darkness of a doorway, and then he stopped and ran back. The front of the man's coarse tunic was dark and wet. It was Bucco, the fat Sicilian baker, his friend. He knelt and laid his hand against Bucco's cheek. It was as cold as wet clay. He moved Bucco's head slightly, and it fell awkwardly to one side, revealing a ragged gaping slash across his throat. Nearly gagging, the boy reeled to his feet and ran on. Why Bucco? Why a simple slave?

Now things came to him, through the haze of fear. There was nobody around. Even at this late hour, there should have been palace guards patrolling the courtyards, night slaves working, *aquarii* replenishing the water butts, priests and deacons in the service of the imperial family on their way to chant the early morning offices of Lauds and Terce in the cold and incense-filled chapel. But there was no one. It was as if the palace were suddenly deserted—and yet sounds carried from afar on the hot night air.

From deep within the palace he heard that cry of the bird again, only now he knew it was no bird but a woman's screams. Then rounding a corner into a small courtyard he almost ran into another woman standing beside a small fountain. He had never seen her before. She was dressed all in white, like a priestess, but she held out to him at arm's length a dead kitten, her mouth hanging open in a silent scream, her eyes staring unseeing at him. None of it made any sense. He stumbled away from her. Madly he wanted to laugh. It was all as meaningless as a nightmare, but it was real, it was all too real. He was wide awake.

He heard running footsteps coming closer and then fading, he heard doors slamming, the clanking of chains being dragged over marble tiles. He came to a bundle of rags slung in a corner, and as he passed by the bundle stirred and a bloody human hand reached out. He ran on.

He could hear the distant clangor of church bells in the city now, and again it made no sense. They seemed to signal some dire and bloody event, sounding to his ears as if they came from deep underground, from the realms of chaos and ancient night. He didn't slink like a wolf through the palace now. He ran with one hand clenched to his chest with the steel weight of his sword beneath. He would need it tonight.

No one seemed to notice him, a mere child.

Two soldiers shoved past him, with a man grasped by the elbows between them. They virtually had to drag him, for his legs were broken. He wore a high-ranking officer's uniform. His face was so bloodily pulped that the boy could not recognize him. Only his teeth showed white from his darkened face, his lips drawn back in some terrible nameless smile.

The boy passed on, down endless deserted corridors and through great hallways, desperate to reach Serena's chambers before someone else did. In one of the great halls of the palace, he found that the vast mosaic of the god Bacchus that decorated the floor had been smashed as if by a lunatic, the face of the god almost obliterated in shards of shattered tesserae. As if some frenzied madman had taken a heavy brass lampstand to it, and attacked it like a living being. Nothing made sense. Always in the air the acrid stench of spilled blood, distant screams, the after odor of oil smoke from lit torches where soldiers had passed by on their murderous task, torches in one hand, drawn swords in the other. Some of them would be well rewarded for this night's work.

Other footsteps were coming closer, and there were more cries in the night.

The boy ran on, and at last he reached the doors to Serena's chambers. He hammered on them. She heard his voice and opened the doors and he ran in to her. He clasped her round the waist and buried his face in the folds of her white stola.

"My darling . . ." she said.

"What is it? What is happening?"

"You must go. You must go now. In the confusion and the darkness, you must try to . . ."

He looked up at her. Her eyes were bright with tears. All distance and formality were gone.

"I promised General Stilicho that I'd never try to escape again."

"Oh, my darling, my darling, it is an oath you need no longer keep." She cradled his head. "You need not keep an oath to a man who is dead."

The boy cried out and the sound nearly broke her heart.

A bottle or a vase smashed somewhere nearby. There was the sound of sandalled feet being dragged over stone.

"He can't be!" cried the boy.

She shook her head. It was the end. They clung together and wept.

"They say my husband is a traitor—he and all his circle."

Who were "they"? But he knew. The Emperor of Chickens, and his cold-eyed sister.

"My darling, you must go."

But he had already turned and drawn his sword when the soldiers came into the room. He walked toward them.

"Attila," said her voice behind him.

He looked back. Two more soldiers had stepped from the doorway and were already flanking her with swords drawn.

He turned away. Ahead came a line of six or eight more soldiers of the Palatine guard, resplendent in their black helmets and cuirasses. They smiled broadly.

"Where's Stilicho?" he demanded.

The soldiers stopped. Their *optio* furrowed his brow. "That traitor? And what's that to you, you little urchin?" He considered. "Well, his head will by now be on top of a pikestaff on the walls of Pavia, I hope."

"And my son?" Serena asked from behind him. "Eucharius?"

At that, even the *optio* could not bring himself to look directly at her. Eyes to the ground, he said, "He sleeps with his father."

Serena fell against the wall, struggling for breath.

The boy stretched his sword out toward the guards. His hand trembled a little but he was unafraid. He fixed his unwavering gaze on them.

Normally the *optio* would simply have walked up to a boy like that, smacked him round the head, and taken his weapon off him sharpish. But there was something in this one's eyes. . . .

He signaled to his men. Almost casually, two of them walked forward with a length of chain, one each side of the boy, and slung it across his chest. Before he realized what had happened, they had walked round behind him, crossed over, and returned, and his arms were pinioned tightly by his sides. He stood as helpless as a trussed fowl in the marketplace.

"Now," said the *optio*, "drop the blade like a good little girl."

Attila told him to do something obscene to his mother.

"Please," said Serena softly from the end of the hall.

The *optio* nodded to the two soldiers holding the chain. They leaned back against it, as if in a tug of war, with the boy no more than a knot in the middle. The chain tightened sharply and he gasped in pain. The sword was squeezed from his hand and fell with a clang to the floor. The soldiers wrapped the rest of the chain round him and hauled him away.

Serena was marched along at sword point behind him.

He glanced back once, and she said something to him. It was too soft for him to hear her words but he knew what they were. And then she was gone.

They pushed him into a cell as black as a moonless night, as damp as an underground cave. He managed to get his teeth into a brawny forearm and tear out a small chunk of flesh as they shoved him in. He spat it back at the guard. There was a roar of pain and fury, and he was slammed against the wall, his head reeling with red stars. He fell in a bundle of chains into a fetid corner of the cell, his head dropped onto his chest, and he lost consciousness.

When he came round, he could see nothing. From a far dungeon he heard a woman's voice, almost deranged with terror, crying, "No, no, no!" But he knew it was not her. They were both dead. His only friends, his beloved. . . . His head throbbed abominably, enough to make him weep with pain. Worse still, the constriction of the chain round his arms was a perpetual agony.

But his anger outweighed his pain. He saw them clearly in the blackness of his cell. Stilicho with his long, lugubrious face. His gravelly voice calling him "my young wolf cub." And her: her large dark eyes, her gentle smile. His last sight of her.

"*My darling . . .*"

"But my people will come," he said quietly to himself, despite his pain. "They will not tolerate this insult." And then, more loudly, so that even the jailer down at the end of the row heard his words and frowned, he said, "The Huns will come."

9

RAIN DOWN TONIGHT,
DROWN EVERY LIGHT

Such was the night on which General Stilicho and his entire circle were savagely destroyed.

An official version was put out by the imperial court, saying that he had been secretly plotting with the barbarian tribes, perhaps with the Huns themselves, to overthrow Honorius and all his family, and to install his own son, Eucharius, on the throne instead. But few believed this, for they knew that Stilicho was an honorable man. And for my part, I do not think he had a traitor's heart. I think that Honorius, encouraged by his sister Galla Placidia and unscrupulous and self-seeking courtiers such as Eumolpus, Olympian, and the rest, came to see Stilicho as a rival in the affections of the people.

In his encampment outside Pavia, the great general, so many times the savior of Rome on distant battlefields, could have taken up arms against the small troop of soldiers, under the command of the pusillanimous Count Heraclian, who came to arrest him that night; for the great majority of the army would certainly have fought and died for him. Their loyalty was to Stilicho, not to the emperor. But Stilicho could not find it in himself to take up arms against his beloved fatherland, even when his fatherland sought to kill him. Instead he rode from Pavia to Ravenna, and sought sanctuary in a church there. Count Heraclian stationed his troops around the church, lured Stilicho out with false promises of safe passage, and then, as soon as he was in his clutches, shamefully had him beheaded on the spot, according to the strict but secret orders of the emperor himself.

Rome always kills its finest servants, its bravest sons—or so it sometimes seems.

Along with them, the emperor also had killed Stilicho's young son, Eucharius; the praetorian prefects of both Italy and Gaul; two masters general of the army who were devoted to Stilicho; the quaestor Bonaventura; the imperial treasurer, and many others, their names now forgotten to history, though not to the hearts that loved them.

Following the massacre, every fawning courtier who had previously sung Stilicho's praises suddenly saw the light, admitted that they had always mistrusted him from the start, and fervently agreed that he had indeed been the most heinous and malicious of traitors.

The many friends of Stilicho were horribly tortured, to make them confess to treachery. Without exception they went to their graves in silence, nobly justifying by their deaths Stilicho's friendship with them in life.

Stilicho's wife, Serena, was also killed, strangled in a dungeon with a ligature of silk. They say that she went calmly to her end, praying to Christ for the souls of those who killed her. They say that she died with a strange serenity, as befitted her name. As if she could already see her beloved husband waiting for her there, on the shores of that eternally sunlit country, beyond the cold dark river she must cross.

But Stilicho's troops, at least, refused to believe that their commander had been a traitor. And the only immediate result of the massacre was that thirty thousand of them, in their furious indignation at the behavior of the imperial court of Rome, promptly went over to join Alaric and the army of the Goths. Whereupon Alaric, sensing that the empire was once more coming apart, turned his eyes again on the prize of Rome.

A mood of festering hatred settled over the courts of the city. A mood of sullen coercion, abject flattery, and naked fear showing through the ghastly smiles.

Attila did not smile. Still a prisoner, his life spared, still the best guarantee that the Huns would not turn against Rome.

Honorius spent more and more time in Ravenna with his chickens.

Galla Placidia spent more and more time in Rome giving orders.

And the Hun boy spent more and more time alone in his dim-lit cell, his fists bunched up and pressed against his ears, or into the red stars of his eyeballs. Torn apart by the promises he had made to Stilicho, by what he knew Stilicho would have wanted of him, and yet also by the knowledge of what had become of Stilicho himself. That most loyal servant. *"Do what is right, Attila."*

But another year passed, and the Huns did not come.

Although at all times the boy remained under strict guard, his lessons were resumed, his regime was relaxed, and he was even given a slightly larger chamber.

Other hostage children came and went, depending on what diplomacy had achieved with the various Germanic peoples who threatened the empire's borders. But Attila would mix with none of them. He despised them all.

He especially depised the two Vandal princes, Beric and Genseric, the most willingly and thoroughly Romanised of the hostages. They had been released before back to their people, and now returned to Rome quite eagerly, under some new diplomatic deal.

They were a few years his senior, perhaps sixteen and eighteen respectively, and very much convinced of their own superiority and their urbane and raffish wit. On one occasion, Attila heard them making a cynical joke about the deaths of Stilicho and Serena. He turned to them and, fixing them with those eyes of his, which even at this age were beginning to take on a terrible aspect beneath his lowering brows, said that if he ever heard them saying such things again he would see to it that they were both dead before nightfall. The brothers looked at each other and laughed at this outrageous threat. But their eyes betrayed more than a little anxiety; and they never mentioned the murdered general or his wife in front of the boy again.

Nevertheless, the Vandal princes, perhaps under pressure from more highly placed palace courtiers, continually tried to persuade the boy to relax and enjoy the soft delights that Rome had to offer. For it is well known that the Vandals are the most slothful of people.

"Do you have hot baths, and fine wines, and robes of silk, and such foods as we eat here, back among the black tents of your people?" Genseric asked him mockingly.

Beric added, "I have never yet seen a Hun in a robe of silk, have you, Genseric?"

"Indeed not," murmured Genseric, stroking his own silken robe as he spoke. "In a motley of dusty leather leggings and, I think, *rabbit* fur, perhaps, but in silk? No."

And they smiled mockingly at the bristling boy.

Attila rejected their approaches with contempt. Indeed the brothers, like all the other hostage children, seemed to him as blissfully foolish and unaware of the truth about their world as sleek and fattened cattle in rich pasture, feeding and lolling complacently in the warm summer sun, oblivious of the fact that when winter set in their keepers would in a trice become their killers.

He kept himself even more isolated than before, and one rolling glare of his eyes was usually enough to make even the stoutest adversary back off.

The other children plumed themselves on their ability to speak Latin and Greek, seduced by what they saw as the superior culture of their hosts. They would quote Horace or Virgil to each other, or the exquisite couplets of Sappho; and they would half close their eyes, and sigh, for all the world like the most enervated aesthetes of Baiae or Pompeii. Attila continued to learn Latin doggedly, and with grim determination, just as he continued to learn his Roman history, while regarding his Greek pedagogue, poor, put-upon Demetrius of Tarsus, with scorn.

He learned of the great victories of Scipio Africanus, of Caesar in Gaul, of Fabius Cunctator, Fabius the Delayer, who defeated the Carthaginians by refusing to engage, but by harrying them with constant guerrilla warfare.

"That is how my people would fight Rome," said Attila. "With patience and guile."

Demetrius snapped, "You will desist from—"

"All these great heroes of Rome defeated other peoples and extended Rome's boundaries so gloriously," queried the boy. "Does that mean that warfare and conquest are always glorious?"

The pedagogue was wrong footed, as usual. "Only if the victor is also the party of superior laws and culture," he said carefully. "As is Rome, compared to the uncouth tribes beyond its borders. Indeed, if Rome were not a superior culture, Providence would never have permitted her to win such an empire in the first place."

The boy considered briefly, then smiled. "In philosophy," he said, "that is what would be termed a circular argument. And logically it is quite worthless."

Demetrius was rendered momentarily speechless. The boy laughed.

Once, Rome had been great. That much the boy perceived, and grudgingly admired. When he read of Regulus, or Horatius, or Mucius

Scaevola, those strong, grim-faced, relentless heroes of ancient Rome, his blood thrilled in his veins. And when he gazed up at the lofty buildings of the city, he admitted greatness when he saw it. But that was long ago and from another world. Now it was all decadence: a rotten fruit, a hollow shell. The Romans had lost their way, and did not even know it.

As for the barbarian peoples whom Rome continued to cultivate and disarm, they forfeited their barbarian virtues without gaining any of the countervailing old Roman strengths: fortitude, stoicism, self-discipline, warrior hardihood; a pride in self and nation and race; and that humility before the gods which is the mark of true wisdom: a proud and even joyful acceptance of whatever fate the gods have decreed for you, no matter how terrible that fate might be.

Instead, the princes of the Vandals or the Sueves or the Burgundians were wretchedly seduced, passing their wasted days in listless self-indulgence, like Beric and Genseric. And when they were released back to their people, they took with them chefs and court dancers and masseurs, tailors and musicians and poets, and established them in their barbarian homes in a clumsy and ludicrous aping of Roman ways. They even took back with them their own personal hairdressers.

The only time a court hairdresser ever tried to get close to Attila's shaggy mop, he ended up regretting it.

The Goths at least, it was said, were made of sterner stuff. And in the fitful skirmishes between the Huns and those tall Germanic horsemen, with their mighty ashen spears and their tawny plumes nodding in the wind, it seemed that their reputation was deserved. But many too many of the barbarian tribes were being destroyed: not by weapons of war, but by baths, and wine, and silk.

Attila gagged on the perfumed courts of Rome, even as he saw that those courts were tottering. Within, amid the vast colonnaded state rooms of marble and gold, malachite and porphyry, the emperor and empress and their fawning courtiers might dress in brocades heavy with rubies and emeralds, their white arms wreathed in gold bracelets, their hair piled high with pearl diadems, as they glided in sinister silence beneath their vast, self-laudatory mosaics gleaming through clouds of incense. But close up the barbarian boy, the little wolf cub in their midst, saw with his unblinking yellow eyes the fissures in the great buildings and abandoned temples of the city, and he observed the many drafty and untenanted rooms of the palace. He saw the people beginning to starve, while still the Roman rich wore silk. Attila scorned silk robes as unfit even for women— was it not Heliogabalus, the monstrous boy-emperor Heliogabalus himself, who had been the first in Rome to wear robes of pure silk? After three terrible years, sickened by his insane cruelties, the people had risen up and killed him. But now they aped him—and not only in his dress: in his greed and his depravity, too. So it seemed to the boy. Aesthetes even told tales of Heliogabalus's exquisite jests, and reminisced with a fond nostalgia about how he had murdered his guests at a banquet by suffocating them in falling clouds of rose petals. The guests had gasped and expired beneath deep drifts of flowers, crying out for mercy. The emperor had looked on and laughed. The aesthetes, too, now laughed.

The boy longed instead for the banks of the wide brown Danube, and the Kharvad Mountains, and the plains beyond. He longed for simple mare's milk and meat, loathing the rich novelties, the ridiculous, contrived delicacies that the Romans ate. He longed for the sound of the wolves in the high mountain passes, and the sight of the black felt tents of his people, and the great royal pavilion of his grandfather, Uldin, hung with animal skins and decorated with carved and painted horses' heads.

He watched and waited. Patience was always the supreme virtue of his people. "Patience is a nomad," they said.

In time, the Huns would come.

One evening he was making his way to the kitchens for dinner when he was accosted by one of the palace chamberlains.

"Tonight you will be dining in the private chambers of Prince Beric and Prince Genseric," he purred.

The boy scowled. "No I will not," he said.

"By orders of Princess Galla Placidia," said the chamberlain icily, not even looking at him.

The boy considered for a moment, then his proud shoulders slumped a little, and he turned and allowed himself to be led to the private chambers of the Vandal brothers. The chamberlain knocked, and a languid voice called, "Enter."

The chamberlain opened the door and pushed Attila inside.

So, thought Attila, staring around, this is what you get if you behave yourself. This is how Rome seduces its enemies.

The door slammed shut behind him.

Before him was a large chamber with a colonnade of pillars running round three sides. Although it was still broad daylight outside, the long summer evening not yet run, in here the drapes were already drawn and the only light was artificial. It also felt as if the underfloor heating was on, even at this time of year. He was suffocating already. Especially as the overheated air was perfumed with attar of roses.

The floor was elaborately decorated with mosaics and black marble, and the chamber was dimly lit with multiple candelabra—not smoky clay oil lamps such as he had in his own chamber, but the finest, most expensive, creamy-colored beeswax candles, set in silver candelabra that towered over his head. At the back of the chamber, in the dim light, farther rooms opened off, and there came the sounds of laughter, high-pitched shrieks and giggles.

In the center of the room were three couches set round a low rectangular table piled high with elaborate dishes of the rarest fish and meat, fine wines, and exotic eastern fruits. They were privileged indeed, the two Vandal princes. Such exquisite dishes must have come from the imperial kitchens themselves.

There was no sign of Genseric, but Beric sat, or rather sprawled, on one of the couches, a sozzled-looking blonde with high-piled hair leaning against him. The Vandal prince wore a white silk robe belted with a golden sash, his eyes were rimmed with kohl that had begun to blur and run, and he had gold bangles on both wrists. He rolled over on the couch and smiled blearily up at the boy, raising his goblet and burping softly at him.

"Comrade," he said, "drinking partner, wenching fellow, I salute you."

Through the darkened door of the farther chamber came more squeals and giggles. Beric turned in the direction of the noise. Then he turned back again and beamed at the boy. He patted the couch next to him. "Come along, then. Tonight is your special night."

Attila went and sat down. His throat felt parched and dry but he wanted to drink nothing. He imagined cool mountain streams that caught the sunlight in droplets as they fell. And the slow-moving rivers of the steppes, the herons in the reeds, waiting with their endless ancestral patience for their prey. . . .

A plump slave-girl appeared with downcast eyes, carrying a big jug of wine. Beric held his goblet out toward her. She stopped and poured the wine, but her hand was shaking so much that she spilled a little over his hand.

Beric stared up at her. "You stupid fucking bitch," he slurred very softly.

The blonde beside him giggled at this witticism.

Beric continued, "And so ugly too. Christ, you're never going to get so much as a *poke* with a face like that, let alone a husband."

The blonde positively squawked with laughter.

Beric turned and added, to Attila, "Even with my standards lowered by wine as they are, there's no way I could give her one, could you?" He looked back at the trembling slave girl, as if in wonder. "Not for all the wheat in Africa."

The girl kept her face lowered. She didn't look ugly to Attila. She had a round, gentle face and scared eyes.

"Why are you still standing there?" said Beric, suddenly raising his voice. *"Go away!"*

She started with fear, but Attila interrupted and said, "I . . . could I have a bit of wine, too?" He reached out and took a goblet from the table and held it out toward her. She came over to him, her hands shaking badly, and poured the wine as carefully as she could. She had poured only a little when Attila nodded and said, "That's enough. Thank you."

He looked up to smile at her but she was already scuttling away like a frightened animal.

"You don't say thank you to slaves, you idiot," said Beric. "Sound like a peasant. Christ." He gave another tremendous belch. "Been drinking since noon." His mouth turned sourly down. "Think I'm gonna puke." He hawked, leaned forward and spat on the floor in front of him, then settled back and grimaced. "Ugh," he said. "I need a bath."

"Have a bath with me, baby," said the blonde girl beside him.

Beric grinned at her and, slipping one hand inside her tunic, began to gently caress her breast. She crooned at him.

Attila looked down in shame.

Beric held his bulbous goblet aloft, and cried, *"Usque ad mortem bibendum!* Let us drink until death!"* looking very pleased with himself that he knew this Latin tag. Then he took a huge mouthful of red wine. Still holding it in his mouth, he lowered his lips to the girl's now exposed breast, and dribbled it over her smooth white flesh. The blonde gasped as if in ecstasy.

Attila kept his eyes on the floor and took a sip of wine. He had never liked the taste and he didn't like it anymore now. The food did nothing for him, either, hungry though he was. In the center of the table was a roast swan, stuffed with a roast peacock, stuffed with a roast pheasant, stuffed with a roast partridge, stuffed with three or four tiny roast larks, laid out in the very heart of the dish as if they were in a little nest. The whole elaborate creation appeared to have been hacked into pieces with knives by the brothers, and then left uneaten.

Why had he been commanded to dine here? He didn't understand. Was he supposed to be *seduced* or something? He glanced over the big silver knives that still lay in the remains of the dish of roast swan, considering. Then he looked away.

"You should eat something as well," said Beric. "You won't get pissed so quickly then. And you've got something to throw up, too, if you need to—which you will soon enough, the way this party's going to go. The two buggering Burgundian brothers are supposed to be joining us soon, and you know how they knock it back. Nothing worse than retching up a bellyful of nothing but wine. Christ." He ran his hand across his heavily sweating forehead. "I feel unusual," he said.

"Well, hello, dear boy," drawled another voice from across the room. It was the older brother, Genseric.

He was wearing a dark red robe elaborately embroidered with hunting scenes in finest gold thread, and belted so that it hung far too high on his thighs. He wore a big silver cross on a chain around his neck—the Vandals were very proud of the fact that they were Christians, regarding the religion as a badge of true civilization and *Romanitas*. Genseric also had some kind of pearls or even a pearl necklace draped round his head, and he had his slim, languid arm round a girl who was giggling and looking across at Attila from under lowered eyelashes.

"My," she said softly, "look at your *scars*. How barbaric!" She spoke as if scars excited her.

She was perhaps eighteen or nineteen, with wide blue eyes and very long, straight black hair. She wore bright red lipstick like a harlot on the street, and thick dark kohl round her eyes, and a white tunic which was slit right up the side of her thigh, and hung half off her shoulder, just revealing the roundness of her breasts.

Genseric let go of his girl and flopped onto the couch opposite. "God's bollocks," he said. "I'm finished." He leaned his head back and gazed at the ceiling, and sighed, and murmured under his breath a couplet from Martial.

Balnea, vina, Venus corrumpunt corpora nostra,
Sed vitam faciunt, balnea, vina, Venus.

Which is to say,

Venus and baths and wine, they say, corrupt us,
but they make life taste so sweet—wine, baths, and Venus.

Then he raised his head and grinned across at Attila. "This is Lollia," he said. "Lollia—Attila. May the evening see you better acquainted." And he winked over Attila's shoulder.

Beric laughed and burped.

Lollia went over to the blonde girl and started to kiss her on the lips. The girl responded drunkenly, and their lips and tongues intertwined. They ran their fingers through each other's wigs and emitted theatrical little moans. The two Vandals looked on and grinned.

Attila eyed the knives.

Then Lollia detached herself, and he felt her walk round behind him. She stopped, laughing silently, perhaps. Her hands closed round his face and covered his eyes from behind. They were damp with perspiration, but he could smell her perfume, too. He felt her hair on his cheek, tickling him softly, and her lips nibbling his ear, the tip of her tongue flicking back and forth, and he pulled away and looked down, his cheeks burning with shame.

"Aw, the lickle boy's shy!" shouted Genseric.

"Don't tell me you've never . . . ?" said Beric.

He longed to get up and go. He longed to run. But something held him back.

Lollia was flopping down on the couch beside him, and resting her head on his shoulder. She sighed and stretched out, and her slit skirt left her legs bare up to the tops of her thighs. So bare and brown. Her toenails were painted the same color as her lips, and her sandals were no more than delicate strips of soft leather, studded with silver, and laced almost up to her knees—which made her legs appear more naked than ever. The boy tried to look away but he couldn't.

She reached out for a goblet of wine on the table and drank a little, then she turned to him and held the goblet to his mouth and made him drink from it, too. She forced it back between his lips, and laughed when it ran out over his chin. She set the goblet down, turned back to him and licked the wine from his chin.

"Juno's tits, I think she likes you, boy," drawled Genseric.

Lollia's hands were stroking and circling his bare knees now, sliding by slow degrees up the inside of his thighs. He pulled away abruptly and leaned forward.

"Aw, lickle boy shy," said Genseric again, watching them through red-rimmed, half-closed eyes.

"Aw," said Lollia, even more softly. She caressed his hair and trailed her fingertips down the side of his neck. He felt a scintillating thrill run up his spine and his skin broke out in goosebumps. He imagined cool mountain streams that caught the sunlight in—

He pushed her away again. Lollia sniffed crossly.

"Maybe you'd prefer something more like what the Huns are supposed to," slurred Beric, grinning stupidly at him.

Attila glared at him furiously.

"And what's that?" asked Lollia.

"A horse!" cried Beric.

The three of them, Lollia and the two brothers, found this hysterically funny. The blonde girl had fallen asleep now, pinkish saliva dribbling from the corner of her mouth and onto the fine silk covering of the couch.

Beric prodded her harshly. "Oi, wake up you stupid tart, we're not paying you to sleep."

But the girl slept on.

"You know nothing about the Huns!" hissed Attila. He could feel his blood pumping furiously. But no one was listening to him.

"And they tie up the horse's back legs first, so it won't kick!" shouted Beric.

"Oh, that's how you do it, is it?" laughed Lollia. "I must remember next time. I got awfully bruised in the stables only last week."

"Then they roll it on its back," said Genseric, "and they're away— these funny little yellow men, pumping away between the huge thighs of their favorite mare, like Cupid giving one to his mummy, Venus."

"It's true—I've seen pictures of it," declared Beric.

They almost choked with laughter.

When the hilarity finally subsided, Beric collapsed into the couch. Lollia turned back to the angry boy by her side and began to whisper sweet nothings in his ear. His fists were bunched but he managed not to strike her. And after a few moments, even against his iron will, he began to relax again. Her warm fingers began to sidle up his thighs and under the hem of his tunic. And this time, although he hated her, hated them all with a fury—he couldn't stir, but only close his eyes. The wine was beginning to make his heartbeat faster and faster, as if he were running. He felt unable to move. Then he felt where her soft hand had reached to, and he gasped.

"Ganymede's asshole," added Beric, "I think she really likes you."

"Talking of Ganymede and his delectable . . . you know what," said Genseric.

Attila opened his eyes and saw the two brothers exchanging leery looks, and Genseric nodding toward the darkened chamber at the far end of the room.

"Right you are," guffawed Beric, staggering to his feet and draining his goblet of wine. "Hold on to your ears, boys. I'm a-coming in!"

A few moments later, Lollia took Attila's hand a little more firmly and pulled him to his feet.

"Let's go back there too," she murmured.

Bewildered and thrilled and terrified, he allowed himself to be pulled over toward the darkened chamber. "But, but . . . aren't . . . I mean, isn't Beric already . . . ?"

But the girl just glanced back at him, and smiled wickedly at him from under her long black eyelashes. "The more the merrier," she said.

They were at the doorway of the chamber. At first he could see nothing in the gloom. He felt Lollia's arm round his waist, and she turned to him and he felt her warm breath against his ear. "Can you see what I can see?" she purred. "Can you see what *wicked* things are going on in there? I bet you like to watch. I know *I* do."

But he was more agitated now. For inside the chamber he could see that there was nothing but one huge bed, and on the bed he could dimly discern shapes moving about. As his eyes became accustomed to the darkness, he saw that there were two more girls upon the bed, both of them naked, and making soft noises to each other, and taking it in turns to kiss Beric, who had disrobed as well. But although Beric was taking it in turns to kiss each of the naked girls, Attila could see that there was another figure underneath him as well. And then he realized to his horror that the fourth figure was also a boy, his face pressed down into the bed, and wearing nothing but a gold chain round his waist, and pearl bracelets around his ankles. Like a girl. Like a helpless slave girl, dressed by her leering master. The boy on the bed raised his head and glanced up from under his horrible, cheap wig of flaxen curls, which they had made him wear so that he would look like Ganymede, and Attila saw how young he was. . . .

"No!" he cried, pulling violently away from Lollia.

"Honey," she said, losing her sensuous purr, "what—"

"Get off me!"

He started to run back toward the door, but Genseric had lurched to his feet, laughing hysterically, and was standing in front of the door, blocking his exit.

"Aw, lickle boy don't like it? Lickle boy too young!"

Attila stopped in front of him, his eyes flashing furiously. "Let me out."

Genseric shook his head sadly. "Not allowed. By order of the Princess Galla herself."

"Princess Galla didn't order *that*," spat the boy, gesturing toward the darkened chamber.

The Vandal prince raised a sardonic eyebrow. "Is that a fact?" And he began to laugh out loud again. "Is that a fucking fact?"

Behind him, he could hear the laughter of Lollia as well.

"I have always thought," said Genseric, resuming his languid tone, "that the princess's greatest strength is that she understands human nature so very well. Don't you think, my darling?"

Lollia had reappeared by Genseric's side, and he put his arm round her. They began to kiss again, in full view of Attila, each of them watching him out of the corners of their eyes, and smiling through their kisses.

"You're disgusting," said Attila quietly. "You're just slaves of the Romans. You're just monkeys in a cage."

Genseric pulled back from Lollia and grinned. "Yeah, whatever—but look what they've given us in return. What a cage! What playmates! And this one, in particular—my beloved Livia—"

"Lollia," said Lollia.

"Lollia, sorry," drawled Genseric, pulling her toward him again, his hand sliding up under the back of her tunic and caressing her bare buttocks. "This one really is the most delectably *filthy-minded* little whore you could ever wish to meet. I tell you, she could *really* teach you some things—things you'd never dream of."

Slowly and languidly they began to kiss again.

But they stopped abruptly when Attila put his head down and ran full tilt into Genseric's stomach. The air whooshed audibly from his lungs, and he fell to one side, gasping. Lollia gave a little scream. Then she reached out and tried to grab the boy by his hair, but he was too quick and too sober for her. He ducked under her snatching fist, hauled open the heavy oak doors of the apartment and ran out into the courtyard. The last things he heard as he fled, toward his small, silent, oil-lit chamber, were Lollia swearing foully and Genseric vomiting onto the marble floor.

He stopped by a water fountain where a slave was rinsing out a jug. The long summer day was now almost dusk. It was about the sixteenth hour since dawn.

"Cup," gasped Attila.

The slave shook his head.

So he grabbed the jug from him and drank deeply. It was no cool mountain stream, but at least it was water, and it calmed him. He thrust the jug back into the slave's hands and wiped his mouth.

"Frightening, isn't it?" whispered the slave.

In ordinary circumstances, a slave was strictly forbidden to address anyone unless first addressed himself. But circumstances were far from ordinary.

Attila frowned. "I'm not frightened," he said haughtily. "Just disgusted."

It was the slave's turn to frown.

Attila waved toward the princes' chambers. "Some of the other hostages I'm supposed to mix with," he said. "Scum."

The slave allowed himself a very slight noncommittal smile.

"Why should I be frightened, though?"

The slave's eyes widened. "You mean you haven't heard?"

"Heard what?"

"About Alaric?"

"What about Alaric?" He could almost have shaken him. "Tell me."

The slave drew in a deep breath. "He's marching on Rome. At the head of a hundred thousand men."

At the news, the strange Hun boy looked anything but frightened. Instead, to the slave's astonishment, a slow smile spread across his face as he digested the news.

"Like Rhadagastus all over again," he murmured.

"Except that Alaric is no Rhadagastus," said the slave quietly. "By all accounts he is a great leader, who has the absolute loyalty of his men. And besides, who does Rome have to command her own armies, now that . . . you-know-who is gone?"

Attila nodded. He reached for the jug, took another long draft, and set it back in the slave's hands. "Thank you," he said. "Apparently it's not done to thank a slave. But thank you anyway."

Then the strange Hun boy turned to walk back to his chamber, and the slave could have sworn that he actually heard him *whistling.*

The rest of Rome cowered in fear. In the palace at Ravenna, there was outright panic. People ran around like the emperor's own chickens at the scent of a fox. For with General Stilicho so recently murdered, and no fewer than thirty thousand of his men consequently gone over to join Alaric and his grim-faced Goths, who was there now to save Rome? Count Heraclian, they said. But Heraclian was a far lesser man than Stilicho; just as Alaric was a far greater man than Rhadagastus.

"That fool Emperor Honorius," they whispered in the shadowy courts of the palace. "He has cut off his own right hand with his left."

Throughout Rome, and Ravenna, and throughout all of Italy, from the plains of the Po and Cisalpine Gaul to the high hill towns of Calabria and across to the golden hills of Sicily, there was the hum of fear and imminent panic.

Except in one small, silent chamber, lit only by cheap and smoky oil lamps. There a boy of some thirteen or fourteen years, but small for his age, his cheeks deeply riven with strange blue scars, knelt and prayed.

He prayed to the god of the Huns: a bare sword driven into the earth, forming a cross like the cross of the Christians, but of hard steel. He prayed to his father Astur, the Lord of All that Flies, and in the name of the murdered General Stilicho and his wife, Serena. He clenched his teeth and set his jaw and prayed for vengeance upon their murderers, and remembering them he wept again.

And he prayed that the Goths might come and do the work that the Huns had so far shamefully failed to do. Even though they were the immemorial enemies of his people, let the Goths come, and raze Rome flat in the red wind from the steppes.

See the Tiber foaming with Roman blood.

See the buildings fall like broken bones.

Let it all fall. Let it all be destroyed.

And when it was razed flat, let the very dust be trampled beneath the barbaric hooves of a hundred thousand horses. Leave not one stone standing. Nothing but seven bare and desolate hills beside a blood-red river where great Rome once stood. Nothing on those hills but a single tomb beneath the wide bare sky. A tomb for a murdered general and his beloved, murdered wife.

He heard her sigh again, through his ragged tears: *"My darling . . ."*

He closed his eyes and prayed to Chäkgha, the horse god of the plains, and to the *kötü ruh,* the demon spirits of the wind, and to the *kurta ruh,* the wolf spirits of the holy Altai Mountains, and to the Father Spirit of the Eternal Blue Sky:

O Lord, I pray,
Rain down tonight,
Drown every light,
Rain down tonight.

PART II

THE FLIGHT AND THE FALL

1

OF THE ARIMASPIANS, OF GRIFFINS, OF THE HUNS, AND OF OTHER WONDERS OF THE VAST AND UNKNOWN LANDS OF SCYTHIA

As far as China, meanwhile, the tribes were stirring. . . .

They say that the northern boundary of the Empire of China is defended by a great wall, greater by far than the wall that cuts across the north of Britain in defiance of the attacks of the blue-painted men of the Caledonian wastes. But they say many things, and the historian must be judicious in what he believes and records. Does not Herodotus himself record that toward China, in the endless wildernesses of Scythia, there live a tribe of men called the Arimaspians, each of whom has only one eye? And also that in those regions there dwell griffins, which defend great treasure troves of gold? That there is a tribe there called the Pedasians, among whom, when danger is about to threaten the people, their priestess grows a luxuriant beard?

We are furthermore told that toward the mountains that divide Scythia in two from east to west, there live the Argippaeans, who subsist on nothing but cherry juice, which they drink from little bowls with lapping tongues, like cats. They know no weapons of war for they are utterly peaceful. They are regarded as sacred by all the other tribes of Scythia, and never harmed. For my part I long to meet such a gentle people, but I fear they are as much a childish fairy tale as the gold-guarding griffins, and that there is not a tribe in the world, howsoever remote, which knows not war or the sorrowful weapons of war.

Farther north from these mythical peace lovers, historians tell us, the air is full of feathers; and then north again, and there live a people who sleep six months and wake six months, for that is how their year is made up, half day and half night. But this is plainly absurd. And among a people called the Issedonians, Herodotus tells us, women have absolute equality with men—which is even more absurd than the idea of a people subsisting entirely on cherry juice! No society could survive for long which practiced *that* kind of lunacy.

I for my part do not believe such myths and fairy tales, and am astonished that Herodotus, who called himself an historian, should trouble himself even to record such extravagant oddities. Yet it is not only Herodotus, the Father of History (or the Father of Lies, as some wits have called him), who records such things. In that immortal epic *The Voyage of the Argo,* by Apollonius of Rhodes, do we not read of the strange Mossynoeci, who inhabit the remote region of the Sacred Mountain in Asia Minor? Everything that other people do in public, these people do in private, and everything others do in private, they do in public. But of course Apollonius was a poet and, as Plato said, all poets are liars. Apollonius drew his story from Xenophon's *Anabasis,* whose account of the Mossynoeci is even more outlandish. He tells us that they use dolphin fat where the Greeks would use olive oil; and that their pale skins are beautifully tattooed all over with brightly colored flowers; and that if they laugh in public they are deeply ashamed, and generally go into their own houses to laugh in secret; as they do also to dance, all on their own, like madmen. They will only eat in absolute solitude, for they regard the act of putting food into an orifice in their face as quite disgusting. On the other hand, these topsy-turvy people defecate quite freely in the streets, without embarrassment; and most shamefully of all, they see nothing wrong with enjoying sexual congress with their own wives or, it seems, like the Etruscans of old, with each other's wives, most lasciviously, in the open. As Apollonius says, "like swine in the fields, they lie down on the ground in promiscuous intercourse and are not in the slightest bit troubled by the presence of others watching them." One wonders if the poet of Rhodes has not let his imagination run away with him here, and exchanged the inspiration of the Muses for inspiration of a more salacious kind. . . .

Despite all these evident absurdities a deeper truth comes back to me, and a wiser, still older voice. Gamaliel, whom it has been my pleasure also to know, would say that anything whatsoever that men have anywhere believed may yet instruct us. For while tales of gold-hoarding griffins do not in truth tell us anything about the mysterious and uncharted wastes of Central Asia, they do tell us much about the beliefs and the hearts of men.

So Gamaliel would say, his eyes twinkling with mischief and delight. Those eyes that have seen so many wonders and horrors, yet still shining with the light of life. Those ancient, glittering eyes. Gamaliel, Fire bringer, Sun singer, last of the Hidden Kings—he has traveled so far and lived so long, yet would still express his faith in the mysterious words that he loved: *Everything is God.*

But I digress. There will be tales of Gamaliel later. And indeed, in time, I shall introduce into this history my own self, Priscus of Panium—not from vulgar immodesty but rather because, for a short time, I truly did take my place upon the stage of the world, and in the great and terrible drama of history. But that is not for many years yet. Our theme for now remains the boyhood of Attila, and how his turbulent, iron-willed, earth-shaking character was formed; and the dark, tumultuous years of the early fifth century since Christ. Dark years, which some said would pass; and others said would only lead to darker yet. But a few, a very few, wise ones, who could see further than either optimist or pessimist, foretold that the years to come would be both for better and for worse; for in the tangled skein of history, which is the work of the God Who Loves Stories, there is very often no telling the two apart.

I resume: as far as China, the tribes were stirring.

Across the vast and measureless grasslands of Central Asia, the rains had started to fail. The deserts of the south had started to creep north, and in the autumn the renewal of the parched grasslands before the coming rains grew later and later with each passing year. And the nomad peoples of those regions, finding only lifeless desert to the south, and the dark and impenetrable forests of Scythia to the north, and to the east only the great Empire of China and its implacable, impassable wall, were forced to turn in the one direction left to them: to the west, and the warm, fruitful, and temperate lands of Europe. Toward the Mediterranean: the sea at the center of the world, with all its ancient, lion-colored promontories sleeping in the sun.

So began that great migration of peoples which lasted for centuries, and indeed is not abated yet. And among them came the most feared and savage tribe of all: the Huns.

They came from the east with dust-parched throats, and wind-parched eyes set on the western horizon. They rode on small, tough ponies with big, ungainly heads, driving before them their flocks of sheep and their herds of lean and starving cattle.

They carried bows and arrows. Their arrows were no different from those of any other people. An arrow is no more than a feathered stick with a barbed iron tip. But their bows would change the world. Their bows were weapons of a range and terror such as no opposing army had ever faced before.

They were made of a number of materials rather than a simple length of wood, and at a glance were unimpressive in appearance: a mere three feet in length, and resembling something like a piece of polished animal horn. But to flex one in your hands and bend it against your thigh was to feel its extraordinary latent strength and power. How their bows were made was a closely guarded secret, passed down through the generations.

The main elements were horn, wood, sinew, and glue boiled up from the tendons of animals, or from the parts of certain fish. The incomparable Hun bowyers had learned, over the long generations of their people, that horn resists compression, snapping back into shape if it is bent, while sinews of a certain kind—the Achilles tendons of antelope, most powerfully—resist extension. The Hun bowyers, therefore, learned to glue horn to the inside of their wooden bows, and lengths of antelope sinew to the outside. Such a task sounds simple, but it took years for a man to perfect his art. When it was done, the bow he had crafted was a thing of astonishing power.

It is said that every time a Hun warrior draws back his bowstring and lets fly an arrow, he exerts a force equivalent to pulling up one's entire weight, from a tree branch, say, by only one arm, and indeed by only three fingers. When you consider that, in battle, a Hun warrior might fire as many as fifteen arrows a minute, while riding at full gallop like a whirlwind past the ranks of the hapless enemy infantry, you will understand what toughness and hardihood these fierce people possessed. A toughness in every way a match for even the most hardened, grim-faced Roman legionary in his iron helmet, but with an additional speed and flamboyance. No wonder that every foreign tribe they encountered feared them as demons out of Hell. Even the Goths, the mightiest and most lion-hearted of all the Germanic peoples, had a grudging respect for the Huns.

The bow used by the Romans could fire an arrow a respectable three hundred and fifty yards or so. A Hun bow could fire an arrow over nine hundred yards—an incredible half a mile. When this was first witnessed in battle, it simply wasn't believed. Their enemies said the Huns could not be men, but must be the infernal offspring of sorcerers and witches of the desert. But they were men, after all, like any other.

The arrow flies from a Hun bow with a staggering force, so that at a range of two hundred yards, when many a Roman arrow is already falling from the air and dropping into the grass, the Hun arrow can still punch effortlessly through an inch-thick plank of wood. When riding out against the Huns, there is little point in wearing armor. Even tempered steel is just so much dead weight against those terrible, springing bows and those hurtling arrows.

The Hun warrior also exhibits a breathtaking skill in horsemanship. He can ride at full gallop while despatching one of those deadly missiles every four or five seconds. His speed makes him almost impossible to hit in return, and the strength and stamina of his sturdy little horse means that it can carry a man at a gallop for up to an hour. The refined Spanish or Cappadocian mounts of the empire, or the beautiful, headstrong horses of the Armenians and the Parthians, would be winded in a quarter of that time.

When riding close to the enemy, the Hun warrior can slip from his saddlecloth, and down the side of his horse, holding on only with the strength of his thighs, still galloping, still firing. He can even lean down so low as to fire underneath his horse's neck, using the body of his mount for cover.

Is it any wonder that, all across Scythia, every tribe feared the Huns? Or that, in time, every empire in Europe and Asia came to fear them too?

These, then, were the people who came across the great plains in their skin-covered wagons, their women and children at their sides, every bit as tough as their menfolk. The wagons came in file, stretching back as far as the eye could see, spreading out over the waterless steppes, the dust in the reddening light of the setting sun raised by the turning wheels of the creaking wooden wagons. The fording of the great rivers of that country could take weeks: the songs of the nomad drovers rising above the bellowing of the cattle as they were driven deep into the water, the snorting of the horses, the splashing of the great wooden wheels through the fording places, the shrieks of women and the yells of men and the excited laughter of children.

As the tribe moved west, so it encountered, and fought with, and generally in its fierceness and desperation displaced, the tribe that went before it. None of those tribes made any distinction between citizen and soldier. When the time came to fight, they simply formed their wagons into a circle, to shelter their women and children within; every man took his bow, and his spear, and mounted his pony; every man fought. Every man a warrior—as it was with the citizen army of Rome, long ago, in the days of its republican greatness.

But do not think that these tribes occupied any territory in the sense that Rome occupies a territory and an empire. These peoples had no boundaries, and no empires, they were nomads, and worshipped the earth itself as their ancestral home. Although one group of the Huns— the Black Huns, Attila's people, and the most feared of all the tribes— had been seen encamped upon the northern and eastern banks of the Danube, in Trans-Pannonia, ever since their own King Balamir had led them into Europe, three or four generations before the time of King Uldin, at other times their camps simply vanished from sight. Then even the rich pastures of the Danube floodplain had tired, and the Huns had moved east again, over the Kharvad Mountains, which the Romans call the Carpathians, and beyond, to the plains of Scythia proper. Many of them still looked back toward the east, even when west of the Kharvad Mountains, to where many of their Hun brothers still lived. Although they looked with greed upon the marble and gold of the empires of the Mediterranean, their dreams still tended toward the open steppes of Asia as their true homeland. And as the days lengthened each year, if they were not fighting in wars with their neighbors, many Pannonian Huns would ride east for a summer of hunting in the empty and desolate expanses of Asia which only they understood and loved.

There they lived a life on horseback for many months, intoxicated by the boundless freedom and lawlessness of those ungoverned lands. Or whose only laws, shall we say, were the laws of the bow, and the noose, and the spear. Over the wide plains they rode, into the valleys and over the mountains, through the narrow passes, down the narrow, sunless gorges beside rivers in full, white spate. They hunted the wild animals, contemptuous of the weak and settled lives that others lived in the world of law and civilization. They hunted bear and wolf, lynx and leopard and auroch. When winter came, and the fur of the wild animals thickened with the cold, they hunted ermine and beaver and mink. They returned with sleds creaking on their runners of wood and bone, piled high with furs, the rich, glossy pelts sparkling with Scythian frost. These furs they sold to the crafty-eyed fur merchants in the Greek trading cities on the shores of the Euxine Sea, at Tanais, and Chersonesus, and Ophiusa. Or farther west, at the markets on the Danube, and at Margus Fair.

Margus Fair, where in time, it would all begin. Where the end of everything would begin.

2

INTO THE MOUNTAINS

The boy was awoken roughly in the midst of his dreams by one of the Palatine guard. The man carried a torch. It was still dark outside.

"Get yourself up and dressed. We leave at dawn."

"Leave? Where for?"

"Ravenna."

Only a few minutes later he found himself seated beside Olympian, one of the senior palace eunuchs, riding in a high and overdecorated Liburnian car through the dark and silent streets of Rome.

Olympian was evidently reluctant, even personally insulted, to find himself sitting beside the half-savage Hun boy for the duration of the journey, and had insisted that Attila be submitted to a full body search before he would consent to ride with him. Why, the little barbarian might be carrying a dagger or something. The soldiers had made sly asides to each other, to the effect that a dagger thrust in Olympian's mountainous rolls of flesh was hardly likely to prove fatal. The boy had duly been searched, and given the all clear. Now Olympian sat beside

Attila, touching his mouth from time to time with a little white silk cloth impregnated with oil of rosemary so as to ward off the ghastly, disease-bearing fumes that the boy must surely give off, and refusing to speak a word to him. That was fine by Attila. He could think of nothing that he wanted to say to Olympian.

All the same, he wasn't mad about sharing a carriage with the eunuch. Unlike the lean and hungry Eumolpus, but in common with the great majority of those who had been deprived of their seed-bearing parts in their youth, Olympian was grossly fat. In the absence of other fleshly pleasures, food had become very important to him. The loose swathes of midnight-blue silk that he wore did little to conceal his massive torso. Indeed, they showed a terrace-like effect, like the Emperor Hadrian's celebrated gardens at Tivoli, each descending terrace being composed of a greater and greater roll of fat. In consequence, the eunuch perspired heavily, and runnels of sweat ran down his puffy cheeks, playing havoc with the white lead powder that he had carefully applied to his face that morning. Never mind whether the barbarian boy was giving off disease-bearing fumes or not. The eunuch himself was soon giving off fumes of quite another sort. The boy held his nose close to the window, and hoped it wasn't far to Ravenna.

Either side of their carriage rode a mounted guard. The boy's previous attempts at escape were well known, and no chances were being taken.

The vast and unwieldy column trundled out of the palace gates and northward through the city along the great Flaminian Way. Carriages were not normally allowed within city precincts by day, ever since Julius Caesar himself had passed a law to that effect. But this was a very special occasion.

Immediately behind Attila rode Beric and Genseric in another ornate and impractical carriage. They were both nursing hangovers, and they felt every queasy rocking of the cabin on its broad leather straps. They chewed fennel but it did little good. Near the Flaminian Gate, Beric leaned from the carriage window and vomited.

Ahead of the column rode a detachment of the frontier guard, some

eighty in number. The roads were bad these days, and the forests dangerous, particularly after one had crossed the River Nera on the great
Bridge of Augustus and begun the slow ascent into the Montes Martanis.
But no troop of bandits, no matter how desperate, would dare to attack a
company of trained soldiers.

As they passed out of the Flaminian Gate their numbers were swelled
by a further detachment from the Palatine camp: fifty or so black-
armored Guards, who immediately took up the position of honor at the
head of the column, relegating the frontier guard to the rear. At the head
of the column rode Count Heraclian himself. He seemed keen to leave
Rome behind, and make for the safety of marsh-bound Ravenna.

Galla Placidia stayed behind in Rome.

Her advisers had pleaded with her. Eumolpus suggested that her regal
presence was needed with the column to maintain order.

She laughed dryly, without mirth. "I remain here," she said. "As do
you."

Eumolpus paled visibly. The Goths were not known for their gentle-
ness to captured eunuchs.

Count Heraclian had told her, before his departure with the column,
that she must flee to Ravenna: the only safe haven in Italy now.

"Ravenna is Italy's Constantinople," he said, "the only city we can easily
defend. Rome has always been vulnerable to attack. Remember Brennus
and the Gauls."

"Remember Hannibal," Galla snapped. "Do not presume to lecture
me, Count Heraclian. I may be only half your age still, but I am no
schoolgirl. What of the rest of the Palatine guard? They number upward
of thirty thousand, do they not? Since when did an army of five Roman
legions have anything to fear from a rabble of barbarians, no matter how
numerous? With how many legions did Caesar conquer Gaul? Or the
Divine Claudius conquer the whole island of Britain?"

"Your Sacred Majesty—"

"Tell me."

Heraclian shook his head. "The Palatine guard did number thirty thousand . . . but Alaric commands over a hundred thousand. And the Goths have fought and won many battles, from Scythia to Gallia Narbonensis and the very foothills of the Pyrenees. They are a nation of great warriors, Your Majesty. Already many of the Palatine guard have left for Ravenna, and others for the south."

She sneered. "*Left* for Ravenna? You mean *fled*." She settled her hands in her lap and looked up at him again. "You are leaving for Ravenna, too, I assume?"

Heraclian stammered. "My, my . . . I am needed, Your Majesty, to command the column."

"I would have thought a junior officer of the frontier guard was quite capable of steering it toward Ravenna?"

Heraclian flushed and said nothing.

"So," said Galla, "the Palatine are proving just as loyal to the empire as the praetorian guard that preceded them. And we know how they ended up behaving, don't we, Count Heraclian?"

Yes, he knew. They ended up butchering Emperor Pertinax, and then auctioning off the empire itself for fifty million silver pieces. It was bought by a wealthy businessman, one Didius Julianus, who promptly declared himself emperor. He lasted just sixty-six days, until he was killed as well: beheaded as a common criminal in the baths.

"Let them all flee," she said. "Galla Placidia does not flee."

She spoke with all the composure and the grandiose sense of self that you might expect from an empress who had reigned for half a lifetime. Once again, Heraclian had to remind himself that this tall, bony, pale-skinned woman, in her long, stiff dalmatic and her glittering tiara, was only a girl of twenty-one. Yet she had the will and the presence of a dozen Caesars.

"What will happen when Alaric arrives?" he asked.

"You tell me," said Galla. Her ice-cold eyes drilled into him. "You are now the master general of the army, are you not, since you presided over the death of your former colleague, the traitor Stilicho? I would have expected a commander to have a rather greater air of determination and resolve about him than you seem to exhibit, Count Heraclian."

Her voice dripped with contempt. Heraclian closed his eyes momentarily, as if in self-defense. He felt cold fury rising. How he hated this woman! And how he feared her. He tried to hide his feelings, but she saw them anyway. Her eyes were like needles.

She smiled. "Hm?"

It was she who had ordered the death of Stilicho, he thought furiously. He had only been carrying out orders. And now he was in command of the Western Army himself, and she was trying to blame him for everything. It wasn't fair. Everything was slipping away. . . .

"When Alaric comes," said Heraclian, struggling to control the tremor in his voice and failing, "you will be taken into captivity. You will be led from Rome in chains."

"No," said Galla. "Rather, the barbarian hordes will see how an Imperial Princess of Rome can die."

Heraclian stood and bowed. "I must leave," he said. "I must ride out and join the column. My first loyalty is to—"

"The emperor." Galla smiled. "Yes, of course. *Ubi imperator, ibi Roma.* Where the emperor is, there is Rome."

Heraclian bowed again. "Your Majesty," he said, and he turned and left the room.

Galla watched him go without expression. Then she summoned Eumolpus to her side.

"Your Majesty?"

"Tell my maids to prepare my bath."

"Yes, Your Majesty."

Well, she thought, Galla Placidia should look her best for the occasion.

She also summoned a scribe to write a letter, to be sent after Count Heraclian immediately.

As the grand column departed from the city, there was no cheering from the crowds that gathered along the roadside. Instead the retreating column was watched with sullen contempt, or even outright hostility. Suddenly the great triumph of Honorius over the Goths, which seemed to have taken place only a few days before, although really it had been a year ago—and the declaration on the Triumphal Arch, that the barbarian enemies of Rome had been destroyed forever—all began to ring a little hollow. One or two spectators shouted insults, or even threw clods of mud at the passing carriages, until a couple of mounted Palatine guards rounded on them with drawn swords and they fled. There could be no such escape to Ravenna for the majority of Roman citizens. They must simply sit and wait for the Gothic wrath to come.

Beyond the city lay the great cemeteries all along the Via Flaminia, with their huge limestone tombs, ornately carved with a mix of Christian and pagan symbols, fishes and birds and crosses and scallop shells, interspersed with the dark and mourning shapes of cypress trees. Attila gazed at them and brooded. It was Roman custom to bury the dead beyond the city walls. To bury anyone within the city would bring bad luck, they believed. Except for the great Emperor Trajan, conqueror of Dacia, Rome's only territory beyond the Danube. When he died suddenly on campaign, and contrary to his dying wishes, the soldier-emperor's ashes were brought back to the city, and buried in a chamber beneath the mighty column that bore his name and whose carved stone bas-reliefs gave such eloquent witness to his Dacian victories. But the interment there of his mortal remains was against all custom, some said. And since that moment, three long centuries ago—since that high noonday of the Antonine emperors, Hadrian, Trajan, and the philosopher Marcus Aurelius, when the Roman Empire comprehended the fairest part of the earth, and the most civilized portion of mankind—some said that it was at that moment that the empire had started to shrink again, and begun its long and slow decline. Now the city was facing an army of a hundred thousand blue-eyed Gothic horsemen, already far into Italy. . . .

The boy longed to see Alaric ride into proud Rome, even though the Goths were the ancient enemies of his people. But he had other plans. When the Flaminian Way rose up into the hills . . .

The late summer air was stifling, and thunderbugs crowded the air. They flew in the faces of the cavalrymen, who swatted them away angrily, tilting back their helmets to wipe the sweat from their foreheads.

The country opened out into the market gardens that supplied Rome's endless needs and greeds, and then the vast estates and villas of the upper Tiber valley. Sun-dried pinecones crunched under the turning wheels of the carriages, broom pods exploded softly in the dense August heat, and the songs of the basking cicadas arose from the long grass.

Olympian insisted that the little red curtains be drawn across the windows to keep out the sun, and the interior of the carriage was as dim as a church. The boy dozed. He dreamed fitfully of Stilicho and Serena, and even awoke at one point believing they were still alive. When he remembered, it felt as if the memory was burning into his flesh like sunburn, or as if his eyes were sun blind with sorrow. He squeezed his eyes shut and took refuge in sleep again. He dreamed of Tibir, the god of fire, and of Otütsir, the god of the sun and the Cause of the Years. He dreamed of his homeland.

The carriage rolled to a halt. He started and pulled the curtains and leaned out of the window. Olympian tried to tell him not to, but he ignored him. The air was hot and still and ominous. From far off, way up toward the head of the column, he could hear shouting. The sound of a horseman from the frontier guard galloping up from the rearguard of the column. Finally he returned, and Olympian hailed him as the column began to roll slowly onward again.

"I say, my man!"

The cavalryman reined in his horse, his bunched fists pulling toward his chest, the muscles in his arms bulging. He slowed and turned his horse to walk beside the carriage, while the mounted guard fell back, and noted sourly that it was that fat palace eunuch inside. He said nothing for awhile, his gaze fixed ahead on the road and the far horizon, his expression one of grim foreboding.

"Soldier? What is your name?"

The soldier glanced sideways at the eunuch and grunted. "Centurion. Centurion Marco."

"Marcus?"

"No," replied the soldier slowly, as if to a particularly stupid child. "*Mar—co.*"

Marco indeed, thought Olympian crossly. It wasn't even Latin. It was *barbaric.*

"Well, Marco, what seems to be the matter?"

"Trouble on the road ahead."

"What, bandits?"

Marco snorted. "Bandits, my ass. Begging your pardon, sir. But I think we could handle a few bandits, don't you? No. Bigger trouble than that, a lot bigger." He hawked and spat, and they rode on a little while.

"Come along, man, speak up," said Olympian, his voice petulant with impatience and fear.

"Well, sir, it's like this. There's us going north along the Flaminian Way." He sliced forward with one hand. "And there's Alaric coming south along the Flaminian Way. And somehow I don't think the road is wide enough for the both of us."

Olympian clutched his little white hanky to his mouth, and Attila could have sworn he gave a muffled shriek.

The boy leaned across the quivering eunuch and said, "But Alaric was still camped up in Cisalpine Gaul, wasn't he?"

The centurion stared into the carriage and jerked his head back with some surprise when he saw the boy. "You're very well informed," he muttered. "You're the Hun lad, yes? Uldin's lad?"

Attila nodded. "My father's father."

The centurion shrugged. "So he was. Alaric was only just over the Alps a month ago, but he's marched south already. Those horsemen are no slouches. They'll be outside the gates of Rome by dusk tomorrow, it's reckoned." He hitched back his shoulders and set his mouth grimly. "Well, what will be will be. Our job is to get to Ravenna first. So we're going to have to turn east."

The boy tried not to appear too eager. "Into the mountains?" he asked.

"Into the mountains," nodded Marco.

"Into the mountains!" cried Olympian.

The boy craned and looked up at the sky: the heavily bruised and swollen sky that precedes a violent summer downpour. The rain-filled clouds seemed to hang down from the heavens like great gray bellies ready to burst.

The boy slapped more thunderbugs away from his sweat-slicked arms. "There's a storm coming," he said.

The centurion looked not up at the sky but ahead, northward along the road and toward the far horizon. "You're not fucking kidding," he growled. Then he shouted *"Hah,"* dug his heels into the flanks of his bay mare, wheeled, and galloped back to the rearguard of the anxious column.

"Well well," thought Attila, settling back into the luxuriously padded seat, almost unaware of Olympian's presence anymore. "A storm. It just gets better and better. Into the mountains we go."

The boy liked mountains. You can hide in mountains.

They rested the first night at a simple marching camp on the Flaminian Way, and the second night at Falerii Veteres. At midday on the third day they crossed the Bridge of Augustus over the Nera, and then turned east almost immediately, leaving behind them the wide plains of the Tiber and ascending a narrower road into the Sabine Mountains, toward the town of Terni. The road became bumpier, and beyond Terni they turned onto a minor road, barely a track across the hills, and the column could manage no more than a slow walking pace. They would be pushed to cover so much as fifteen miles a day at this rate, even allowing for every hour of summer daylight. Which they couldn't, as they would have to make safe camp each night they couldn't make a fortified town. Nevertheless, the boy guessed that this route was reckoned the least risky, because the least likely for an imperial column to take.

"Where's Galla?" he asked.

"The Princess Galla Placidia, to whom I assume you are referring in that peculiarly familiar style," said Olympian acidly, "has remained behind in Rome."

"What will the Goths do to her?"

Olympian crossed himself piously, rolled his puffy eyes up toward the roof of the carriage, and said, "Nothing that is not already ordained of God."

He leaned forward and plucked back the little velvet curtains to let in the cooler mountain air.

The hillsides were covered in sheep and fattening lambs, and the occasional shepherd. One stopped and stood right in the road, gawking at the approaching column, until a couple of guards rode out and shoved him out of the way.

"Of course, it is well known," began Olympian, hardly noticing whether the boy was listening to him or not. In fact, the only reason he had begun talking at all was to try to calm his own nerves, which by this time were feeling very frayed indeed, what with the soldiers, and the mountains, and the Goths.

"Of course," he said, "it is well known that the shepherds of these hills are absolute beasts of men, who never take a bath from the day they're baptized to the day they're buried. *If* they ever are baptized." He gazed hesitantly out of the window upon the sun-parched land, his hanky held tight in his fat, white, delicate hand. "They probably still worship goats out here, most of them."

He settled back into his seat again. " 'All buggers and bandits,' as they say in Rome of the country people of the Sabine Hills. Or, even more vulgarly, 'sheep shaggers.' One knows what they mean. Why, it wasn't so very long ago that the Sabine peasants were notorious for having the barber shave not only the hair on their heads but their pubic hair as well. *In public.* In the market square, before the eyes of their own wives, and other men's wives as well! They have as much sense of shame as the animals they tend."

The boy snickered, and Olympian glared at him.

As if to prove the eunuch's point, however, a little farther on the column passed another shepherd, standing and staring at them as if they were the first human beings he had seen in months. Perhaps they were. He stood stark naked but for a sheepskin wrap round his shoulders. His deep brown skin was like leather dried out and cracked by a desert sun, his legs were misshapen by childhood starvation or adult accident, and his eyes were wild and bloodshot. The boy thought of Virgil's *Eclogues,* drummed into him by his Greek pedagogue. So much for the romance of shepherd life.

Olympian tutted.

The boy grinned. These Italian *barbarians.*

He looked back and saw, with some surprise, that the shepherd had jogged back to a clump of brushwood, and led out from behind it a starveling mule. He hauled himself up onto the mule and, turning it toward the valley below, he glanced back only one more time at the imperial column.

Then he kicked the mule forward with some ferocity, and disappeared over the brow of the plateau.

Attila sat back and wondered.

They climbed higher and higher into the mountains, up a stony ravine, which in winter must have been a river in spate but was now only a dry riverbed, steeply banked on either side. Thornbrush clung to the crumbling slopes, and cicadas trilled in the hot summer air. Otherwise the silence and loneliness up here were oppressive. Already they felt a long way from Rome.

The boy couldn't resist it. Gazing up at the high rocky banks on either side, he murmured, "Good place for an ambush."

"Oh!" said Olympian, quivering. "Oh, don't say that!"

"Well, you never know," said the wretched boy, apparently enjoying himself immensely.

"Anyway, our man back there, Marcus, said we had nothing to fear from bandits," went on the eunuch, talking nervously fast. "We are with a column of heavily armed, professional soldiers, after all."

"What about a gang of ex-gladiators?" said the boy. "Not slave gladiators, I mean the professionals. A lot of them have turned bandits, so people say, now that they're all out of a job in the arena. They'd be pretty tough opposition in an ambush, wouldn't they?"

"Don't be ridiculous," said the eunuch. "You must have been listening to too many silly stories from the slaves." He held his hanky to his face again and mopped up the drop of sweat that had formed on the end of his bulbous nose. "Gladiators, indeed," he huffed.

But the boy was right. He always listened to the stories from the slaves, and found them a very good source of information. He liked information. It was a kind of power.

Emperor Honorius had abolished the games back in AD 404, after the self-sacrificing protest of the monk Telemachus; at the same time, he had shut the gladiatorial schools. Unfortunately, it didn't seem to have occurred to either Honorius or his advisers that an unemployed gladiator, like an unemployed soldier, is a rather dangerous individual. Five thousand professional gladiators finding themselves unemployed overnight are very dangerous indeed. After their well-remunerated careers of bloodlust and carnage in the arena, it was somehow unlikely that these men would quietly settle down as good citizens, and get jobs as water carriers, fresco painters, fig merchants, or whatever. Some went into the army, but most of them were too old. The army only wanted young men up to the age of twenty-one: fit, malleable, and easily trained. After their years of individual heroics, gladiators, for all their toughness and predisposition to extreme violence, were regarded as poor-quality soldier material.

The best-looking ones were snapped up by some of the wealthier ladies of Roman society, to be their "personal assistants," "litter bearers," or even, in one instance which caused great hilarity among the city's satirists and literary salons, her *ornatrix,* or "hairdresser." The word was of the feminine gender, but was now peculiarly applied to male hairdressers, who had become fashionable of late. They were mostly eunuchs, of course, or else interested strictly in boys. Upon hearing of the gladiator-hairdresser, the satirists sharpened their goose-quill pens. Soon there were circulating little squibs about how strange it was that an *ornatrix* should be required to attend upon his mistress in her private chambers only after having stripped naked, oiled himself all over, and performed vigorous weightlifting and strengthening exercises in the gym with his *membrum virile.*

But the laughter died on their sophisticated faces when they learned that the great majority of the gladiators had taken to the hills to become bandits.

"Remember Spartacus," said the pessimists.

"Yes, and look what became of him," said the optimists. "Crucified along with his men all along the Appian Way."

"Yes," said the pessimists, "but only after they'd wiped out two Roman legions."

"Ah," said the optimists. "Well, yes. . . ."

Which was why Olympian was so disturbed by this wretched barbarian boy's suggestion that they might be ambushed. As the eunuch well knew, this was a real possibility.

In general, however, the bandit gangs of the Sabine Hills and beyond were not reckoned to be any great threat, but operated as cowards, attacking lonely, isolated farmsteads, or wealthy merchants foolish enough to travel without a decent armed escort. Whoever they were, it was inconceivable that they should have the temerity to attack a fully escorted imperial column, even in these remote hills.

3

FIRST BLOOD

The first arrow struck Marco in his upper arm.

"Fuck!" he roared, looking down. The arrow had punched almost through his tricep and out again. He ordered his *optio* to snap off the haft, and push the arrowhead through and out the other side, while he clenched his teeth furiously on the leather strap of his reins and bit down. Another arrow whistled over his head as their horses skittered, and the *optio* struggled to tie the tourniquet tightly above the wound.

His lieutenant came galloping back. It was Lucius, the gray-eyed British lieutenant.

"First blood, centurion," he called cheerfully. "Good man!"

"Yeah, unfortunately it's *my* blood, sir."

Another arrow fell short and clattered over the rough ground at their horses' feet. Lucius squinted up. There was nothing in the silent air but the trill of the cicadas, nothing to be seen up on the ridge but the blue sky beyond. Not a plume of dust, not a scuffle.

"We're being ambushed by . . . what? A solitary six-year-old boy? What in the Name of Light is going on?"

Marco shook his head. "No idea, sir. Feeblest ambush I've ever been in."

The column had come to a halt, even though it was in a narrow defile. No more arrows came. There was no need to panic.

"When you've finally stopped bleeding—" said Lucius.

"Stopped already, sir," interrupted Marco, patting the tourniquet. "Tight as a virgin's—"

"Okay, Centurion, I get the message. Now ride on up to the Palatine vanguard and ask Count Heraclian, respectfully, what he wants us to do."

Marco soon returned. "He suggests you're in a better intelligence position than he is, sir."

Lucius stared at him. "He wants me to give the orders?"

"Seems so, sir. He also suggests that you and your frontier guard ride at the head of the column from now on."

"Jesus the Jumping Jew." Lucius turned away. "Master General Heraclian," he said under his breath, "you are one useless pile of mule shit." He turned back. "Okay, Centurion, we ride on. At the end of this defile, when we come to that stand of cork oaks there—see?—you and me and First Squadron turn sharply back and ride round to the left and see what we can see. How's that for a plan?"

"Tremendously complex, sir, but it might just work."

"Okay, you cheeky bastard. Ride on."

As they rode, Marco gave the silent signal to the first troop of eight cavalrymen to be ready to split off from the column and climb the slope to the left. At the given moment they did so, without Lucius needing to bark a single word of command. The horses strained to get them up the steep slope, their heads held low and their nostrils flared, until at last they reached the summit, and reined in and stopped, and looked away across the blank escarpment.

Nothing. Not even a plume of dust.

"What the fuck *is* going on, sir?"

Lucius squinted across the plain. At last he said softly, "What kind of bandit gang, Centurion, launches probing, reconnaissance attacks, to test the strength of its chosen target? Not even a volley, just a few well-aimed arrows, and then has the discipline to retreat and vanish before the enemy can counter?"

"None that I know of, sir."

Lucius scanned the hazy horizon again with eyes almost closed.

"Gladiators?" said another, younger trooper, wide-eyed Carpicius, all boyish excitement and dread. "Turned bandits?"

"Gladiators," snorted Ops, a bull-necked Egyptian decurion in his early forties, due for retirement soon but as tough as any in the legion. His real name was Oporsenes, but Ops suited him better. "Don't give me fuckin' gladiators. Gladiators, sunshine, is a bunch of actors with swords in their hands. They're just celebrity fuckin' murderers, they are."

Like any other soldier, Ops had nothing but contempt for gladiators, unemployed or not. Overpaid sex symbols, girly boys, showy individualist fighters who wouldn't last five minutes on a real battlefield, where the mutual loyalty and trust between you and your men was what kept you all alive. Not fancy blade work in front of a roaring crowd of thousands.

"Okay, men," said Lucius, wheeling his horse round again. "Back to the column and ride on, eyes skinned. This isn't over yet."

"What on earth is going on?" whispered Olympian as the column rumbled forward again. "We can't be under attack, can we?"

"Looks like it," said the little barbarian, settling back comfortably in his seat. "Pretty disciplined attack, too, I'd say."

Olympian turned his fear into scorn. "Oh, so you're a military expert, too, are you now? Closely acquainted, no doubt, with the military treatises of Aeneas Tacitus, Frontinus, and Vegetius?"

The boy eyed the eunuch and nodded evenly. "Yes, I've read them," he said. "And that anonymous one, *De re militari,* which shows you how to drive a boat using paddles powered by oxen. Interesting idea—be good for attacking upriver. Do you know it?"

The eunuch gaped at him like a dying mullet.

Attila smiled and closed his eyes. "They'll be attacking again soon," he promised. "Better say your prayers."

They climbed out of the gully and onto a high, barren plateau. Perfect for a hit-and-run cavalry attack on a heavy, slow-moving column. But the outriders Lucius had posted—Heraclian, for some reason, hadn't got round to it—reported no sign of life except lizards and cicadas. And the ground was far too hard and rocky to leave any decent trail signs.

They crossed the plateau in tense silence, the frontier guard riding in the van, the Palatine guard in the rear. Then they began to drop down again, into a vast natural amphitheater of grassland. The track itself curved away, round and down the flank of the hill, the terrain rising steeply to the left and falling away just as steeply to the right.

Lucius called a halt.

There was no sound but the soughing of the wind in the dry grass.

Ops growled something. Lucius told him to be quiet.

He was thinking of the day Hannibal slaughtered the Romans at Lake Trasimene, ambushing them side on when they were in marching file, unable to turn round into battle order, pinned against the lakeside. He was thinking how good a place this would be to launch a similar ambush. To their left a steep ascent, and to their right an even steeper descent. There was no way they could get themselves into decent formation on this slope.

Then Marco said, "There are horses coming. That way, over the rise."

"Shepherds?" suggested Lucius. "Goats?"

"No, horses. Men on horses."

They listened. Lucius could hear nothing. The tension was unbearable. A soldier's desire to get stuck in, as Lucius knew, often made him attack too early. There was nothing worse than waiting for the enemy—especially for an unseen, uncounted enemy.

But Marco was no novice. He nodded again. "They're coming."

"How can you hear that?" said Lucius.

"I can't. But our horses can."

He was right. Their mounts were skittish anyway, smelling their riders' sweat and fear. But there was something more than that on the wind. Their ears twitched back and forth, and their nostrils flared to pick up the scent of their approaching kind.

Lucius leaned forward and spoke into the flicking ear of his fine gray mare. "What is it, Tugha Bàn? Trouble ahead?" He sat back, oblivious of his centurion's skeptical stares. "I think you're right."

He squinted up the slope to their left. Then he signaled to Marco to give the general order to dismount. "And that means the Palatine, too—*if* Master General Heraclian doesn't mind. So ride back and tell them to get off their fat asses."

"We're not going to ride on down?"

"At our speed? With those wretched, overweight carriages?" Lucius shook his head. "We'll be cut to pieces if we stay mounted." He slid to the ground and fingered the pommel of his sword. "We're going to have to fight." He stood and scanned the steep slope again and the shimmering heat haze above. "Where are those fucking outriders?"

Marco said nothing. They both knew where the outriders were by now.

And they both knew what it meant when a troop of cawing rooks took flight and arose from the oak forest below them and flew away down the valley. Rooks are clever. They don't fly away at the approach of horses, or sheep, or goats. But they fly at the approach of men, and they can tell a man armed with a bow from a man without. When rooks take flight, trouble is coming.

Marco drew his sword and touched its edge.

Lucius had them line up two deep to the left of the column, facing uphill.

"That's quite a climb," muttered Marco.

"Certainly is," said Lucius. "Hope you've been doing your exercises."

Marco hawked and spat. "Yeah, yeah."

But he knew his officer was right. His officer was generally right, he had to admit it. Lieutenant Lucius was okay. In a situation like this, if they were about to be ambushed from above—and they were—the best thing to do was, as so often in warfare, the thing the enemy would least expect: counterattack uphill.

Marco glanced up, and there they were. He gave a low whistle. Counterattack uphill and with a lot fewer men. Jumping Jesus.

Along the ridge above them stood perhaps four hundred men, arrows already notched to their bows. They wore motley clothing, though many would fight naked to the waist. What little armor was in evidence was no more than leather breastplates. They stood unshaven, tattered, wild eyed. But their weapons were serious. As well as bows and arrows they bore shields, swords, and a few carried heavy pikes. This would be no picnic. They stood in orderly formation, looking down on the hapless column without expression, waiting for the order.

Then a solitary figure in a white robe stepped forward and tossed a sack down the slope. As it bounced and tumbled, the mouth of the sack opened, and out rolled two severed heads. One clunked against the wheels of a carriage and stopped. The other bounced right across the track and then on down the slope beyond. The outriders.

There was no point waiting any longer. Lucius gave the order, and they charged.

He felt his leg muscles burning and trembling with the strain as he struggled up the steep slope for twenty or thirty yards, in the front line with his men. Above their bellowing, he heard with sickening frequency the hollow thunk of arrow after arrow hitting men in the chest. At this close range armor was useless, and the wound would almost always be fatal. Five men had already gone down, ten, even twenty. And they were only eighty in all, plus the fifty Palatines over on the left flank. At last he was five yards from the line of bowmen, and he could see the surprise in their eyes. Their leader had still given no command to pull back or draw swords, and most of them were still encumbered with bows, astonished to see how quickly the soldiers had sprinted up the steep hill. Lucius looked up at the bandit who towered above him, and saw that his eyes were bloodshot, his lips cracked with the parching summer sun, his cheeks sunken and his hands shaking. These men were not in peak condition. His own men were.

Then they slammed into them. Lucius stepped up and barged his man backward off the ridge. He stepped forward again and thrust his sword forward with all his weight behind it. The startled bowman tried to fend off the thrust, absurdly, with his bow, but the thick steel blade plunged past and went into his guts up to the hilt. Lucius gave the blade a smart twist and pull, and the man fell at his feet, choking out his lifeblood, his intestines oozing from the ragged hole in his belly. Behind him another man came on, drawing his sword. He got no farther. Lucius raised his sword in a flash to shoulder height, his shield held across his chest and belly for defense, and drove the point into the man's throat. His blade grated against the man's neck vertebrae, and he could feel them coming apart as he twisted the blade and pulled it free. His hand and arm were covered in blood. The man lolled lifelessly against him, and he shoved the corpse back ferociously with his shield, into the man who came on behind.

All along the line it was the same story. On the left flank, the silent, orderly Palatines were making mincemeat of their malnourished opponents. You had to hand it to them: they were tough enough soldiers when it came to it.

Though they had lost perhaps a quarter of their men on the ascent, now they were fighting in deadly, close-packed formation as only Roman soldiers knew how, offering their enemy nothing but a solid wall of shields and shining blades. There was nothing for the ragged bandit army to attack but hard steel.

Marco was fighting to Lucius's right. Although the battle-scarred centurion would never dream of uttering a word of complaint, Lucius could see that the arrowhead wound in his left arm was bleeding afresh. He was trying to keep his shield up to cover his flank as he thrust forward with his sword arm, but his arm was weakening steadily, his shield trembling and gradually sinking lower and lower. Any moment now the enemy was going to spot it and drive in over the top, straight into throat or lung. Lucius said nothing but made sure he kept him covered, too, fighting a little in front of Marco, covering his left. They had always made a good team.

Along the line, he saw the lad Carpicius stumble and fall. A bearded, beggarly looking brute raised his short stabbing spear above his head, ready to drive it into the back of the boy's neck. Lucius turned, but it was too late. And then, even as the spearhead was coming down through the air, Ops, the burly Egyptian, flung himself forward, almost covering the boy, with his shield raised on his hefty arm. The spear went straight through the shield, of course, and from the roar Ops gave it must have gone into his arm as well. But Carpicius was saved, by the skin of his teeth, scrambling clear and sticking his sword smartly into his opponent's side while he was still wrestling to free his spear from Ops' shield. Lucius felt a momentary lump in his throat. He had some good men in his command. He was damned if he was going to lose any more. He fought on with mute ferocity.

The bandits were coming apart all over the place. And foolishly, they had left their horses immediately behind them. Now they were stumbling back against their whinnying mounts, trying to get past, under them, even over them, mounting up and riding chaotically away. The line of soldiers came mowing into them still, the close-packed bandits utterly outfought. At the back, Lucius glimpsed the man who had tossed down the sack containing the two severed heads. He was trying to pull his horse round by the reins so he could mount.

He punched Marco on the arm. "With me!"

He fell back and sprinted round the rear of the line to the left, heading for the bandit leader. Marco sprinted at his heels, roaring at the top of his voice. Lucius grinned as he ran. That was Marco all over.

In fact, Marco was roaring because his wounded arm was flaming with pain where his officer had just punched him. If Lucius didn't keep running, Marco would be strongly tempted to deck him.

They reached the bandit leader as he swung up onto his horse and wrenched the reins round to the right. Marco didn't muck about. He hurled himself forward and thrust his sword into the horse's neck. Its carotid artery was cleanly severed and blood spurted with extraordinary force into the faces and chests of the two men. The rider wrenched the reins again, trying to control his dying mount, but it was futile. The poor beast was already done for, wheeling and staggering in a circle, its great heart driving the blood gushing from the gaping wound in its neck, as its back legs crumpled and it folded into the dust. The bandit leader rolled clear and scrambled to his feet, only to thump back down into the dust again as Marco planted a hefty hobnailed boot in the small of his back. He stuck the point of his sword firmly into the back of the man's neck and waited, panting, for Lucius.

He saw that the skirmish was already over. Perhaps two hundred bandits lay cut up on the ground. The few who were wounded were being rapidly despatched. The rest were streaming away over the plateau toward the oak forests beyond. Some of the men gave brief chase. But it was hot, and the battle had been won.

Lucius put the dying horse out of its misery, setting his sword point just behind the horse's still twitching ear and then driving it down into its brain. He always was soft about horses. Then he went over and ordered its rider to his feet.

Their captive was dusty and emaciated, but something proud still flashed in his eyes. He was oddly dressed, too, in only a long white robe, filthy and tattered around the hem. No armor, no arrow guard. Nothing to give him away.

"So," panted Lucius, shaking his head and blinking to clear the horse blood from his eyes. "Your name?"

The man lowered his head.

"You've had training. That wasn't a bad attempt at an ambush."

The man glared up at him with hatred burning in his eyes.

Then Lucius caught sight of something. The man was trying to hide his left hand. Lucius grabbed it and pulled it toward him. A signet ring flashed on the forefinger.

He looked at him sharply. "So you were a soldier? Soldier turned bandit, eh? Got cross one day that you hadn't been paid for a few months, is that it? Got a bit peevish? So you turned on the Rome that nurtured you, that you owed everything to, and went back to live in the forests like a wild animal?"

The man turned aside and spat in the dust, and then looked at Lucius again, eyes still blazing with that strange hatred. "I served Stilicho," he said.

Lucius nodded, slowly. And then at last he said, very softly, "I served Stilicho, too. I like to think I still do."

The two men stared at each other a while longer.

"Well," said Lucius at last, sighing and letting the man's grimy hand drop. "Enough of that."

"String 'em up, sir?"

Lucius turned wearily away. "String 'em up."

Only eight bandits, including the leader, had been captured alive. They would be used as examples, and were led away across the plateau to the edge of the forest.

At the head of a small ravine running down off the plateau stood an ancient and battered pine tree. The prisoners were taken to the foot of the tree and stripped naked. Lucius's men were throwing ropes over the mighty lower branch of the tree and setting nooses round the prisoners' necks, ready to haul them up and hang them, when Heraclian came riding up and assumed command.

"I think a special lesson is needed," he said.

Lucius turned away. He had no desire to see the Palatine go to work. But Marco made himself watch.

The Palatine guards tied the prisoners' hands behind their backs, made them kneel in the dust, and beat them savagely with a whip of knotted leather thongs. They beat the leader with special savagery, but, like his fellow outlaws, he made not a sound. After the beating, the leader was kicked down into the dust, and his ankles were bound tightly together. A rope was passed between his shins and knotted round his ankles, while the other end of the rope was thrown up over the lower branches of the tree, and he was hauled up with his head toward the ground. One of the guards climbed up and hammered in a nine-inch iron nail through his crossed ankles, pinning him to the branch. And there he was left, silent but conscious, trembling with exhaustion and pain. Blood ran down from his ankles and his back, and dripped from his nose and from the ends of his hair.

Marco knew what was worst about this reverse crucifixion. The nine-inch nail through the anklebones was bad enough, but it didn't kill you. No, the worst thing was to be suspended upside down like that, unable to move, until you died. It would take about three days, maybe more. The bandits were shaded by the pine, so they wouldn't die of thirst that soon. The blood would rush to their heads, and not return. Within an hour they would have headaches worse than you could imagine. Within a day, their lips and tongues would be purple and swollen, the whites of their eyeballs would be as purple red as ripe plums. It wasn't unknown for a man's eyeballs to burst open with the pressure. But that still wouldn't kill you. A brain hemorrhage might, or dehydration. If nothing else did, within three days you would die of agonizing suffocation, unable to raise your rib cage any longer to breathe. And you would die gratefully.

If you were lucky, the crows wouldn't find you before you died. Those gallows birds with their strong black beaks and their bright, unsmiling eyes. But if you were unlucky, they would spot you hanging there from afar off, and come and flutter on your upturned chest, and peck out your eyeballs for a dainty treat as you still lived, or rip away the soft flesh of your lips. It was no good closing your eyes to them. They would simply devour your eyelids as well, tearing them delicately away as if they were silk. No wonder crows were thought to be the wandering souls of the damned.

The Palatine guards nailed the eight bandits upside down like this, one by one, from the creaking, bloodstained branch of the ancient pine. The tortured men groaned, and some of them pleaded, but to no avail. The guards had no time for them, only contempt.

"Now, now, madam, do stop your whimpering," said one of them cheerfully as he banged in another nine-inch nail. "You'll soon be in Hades with a wooden sword up your ass."

Lucius sat on his horse and looked out across the valley to the south, toward Rome. He knew these scum deserved no better. It was perfectly just punishment for a criminal. But all the same, he didn't have to enjoy it.

Then they rode back across the plateau and down toward the waiting carriages of the column, leaving the tall tree behind them with its ghastly decorations of living but dying men.

Some of the soldiers had dragged clumps of brushwood from the edge of the forest, and piled them up into a pyre for burning the bodies of the slain. The stench from the battlefield was already terrible: blood and sweat and the contents of ruptured bowels mingled foully on the hot air. The men covered their faces, dragged the bandits' corpses onto the pyre and set it burning. The bodies burned slowly, sizzling like roasting meat, a plume of black, oily smoke rising high into the air.

"A warning signal," said Heraclian with approval, "to any other robber bands in the area."

Molten human fat was beginning to run from under the pyre and trickle away into the crevices in the earth. Lucius moved on, ordering the Roman dead to be laid on travoises and taken down into the valley. The ground here was too hard to dig. They would be given a decent burial in the soft earth below, as befitted any who had died in the cause of Rome.

They had lost a quarter of the force. Lucius had made the right decision, to attack when he did. But it had been a victory dearly won.

More soldiers lay injured. Those who could survive were bandaged and dressed by their comrades, and mounted on their horses.

Another lay with an arrow deep in his lungs, bubbling out his lifeblood where he lay. It was Carpicius, the new young recruit. All of eighteen summers. Even Ops's mulish heroism hadn't saved him in the end.

Near the boy lay Ops himself. His arm had been badly cut by that spear thrust through the shield. It had hit an artery, and the burly Egyptian had lost a lot of blood. He clutched his arm across his chest, his other hand a rusty brown where it was encrusted with dried blood. His face was ashen pale, and his breath was shallow and uneven.

"Come on, soldier, let's get you fixed up," said Lucius.

Ops ignored him. He only gazed at Carpicius.

The lieutenant well knew that they'd been bedmates as well as messmates. It was common enough. The men might mock a comrade, give him a scornful nickname like Mincius Flabianus if they found him in bed with another, but most of them took a bedmate from time to time. Ops would have died for the boy. Now it looked as if he was going to. And they couldn't afford to lose such good men. Not now. Lucius turned aside and cursed under his breath. If he didn't curse, he might weep.

Marco knelt by Carpicius's side. Why was it always the youngest who got it first?

"Sit up now, boy," said Marco gently. "We'll have to get your breastplate off to get you bandaged."

The tenderness with which soldiers cared for each other after a battle. Lucius heard but he couldn't look.

Seeing great Hector slain, says Homer, even Lord Apollo cried out at his fellow Olympians, "Hard hearted you are, O you gods! You live for cruelty!"

And he thought of the words of the ancient song.

For hard is the gods' will,
My sorrows but increase,
And I must weep, my lover,
That wars will never cease.

Carpicius gazed up at his centurion with watery, half-closed eyes and shook his head. "Wait a bit," he whispered, blood bubbling on his lips. "Just a bit more."

Marco waited a bit. The rest of the men stood near with bowed heads. After a few minutes, Marco stood and signaled, and the body of Carpicius was laid gently on another travois along with his fallen comrades.

Riding back down to the column, Lucius looked in at Olympian, who was sweating profusely in the gloom of his ornate carriage.

"Where the hell's the boy?"

"The boy is not *my* responsibility," snapped the eunuch. "He's gone."

Lucius's blood froze. "Gone?"

"Here I am!" called a voice behind him cheerfully. Looking round, Lucius saw Attila slithering down the grassy slope toward the carriage.

"Where the Hell have you been all this time?" Lucius demanded.

The boy stopped at the carriage door and looked up at Lucius on his big horse, shielding his eyes against the sun.

"Watching." He grinned, wolfishly. "Learning."

Lucius was in no mood for jokes. "Get in the carriage," he said.

He dug his heels into Tugha Bàn's flanks, and the column rolled on.

They made camp that night down in the valley, after they'd buried their dead. They dug a rough square trench and mound, put up a stockade and set out staves. A defensive camp, in the heart of Italy! But times were strange.

The men were exhausted, and still they had to keep nightwatch, changing every two hours. Lucius and Marco kept the first watch with them, their eyelids almost dropping with weariness. As soon as their watch was relieved, they went down to the river with their men and bathed before they slept.

They washed the encrusted blood from their arms and faces and tunics, then took deep lungfuls of air and sank underwater for as long as they could bear, resurfacing with grateful gasps. None of them spoke in the darkness, as the river flowed coolly round them and cleansed them. They scooped up handfuls of the clear, cold water and poured it over their heads, as if anointing themselves. They prayed to their gods, to Christos, and Mithras, to Mars Ultor, and to Jupiter Optimus Maximus. They raised their eyes to the heavens and saw the wheeling stars: the Dragon coiling about the North Star, the Eagle and the Shield slowly sinking toward the western horizon; the crescent moon on her back, like the crown of Diana the Huntress; and Orion the Hunter, whom she cruelly slew, slowly rising toward dawn.

Lucius thought of his wife, and how she would see the same stars as he. Orion fading from the sky as she went outside to bring in the new-laid eggs in her white apron, and the sun rising in the early morning over that gentle Dumnonian valley. His children, Cadoc and little Ailsa, herding the chickens out into the yard with hazel twigs, their big brown eyes serious and intent, chattering to each other all the time. He smiled in the darkness, felt his beating heart. He saw the clear, trickling stream that ran down to the gray Celtic sea; the hillsides of lush meadows, full of plump white cattle, and the high ridges crested with ancient oak woods. That country knew nothing of war and killing. His wife and children had never seen so much as a sword drawn in anger, let alone the foul aftermath of battle. It was right that it should be so. But for the future of his country, now, beyond the frontier of an enfeebled Rome, with tales of those brutal Saxon pirates drawing ever closer . . . He should be there, with them. He feared for everything that was.

Before he had departed from Isca Dumnoniorum to join the waiting ships at anchor in the estuary, with the last few threadbare centuries of the once mighty Legio II "Augusta," he had taken her in his arms and they had sworn that they would look at the moon and the stars every evening and every morning, wherever they were, and their love would fly to each other through the night air, far apart as they were, over whatever endless plains and mountains and deserts might separate them. Whatever lands might lie between them, the same sun and moon shone down on them both. Lucius gazed up at the crescent moon, and prayed his prayer of deepest longing.

Then the soldiers returned to their camp, and slept under their blankets like newborn babes.

4

THE FOREST

The next morning Lucius washed in the river again, and saw the brilliant flash of a bee-eater flitting over the wide grasslands beyond. He crossed himself and muttered a prayer. If bees were lucky, what did a bee-eater mean?

He returned to see a fast-riding messenger of the imperial *cursus* pulling up outside the camp. He went over to ask him what the message was. The expressionless rider shook his head. "This is for Count Heraclian only."

Lucius shrugged and allowed the rider to dismount and go to Heraclian's tent.

A few minutes later he reappeared, remounted, and vanished back down the track.

Heraclian informed Lucius that the Palatine guard would ride in the van again from now on.

They ate bacon and hardtack and broke camp and rode on. They ascended out of the valley and onto the track again. They rode over further rough plains, sun parched and bare, dotted only with the occasional broom or kermes oak, the air heady and aromatic with juniper and wild thyme. They rode on until midafternoon over the parched tableland. Storm clouds began to mass again to the south, but still the storm did not break. The air was hot and oppressive, even in these mountains. Then they began a slow descent, when the track entered a dense pine forest.

Everything was dark and claustrophobic, and the heavy, thundery atmosphere that had haunted them on the day they left Rome had returned. Surely a storm must break now. And in the darkness of the forest, the weight and silence of the brooding summer air felt more ominous still. Some of the horses grew skittish and rolled their eyes to left and right of the narrow track. They showed their frightened whites, and their ears flicked furiously, their nostrils flaring for danger, for they could see nothing among the dense, dark trees that crowded in like malevolent sentries on either side of the track.

Lucius noticed Marco gazing intently into the forest to their left as they rode. He followed the direction of his gaze. "What is it, Centurion?"

Marco shook his head. "Nothing."

They said no more.

Count Heraclian, riding with his Palatine guard at the head of the column again, found himself thinking of Varus and his legions in the dark Teutoburg Forest, even though they were still in the heart of Italy. There was no safety left in Italy. He found himself thinking, too, of Stilicho. Sometimes, he longed for the company and the steely optimism of that man, that murdered hero of Rome, whom he had always resented and whose killing he had commanded and condoned. Worst of all, he knew himself to be a weak man. He knew also that it was the most dreadful thing for any man to feel. To be a galley slave, to be crucified, to be the "entertainment" in a show of wild beasts—these things were as nothing to the torment of waking each morning and knowing yourself to have a weak and timorous spirit, beneath your shell of resplendent bronze and scarlet. Heraclian tightened his hold on the reins and rode on.

The dark pine trees almost met over their heads, and what slender sky they could see between them was as heavy and gray as a shield. It was getting so dark that they could hardly pick out the track before them, when suddenly everything was illuminated in a stab of forked lightning which struck the forest perilously close to the track. A clap of thunder followed only a fraction of a second after, showing how closely the lightning had missed the column itself. The horses whinnied and reared, and their riders reined them in with savage cries.

In the creaking Liburnian carriage, its ornate gilding and its swathes of crimson curtains seeming ever more ridiculous in this harsh and ominous landscape, Olympian actually reached out and snatched Attila's arm for comfort, giving a gasp of fright as the bolt of lightning detonated close by in the forest. The boy carefully detached himself.

"But we should be safe enough under the tall trees," stammered Olympian.

He sounded as if he was complaining about the lightning, about the way things were, petulantly, to the gods who made the storm. The mark of deepest foolishness. Attila smiled to himself.

Olympian could not understand the Hun boy. He smiled often—that wolfish grin—and yet there was no happiness in it. He was full of anger, even hatred. He smiled like a little god overseeing the sacrifice.

Count Heraclian signaled that the column should ride on, and they did so grimly. Experienced soldiers like Marco and Lucius lowered their spears, and took off their iron helmets, even if it did mean getting a soaking. But pity the standard-bearer in a storm. No lowering *that* for safety's sake. Poor bugger was a human lightning rod.

A chill wind had arisen, tossing the branches of the trees about above their heads, and whipping their cloaks round them. And then it began to rain, great gobbets of water smacking down on their heads and shoulders and drumming on the roofs of the carriages housing the lucky few. After the initial noisy cloudburst, the raindrops grew finer, and gusted down in an unbroken sheet, and the soldiers at the front of the column could barely see their way forward though the veils of water. In their carriage toward the back, Genseric and Beric finally woke up. Olympian crossed himself furiously, and throughout the column soldiers and officers variously crossed themselves in the name of Christ, or made promises of future sacrifices to Mithras or Jupiter, should they reach Ravenna safely. Not a few of them made vows and promises to all three gods. No point not spreading your bets, when the stake is always the same.

The rain pelted down and slicked their hair to their heads, and plastered their red woolen cloaks to their shoulders, and the horses' manes clung to their withers and streamed with chill mountain rain. Puddles formed quickly on the dry summer track, at first as hard and unyielding as concrete, and then turning to yellowish, unctuous mud. Men and horses alike bowed their heads in obedience and fear and exhaustion to the superior force of the storm and the gods of the storm, and they rode on.

But Attila leaned out of his carriage window and grinned into the rain.

"Back inside, boy," scolded Olympian. "Draw the curtains."

The boy ignored him.

Every other man in that column felt that the storm was around and about him like a raging animal, threatening to extinguish him with a single toss of its white-light horns. But Attila knew that the storm ran through him, and that he was a part of it, and it could do him no harm. Every other man, huddled in his own private universe, felt smaller in the face of the storm: less powerful, threatened, diminished. But the boy felt stronger, greater, more powerful: one with the thunder, one with the universe. And looking at him, and seeing something of this truth in him, something unnatural, Olympian closed his eyes and crossed himself again.

Attila grinned out into the rain and into the black rain-drenched forest that closed in around them. When another terrific bolt of lightning hit the pines nearby, and sent one crashing to the ground in a cloudburst of sparks and smoke and brief flame, and the horses throughout the column had to be kicked hard and reined in tight as they skittered to left and right with white and rolling eyes, ears pressed back, and every other man there crossed himself and worked his lips again in furious prayer, Attila only gazed in rapture into the forest and upward into the chaos of the dark and angry heavens and prayed, *Astur, my father . . . Lord of the Storm . . .*

Then a fork of lightning hit Beric and Genseric's carriage immediately behind them.

As is the unpredictable way with lightning, it left the main carriage untouched but burst the leather straps that supported it, and the entire unwieldy apparatus buckled in the middle and sank down upon its axles. Then the back axle broke with a terrific crack. The terrified horses whinnied and reared and tried to break free, but they were still yoked implacably to the shattered carriage. The coachman lashed them down again and they subsided into nervy silence.

Gradually the rest of the column ahead slowed and then stopped, and the two mounted guards who rode alongside Olympian's carriage wheeled and turned back to inspect the damage. They quickly concluded that the broken car would have to be pushed off the road into the forest, and the two Vandal princes would have to pack into the carriage ahead.

At that moment, Attila looked round and saw that Olympian was sitting forward, curiously hunched, with an arrow's shaft and fletching sticking out of his vast belly. The eunuch was clutching his flesh bunched up around the arrow, and muttering, "I've been shot!" Then he looked up at the boy and said, "I've been quite appallingly shot!"

"It does look like it," Attila agreed.

Much of the arrow was still visible, however, and the boy reckoned that only an inch or two, including the head, had gone into the eunuch's belly. Given his bulk, that would almost certainly make it only a minor flesh wound. He spared the poor man a glance of very momentary pity, and then leaned out again. To the side of the window, sure enough, was another arrow embedded in the gilded woodwork of the carriage wall. As he watched, more arrows arced silently out of the dark forest and the rain, like eerie messengers from another world. Evidently the rain had done little to dampen their unseen enemies' bowstrings just yet. One arrow struck a horse at the top of its leg; another went through a trooper's throat and he reeled forward on his horse, clutching its neck and gargling blood all over its rain-sodden mane.

"We're under attack!" cried a young *optio*. "From the left! Second squadron, to me!"

The eight cavalrymen turned and began to force their way into the dense forest, hacking at the low, spindly pine branches with their swords.

Lucius came galloping back alongside the column and reined in Tugha Bàn furiously, her front hooves slithering forward in the yellow mud. He was apparently oblivious of the flying arrows.

"Dismount, you fucking idiots!" he roared. "Get off your horses and use your fucking legs. We're under attack from left and right, in case you hadn't fucking noticed. And you lot, get this fucking thing off the road— *now*!"

Immediately the soldiers obeyed. The horses were cut loose from the shattered carriage and reined in by fresh cavalrymen called up from behind. An arrow thumped into Lucius's leather saddle just below his thigh, but he reached down and snapped it off without even looking down. He tossed the shaft contemptuously aside and continued to bellow commands. From the front of the column and Count Heraclian came no sign of life at all.

The broken carriage was levered and poled off the side of the road, where it crashed heavily into the trunk of a tall pine and fell still.

"You two buggers," Lucius yelled at the startled Vandal princes, "get in the car in front!"

Beric and Genseric, huddled in their cloaks, ran forward to join the next carriage.

Lucius wheeled his horse again and glared into the rain from under the brow of his helmet. "Jesus, what a farce. They're only *bandits,* for Christ's sake. Fucking amateurs."

"Under attack *again*!" yelled Marco, reining to a violent stop beside him. "I don't fucking believe this."

"Me neither," Lucius shouted.

"Remnants of the last lot?"

Lucius shook his head. "These are no ex-soldiers. They're firing from both sides."

Even as he spoke, arrows were slamming into shields and carriage walls around them, but the two soldiers ignored them.

"Anyone would think," said Lucius, "that somebody didn't *want* us to get to Ravenna."

"Is Count Heraclian . . . ?" asked Marco.

Lucius pushed himself up in his saddle and craned to see if there was any sign of decisive action from the front of the column yet. He sat down again. "Jupiter's balls," he breathed with exasperation. "What we have here is, in technical army parlance, a bunch of fucking amateurs. And we're running around like ants on an anthill." He reined his horse round angrily again and started bawling fresh orders.

"Okay, you, Ops, get twenty men, *on fucking foot,* and get into those trees and cut down those bastards. And you there, Trooper Shit-for-Brains, dismount the rear two squadrons and do the same on the right. I don't want to see any more arrows coming out of that forest there by the time I count to ten."

The tough-looking trooper and two more squadrons quickly formed up on foot.

"Come along then, ladies!" he addressed them cheerfully. "Playtime in the woods. Anything you find alive, cut its guts out and hang 'em off the nearest tree."

He and his men vanished into the trees, and soon there came loud cries and screams from the forest. Another bandit gang was indeed being despatched.

Lucius rode back and stared in at Olympian and Attila.

"Is it bandits again?" wailed Olympian. "And ex-gladiators, too?"

"Yeah, yeah, whatever," growled Lucius. "I'm quaking in my boots. Fucking amateurs." He glared angrily down at the eunuch and Attila from his skittish horse. "Trained soldiers attack a marching column from one flank only. Fucking amateurs attack from both sides simultanously." He leaned over and spat. "And why do you think that might be?"

Olympian groaned that he had no idea. The boy thought for a moment and then said, "Because they might just as likely be shooting across into each other."

"But, my good man," wailed Olympian indignantly, scarcely able to believe his ears that this conversation about military tactics was taking place, while he had an actual *arrow* embedded in his person, and was actually *bleeding,* slightly. "But, my good man, I am wounded!"

Lucius flung open the carriage door and leaned in. "One in the gut, eh? Lift your robe up."

"I couldn't possibly countenance such—"

Lucius leaned forward and nicked the eunuch's robe open neatly with his sword point. The head of the arrow was in fact buried only half an inch into the eunuch's rolls of flesh, and the barbs were visible under the skin.

"Okay," he said. "Shallow breaths—stop the arrowhead going in deeper. And clench your teeth."

"I beg your pardon?"

"I said," repeated Lucius—he reached forward, grabbed the arrow just behind the head with his fist, and gave it a sharp tug; with an unpleasant slurping sound, the arrowhead came free of the eunuch's stomach and Olympian began to bleed profusely—"clench your teeth. Ah well, too late now. It's out anyhow. Get some pressure on that wound, and we'll clean you up when we get out of this bloody ruckus."

But Olympian had fainted.

Lucius looked at Attila. "Looks like you've got a job to do."

"You're kidding."

The lieutenant shook his head. "Just till he comes round again. Lard ass like that will have sluggish blood—it'll soon clot. But till then, keep your hand pressed on the wound." He punched the boy on his arm. "Tough job, I know, but someone's gotta do it."

And then he was away into the rain, bawling at the top of his voice to get the column organized.

Attila stared at the unconscious eunuch, blood flowing freely from the hole in his belly, and thought for a moment. Then he leaned over and ripped a wide strip of silk from the bottom of Olympian's priceless blue robe, passed it round the back of the vast, sweat-soaked waist, and tied it in front. But being silk, it was soon saturated in blood, so he made a pad from his own linen sleeve, though he didn't think lard ass deserved it. He ripped the robe open a little wider and bound this in a compress tightly under the silk bandage. He watched for a few moments, and, after absorbing a little more blood, the white linen showed no more sign of flow.

He dusted his hands together with satisfaction.

Then the eunuch groaned and woke up.

That wasn't what the boy had been planning at all.

He could hear the troopers shouting in the driving rain, and another distant rumble of thunder, and he knew his chance had come. His palms were sweating and his heart was hammering in his skinny chest, but it wasn't fear. He glanced at Olympian out of the corner of his eye, but the eunuch was oblivious of him, clutching his belly and peering out of the window anxiously. He nearly addressed an apology to the man, but decided that would be dishonest. Instead he got to his feet, seized Olympian's great bald head and rammed it repeatedly against the wooden wall of the carriage.

Unfortunately for the eunuch, the boy didn't quite have the strength to knock him out cold. But he felt blood trickling down the back of his neck, and a sick, chilly feeling and his head was spinning and dizzy and green spots danced before his eyes, and all he could rasp was a hoarse and confused "Spare my life, I pray you, whoever you are. I will recompense you profusely. The rest of this rabble are nothing to me, nothing but soldiers and slaves, but I am a very wealthy man, ranking high in the courts of Rome. . . ."

He sank back in his seat, gasping for breath. His eyes were closed when he heard the carriage door kicked open, and the sounds of the storm came to his ears more strongly than ever. And then the door was slamming jerkily back and forth on its hinges in the wind, and he knew that the boy was gone.

One of the troopers saw the boy run for the trees, and immediately cried, "Man escaped!"

Lucius whipped round and gave a cry of despair. "Those slippery . . . Okay, Marco, our attackers are cleaned up, pretty well. Keep some of them back for questioning, though. The little prince won't get far in this weather." He wiped the sweat and rain from his forehead. "Ride to the front and inform Count Heraclian. Tell him—I mean, *suggest* to him—that he lead the column on. We'll catch them up later."

"They'll make good progress, I'm sure," said Marco sardonically. "The Palatine vanguard didn't take a single hit."

Lucius stared at him. "What do you mean?"

"Don't mean anything, sir. Not for a simple, boneheaded soldier like me to offer interpretations of anything. I'm just reporting the facts: strange that not a single arrow went into the Palatine guard, or Count Heraclian. All reserved for us, sir."

They eyed each other levelly. There was no man in the world whom Lucius trusted more than his centurion. They had saved each other's backs more times than he could count.

"What's going on, Marco?" he said. "Why are they after us?"

"Is it us, sir?" said Marco. "Or is it those we're guarding?"

Lucius frowned and shook his head. "Ride forward, Centurion."

"Sir."

The lieutenant arched his arm forward for the squadron of eight to follow him. He expected to be back in a minute or two, with that little bastard bound in ships' hawsers if need be.

Behind them the column began to roll forward again at its painfully slow walking pace, and the nine horsemen plunged into the inky depths of the pine forest.

The storm was violent and brief, like all summer storms, and its force was already beginning to abate. The sky above was brightening, although in the gloom of the pine forest the troopers still struggled to see their way ahead clearly. The trees dripped with rain, but it was no longer falling from the sky. Every few seconds the troopers stopped to listen, or mark the tracks. The boy's trail was slight but unmistakable on the damp, needle-covered floor.

"How's he going to get away? Climb a tree?" one of the troopers chuckled.

"Shut up," ordered Lucius. "Not a sound."

They rode on.

After some minutes, the trees began to thin out, and through the gaps between the dark trunks they could see the sunlight breaking through the clouds, and falling on the bare limestone hills ahead.

They emerged from the edge of the forest, and there even those hardened soldiers, who between them had done service from the Wall to the sands of Africa, and from the wild mountains of Spain to the reedy banks of the Euphrates, stopped and stared with something like awe. Below them stretched a beautiful valley, green with vineyards and olive groves. Beyond it rose further ancient limestone hills, gray gold in the breaking sunlight, dotted with sheep and small farms. Above and beyond them arose still greater peaks, even now capped with snow, and bathed in an extraordinary luminous light as it reflected off the last of the storm clouds and echoed back and forth across the vast expanse of sky. And there arced a great rainbow over the distant hills, set by Father Jove after the Flooding of the World, from which only Deucalion and his wife Pyrrha were saved.

Yet here, in the heart of Italy, it had begun to feel as lawless and dangerous as the wilds beyond the Wall.

The men and horses sat and steamed in the sun. Then one young trooper shot forth his arm and pointed. "There he goes."

Lucius looked witheringly at him. "Well done, Salcus. I've been watching him for the last five minutes."

The trooper bowed his head in shame, and the other men guffawed.

"Game little bugger, all the same," said another.

The men harrumphed in grudging acknowledgment.

"He'd have kept to the forest if he had any sense," muttered Salcus.

"Shows how much you know," said another. "He's a Hun. He's bound to make for open country. Even forests feel like a prison to them."

"Then we've got him."

The other nodded. "We've got him."

Lucius had been screwing up his eyes, trying to discern the distant figure better. "That's the Hun boy? I thought it was one of the Vandal princes who'd escaped. You mean it's the one they call Attila?"

The trooper was a little taken aback by the sharpness of his officer's reaction. "Yes, sir."

"The one who's *always* escaping," said another.

The lieutenant's pale gray eyes gazed out across the valley, his expression inscrutable. Far below, they could see the little figure of the boy, running desperately across the fields and between the rows of vines. Every now and then he looked back toward the troop of nine horsemen sitting up on the hill on the edge of the forest, knowing they had him clear in their sights. They could bide their time; there was no hurry. What chance did a mere boy have against nine cavalrymen?

"Come on then, you bastards!" he yelled angrily, bending at the waist and clutching his sides as he gasped for air, his voice high and shrill. "Come and get me!" He stood straight, gave the obscene fig sign with his forefinger and thumb. "What are you waiting for?"

His thin voice carried across the valley to where the troopers sat their horses, and they grinned at each other, despite themselves.

"You've got to hand it to him," said one.

Lucius turned to his men. "Ride back to the column."

His second looked puzzled. "Sir?"

"It doesn't take more than one to bring in a little shrimp like that. Now ride back to the column and inform Count Heraclian that I'm bringing him in."

A little deflated, the troop wheeled their horses and rode back into the forest, heading north for the track. Lucius kicked his horse forward and rode on down into the rain-washed, sun-bright valley.

Once off the steepest and rockiest slopes, he heeled Tugha Bàn into a fierce gallop, down through the rain-wet meadows lush with late summer flowers and ripe for the scythe, and then crashing through the vines to where he had last seen the boy. He glimpsed him up ahead, but by the time he had reached the spot the boy had ducked under the row and was into the next. Infuriated, Lucius had to gallop to the end of the row and up the next one. By which time the boy had ducked under again. The lieutenant reined in his panting horse and reflected. He leaned down and plucked a fat, juicy ruby grape. Arcturus was rising, and soon it would be the harvest.

After a few moments of pleasurable munching, he called out in his most languidly authoritative voice, "You can't get away, you know."

There was a pause while the boy considered whether it was worth giving his position away just for the pleasure of answering back. But, as Lucius had guessed, he was proud and reckless. "And you can't catch me, either."

Before he had finished his sentence, Lucius was slipping from his horse and leading it by the reins as he crept forward down the row of vines.

"I could just have my men set fire to the vineyard," he said.

"Your men have gone back to the column," said the boy.

Lucius grinned, despite himself. The lad's military intelligence was pretty impressive. "How are you going to get anywhere on your own?" he asked. "Winter comes early in these mountains. You've no money, no weapons. . . ."

"I'll survive," called the boy cheerfully. It sounded as if he, too, was chomping the irresistibly ripe, juicy grapes. "I've seen worse."

"And the Julian Alps by October, November? You'll just stroll over those into Pannonia, will you?"

The boy paused. He was surprised that the lieutenant had read his plans so precisely. How did he know that he was heading north and home?

Lucius meanwhile had stationed his horse at the end of the row, so that its head appeared at the head of one and its rump at the next. Its middle was hidden by the vines. The boy turned and saw the horse's muzzle appearing round the end of the row, assumed the obvious, and ducked to safety into the next one. He lay low in the sopping wet grass, under the late dark green leaves and the heavy clusters of grapes. Lucius crept toward him on foot. The boy did not stir. He bit into another grape, the purple juices exploding in his mouth. He only had to keep an eye on that horse. . . .

Then he felt the edge of cold steel at the back of his neck and he knew that it was over. His head sank down into the grass, and he spat out the last mouthful of pulped grapes in his mouth. He felt sick.

"On your feet, son," said the lieutenant. His voice was surprisingly gentle.

Attila bowed his head. "Fuck you," he said.

The lieutenant didn't move. "I said, on your feet. I'm not here to kill you. I know well enough who you are: Rome's most valuable hostage."

The boy squinted up at him into the sunshine. "Up your ass," he said.

Something in his voice told the lieutenant he really wasn't going to move for him, no matter what he threatened. So he reached down, grabbed him by the scruff of his neck and dragged him up onto his knees, where the boy knelt in sullen silence, staring into the vine leaves before him. A drunken late-summer wasp buzzed angrily round his face, and even settled briefly on his hair, but he did nothing to swat it away.

Then the lieutenant did a very curious and unmilitary thing. He sheathed his sword again, sat down beside the boy, cross-legged in the wet grass, reached out and picked a whole bunch of shining grapes, and began to eat them as if he had not a care in the world. The boy glanced at him, and then something held his gaze.

At last, the boy said, "II Legion, the 'Augusta,' Isca Dumnoniorum. Your father was a Gaul, though."

Lucius nearly choked on a grape. "Christ's blood, lad, you've got a memory."

Attila didn't smile. It was him, definitely. The tall, gray-eyed lieutenant with the ragged scar on his chin, who had arrested him that time in the street after the knife fight. The boy glared, but not at the lieutenant. At an imaginary image.

"And you're Attila, right?"

The boy grunted.

"I'm Lucius."

"Sounds like a girl's name to me."

"Yeah, well it isn't, okay?"

The boy shrugged.

Lucius quelled his rising temper. "It's Lugh in Celtic," he said. "Or you can call me Ciddwmtarth, if you prefer. That's my real Celtic name."

"What does it mean?"

"Wolf in the Mist."

"Hm," said the boy thoughtfully, slitting a grass stem with his thumbnail. "Sounds better than Lucius, anyhow. S'more like a Hun name."

"What does Attila mean?"

"Not telling you."

"What do you mean, you're not telling me?"

The boy looked up at Lucius, or Ciddwmtarth, or whatever he was called. "Among my people, names are sacred. We don't give our real names away to any old stranger. And we certainly don't tell them what they mean."

"Christ, you're an awkward bugger. And my wife says *I'm* awkward."

The boy started in surprise. "You're married?"

"Soldiers can marry now, you know," said Lucius, with amusement. "Although some say it's when we started getting married that the rot started to set in—sapped our vital and manly juices and suchlike."

The boy was shredding the grass stem to pieces.

"You believe, I take it," went on Lucius, "that only idiots marry? And you hadn't thought me stupid enough to shackle myself to a woman for all eternity?"

Attila had sort of thought that, yes.

"Ah," said Lucius softly, looking westward toward the hills. "But then you haven't seen my wife."

Now the boy was embarrassed, his cheeks flushing red under his coppery skin.

Lucius laughed aloud. "You'll see. Give it a few more years and you'll be as enslaved as the rest of us."

Not bloody likely, thought Attila, staring down at his grubby feet. Girls! He thought back to those giggling, half-clothed girls in the Vandal princes' chambers, and how they had stirred him despite himself. And he feared that what Lucius foresaw was already coming true.

"I've a son your age as well," said Lucius. "A son and a younger daughter."

"Among my people, if a man like you were asked what children he had, he'd say, 'One son and one calamity.'"

Lucius grunted.

"What's his name? Your son?"

"Cadoc," said Lucius. "A British name."

"Is he like me?"

Lucius saw his son's dreamy brown eyes, and pictured him creeping through the sunlit meadows of Dumnonia with his little sister Ailsa in tow. Clutching his toy bow and arrow in his grubby hand, trying to hunt for squirrels and voles, or telling his sister the names of the flowers, and which plants were good to eat.

"Not really," he said.

"Why not?"

Lucius laughed. "He's gentler than you."

The boy made a guttural sound in his throat, and tore up another fist-ful of grass. This Cadoc sounded like a calamity, too.

"Well," said the lieutenant, getting to his feet and standing tall over the boy. He reached inside his cloak and drew out a shorter, broad-bladed sword, the kind you'd use for up-close, short-term work. Then he took the sword by the blade end, turned it round and offered the handle to the boy.

Attila looked up, his mouth agape.

"This was taken off you, along with your freedom," said the lieutenant. "Time you had it back."

"It's, it's . . ." the boy stammered. "Stilicho gave it to me. Only a few nights before . . ."

"I know. I knew Stilicho, too."

"Did you . . . ? I mean, what did you . . . ?"

"Stilicho was a good man," said the lieutenant. "And I made him certain promises once."

Their eyes met briefly. Then Attila reached out and took the precious sword. The blade was as keen as ever.

"You've looked after it," he said.

The lieutenant said nothing. Instead he reached down and unbuckled his scabbard belt. "And I expect you to do the same," he said, handing it to the boy. "I don't know why Stilicho made you this gift. He made me a gift, too." He smiled distantly. "Both lighter and heavier than yours. I don't understand it, any more than you do, but it meant something to him. Which still means something to me."

The boy struggled with the belt, until Lucius told him to turn and buckled it on for him. But it was too loose, so the lieutenant showed him how to twist the belt a couple of times to shorten it, and then it buckled good and tight. Attila slipped the sword into the scabbard, looked up and nodded.

"It's good," he said.

The lieutenant smiled. "Now mind how you travel," he said.

Attila stared at him. "What do you mean?"

Lucius gestured impatiently toward the hills beyond. "Time you were off, lad."

"You're letting me go?"

He sighed. "And I thought you were quick witted. Yes, I'm letting you go."

"Why?"

The lieutenant hesitated. "You might be safer on your own. Not with the column."

"Won't you . . . won't you get into trouble?"

The question was ignored.

"Travel by night if you can. The moon's only crescent now but use it when it comes up full. The country people are all right, but remember that most of the shepherds are part-time bandits as well. Or they might take fancy to you in quite another way, if you get my meaning— something a bit exotic. So steer clear of them, I would. Don't use the sword unless you have to. Otherwise, keep it hidden under your cloak. Look poor, or even better, mad. No one bothers to rob a madman."

The boy nodded.

"Shake," said the lieutenant.

The boy held out his hand.

"Your sword hand, dummy."

"Oh, sorry."

The boy held out his right hand, and they shook.

"How do I know you might not stab me in midshake? You're no real friend of Rome, are you?"

Attila grinned.

"Right," said Lucius, "now bugger off. I never want to see you again."

"Me neither," said the boy. He grinned up at the tall lieutenant again, one last time, shielding his eyes against the sun. Then he turned away and started to jog-trot down the rows of vines and into the field beyond. At the last minute he turned and called back, "I'd go back to Britain if I were you! Rome's all done!"

"Yeah, yeah," Lucius called back, waving him away. "Watch out for yourself."

The boy ran up through the neighboring meadow and over the crest of the hill and turned back and waved one last time and was gone.

Lucius walked back to his horse, remounted, and rode back toward the forest.

5

CLOACA MAXIMA

Well?" said Marco.

Lucius fell in beside him. "He got away."

Marco nodded. "Thought he might."

"Get anything out of the captives?"

"General Heraclian ordered us to let them flee. Said it wasn't worth risking our necks for."

"Did he indeed?"

"He did. One thing we learned, though: they spoke good Latin. Fluent, in fact."

Lucius frowned. "Why shouldn't they?"

"Well, they were Goths."

Lucius reined his horse to a halt. "They were *what*?"

"A Gothic war band."

Lucius stared ahead between Tugha Bàn's flicking ears. This was making less than no sense. "Where's Heraclian now?"

Marco harrumphed. "He and the Palatine have gone on ahead, along with all the other hostages, mounted up now. In fact, we've lost sight of them. For some reason we're stuck with the carriages."

"The fat eunuch?"

"Gone, too."

"What, mounted? How . . . ?"

"Don't ask. It wasn't a pretty sight."

"But as far as they know we've still got Attila?"

"As far as they know."

Lucius kicked his horse forward again and they rode on in pensive silence for awhile.

Then Marco said, "Permission to, sir?"

Lucius nodded.

"Well, sir, do you ever get the feeling somebody doesn't want us to get to Ravenna?"

Lucius shook his head. "I don't know what I think. I don't know what the Hell's going on. One thing I do know: I'm glad I'm just a poor, dumb bonehead of a soldier. Not a bloody politician."

His centurion grinned.

When it became clear to Lucius that they had lost the Palatine guard for good, he sent two of his men on for reinforcements. They were to ride forward at all speed to the next main road and imperial *cursus* station, and there send out for more reinforcements. From Ravenna, if need be.

"You think we're going to be attacked again?" asked Marco quietly.

"I know we are. So do you. In fact," said Lucius, looking at his depleted column: forty cavalrymen, a handful of wounded, and two lumbering great Liburnian cars. "In fact, we are in serious trouble." He turned back to Marco. "But keep it under your helmet."

They had ridden for about a further half an hour when the column shuddered to a halt.

The two troopers hung from a branch across the road. They had been stripped naked and then flayed. One had had his right hand cut off and stuffed in his mouth, his fingers splayed obscenely over his raw and bloody face. The other's mouth was stuffed with his own genitals.

"Cut them down," ordered Lucius quietly.

They were lowered into blankets and buried at the side of the road.

Lucius addressed his horror-stricken men, trying his best to keep the horror out of his voice and eyes. He told them they were in deep shit. He told them they were up to their eyeballs in the Cloaca Maxima. He told them he didn't have a clue what was going on, and they might not survive at all, let alone get to Ravenna. But they must keep together, and then they'd have a chance.

"Don't start running," he said. "We've been through worse than this before."

The men knew their lieutenant of old. They set their faces grimly, shouldered their shields, hefted their spears, and with renewed resolve the column moved on.

Attila had already stolen a mule.

He had crept into a little farmyard in late afternoon, and set the ducks quacking furiously at his intrusion. But nobody stirred. An ancient, fly-blown mule was standing sullenly in the shade of a stone barn, tethered to a fence. Attila untied the frayed old rope and began to lead the animal out of the farmyard as silently as he could. The cobbles were thick with straw, so the boy and the mule made little sound.

There was a narrow window at the end of the barn, and he could hear noises inside. Unable to resist the risk, he turned the mule alongside the barn wall and hoisted himself up on its back to peer in through the window. The scene within was lit by a slash of late afternoon sunlight coming in through the open doorway.

An older man was bucking up and down in the hay, naked but for his shirt, while underneath him lay a young girl on her back, similarly undressed. There must have been thirty years between them. Maybe they were father and daughter. Such things were known to be as common as sunshine in these remote rural parts, and the long, lazy hours of summer had to be passed somehow. The girl seemed to be enjoying it well enough, anyway, judging from the urgency of her thrusts beneath him, and from the give-away curling of her toes, and from her sweat-streaked face, and from the little gasps that came from her open mouth. The boy felt the warmth of the mule underneath him and a stir of hot longing in his belly and below, and he slid dry-mouthed and wondering from the ancient and indifferent mule and led it silently out of the farmyard. He draped the frayed rope over its withers for a rein, hauled himself up again, using a fence post for lift, and sat astride its bristly, mud-flecked back and rode away.

He rode on down the valley into a wide champaign country, through tall grasslands and meadows still bright with the last flowers of the year, crown daisies and mayweed, centaury, yarrow, and feverfew.

He should have sensed them; or he should have taken note of what his senses told him. But now he was away from the column and free at last, with nothing between him and his far, beloved homeland—so he thought. It made him careless, light hearted, light headed. He even whistled as he rode.

He should have noticed his sullen mount's ears flicking back and forth. He should have heard the muffled sounds of pots and pans clanging, should have smelt the woodsmoke, and the unmistakable smell of a camp of men and horses. But he rode down through the meadow with his legs hanging loose and his hands loose on the rope, whistling like the boy he was. When he rode round the end of the copse he saw before him a camp of some two hundred men. Tents, campfires, horses tethered to stakes. And no more than a hundred yards between them.

One of the men happened to look up from where he was kindling his campfire, and stared. He stood up and stared some more. Then he turned to his comrades lounging near the tent.

"Well, would you look at that?" he said.

They looked, and saw at the far edge of the meadow, the tousled-looking boy with the unmistakable slanted eyes and the blue tattooed scars on his cheeks. They scrambled to their feet in an instant.

"The lamb walks straight into the lion's jaws," said another.

They grinned.

Then they scrambled fast for their horses as they saw the boy wheel his ancient mule round and urge it forward into a trot as hard as he could.

He wouldn't get far. But they didn't want to lose him again.

Lucius was becoming more anxious with every mile they covered, though he betrayed nothing to his men. Now the sun was going down, and they still hadn't struck camp. The terrain was difficult. They had passed through dense woods, and emerged onto a flat but rocky plateau, surrounded on three sides by dark forest and on the fourth by a steep drop into the valley. It was no place for a secure camp, but if they went on they'd be in deep forest again. The light was failing fast, and his men were exhausted. So, for that matter, was he.

Halfway across the plateau, he raised his hand and called a halt. Something had caught his eye in the trees ahead, maybe half a mile away. Marco stopped beside him.

"See anything?"

"No, sir."

They stared a little longer. They were about to move forward again when an unlikely figure emerged from the shadows of the trees and came trotting furiously toward them. No more than trotting, but there was an urgency to it all the same. The mount was an ancient, dusty mule, and the boy who clung to its bony back was jolted around like a rag doll. But he clung on with fierce determination, kicking his heels into the mule's skinny flanks all the way.

"Can't shake this one off even if we wanted to," growled Ops close behind. "He's like a nasty dose of Syrian clap, he is."

As the boy drew closer they could see the fear in his eyes. He came to a panting halt before them at last, his mule wheezing beneath him as if it were about to expire where it stood. The boy twisted round to look back into the trees. He could see nothing. He turned back and collapsed, gasping, along his ungainly mount.

"Back so soon?" said Lucius. "What's up?"

The boy hauled himself upright. His face was streaked with grime and sweat. "They're coming this way."

"Who?"

Attila shook his head. "I don't know. But it's me they want."

"*You?*"

"I don't know why."

"Me neither," growled Ops.

"Shut it, Decurion," said Marco. "Have you had that arm of yours stitched up yet?"

Ops shifted uncomfortably in his saddle. "Will soon, sir."

Marco shook his head. It was a standing joke in the century that, while Ops was quite happy to face a line of howling Picts and not flinch, he hated needles.

Marco turned back to Attila.

Shielding his eyes from the setting sun, the boy looked up at the two grim-faced Roman officers in their tall, scarlet-plumed helmets. "I thought I might be able to outride them, but. . . ."

Lucius shook his head, smiling at the thought. That mule couldn't outride a lame tortoise. "Not a chance. They'd track you, anyway."

The boy lowered his eyes. "I'm sorry," he said, almost whispering.

It was Marco who replied, leaning down a little to the boy's level, his bearlike growl softened for once. "Sorry's got nothing to do with it, lad. You're our responsibility, and any bunch of marauding barbarians, begging your pardon and all that, that wants to get their hands on you, is going to have to come and take you. *Without our permission.* Is that understood?"

The boy nodded. "Understood."

Marco straightened his back again. "So. How many of them?"

The boy had finally got his breath back. "Two hundred? Maybe twice as many horses, and fresh looking."

Once again, Lucius admired the boy's military eye. But the situation was desperate. It would take the Goths only a matter of minutes to saddle up, don their armor and ride out after him. He turned to Marco.

"I know, I know," said the centurion.

Lucius wheeled back and roared at the column. "Century, dismount! Packs off, spades out, picks at the ready. There's work to do."

Even after eight years of service, he could still be impressed by the speed and stamina of his men. Soon they had gouged a circular trench out of the ground deep enough to trip a horse and rider, and thrown up an earth-and-stone rampart within. They left only a narrow opening, wide enough for a single mounted man. Exhausted, caked with sweat and dust, every muscle in their bodies burning, they set to beating the rampart solid with the flat of their spades, and putting up a rough but effective stockade on top. Not a man complained. Not a man went slow. Not a man stopped for water till the work was done. Even Ops, with his wounded arm and his face still pale with blood loss, slaved as hard as the rest of them. Even that skinny new lad Salcus set to with a will. And Marco as well. Lucius looked them over, and thought of the two hundred Gothic horsemen coming their way. And for the sake of this one inscrutable boy, all their lives would be spared. But he and his men had a job to do, and not a man here would shirk it. He knew them well enough. The *Caligatae*: the Boots, the Iron Hats, Marius's Mules, the Poor Bloody Infantry. He wouldn't swap his century—what was left of his century— for any other band of men in the world.

He scanned the treeline continually, but there was still no sign of their attackers. What was taking them so long?

"Use the wagons, too," said a voice.

Lucius looked round. It was the boy.

He frowned. "I don't usually take tactical advice from twelve-year-olds, but . . ."

"Fourteen."

"Whatever."

Lucius considered again. Then he started giving orders for the two carriages to be dragged into the defensive circle.

The boy interrupted again. "On their sides. You need to tip 'em over."

Lucius growled, "You're beginning to try my patience, boy."

But Attila was unperturbed. "Leave 'em upright and it's the easiest thing in the world for your enemy to come in close under cover, lasso them, hitch them up to a team of horses and just trundle them away on their own wheels. And then your circle's wide open. Tip 'em over on their sides and they won't budge."

Lucius harrumphed. "It's not the Roman way."

The boy grinned. "No, it's the Hun way. Oh, and tip 'em over with the wheels on the inside, so they can't use 'em for climbing."

So Lucius barked further orders, and soon the two great gilded carriages were roped up to teams of straining horses. With a lot of creaking and cursing, and then an almighty crash, they toppled over into the dust. Lucius had to admit they made a useful extra barrier round about one third of the circle. And with only forty men to defend the perimeter, they needed all the extra help they could get.

They drove the horses in through the narrow gateway, along with the boy's rickety stolen mule, tethered them in the center, and closed the gap off with a further rank of bristling staves. Lucius had a quiet word in Tugha Bàn's twitching ear, and she settled down on her hooves and lowered her head to sleep.

Silence settled over the circle of men.

A few had gathered enough kindling to light a couple of small campfires, and they sat cross-legged in the flickering orange firelight, taking careful swigs of water and mouthfuls of ground-up hardtack. It wasn't much, but it was all they had left. None of them felt much like leaving the circle to do a bit of twilight hunting. The sun was almost gone, and darkness was settling over the face of the world. The little summer birds were already sleeping with open eyes in the forest, and in the valleys below the cattle were settling into silence for the night.

Lucius and Marco stood side by side on the earthen rampart, straining to see into the forest beyond.

"They're there," said Marco softly.

"You can see them?"

"A flash of something. They're watching and waiting."

"Why didn't they attack earlier? They just sat and watched us throw up our defenses."

Marco grunted. "Such as they are."

"So it'll be a night attack?"

"Darkness usually favors defenders, as does twilight. Maybe that's why they're waiting."

"Attack at dawn, then."

"I reckon."

Then Lucius's blood ran cold. The last of the sun was slanting in low across the rocky plateau, the trees beyond almost black in the failing light. And the Gothic horsemen were riding out of the forest.

But it was no attack. Not yet. It was an embassy.

There were three of them. They rode tall, high-spirited horses, and each held a long spear in his right hand, a fluttering pennant just below the spearhead. They carried no shields, but their burnished steel breastplates caught the dying rays of the sun, and their tall, conical helmets with their flowing horsehair plumes made them look still taller.

Both officers thought: against two hundred of them, like that? We've got no chance. But both had the tact to keep silent.

The three horsemen rode fearlessly up to the edge of the circle, and the one in the lead nodded to Lucius.

"This is your command?"

"It is," said Lucius evenly.

Their leader's horse, a leanly muscled young black gelding, circled skittishly in front of them, mettlesome and full of fire. His gait was high stepping, free floating, as if he had Spanish or Berber in his bloodline, though the Goths usually rode the shaggy, enduring horses of the plains.

The warlord spoke again, his Latin excellent. "Hand the Hun boy over to us, and the rest of you will go free. Resist, and none of you will live to see tomorrow's sunset."

Lucius turned to Marco. Marco summoned Ops, who came shambling over from the fireside.

"Hear that, Decurion?"

"I heard."

"What do the men say?"

Crates, the wiry little Greek who served as the century's doctor, sitting cross-legged by the campfire sharpening his dagger on a whetstone, spoke up for all of them. "Tell him to go fuck himself," he called.

Lucius grinned and turned back to the Gothic horseman. "The answer is: go fuck yourselves."

The horseman was unperturbed. He said quietly, "You will regret that."

Lucius kept his eyes locked onto the eyes of his enemy. "Maybe. And maybe not."

The three tall horsemen wheeled their mounts and rode back into the forest.

Lucius sat with his men. Attila sat close by.

Crates the Greek was gouging at the dust with his knife. He said, his usually sardonic voice softened with puzzlement, "Goths don't skin people alive. Of all the barbarian peoples, they're the ones with the greatest sense of honor. They don't raze villages flat, they don't perform human sacrifices." He shook his head.

Lucius glanced at Attila, but he was saying nothing, his gaze inscrutable.

Marco, who had done service on the Danube earlier in his career and knew the Gothic peoples well enough, nodded in silent agreement. "One of our men, when I was out in Noricum with the Legio X 'Gemina,' getting seven different kinds of shit kicked out of us by those tall, gorgeous horsemen with their long blond hair—"

The rest of the men guffawed.

"Well, one of our men there, he got caught by a Gothic war band, hunting across the river. He came back alive okay. But you know what had happened?"

The men settled back to listen, the threat of tomorrow temporarily forgotten. Marco always told a good tale.

"This man, he was a young *optio,* not an ounce of common sense in his body. But he'd read a lot of books, and even sitting in camp down by the river he'd be talking poetry and philosophy and suchlike. Rest of the men sitting round stuffing their faces with lentil stew and farting at him from time to time, but he'd chatter on anyhow, regardless. So this one time he goes out hunting on his own—wildfowling—needed some duck, too many lentils playing havoc with his guts—and he gets caught by this Gothic war band. So they form up in a ring around him like they do, spearheads straight at his throat. And he told us he'd read about this Greek philosopher, who'd been threatened with execution by some tyrant—I forget his name. And this Greek philosopher, in true philosophical style, he sneers at the tyrant, 'How marvelous it must be for you to have as much power as a poisonous spider.' The tyrant had him executed anyway. But you have to admit, the philosopher went to Hell with a certain style.

"So now this Gothic war band has our man surrounded, not a cat's testicle of a chance, all on his own out there. And their leader says something about how he has strayed into their kingdom and domain, and the penalty for that must be death. And this young bookworm of an *optio* sits up proud in his saddle, and comes out with the very same line: 'How marvelous it must be for you to have as much power as a poisonous spider.' Straight to their faces. There's deathly silence as the twenty horsemen goggle at this bit of gross impertinence to their chieftain. And then bugger me if they don't all fall about laughing. They laugh so much they look like they're going to fall out of their saddles. Then the leader raises his spear, and the rest do the same, and he rides up and claps our daft young *optio* on the back, and demands that he comes back to their tents and gets shitfaced with them on some inferior Gothic mead. Which he duly does, not appearing to have much choice in the matter. Next morning he feels like he's been hammering his head against a wall all night. But he and this Gothic war band are now pretty much blood brothers for life."

Marco paused. Then he said more seriously, "Point is, that's the kind of people the Goths are. They're warriors and they have that old Germanic heroic code. You know? They don't skin prisoners alive, like the little Greek here says, and they don't slaughter whole villages of women and children. I'm not saying it's because they're tenderhearted, exactly. It's more because, as warriors, they'll only draw their swords against a worthy opponent—in other words, another man with a sword in his hand. You'll never hear about any Gothic atrocities, unlike with some tribes I could mention."

There was an awkward silence. The soldiers resisted turning to look at Attila. Still he remained impassive, listening to every word as he gazed into the orange firelight.

Lucius stood up. "Okay, ladies. Enough learned talk for the night. Time to get some sleep. It'll be dawn in a few hours, and tomorrow's going to be a long, hard day."

Marco and Lucius stood a while longer on the rough earthen rampart and looked out into the silent darkness.

"What are our chances do you reckon, Centurion?"

Marco took a deep breath, and when he answered he was uncharacteristically indirect. He said, "Another thing I know about the Goths is that when they charge they cry, 'Ride to ruin and the world's end!' So who fights harder, a man with a healthy dread of death or a man with no fear of death at all?"

His lieutenant brooded.

"I even learned a bit of Gothic poetry," said Marco.

"You never cease to amaze me, Centurion."

Marco went over it in his head, and then he said, his voice soft and guttural with the ancient Germanic sounds:

Hige sceal þe heardra,
Heorte þe cenre,
Mød sceal þe meara,
þe uns mahteig lytlað.

"Meaning?"

Meaning:

Heart shall be harder,
Will shall be stronger,
Fight shall be fiercer,
As our strength fades.

"That's the old, heroic Gothic soul for you."

"Very heroic it is, too."

Marco straightened. "But then, look at us. Look at what we're facing, now and in the hard years to come. Are you telling me there's any other way of looking at the world that makes sense? The world being what it is?"

Lucius was silent. After a long time he said, "No. It makes sense."

The two men looked into the implacable darkness and spoke no more.

It seemed to them as if all speech and all longing, all love and loyalty, bravery and sacrifice, might vanish and be swallowed up in that profound darkness, and nothing come out of its depths but more darkness yet.

A shiver ran down their spines. A voice began to speak close behind them:

Our mother the earth, there on the birch tree!
Amber-dark butterfly, that gave us birth!
As we go singing over endless plains,
Riding our lives away, shadows on the steppe.
Here she comes now, plumed with white horsehair,
Dressed for the sacrifice, our mother the earth.

Lucius turned then, but he knew who it was. The Hun boy stood close behind them, a blanket over his shoulders, his teeth gleaming in the darkness.

"But of course," said the boy, "the Huns have no poetry. It's a well-known fact. They are the most barbaric of peoples. The people who are born on a smoking shield, the people who shoot arrows in search of the gods."

His eyes held them for a little while longer. Then he walked silently away, back to the center of the camp, and lay down and closed his eyes.

Marco shook his head, looking over to where he lay. "That boy . . ."

"I know," said Lucius. "Something about him, isn't there? Something special."

Marco nodded. "And the Goths know it, too. Why are we waiting? What are we fighting for? *Who* are we fighting for?"

"Damned if I know." Lucius laid his hand on Marco's shoulder. "Come on, Centurion. We need some sleep, too."

Marco grimaced. "Yeah. Long day tomorrow."

6

DRESSED FOR THE SACRIFICE

They came out of the forests to the east with the rising of the sun, knowing their enemies would be blinded by that sun. Their striped and serrated and many-colored pennants fluttered proudly from their lofty ashen spears. Their long diamond-shaped shields were decorated with every kind of heraldic device, with every totemic animal that haunted the fierce imaginations of these warlike people and their measureless forests of the north. Outlined on their great shields were the shapes of bear and wolf, boar and the huge, shaggy European bison, each one circled and embossed in barbaric bronze. Long plumes of flaxen horsehair swayed from the peaks of their high, quartered helmets, and their fearsome long swords in their scabbards hung glittering from their sides. They sat tall and proud on their horses, and their horses raised their forelegs as they trotted forward, champing eagerly at their bronze bits.

They rode in perfectly ordered array—no howling tribal charge for them. At a distance of some two hundred yards, well within bow range, they pulled up their reins and halted. Their horses high-stepped skittishly where they stood. Their leader rode forward from their ranks. It was the warlord who had spoken to Lucius last night. He wore a bronze face mask beneath his helm, making him appear as metallic and terrifyingly impassive as an Olympian god. Even his horse wore a chamfron, a beaten bronze visor.

Again he said that they had no quarrel with the Romans. They wished only to take the Hun boy. And again Lucius said that the boy was in their charge, and they would not hand him over. The Gothic leader nodded, returned to the head of his ranks and wheeled about.

The soldiers within the flimsy circle clenched their teeth, gripped their spear shafts still harder and raised their jaws belligerently. They looked at each other wordlessly, for no words would suffice. These were men who had drunk together, fought together, whored together, all across the empire. They had stood back to back with shields raised under a rain of arrows, or ridden out to fight mounted against raiding parties of Attacotti pirates from Hibernia, looting the coasts of Siluria or Dumnonia for slaves. They had fought Franks on the Rhine and Vandals in Spain and Marcommans on the Danube, and not one of them lacked a scar in his flesh or a scar on his heart for a comrade who'd died in his arms in battle.

The Gothic horsemen dismounted. They were going to fight on foot. Lucius and Marco exchanged looks: unusual. They formed up in strict rank and file, three deep, curving round to cover as much as two thirds of the circle. They moved quietly, without fuss. Two hundred? thought Lucius. More like two hundred and fifty, maybe three.

Ops leaned and spat, and muttered something obscene about barbarians. Salcus, the young recruit, stood nearby, milk white.

Crates nudged him. "All right, lad?"

"All right."

There wasn't much more to be said by way of comfort.

"Can't wait to get stuck in, that's all," said the lad, speaking far too rapidly.

Crates managed a sardonic grin. "Me, too."

It would be the last time the Eighth Century, First Cohort, Legio II "Augusta" ever fought together. It would be the last time they ever got stuck in. They knew that. It would be their last stand. For reasons they did not comprehend, this was where it would all end for them. A small army of Gothic horsemen had brought them to a standstill, here in the once-peaceful heart of Italy, and demanded that they hand over one of their hostages—who was no more than a boy, and a barbarian to boot! No, it made no sense. But they would go down fighting; and then, they supposed, the Goths would take the boy for themselves anyway. But they would have to pay in blood.

It was not what they had envisaged. This was not the long and happy retirement so many of them had fondly foreseen for themselves, after twenty years' loyal service with the legion. Pensioned off with a nice bit of farmland in the mild south country of Britain, with a plump young rose-cheeked girl for a wife, with good round hips and a willing smile. Or, now that Britain, too, had been taken from them, maybe some place in Gaul, or the rich vinelands of the Moselle.

But here they were, here because they were here, and orders were orders. Anyway, they were not going to take orders from a Goth. So, let it be. They'd never live to see retirement, as it turned out; or know gout, or arthritic hands, or the palsy, or old man's staggers, or creep with bent and crooked back to a cold grave. They'd die here, after all, with sword in hand. It wasn't so bad. All men must die.

The Gothic warlord alone remained mounted. He turned to look at the small, grim circle of Roman legionaries. He glanced back to salute his father, the sun, climbing slowly up the eastern sky. Then he looked out over his ranks of men. He dropped his gauntleted hand. They broke into a run.

"Bows at the ready," ordered Lucius evenly.

Forty bows were raised aloft over the stockade.

The Gothic warriors were a hundred and fifty yards away. One hundred. Closing.

"Take aim," said Lucius, raising his *spatha*.

They were fifty yards distant now, running at full tilt, knowing that the arrows would be coming soon.

"*Fire!*"

The volley flew out into the enclosing circle of warriors, arrowheads finding their targets, burying themselves in the chests and legs of men. A few sank to their knees clutching the arrow shafts, a few more stumbled and fell full length, tripping their comrades who came on behind. More arrows glanced off the side of heavy shields or burnished helmets, or fell short and slithered into the dust. The mass of warriors came on.

"*Fire!*"

There was time for one more volley, then Lucius gave the order to take up arms. The bows were thrown aside and men took up swords and shields, or else their spears, and held them high over the trench below. Lucius sensed a figure at his side. He started. It was the boy. He had stripped to the waist, and daubed himself from the crown of his head downward with mud. His slanted eyes glittered in his blackened face like some forest animal's. He had tied his shaggy hair up in a Hun-style topknot, bound with plaited grasses, which made him look a little taller. Still, short though he was, his tattooed torso was tightly muscled and his biceps bulged as he held his short sword two handed.

"Back in the middle with the horses," Lucius ordered curtly.

The boy shook his head. "You're fighting for me. So I'm fighting for you."

And then he was away, sprinting across the circle and hurling himself at the stockade opposite.

The Goths were upon them.

Without the trench and the stockade, the fighting would have been over in minutes. But every Gothic warrior, no matter how tall, had to fight from below, stabbing his long spear upward, while the legionaries thrust down with their weapons in response, to deadly effect.

Lucius and Marco fought side by side as always, flanking each other, and moving readily to fill the gaps. A Goth had one leg over the stockade when Marco rushed at him, bellowing, and planted his foot in the warrior's chest. The warrior flew backward into the trench, and Marco leaned over to thrust his spear down into his exposed midriff. Another warrior slammed up against the stockade and drove his long sword at Marco's side. The centurion gasped and twisted, and the sword thrust grazed past him. Lucius grabbed the warrior and rammed his head down against the stockade, then despatched him with a clean thrust of his blade to the neck. The corpse rolled back into the trench.

As the trench filled with corpses, so more came on behind, treading across the bodies of their fallen comrades and approaching the stockade on the level. It was grotesque but effective. Some of the warriors crossed themselves as they trod on the dead, and Lucius had to remind himself that they, too, were Christians now, so they said.

He looked back and saw the lad Salcus curling back from the stockade and then, gently, sitting down cross-legged like a schoolboy in the dust, cradling his belly. He heard Ops roaring nearby, seizing two warriors by the throat, one in each hand, and wrenching their heads down onto his upraised knee. Then he rolled them back contemptuously into their comrades.

Attila was climbing up onto the stockade opposite. Lucius roared at him to fall back, but then he saw what had happened. A knot of warriors had thrown a grappling hook over the top and were passing the rope back to a team of horses just behind their lines, ready to pull away and tear a breach in the defenses. An instant before the rope was attached to the team, Attila leaned down and cut it clean through with a single swipe of his sword. He moved so fast, it was a blur, but then he wrenched the grappling hook free from the splintered wood at his feet and swung it furiously into the head of a Gothic warrior who was swinging his shield edge at the boy to knock him down. The grappling hook connected first, and the warrior's head spun round, his unconscious body sagging across the top of the sharpened staves. The stockade was saved, at least for a time.

Then, to his horror, Lucius watched as the boy, again moving faster than any man would have been able, aimed three rapid strokes in quick succession at the comatose warrior's neck. He kicked the warrior's helmet from his head, grabbed a fistful of his hair and, with a fourth stroke, separated his head cleanly from his body. He gave an unearthly cry of triumph and, whirling round, flung the severed head into the crowd of Gothic warriors massing beyond the sharpened staves. The bloody head whirled through the air, a tendril of spinal column hanging obscenely loose, gray pulp and crimson gore flying from the neckhole and spattering the chests and faces of the aghast warriors. The boy howled at them again, his teeth bared like a wild animal's, his sword held aloft, his face and chest smeared with a paste of earth, sweat, and blood, and for a single, frozen moment the mob of Gothic warriors stopped dead in their tracks at this figure of nightmare. Then they braced themselves and came on, and the boy stooped low beneath the clumsy swing of a long sword, and drove his own blade deep into the man's guts. He wrenched his sword free and fresh blood welled over him as the dying man fell against him. Attila twisted away and slashed his blade across another man's belly. Another corpse fell into the dust.

The boy had grown up since the night in the Suburra, two years since, when he had stabbed his drunken attacker, and then shed tears of remorse for it. In the fury of battle he had found his vocation, and the voice of remorse was quickly drowned in other men's blood.

All around Lucius, the hopelessly outnumbered men were fighting furiously, and the fighting was close quarter, messy, and chaotic. So far the defenses had not been breached. But his men were tiring fast. And, with uncharacteristic control, the Gothic warlord was sending in his men in separate ranks. When one rank began to tire, they drew back and the next rank took their place. Then they gave way to the third, and so on. None need fight to the death. None need even tire. But for Lucius's men there could be no such respite. Several lay dead already; more were wounded; and every one of them who could still stand and wield a sword did so. He saw that Crates had his left arm bandaged, at the end only a bloody stump where his hand had been. But still he fought on.

He smelt something oily burning, overlaying the denser odor of blood in the air. The Gothic archers had started firing arrows high into the bright morning air, and dropping them down into the circle. A risky strategy as they might well hit one of their own. But the arrows flew true, some wrapped in flaming cloths soaked in pitch, and soon the two great Liburnian carriages that formed so vital a part of the Roman defenses were aflame. More arrows fell into the center of the circle, where the horses were. The horses bucked and reared, straining white eyed and terrified against their guy ropes. The Goths were trying to start a stampede.

One of the horses was hit in the eye.

The sound it made was terrible. Lucius had heard horses scream before, on battlefields other than this, but the sound never ceased to wrench his heart. The agonized beast tore loose from its guy rope and reared, with its great head and its corded, muscled neck thrown back, its front legs dabbling helplessly at the empty air, its vocal chords stretched and tearing with the terrible screaming that arose from deep within. The arrow bristled from its right eye, and the animal's screams seemed to cry out to heaven in despairing protest that anyone, anything, should feel such pain in this world. Lucius was at the horse's side even as it reared, and as it came crashing down again he ducked beneath its neck and drove his sword point with all his might, two handed, into its carotid artery, just below its jaw. The blood spurted out in a hot jet, and the horse was dead by the time it hit the dust.

But it was hopeless. The arrows came down in a cruel rain upon the wretched beasts' backs and withers, and they began to tear loose and panic. Tugha Bàn was somewhere in the center. Lucius ran across the stockade to the eastern edge of the circle, trying to block out the sound of the horses' screams that filled the air. He plunged into the mêlée with a roar, driving back a knot of Gothic warriors, seized the stockade poles and began to wrench them out of the earth. He found Ops nearby and bellowed at him to do the same. Soon they had torn a breach five or six feet wide in their own defenses. Lucius returned to the milling, rearing horses, and drove them toward the gap. The stricken beasts stumbled through the breach and out across the battlefield, the boy's stolen mule following stiff legged after them, breaking up the lines of Gothic warriors and trampling one or two under their hooves. The Goths closed ranks, set the butts of their pikes into the earth, and drove the long iron heads into the horses as they came. Lucius could no longer watch. He hardly knew which was worse, the slaughter of men or the slaughter of horses.

He and Ops set the staves again and closed up the gap. The Gothic onrush was temporarily broken by the stampede, but it wouldn't last. His men slumped against the wooden barrier, exhausted. Their mouths were cracked and dry with thirst, their throats as rough as sharkskin from shouting; but the water was all gone. Ops was drenched from neck to waist in blood; it was unclear whose.

Lucius felt every muscle in his body burning, and could scarcely believe he could still muster the strength to raise his sword arm. His hands trembled uncontrollably with strain, his eyes were blurred and stinging with sweat and dust. He had long since thrown aside his heavy shield. They could only hold back one more onslaught, he knew. A second would destroy them all.

Then it came.

His men dragged themselves to their feet for the last time, uncomplaining, unsurprised and in silence, too exhausted even to give the battle cry. They fought with astonishing ferocity, with the fury of despair, of men who know they are going to die. In such a mood, a man can take a wound which would bring him to the ground in any normal circumstances, and yet fight on. So, yet again, the Goths' charge broke against the ranks of Roman swords and spears, what few remained, and they were forced to a standstill at the stockade; where, yet again, it came to a grim exchange of grunting blows, of wounds taken and wounds received and no quarter given on either side. Again, to the exhausted relief of the soldiers, the Gothic line fell back to regroup once more. Their retreat was slow and stumbling, the ground strewn as it was with the corpses heaped up in stark and scarecrow attitudes. A slain Gothic warrior sat in the dust bolt upright, facing the stockade where he had died. His severed head lay in the dust close by. Another lay cloven from the crown of his head to his belly, his intestines dragged out over many yards of ground where they had been caught by the hooves of passing horses. The air stank with the odor of spilled blood and of the ruptured bellies and bowels of men and horses.

An eerie silence fell over the battlefield as the dust settled between the two opposing war bands. Lucius saw to his despair that, although many Goths had fallen, many remained. They formed up three ranks deep, curving round to left and right; soon they would come again, and this time they would triumph. It would be a victory dearly bought, but it would be a victory none the less. All for the strange and glittering-eyed boy from the steppes of Scythia, who even now, to Lucius's disgust, was sauntering round the perimeter of the stockade, whistling to himself and taking scalps.

The Gothic warlord sat mounted and still on his black horse to the far right of his ranks. He surveyed the chaos of the battlefield with apparent serenity.

Lucius looked around. Crates was on his knees in the dust, cradling his stump of an arm. Lucius called out to him, and the lithe, clever little Greek looked up at him very slowly, his mouth hanging open as if he were an idiot, all his sharp, sardonic wit drained from him with his lifeblood. And then, like a moment from a nightmare, his eyes still fixed on his commanding officer, Crates slumped sideways and fell dead into the dust.

Young Salcus lay dead nearby, a spear driven through his skinny ribs and deep into the ground below. And there lay Ops, too, Ops Invictus, Ops the Unvanquished from Caledonia to Egypt, from Syria to the banks of the Danube. But he was vanquished now, at last, in the very heart of Italy, arrows bristling from his great mound of a belly like a porcupine's quills. Marco sat hunched, tawny with dust from head to foot as if he had been perversely anointed, his hands clutching his side. Surely not Marco, too. . . . In a panic, Lucius called his name. Marco looked up at him and then down again. He said nothing. Slowly and painfully he clambered to his feet, one hand still clutching his side, and came to stand near his commanding officer. Marco wouldn't be so easily beaten.

They were the only two men still standing. They and the boy. The boy, of course, the cause of all this mayhem, was still standing. Nothing could destroy him. Naked to the waist, sword in hand, topknot tied and decorated with a plait of horsehair, his whole body thickly pasted with blood and sweat and dust—and none of that blood was his own, Lucius felt sure, not a drop of his own wild blood had been spilled. The boy eyed Lucius evenly across the corpse-strewn arena of the stockade, drew his sword blade swiftly through the folds of his filthy, ragged tunic, which still hung from his belt, further garlanded with ragged and gory hanks of human scalp. And then he grinned.

The stockade was breached in three places, and the carriages were no more than a heap of ashes. There were three of them left to fight, and a hundred horsemen were about to ride in and slay them. They were finished. And the boy grinned.

Lucius looked at the ranks of standing men across the plateau. "You gods," he whispered, but with deep and bitter accusation. *"You gods . . ."*

The Gothic warlord raised his gauntleted hand for the last time.

Here they came now. The rear, untried ranks of horsemen were mounting up. The walking wounded were retiring to the shade and coolness of the forest edge, but the rest were riding forward. They would fight on horseback now. They would simply ride in and slaughter the last remnants of this troublesome century.

Here they came.

Beside him, Marco looked up. "To the otherworld, sir," he said.

"To the otherworld."

The horsemen did not even break into a gallop. No more than twenty yards from the stockade, the Gothic warlord raised his hand again and they came to a halt.

"What the Hell are they playing at?" growled Marco. "Come on, you bastards!" he yelled at them. "Come on! What are you waiting for?"

The ranks of tall, plumed horsemen sat their horses and didn't stir.

Then their leader heeled his horse and rode forward, just as he had only yesterday evening, many lives and deaths ago. He stopped near the stockade, turned his long ashen spear deftly in his right hand, and drove the head deep into the ground in front of him. His sword remained in his long scabbard. For a moment he bowed his helmeted head, and when he raised it again, Lucius saw to his astonishment that his eyes were bright with tears.

He spoke quietly, but they heard his every word.

"The battle is ended. The boy is yours. We will no longer fight against those who fight so bravely. We salute you, our brothers."

As one, the horsemen raised their right hands, empty now of weapons.

Then they turned and rode away. The dust settled behind their thundering hooves, and the plateau was silent.

In a daze, Lucius wandered out onto the battlefield, Marco close behind him.

After awhile Marco called, "Man alive here, sir."

Lucius went over. The warrior was badly wounded, blood bubbling from a hole in his chest. Marco stooped over him and tore off the warrior's helmet. He had cropped dark hair and, now they looked closely, his eyes . . .

"Never saw a Goth with brown eyes before."

The man begged for water, his voice grating with thirst, but Marco said they had none. Instead he demanded, in the Gothic tongue, *"Hva pata wairpan?"*

The man closed his eyes, ready to die.

"Get off him," Marco growled at his unseen, immortal adversary, gliding over the battlefield in his long black robes. "A minute more." He shook the dying man roughly, and demanded again, *"Hva pata wairpan? Who are you?"*

The man's eyelids fluttered and he groaned. "Don't understand. Speak Latin."

His brain reeling, Marco did so.

The soldier gasped, "Batavian cavalry, second *ala,* Roman auxiliaries, the Danube station."

"Not Goths?"

The soldier smiled faintly. "Not Goths." Blood frothed from between his cracked lips.

"Why? Who sent you?"

"We were waiting for orders . . . The boy . . ."

But the dying soldier's mind was already dimmed, and his inner eye saw nothing but the light beyond, and the outstretched arms of his wife, standing in the sunlit fields across the wide river.

Then his head fell to one side and his breath died.

Marco laid him gently down. His enemy. His Roman brother in arms.

The two officers felt another presence close by, and found the boy standing behind them.

"They were Romans," he said.

Lucius shook his head.

"They were Romans," insisted Attila, "sent to kill me."

"They were auxiliaries, Batavians," muttered Lucius.

"Same thing."

"I knew from how they fought," said Marco. "None of it was right."

He looked at his commanding officer. He had never seen him sunk so low. Lucius had seen his entire, loyal, beloved century wiped out in just two bloody hours—and on the obscure and treacherous orders of Rome. The lieutenant's head sank down upon his chest, as if burdened with a crown of lead.

Marco felt the same. There was nothing left for them here, or anywhere. Nowhere left for them to go. He said, "Suggestion, sir: they didn't expect such a fight, if any. They take the Hun boy here from us. We ride on to Ravenna. We report in all good faith that a Gothic war band has seized the boy. The boy is never seen again." Marco looked aside at Attila. "Sorry, son, but I don't think they'd have given you a hot bath and warm blankets to sleep in." He resumed to Lucius, struggling to hold on. "So word gets back to Uldin that his grandson has been captured, presumed killed, by Gothic raiders. An insult no Hun king would take lying down."

Lucius was ominously silent.

The boy was eager, though. "So he turns on the Gothic army of Alaric?" he said. "Attacking them from behind, as they are attacking Rome?"

Lucius shook his head and gave a deep sigh. "Like I've said before," he said very quietly, "I'm glad I'm only a dumb, boneheaded soldier, and not a politician."

He felt unspeakably weary. And he realized that they shouldn't be having this conversation in front of the boy.

But the boy had heard and understood it all. His slanted, leonine eyes were already burning from within. "I know who ordered it," he said softly. "I understand."

Marco tried to straighten up, but instead he gave a weak groan and sank down on his knees again, his hands stretched out in the dirt, clasping at nothing.

Lucius was at his side, urgently. "Marco!"

Marco turned stiffly and sat down, his head dropping. He felt he had no strength left in his powerful neck.

"Marco, not you, too."

"It is time, sir," said the centurion. "It was time for a lot of us today."

It was the wound in his side. He had ignored it, as he always ignored his wounds. "Either they go away," he used to say, "or you do." Until now, he had always got the better of them. But this one was different. His whole body ran cold, and his limbs trembled.

Lucius cried out his name, and ordered him to stand. "On your feet, soldier!" He could almost have struck him in his sudden rage.

"Just a few minutes more, officer," said Marco. Farewell, warm time. Hail, cold eternity. He could no longer see. "May the gods keep you," he whispered. "It has been good to serve with a man like you."

Then he rolled onto his side and curled up on the ground, smiling gently to himself. That great muscled, battle-scarred body, curled up like a baby in the womb. As at my beginning, so at my end. He breathed almost silently now, hands clutched to his stomach, blood seeping afresh from under his tunic. Lucius stood over him, utterly at a loss, speechless with anger. Marco stopped breathing. The blood stopped seeping.

Attila turned away, puzzled at himself, unable to watch, unable to listen. He walked away over the battlefield to find his mule.

Lucius sank to his knees with a howl, and dragged at his centurion's broad shoulders. He raised up his body, cradled his grizzled head in his lap, and wept.

Attila came back a few minutes later, leading his mule by its frayed rope. Lucius was still kneeling in the dust beside his centurion.

The boy stood near him for awhile, and then he said quietly, "I'm going now."

Lucius nodded.

The boy hesitated a while longer, then he said, "Rome's all done, like I said before. You should get back to Britain."

Lucius said nothing. He knew of nothing worth saying. And he suddenly felt that words of Latin, the language of Rome, would stick in his throat like fishbones.

"Your homeland," said the boy with a strange urgency.

Lucius nodded. His homeland. His heartland. Then he said, in the language of his own people, "*Mae hiraeth arnath Britan.* My heart is longing for Britain."

The boy knew nothing of the Celtic language, but there was no need. He understood every word from the longing with which the lieutenant spoke.

Still he hesitated. Then he said, "I owe you my life. I will not forget."

At last Lucius turned round. "Do not forget," he said quietly. "In the years to come." He watched the boy scramble up onto his mule, without a trace of tiredness, as if the morning's desperate fighting had been nothing to him but a stroll in the meadows. "Ride safely, young one."

Attila nodded. "I'll survive."

The ghost of a smile passed over Lucius's face. "I don't doubt it."

The boy kicked the mule's bony flanks and it lurched forward stiff leggedly away over the plateau, northward and into the trees.

Lucius watched him go for a long time.

THE LONG JOURNEY HOME
OF THE BROKEN-HEARTED
LIEUTENANT

In the afternoon heat and silence, amid the gluttonous buzzing of the gathering flies, the solitary soldier of Rome hacked brushwood from the surrounding forest and piled it up in the center of the stockade. He built a great pyre over the brushwood with the uprooted staves of the stockade, and dragged the bodies of his slain men onto it. When he had lifted up the twentieth corpse he knew he could do no more that day, and he slept comatose some distance away without dreaming. The next day, aching in every fiber of his body and his soul, he managed to lay the rest of the bodies on the pyre. Last of all, his centurion.

He fired the brushwood and watched it burn as the sun went down in the west. Over Rome.

He walked away into the forest.

But some unknown god was watching over him. The god who blesses and curses in one breath.

After only a few minutes' walking he saw something like a white shadow through the trees. He emerged into a glade filled with the last smoky rays of the sun slanting in low between the trees, and there in the beautiful light stood Tugha Bàn, cropping the sweet dark grass of the glade. She still wore her saddle, but Lucius's scalp froze when he saw an arrow buried in it.

He went over and let the wounded horse nuzzle his hand gently. He carefully raised the saddle, and his heart sang. For he saw to his unspeakable relief that the arrowhead had only just passed through the leather and then stopped. Tugha Bàn in her innocence wasn't so much as scratched. And it was only right that it should be so. What had his gentle gray mare to do with the violence and treachery of men?

He laid his arms across her broad, strong back, rested his cheek against the dense leather, and gave thanks with an unsteady voice; and then he broke down and wept again. Tugha Bàn looked back at his emotional outburst with some surprise, grazing her damp muzzle over his arm. Then she returned to cropping the sweet, cool grass at her feet. It was too good to miss.

After his prayers, Lucius took off her saddle, snapped the arrow off at the head, pulled the wicked iron barb through from the other side, and threw it deep into the undergrowth. He replaced the saddle and tightened the girth, looped the reins back, hauled himself up, patted Tugha Bàn's long gray-dappled neck, and pulled her gently and firmly away from the grass. She harrumphed a little crossly, and he heeled her forward into a gentle rolling walk.

"You and me, girl," he murmured. "Into the sunset."

Around noon the next day, under a burning sun, he drew his sword one more time.

He rode down a narrow track and round the corner of a grove of stone pines, and there immediately before him stood three men. Momentarily they were as surprised as he was. Then they smiled lazily at each other, and moved out across the path.

"Nice horse," drawled one of them, squinting up at him and grinning.

"She is," said Lucius. "And where I go, she goes."

"By the giant golden balls of Jupiter, is that a fact?"

"It is."

"Well well."

"We don't have no horses," said another, coming in close on Lucius's far side.

Tugha Bàn tossed her long gray mane.

"So I see," said Lucius.

All three men were sunburned and had terrible teeth. The third one drew a dagger slowly from his belt, and ran it through his long, lank hair, grinning at Lucius all the while.

Lucius looked each one of them in the eye in turn. Then he said, "I'm in no mood for it. Now out of my way."

The second bandit stepped back and also drew a dagger from his tunic.

The nearest one gave an obsequious bob of his head where he stood, not moving. "Most certainly we will, your eminence. Just as soon as we've relieved you of that nice bronze cuirass you're wearing. And your helmet, and your sword, and your shield, and your dagger. Oh, and your horse, of course, and all the trappings and accoutrements pertaining thereto." He grinned toothlessly, drawing a long sword from the scabbard that hung from his back. "Then we'll be out of your way in a—"

He never finished the sentence. Lucius whipped his cavalry *spatha* from his scabbard in the blink of an eye, jabbed Tugha Bàn forward a couple of paces and slashed the blade through the air, saying with weary irritability, "Oh, leave me *alone.*"

The bright sword blade slashed across the bandit's throat and he tottered forward and fell, collapsing across the rump of Lucius's horse as he rode by. The head lolled almost free from the neck, attached only by a flap of skin, such was the skill of the blow, and blood gouted across Tugha Bàn's gray flanks. Then the corpse slithered off her rump and fell into the dust.

Lucius did not even spur Tugha Bàn into a trot. He walked on, leaving the two men staring after him, knowing they would not come.

All that hot afternoon he rode on. He felt nothing, except for the bandit's blood crusting over and drying in the hairs on his bare right arm. He didn't even stop to wash, or to clean his sword before resheathing it, or to sponge Tugha Bàn's flanks clean. He cared about nothing anymore.

The sky was filled with blood, and none of it was innocent. The gray dusk fell, and still he rode on west. Tugha Bàn slowed her pace in puzzlement as they rode on into the night. But, as her rider showed no sign of stopping, she ambled on. The moon rose behind them, and the air grew chill, even in late summer, for they were still in the Appenine mountains. Once, once only, they heard the call of wolves in the high mountain passes to the north. A tremor ran over his mare's withers, a tremor of primeval and instinctual fear. They rode on.

They emerged from a deep-sunken track onto higher ground, and there in the moonlight stood a man upon a rock. He stood quite silent, haloed only by the pale moonlight, like some figure out of myth. The broken-hearted lieutenant reined in his horse and stopped. Ready for any new horror or revelation that might come out of the darkness of this world or the world beyond.

The horseman and the man upon the rock stared at each other in the moonlight upon that lonely mountain road, and the only sound was the slow, deep breathing of the horse. The man upon the rock was dressed in a long robe of coarse wool, perhaps gray, perhaps brown, for all colors were indistinguishable in the moon's gray light. The robe was belted at the waist with a rope sash, and a large hood was drawn up round his neck, but his head was bare. His hair was long and unkempt, and his beard straggled down over his chest almost to his waist. He held a long staff topped with a bare wooden cross of the simplest, most spartan design. His eyes glittered in the moonlit night and they never left the eyes of the broken-hearted lieutenant, who returned his gaze with eyes similarly unwavering. The man or hermit or lunatic never stirred an inch. In the gentle night air only the heavy hem of his tattered robe stirred a little and then stilled again. The moon shadow of this silent messenger with his staff and his cross fell across the mountain road, jagged and broken up by the rough stony ground, but still clearly visible for what it was: a man holding a cross. His feet were as firmly planted as his staff.

It seemed that many minutes passed in the silent night as the two men, two refugees from the world of men, looked deep into each other's souls and said nothing. Finally the stillness was broken, though not the silence. The ancient man on the rock raised his skinny arm and touched his fingertips first to his heart, then to his lips, and then to his forehead. Then he held his arm outstretched, so that he reached out into the empty space over the soldier's head, and he carved another invisible cross in the empty air. He let his hand drop, and the soldier and the man or hermit on the rock looked at each other a while longer, with no words spoken. At last the lieutenant turned and looked ahead down the moon-washed road, and dug his heels gently into the flanks of Tugha Bàn, and rode on.

That night he felt unspeakably weary, as if another ten or twenty years had been added in one hour to his bones. For the second night running he fell asleep in his bloody clothes, rolled up in his horse blanket under a creaking holm oak, the stars glimmering through the spearhead leaves, his mouth tasting of dust and betrayal and blood.

He awoke close to dawn with those last stars fading from the sky, and he went down into the valley to the river's edge to wash. He stripped naked and went into the icy water from the mountains and stood up to his waist, then plunged in over his head, resurfacing gasping and shaking his streaming black locks, scraping his eyes clear of the water, and opening his mouth to its purity. He closed his eyes and raised his arms to the clear early morning sun still orange on the horizon, and in his mind he climbed to the portals of heaven and begged Isis and Mithras and Christos and the imperturbable gods to cleanse the blood away. He kept his eyes tightly closed, as if afraid that when he opened them and gazed back upon the mortal world, he would find only that he stood in a river that was a sluggish rusty brown, forever polluted with dust and betrayal and blood.

He submerged himself again and again in the icy water, rubbing his hands and face, his arms and his chest until they were red and glowing with the cold.

Then he stepped back to the bank, took hold of Tugha Bàn's reins and led her gently into the icy water. She whinnied as it streamed around her belly, throwing her head up crossly and baring her teeth. But he held her tight and pulled her in deeper, until the pure mountain water coursed right over her back and washed her clean and dapple gray again. They returned to the bank, and both shook themselves dry as best they could. Lucius dressed again, and saddled Tugha Bàn, and mounted. He buckled on his scabbard belt and shoved his sword round to his right side. Then he sat for awhile and considered.

After some time, slow and dreamlike, as if unable to believe his own actions, he slipped down off the horse again. He unbuckled his scabbard belt and walked back to the river's edge. He held the belt by one end, whirled it round his head, and threw the whole thing, sword and all, into the deepest water. It sank immediately. He picked up his shield by its rawhide rim and hurled it in after. He did the same with his bronze cuirass and his expensive, crested helmet. Then he turned back and pulled his spear from the ground, and sent it hurtling high into the air. It crested and curved and fell, entering the deep, dark water in virtual silence, and was gone. Left in only his hobnailed sandals, white linen tunic, and leather jerkin, the lieutenant mounted Tugha Bàn again, wheeled her, and rode on down the mountainside.

At about the same time, some miles to the north, Attila awoke to the same early sun. He sat up and rubbed his eyes and looked around him at the fresh morning world, as bright as a sword blade with dew, and he grinned. Then he rolled lazily to his feet and took a look around.

There was a farmstead nearby, at the edge of the trees on a warm south-facing slope. He left his mule tethered to a low branch and crept silently over to it. The shutters were wide open, and a dense male snoring came from the gloom within. He stepped silently into the lower room, which served as a barn, and waited patiently for his eyes to adjust to the darkness. Then he grinned with satisfaction. On a peg on the wall opposite hung a good length of strong rope, and leaning in a corner was a long-handled billhook with a decent-looking curved iron head.

The boy noosed the rope with a slipknot and nodded with satisfaction. It would do fine. He looped it over his head and left shoulder, so that his sword was still readily to hand on the right. Into the opposite side of his belt he tucked a pruning knife. He stole a flat whetstone that he found on a bench, and a hessian sack. Then he hefted the billhook, and grinned with satisfaction at the weight of it. He went back outside and remounted his mule, hefted the billhook across his right shoulder, and rode on down the mountainside.

In the mountains they had known nothing of what had gone on in the wider world. But as soon as Lucius came down into the plains and the rich farmland of the Tiber valley, he saw the devastation that the Goths—the real Goths—had wreaked in their righteous anger. Farmstead after farmstead was burned to the ground. Golden fields of ripe corn, ready for the harvest, had been trampled into the mud by the hooves of a hundred thousand horses. Entire orchards had been slashed and burned, livestock slain or herded into the Gothic column and driven off. The landscape was deserted. The country people had gone. He saw only stray dogs whimpering and cowering amid the burned-out cottages, crows and kites circling and feeding on the carcasses of cattle and sheep.

As he neared Rome, he passed the occasional ragged group by the roadside. An entire family, huddled around a single handcart, looking up at him with round, empty eyes. He felt his heart swell in his rib cage with pity, but he could do nothing.

And then he came in sight of the city on the seven hills, and he saw the vast army of the Goths encamped about. Like all barbarian peoples, the Goths made no distinction between soldier and civilian. When they marched, the whole tribe marched: men, women, and children all together in their covered wagons. And when they camped, they spread like a vast nation, as now across the fields outside Rome. The city of a million people was surrounded and cloaked around by a dark shadow of a hundred thousand Goths. And Rome was starving.

Lucius sat and considered for awhile. And then he rode forward.

The Gothic army camp was undefended. There was no Roman force left in Italy that would dare to face them. All that stood between them and the glittering treasures of Rome were the walls and gates of the city itself.

Alaric, that shrewd Christian king of the Gothic people, had sent messengers to the imperial court and to the Senate in Rome some days ago, pointedly lamenting the death of his noble opponent, General Stilicho, and then demanding four thousand pounds of gold in return for his withdrawal from Italy. The Senate had responded with foolish contempt. "You cannot defeat us," they said. "We are many more in number than you."

Alaric sent back a curt message, of the kind beloved once by the Spartans, and now by the tough Germanic peoples. "The thicker the hay," he said, "the more easily mown."

And he increased his demands. Now he wanted all the gold in the city, and all the silver, and the handing over of all slaves of barbarian blood. The demands were outrageous, and the Senators said as much. "What then will we be left with?" they asked indignantly.

Again the reply was laconic. "Your lives."

Nevertheless, although in the open field there was none to stand against Alaric and his horsemen, the barbarian king knew he had no skill in siege warfare. Rome might withstand them for months, and the besiegers, as is so often the case, would soon be every bit as trapped, malnourished, and diseased as the besieged. So, instead, Alaric turned his men away from the walls and made down to Ostia, the port of Rome, where the great grain ships came from Africa and Egypt. And they sacked Ostia, and laid it waste, and burned the massive grain houses, and sank the huge, clumsy ships in the harbor. And Rome began to starve.

Alaric returned to camp outside the walls of Rome and waited for the inevitable surrender that must come soon.

The tall, fair-haired warrior leaned on his spear outside his tent and shielded his eyes from the sun. Across the shimmering fields came a man, unarmored, unarmed, on a fine gray horse. Little plumes of dust arose from the horse's hooves as it trod delicately down toward the Gothic encampment.

Lucius looked neither to left nor to right. Over his head he could feel the sign that the hermit on the rock had made in the mountains by moonlight. His heart was as steady as his hands. He walked on between the first felt tents of the Goths, toward the walls of Rome.

More and more spearmen emerged from their tents to stare. Some of them called out angrily, some hesitated, some even laughed.

"You have a message for us, stranger?"

"What is your business?"

"Speak, man."

Lucius rode on through the camp. Outside these tents, the wives of warriors sat cross-legged before campfires, stirring pots or nursing infants at their breasts. Children ran about in the dust, or stopped to stare at the strange man on the gray mare. One little boy ran across almost under Tugha Bàn's hooves, and Lucius reined in to let him pass unscathed, then rode forward again. At last the road ahead was blocked by four mounted men who lowered their spears toward him.

"*Hva pat waetraeth?*"

He drew up in front of them. They eyed him easily, unafraid, their spears held loose but firm at their sides. Their blue eyes never wavered. These were no bandits who could be brushed aside with a sword stroke. Besides, he had thrown his sword away.

"Do you speak Latin?"

The horseman to his right nodded. "Some." He swiped his hand over his mouth. "Enough to tell you to depart."

Lucius shook his head. "I'm not departing. I have business in Rome."

The horseman grinned. "We, too."

Another horseman, his mount restive and his eyes burning at this Roman's impertinence, pulled up tightly on his reins and said angrily, "*Tha sainusai methtana, tha!*"

The warrior to the right, with the easy smile but the firm and steady eyes, leaned forward. He rested his muscular forearms, banded with bronze armbands, on the pommel of his saddle, and said conversationally, "My friend Vidusa here is growing angry. He says you must go. Otherwise . . ."

"I am unarmed."

"Then we will pull you from your horse and knock your teeth out. But you will not ride into Rome through this camp, without—"

"I will ride into Rome," said Lucius, his voice quiet and steady. "I have business there that cannot be denied."

A sound of furious galloping approached, and Lucius's back and neck shivered with readiness for the cold bite of sword blade or arrowhead. But none came. Another warrior skidded to a halt at his side. From the way the first four sat up and looked respectfully into the far distance, Lucius judged that the newcomer was a nobleman. He glanced to his left. The new arrival wore cross-gartered trousers, and was naked to the waist. His biceps bulged as he wrenched back the reins. His hair was long and fair and his eyes burned keenly into Lucius." He wore no sign of his rank, but the air of authority and power was unmistakable. He bellowed at his four inferiors and they answered sheepishly. They lowered their spears. The newcomer then turned his attention fully on Lucius. His Latin was basic but adequate.

"You are Roman? Answer."

"I was."

The newcomer frowned, his horse curvetting skittishly in the dust. The warrior wrenched the reins so fiercely that its head was pulled round almost to touch his legs, and the skittishness subsided.

"Was?" he rasped. His voice was deep, hoarse with dust, but powerful. "Can a man change his tribe? Can Roman become not Roman? Can Goth become Saxon or Frank? Can man disown father and mother, even people? Answer."

"My name is Lucius," he said. "I am from Britain."

"Britain," repeated the newcomer. "It rains."

"Sometimes."

"Often. Always. But grass is green. Answer."

Lucius nodded. "Grass is green."

The warrior grinned suddenly from under his bushy mustache. He sliced his hands at the walls of Rome. "After Rome burns," he said, "we come to Britain. We graze our horses where grass is green."

Lucius shook his head. "The grass of Britain is for my people. Our land."

The warrior's grin vanished as abruptly as it had appeared. He rode in alongside Lucius and stared at him closely. "You not afraid, Was-Roman?"

Lucius shook his head again. "Not afraid."

"Why not afraid? We kill you. Answer."

Lucius remembered the words of the Greek philosopher: "How marvelous it must be for you to have as much power as a poisonous spider." But Lucius was not a man to borrow another man's words. He spoke his own words, simple and true.

"I am not afraid, because I am not your enemy. You will not kill me. I will ride into Rome. I have business there. Then I will sail home to Britain."

"Where the grass is green."

"Where the grass is green."

The warrior stared into Lucius's eyes a little longer. Lucius returned his gaze without blinking.

"You are strange, Was-Roman," said the Goth at last.

"I don't doubt it," said Lucius.

Then the warrior wheeled away and threw his arm out wide to his men, roaring at them in the Gothic tongue. They parted, and Lucius rode on between them.

Several hundred yards separated the perimeter of the Gothic camp from the walls of Rome, well out of missile range for both. Lucius rode up under the shadow of the Porta Salaria and shouted for entrance. No questions were asked, and there was only a brief delay before the door in the center of the great oak gates was opened. He dismounted and stepped through it, leading Tugha Bàn behind him. He wondered why it had been so easy, but when he saw the guard on the gate he wondered no more. He was starving. His eyes were hollow and red, and his hair had fallen out in clumps from his white scalp. Spittle had dried and crusted round his mouth, and his lips had almost shrunken away with starvation. In such a condition, a man can barely think straight. The city was in a desperate situation.

Lucius led his horse up the street, and everywhere there was the stench of starving, unwashed and, even worse, unburied bodies. He saw people huddled along the edges of the streets or in the shadows of the darkened alleyways, sometimes holding out a clawed hand in beggary. He stopped only once, when he came upon the body of a child in rags, no more than four or five years old, its face of parchment, eyes rolled up in its head, flies settling already around the shrunken lips and the flaking nose. The child would be the same age as his own. . . .

He bowed his head sorrowfully and could walk no farther. He let go of Tugha Bàn and leaned down and gathered the dead child up in its rags. He covered its face—it was impossible to say even whether it was a boy or a girl—and laid the featherlight bundle at the side of the road, brushing away the flies and hiding the drawn, ashen face with a corner of ragged cloak. It was not enough, it was never enough, but it was as much as he could do. Then he and Tugha Bàn walked on.

The whole city lay under an ominous silence, except for perhaps a long-drawn-out, barely audible sigh as it settled into enervation and death. The bodies of the dead were everywhere, and the clouds of breeding flies. It was still August, and in this heat Disease would soon make his appearance, close on the heels of his beloved bride, Starvation, and add to the manifold miseries of Rome.

Lucius and Tugha Bàn walked for half an hour through the starved and haunted streets, the huddled groups of the dying sometimes stirring and chattering as they passed, eyeing with glittering, half-mad eyes the plump, grass-fed flanks of Tugha Bàn. Lucius patted her on the nose.

At last they came to the Palatine Hill and the gates of the Imperial Palace. The guards here looked better fed. He demanded entrance, saying he came from Count Heraclian, from the column that had been despatched to Ravenna earlier in the month, and he gave the correct passwords. There was a long delay, and then at last he was admitted. He insisted on an audience with Princess Galla Placidia, saying that he had a confidential message for her from Count Heraclian himself. He was told to wait, and he waited for two hours. He waited until the evening. And then they said that the Princess Galla would receive him.

"Look after my horse," he called over his shoulder. "I'll be coming back for her."

They gave him their word.

He was escorted by four armed guards into the Chamber of the Imperial Audience, and there in regal splendor on her throne of finest Carrara marble sat Princess Galla Placidia. Close by her stood the eunuch Eumolpus.

The princess let her pale eyes settle upon him for some time. Then she said, "So Heraclian is safe in Ravenna."

"He is. Along with his beloved Palatine guard." The soldier's tone was peculiar, sarcastic.

"Address the Throne as 'Your Excellency,'" hissed Eumolpus.

Lucius turned and gazed at him steadily. Then he turned back and looked at the princess with equal steadiness. He said nothing.

Galla was astonished, but she betrayed nothing. A princess must never betray any emotion, which is weakness; she must never raise her voice, and she must walk with a slow stateliness at all times, as if a cup of water were balanced on her head.

Besides, perhaps this filthy, tousled, bare-legged soldier, whose malodorous presence she must endure for the sake of his communication from that fool Heraclian, had sunstroke, or was weak with hunger or something. No matter. For once, palace protocol could be put aside. All she wanted to know was: "And the rest of the column?"

"Dead."

She nodded. "And the Hun boy?"

"Apart from the boy. He is free now."

She smiled. "As you put it."

Lucius nodded. "He will be well on his way back to his people by now."

Galla hesitated. "You mean . . . his ancestors?"

"No, I mean his people. Out on the Scythian plains. That's clear enough, isn't it?"

"Your Excellency!" cried Eumolpus, snatching up his skirts and hurrying out into the center of the chamber. "This impertinence is grotesque! I must abjure you"—he swung round to the deranged soldier who dared to address the Imperial Throne in such a way—"I must abjure you. . . ." Uncertain of what exactly he must abjure the soldier from, he raised his hand angrily.

"Slap me," said the soldier quietly, "and I will break your neck where you stand."

"Oh!" cried Eumolpus, backing away. "Your Excellency! Guards!"

But Princess Galla waved the guards away. "Bring this man some wine."

"I have no need of your wine," said the soldier. "It might make me puke."

Galla's face began to show signs of revulsion, uncertainty, and fear in equal measure. When she spoke, it was with further hesitancy. "What is your message, soldier?"

Lucius fixed her unblinkingly. "'If Satan cast out Satan,'" he said, "'how then shall his kingdom stand? For then he is divided against himself.' The Gospel of St. Matthew, chapter twelve, verse twenty-six."

Eumolpus retreated to his mistress's side, and the two of them stared at the strange, sun-maddened soldier.

Finally, Galla spoke again. Her skin and her pale red hair looked paler than ever. "You are telling me the boy got away?"

"The boy got away. Heraclian and the Palatine guard got to Ravenna. And the rest of my century—*my entire century*—got wiped out. By a detachment of Batavian cavalry from the Danube station, disguised as a Gothic war band." Lucius kept his eyes on Galla all the time, his voice rising now in volume and anger. "I don't have a message for you from that scumbag Heraclian, may he rot in Hell. I only came here to ask you a question. One simple question, to which I trust you will give a straight answer. Is it true that this whole disgusting business—this *massacre*—was merely a—"

"Your Excellency!" cried Eumolpus, unable to contain himself any longer. "This is outrageous! You, an unwashed hooligan, do *not* put questions to Her Imperial Majesty, and you do *not*—"

Lucius took two deliberate steps toward Eumolpus. "Shut the fuck up," he said. "I want to hear an answer from the one who gives the orders, not a fucking eunuch."

"Guards!" yelped Eumolpus. "Arrest this man!"

This time, the princess was so shaken that she did nothing to stop

them. Two burly Palace Guards soon had Lucius's arms locked up painfully behind his back, but he appeared not even to have noticed. His eyes
never left Galla's porcelain-white face.

"If you do not answer," he said, as he was dragged back from the
throne, "I will assume that my century was destroyed on your orders, as
part of a plot using the Hun boy as a pawn. Am I right?"

Galla said nothing, but her lower lip trembled, and she clenched one
small white fist in the palm of her other hand.

"*Am I right?*" roared Lucius, and his voice echoed deafeningly around
the cavernous chamber like an angry missile.

Still there was nothing from the throne but an aghast silence.

"Then I pray to God that you are punished for it," said Lucius, his
voice quiet again but perfectly clear. "And that the line of Honorius die."

At last it was too much for Galla. She leaped to her feet, all regal
diginity and slow stateliness gone, and she raised her voice and cried with
considerable emotion, "Take this man away! Have him beaten—and
executed within the hour!"

And Lucius was dragged from the room.

"So the Huns will not come?" said Eumolpus, once the obnoxious soldier
had been dragged away.

Galla resumed her seat, still shaken. "If what that madman has just
told us is correct, the Huns will not come. The plan has failed."

"What must we do now, Your Excellency?"

Galla scowled in fury. "We must negotiate with the Goths. At first
light tomorrow."

"And the boy? We do not know how much he really knows. If he
makes it home to Scythia—unlikely, I know, but if he does—and tells
his story, we will make mortal enemies of the Hun nation as well."

Galla turned such a look on Eumolpus that he quailed where he stood.

"Kill him," she said. "Send out orders. Scour all of Italy, and all of

Pannonia beyond, to the very banks of the Danube. He must be destroyed. He must not get away. Rome itself may depend on it. Find him. And kill him."

After ten lashes from the knotted rawhide whip, his back was streaming with blood. After thirty lashes, the flesh hung from his back in ribbons, and soon after that he lost consciousness. By the time the guards were done, the white of his ribs showed through the flesh.

He was not aware of the appearance of two Palatine officers in the cell beside him, nor of the low, urgent conversation they had with the prison guard. He did not hear them say ". . . from Heraclian's column . . . the sole survivor . . . sweet Jesus . . . not ours to ask questions, soldier . . . be criminal to . . . no one will ever know."

Then the two guards who had tied him up and lashed him tended him as he lay belly down for three days not moving. He tried to speak but they told him to shut up. They told him they knew who he was, and he would not be executed. He muttered that they could be put to death themselves for this disobedience. They shrugged.

They sewed up his wounds, where there remained enough skin on his back to do so, and they bathed him every hour, day and night. Sometimes the officers of the Palatine guard came into his cell and looked him over. Not a word was exchanged. And then the officers left again. They, too, could be put to death for this.

The guards bandaged him with fine linen bandages, and made compresses of antiseptic herbs such as garlic and figwort, known to prevent the poisonous miasma that seeps into open wounds from the infected air, and turns the flesh of even the young and the healthy into a stinking pulp like rotting fruit.

He was strong. On the third day he insisted he could sit up. When he did so, some of his stitches burst apart and he began to bleed again. They bawled at him and told him what a dumb bloody idiot he was, and they laid him down again and undid the bandages and sewed him up and re-dressed him with fresh compresses of herbs and bandaged him up again.

He lay on his belly and complained that he was bored.

They grunted, unimpressed.

It was another week before he reckoned he was really well enough to stand. He stood there tottering in the dank cell to prove it.

"But not to travel," they said.

"Out of my way," he said.

"No," they said. "We're not seeing all that work going to waste. You're not well enough. You need another week at least."

He challenged the bigger of the two to arm-wrestle to prove he was well enough. They declined. He argued with them. He argued with them for over half an hour, by which time they felt as if *they* were begin-ning to suffer from exhaustion. At last they shook their heads wearily and opened the gates of the cells.

"And my horse," he said, "Tugha Bàn. Where is she?"

The two guards looked uncomfortably at each other and then back at him. "You serious?"

"Yes."

They shook their heads. "You lead a horse into a city dying of starva-tion, and you expect to lead her out again? You're old enough to know better than that—with respect, sir."

Lucius stared at them. "The guards on the gate gave me their word."

They shrugged.

"Words, words," said one.

"When food is scarce, so is friendship," said the other.

Lucius stared at them a little while longer. Then he turned away, and they watched him walk stiffly up the narrow steps into the darkened street above. There he stopped and called back softly, "Thank you both anyway. I owe you everything."

"Madman," they called after him. "Now scoot."

8

NOT EVERYTHING IS FALLEN

It was night. He leaned against a wall and tried to still the thumping of the blood in his head by force of will. He gave a low moan and rubbed his forehead against the flaking, ancient wall. The air around him stank, and a huddle of rags nearby emitted a low gurgle, but he did not even look round.

Hopes may deceive, but none deceives like despair. Despair is the lowest cowardice of all.

He straightened up against the wall, feeling the tug of the fine flaxen stitches in his skin. He took a lungful of fetid air, pushed himself away from the wall and began to walk.

In a nearby alley, he stooped, holding his arm across his nose, and pulled at a pile of rags. An emaciated corpse rolled out, eyes staring, the nearly bald skull clunking horribly on the ground as if hollow with hunger. He shook the black rags violently again, and a rat ran free with a squeal. The corpse's belly had been eaten open.

He pulled the black, stinking winding sheet round his shoulders, half covering his face, he tied another strip of rag around his head like a Barbary pirate. Then he walked unsteadily round the eastern gate of the Palatine.

The guard saw him coming.

"The answer's no," he shouted. "Now shove off."

Luicus went nearer.

"You come one step closer and I'll put a blade in your guts!"

"Spare a crust for a poor, starving citizen," croaked Lucius. Even in his own ears his voice sounded cracked and terrible.

"You heard. Now shove off."

"A little bread or some horseflesh?"

The guard ignored him.

The beggar stood a little taller and the guard eyed him warily but curiously.

"How much are you paid, soldier?"

The soldier looked defensive. "You know the answer. We haven't been paid for six months. But at least we still—"

"And you have a wife and children?"

"One of each. And maybe even that's an extravagance these days."

"Are they not hungry, too?"

"Now look, I've told you before, I'm not standing here arguing with—"

"How much would you get for a plump gray mare in your stables, sold for horseflesh? A plump gray mare with her belly fat on rich summer grasses, her satin flanks gleaming in the sunshine?" The beggar now stood up fully. "Answer me, soldier."

The guard frowned. "You know what I'd get. Anything I bloody well wanted, and more. But how—"

"And how much *did* you get for my horse?" The beggar let the filthy sheet fall from his shoulders and tore the rag from his head, and the guard recognized him at last. "How much did you get for Tugha Bàn?"

Lucius was unarmed, but he stepped forward menacingly, and the guard stepped back in reply. He slipped inside the gateway and drew the barred gate across.

"You bastard," said Lucius softly. "You treacherous bastard. May all the gold you gained bring you nothing but grief."

He turned and made his way down the grand street of the Via Palatina, moonlit, deserted, starved, already haunted by the ghosts of its former greatness.

He had not gone more than a hundred yards when he heard a cry from the gatehouse. He hesitated, wondering whether to turn round. When he did, he saw a figure standing at the top of the street, a gray mare beside him, saddled and bridled, her reins in his hand. The mare tossed her head and whinnied softly. Lucius felt a profound shudder of emotion—several emotions—run through him. Then he walked back up the street and she settled her muzzle in his cupped hand. Her ears flicked with happiness.

Lucius looked at the guard. "You fool," he said. "You could have got a year's pay in gold for her."

The guard shrugged. "Maybe, maybe not." He looked at the ground. "A year of gold for a lifetime of bad sleep."

Lucius clutched the man's arm, then let it drop. "Thank you," he said, with such urgency that the guard flinched. "Thank you."

Then he stepped up on the stone mounting block beneath the wall, seized the low pommel and cantle of the military saddle, and hauled himself carefully up onto Tugha Bàn's broad back. He nodded once more to the guard and then rode on down the street.

Not everyone is false; not everything is fallen. Though great Rome herself may fall, not everything will fall.

"You look out for yourself, now," the guard on the gate called after him. "We live in funny old times."

So we do, thought Lucius. So we do.

He rode out of the west gate of the city, and through the encircling camp of the Goths by moonlight, riding and looking so steadily straight ahead that those who challenged him did not pursue their challenge in the face of his silence. Some said that he was a ghost. None would stay his flight with sword or spear.

He rode along the banks of the widening Tiber and saw the well-fed water bats skimming the surface of the river, hawking at gnats in the darkness, and he wondered that bats should be better fed than men. Surely Rome was being punished by the gods. He rode on down to the port of Ostia. At dawn he stopped to bathe in the river, only to remount and ride on still sweat stained and travel weary. How could you wash yourself clean in a river where starved and skeletal bodies floated by?

The sun rose over the great stone warehouses and mighty wharves of Ostia, but many of them lay in ruins now, stricken and blackened at the hands of the Gothic invaders. In the harbor, the smashed masts and the sunken wrecks of the great African grain ships still showed above the flat, calm waters where they lay. There were very few people about, and those he encountered looked warily at him and said nothing. Where before, for centuries, sunrise in summer would have seen thousands of workmen arriving or waking here for their day's work, now there were only a handful. The shipwrights and chandlers, caulkers, sailmakers, and netmenders were gone. And the merchants and traders, too, who had come here from all over the Mediterranean, bringing precious marble and porphyry from the east for the buildings and monuments of Rome, and Egyptian cotton and linen, and all the fruits and spices of the Levant—there were none. Where were the hundred different languages of the known world, haggling over prices, rising into the early morning air in a babel of polyglot voices? Where were the lightermen and stevedores, pushing their wooden handbarrows, unloading ship after ship of its treasure store of silks and linen, sacks of grain, ingots of silver and tin? And hefty, roped bundles of furs, and barrels of precious Baltic amber, slaves from Britain, and huge, rangy hunting dogs from Caledonia, straining on their studded leather collars: deer killers and wolf slayers, all ivory teeth and eyes like Baltic amber.

All that great hubbub was gone. Ostia lay under the warm and constant sun, a ghost of her former self. The great quayside cranes with their granite tackle blocks and their huge oak crossbeams stood silent, blackened with fire, some still smoking gently like mournful, extinguished dragons. Only the occasional cry of a lone yellow-legged gull broke the silence.

On the far side of one of the smaller harbors, Lucius could see a small, broad-beamed cargo ship, a square-rigger with a red sail faded by salt and sun. He rode round the cobbled harbor wall and found three men lading her with corked amphorae and crates of fruit. Evidently the Goths had no taste for dried apricots. But everything else that had lain in the warehouses they had destroyed or looted, loaded into their great wheeled wagons, and taken away.

"Where are you bound for?" he called out to the three dogged sailors. They ignored him. He called out again, more strongly.

One of them set down his amphora in its wooden stall. "No place you'd want to go," he said.

"Tell me."

"Gaul," he said. "Port of Gessoriacum."

"Take me. Take me north, to the coast of Britain, and sail me into port at Dubris, or Portus Lemanis. Or Noviomagnus, even better."

"You got money?"

"Not a fig."

The man grinned at one of his fellows: the cheek of it. Then he shook his head. "Out of our way. We've got a load more lading to do before we sail, and we've no desire to cross Biscay in September storms."

Lucius dismounted. Before they could stop him, he had lifted a heavy wine amphora onto his right shoulder and was walking across the wooden gangway on board. It cost him more in pain than the sailors ever knew, the still unhealed wounds across his back cracking and oozing afresh over his straining muscles. But he made not a sound, gave not a sign. He set the amphora down in the rack, and went back to get another.

The sailors eyed each other and shrugged.

They'd reckoned the lading would take all morning. It was done by the fifth hour, thanks to the stranger's willingness and heft.

The captain, the one who had spoken to him, leaned against the gunwale of his ship. "So you want to go to Gaul?"

"No, *you* want to go to Gaul. I want to be set down at Noviomagnus."

"'Set down?' You know what it's like sailing into British coastal waters these days?"

Lucius shook his head. "No, I've no idea. That's your job. But when you set me down at Noviomagnus—"

"If."

"When. Then I'll find you payment of five silver pieces before you sail for Gaul."

The captain debated democratically and in muffled tones with his two crew members for a moment. Then he grunted, "You're on. Only go and get what you can for the horse first. Try the customs office over there. What you get will serve for now as down payment."

Lucius shook his head. "Where I go, she goes."

"No."

"Yes."

"Look, sunshine, I'm the captain of this ship, and a captain on his ship is a little emperor at sea. What he says is law. No one even farts on this leaky old bucket without my permission, see? And the one thing I won't have on my ship is horses."

"Or cats," said a crewman.

"Or women during their periods," said the second.

"Or anything made of linden wood," said the first.

"Or—"

"All right, all right, you twittering idiots, we all have our funny little

superstitions. Yours is cats and bleeding wenches, and mine is horses."
He looked back at Lucius. "And my superstition tells me that ships,
weather and horses go together like wine, women, and chastity. One hint
of a storm, or Jove gets irate and starts hurling bolts at us, and horses
start stampeding all over the hold. Nothing but a bloody nuisance,
horses is. So if you want to keep your horse, then it *stays* with you."

"You don't know Tugha Bàn," said Lucius, patting her on the withers.

"How very true that is. And you know what? I have no wish to make
the lovely lady's acquaintance, neither. Now fuck off and—"

Lucius stepped up onto the ramp, leading Tugha Bàn behind him.

"If she causes you any trouble on the voyage," he said with quiet determination, "I will cut her throat and roll her overboard myself. You have
my word."

The captain scrutinized the strange, gray-eyed horseman. And he saw
that he was, indisputably, a man whose word meant something. "Ten silver pieces," he grunted. "You're aboard."

"Ten silver pieces," agreed Lucius. "When you set us down at
Noviomagnus."

The late summer seas were calm and the voyage was uneventful, but for
one incident when they anchored at Gades to take on more fresh water.
The two crewmen came back staggering under huge amphorae.

When they had set them down, and swiped the perspiration from
their faces, one said, "Rome's fallen. The gates were opened to the Goths
by some bleeding-heart old matron who couldn't bear seeing all the
people starving like that. Like the Goths was going to come trooping in
and open a bloody soup kitchen. So in they march and sack the city top
to bottom."

Neither Lucius nor the captain said a word. It was written.

"Then Alaric their king went off south and died of poisoning, they
say. Dirty work, maybe."

Lucius looked up.

"His brother rules the Gothic nation now. Athawulf, he's called. Just as much of a sharp one as his big brother, they reckon. And you know what? You know who he's gone and married? Or who's gone and married him, rather?" The sailor stretched his aching back. "Times we live in, I don't know. He's only gone and got himself hitched to the emperor's sister, hasn't he?"

Lucius stared open mouthed. "Princess . . . Galla Placidia?" he said hoarsely.

The sailor pointed a forefinger at him. "That's the one. Emperor's sister, and a handful, they say. And now she's only gone and given herself in marriage to the King of the Goths!"

Lucius's head sank down on his chest and he spoke no more.

But that evening, as the ship pitched gently through the waves, and the stars came out in the late summer sky and the moon went down, and the golden shores of Hispania retreated behind them into the night, the captain and his two crewmen sat and wondered at the strangeness of their passenger, the gray-eyed British horseman. For Lucius sat alone in the prow of the old cargo ship, staring up at the stars with his fists raised to heaven, his head thrown back, laughing to himself as if he had just been told the funniest joke in the world.

The sailors' garbled, dockside intelligence was broadly accurate.

On the night of 24 August, 410 years after the birth of Our Savior, Rome fell. For the first time in nearly eight hundred years, the proud capital of empire heard in its streets the tramp of a barbarian army.

They came pouring through the Salarian Gates to the sound of triumphal Gothic trumpets. Many of the starving multitude welcomed them as an end to their suffering. Furthermore, Alaric, the Christian king of his people, gave strict orders that, while any loot belonged to his men by *jus belli,* no churches, chapels, or other places of Christian worship were to be touched. And no holy women were to be subjected to the usual *jus belli,* either. And his Gothic warriors—cross-gartered, long-haired, mousta-chioed barbarians in outward form—conducted themselves with restraint and even nobility.

Sacking certainly took place, and many centuries of treasures were lost—which had been sacked in their turn from weaker, colonized peoples, of course. But tales of atrocity and torture, such as one expects to hear at the collapse of a great city, were few, and often disbelieved. The Goths' reputation for both martial ferocity and a certain proud clemency toward those weaker than themselves was once again confirmed. Indeed, the worst atrocities that took place during those fateful few hours were committed, it was said, not by the fair-haired invaders but by disgrun-tled slaves taking private revenge on cruel masters and mistresses for years of oppression, under cover of chaos and the night.

The houses the length of the Via Salaria were put to the torch, to light the army's way into the heart of the city. And once there, amid the seven hills, many of Rome's great towers and palaces were brought down in ashes and dust. The Palace of Sallust on the Quirinal Hill, beside the Baths of Diocletian, that architectural jewel containing the unnumbered treasures of Numidia, and every miracle of the jeweler's and goldsmith's, the painter's and the sculptor's art, was fired and destroyed in a single night, its contents vanished forever. Likewise the palace of the fabulously wealthy Anician clan was seen from afar off, aflame in the night. Wagons piled high with gold and silver, silks and ornaments and purples, were soon trundling out of the gates toward the Gothic camp.

In the Forum, the mighty statues of the heroes of Rome were roped and pulled down by rearing horses and their drunken, whooping riders. In the fiery light of the burning buildings, those monuments of the ages came crashing to the ground: Aeneas and the early rulers of Rome, the honored generals of the Carthaginian and Macedonian campaigns, the deified emperors, great Hadrian and Trajan themselves. Even Caesar's solemn mask, melting into the flames as he if were no more a man of bronze but only a pitiful figurine of wax. . . .

Some of the wealthier citizens fled ahead of the invaders, and sought refuge on the little isle of Igilium, off the Argentarian promontory. The woods there grew thick with huddled and hungry refugees, still strangely attired in rich robes and gold-embroidered dalmatics. But on those summer nights they shivered like any beggar in his rags, to see Rome burn across the bay, and all their vaunted wealth go up in smoke. Others took ship for Africa or Egypt; still others took the veil. But none truly escaped the wrath of those days.

In Hippo, on the African coast, Bishop Augustine began to brood about the meaning of the Sack of Rome, and to contemplate the writing of his great masterpiece, *The City of God.* For the city of mankind's longing must be a city that endures forever, a celestial Rome. For here we have no abiding city. . . .

And in Bethlehem in far-off Palestine, Holy Jerome in his sky-lit cell wept at the news that the world was at an end. "My voice is choked with sobs as I write these words," he lamented. "The city that conquered the world is now herself conquered."

He also wrote, in a letter to a friend, a line that has become famous throughout the world. "All that is needed for evil to triumph is for good people to do nothing."

The Goths stayed only six days in the city before their creaking covered wagons rolled out again, laden with the treasures of half the world. Alaric marched south, his thirst for gold and glory not yet wholly appeased, and his Gothic horde sacked the city of Capua, the proud, sybaritic and luxurious capital of Campania. Along the Neapolitan coast, that playground of the rich and powerful for centuries, even the gorgeous villas of Cicero and Lucullus were filled with long-limbed Goths reclining on silk-upholstered couches, quaffing huge bejeweled goblets of the finest Falernian, and rejoicing in their mastery of the world. In their drunken vainglory, these haughty German warriors forgot that there were still other tribes—and one tribe in particular—that might envy them their easy conquest of Rome.

Alaric marched south again for Messina, his eyes on the rich pickings of Sicily just across the straits. But the weather was by then turning rough, with late summer and early autumn storms, and rising Sirius presiding as always over the season of storms that sailors have dreaded since man first presumed to travel in Neptune's realm. And that very night, after a fine banquet in his palatial tent, cooked for him by his boasted new Roman chef, Alaric was suddenly taken ill with some mysterious form of poisoning, and died. His chef had in fact been a gift from the household of Princess Galla Placidia herself. . . .

The unfortunate creator of the banquet was put to death, just to be on the safe side. And Alaric was given a burial fit for a conqueror and king. His generals, with massive slave labor from the neighboring townships, diverted the River Busentius from the walls of Consentia, buried their lamented king in a triple casket in the muddy riverbed, then returned the river to its course. All those who had worked on the burial were slain, and to this day the exact place of Alaric's burial has not been discovered. Doubtless it never will be.

To unanimous acclaim, Alaric's capable, vigorous, taciturn younger brother, Athawulf, was made king in his stead. And the Gothic nation, abandoning its dreams of conquering Sicily, which seemed to them foredamned, returned northward to Rome. And there, to general astonishment, and not a little sardonic laughter, it was soon announced to the populace of the city, and to the Gothic nation, that King Athawulf, as a sign of the new concord that now existed between the Gothic and Roman peoples, would take as his bride the beautiful Princess Galla Placidia, sister to Emperor Honorius, and a spotless virgin of only twenty-two summers.

9

THE RUINS OF ITALY

Throughout these tumultuous days for Rome—her last days, so it seemed—the Palatine guard continued to hunt for the barbarian boy with the slanting eyes and the blue, scarred, tattooed cheeks, on his arduous flight through the ruins of Italy.

The boy fought on, hunted all the way.

His ancient mule died under him so he stole a horse. He rode that horse to death in a single day, and the next sunrise he stole another. He could cover a hundred miles between dawn and dusk, or as often by night, riding through the dense woods of the Italian mountains, only coming down into the more populous valleys to steal. He survived through anarchy and war, fighting sometimes like a cornered animal against vagrants or bandits or deserter soldiers with lust or cruelty in their eyes. He fought, cheated, and lied his way through the flames of Roman devastation, and with every victory that he won he grew stronger. He was happier in those desperate weeks than he had ever been during the years of boredom and bitterness in the safe and perfumed courts of Rome.

He had always before him the prospect of his own country: the beloved, windy plains of Scythia, the broad, winding rivers and the vast,
dense pine forests, the tents of black felt and the wagons where his people
encamped. The boar hunts, the wolf hunts, the blue skies of summer
and the terrible snow-bound winters. And he rode with a happy heart,
through the chaos and ruins of Italy, heading north, back to his tribal
homeland. Nothing could destroy him. Not lightning, not bandits, not
street bullies, not hunger or thirst, not summer sun or winter snow, not
even great Rome itself. He was one with his father Astur and with the
immortal gods of heaven, and when he killed he felt he could create as
easily and with as much pleasure as he destroyed. For that is the way of
the unknown and changeful gods.

He did not always travel alone. One chill autumn morning he awoke
to find, to his annoyance, that a crook-backed old man had crept into the
woodland glade where he had camped without his hearing. The ancient
stranger was stooped over his campfire, piled afresh with dry twigs, and
was blowing new life into it through his bony, liver-spotted hands.

The old man eyed the boy impassively as he scrambled from his blankets and reached for his sword. He was bearded and his face, with its
beaked nose and deep-set eyes, was grim and without humor. When he
spoke his voice was a hoarse rasp from disuse, as is the way with hermits
and solitaries.

"No need for a sword, boy. Not in these Latter Days."

Attila laid his sword aside uncertainly, and approached the stranger.
"Your name?" he demanded.

"A servant of the servants of God."

"That's not a name."

The old man said irritably, looking back at the fire, "John, then, if
thou must. Unworthy as I am to share a name with the fourth evange-
list." He crossed himself. "Now give me food."

"I have none."

"Thou liest."

The boy was becoming irritated in turn. "I do not lie."

"And what are those markings on thy face? Those unChristian daubings that stain thy visage in the manner of the most wretched and unhallowed of barbarians?"

Attila touched his fingertips to his cheeks. "My birth tattoos," he said, "cut by my mother ten days to the hour from the day my birth cord was cut. After ten days had passed, it was known that the gods would not call me back to the Everlasting Blue Sky."

The old man looked at him with dawning horror. At last he sprang to his feet and seized the boy's arms in his skinny, clawlike fingers. His eyes were rheumy and watery with age. "The Lord God of Israel save thee, and all the apostles save thee, and all the saints save thee, and the Mother of God intercede for thee, and save thee as a brand plucked from the burning! For thou art in mortal danger of eternal Hell fire!" He threw his head back and cried to heaven, "O Lord, have mercy on this Christless and unshriven soul!"

The boy shook the madman free with some effort, for his grip was like that of a hawk on its prey. "I have no need of your Christ," he retorted.

Holy John reeled back as if from a blow, and put his hands to his ears.

"Astur my father sees all and judges all. I am not afraid of the day of his judgment of me."

"What is this new diabolical name? What is this daemon?" cried Holy John, his voice becoming hysterical. "Surely there are more demons in the earth than there are birds in the sky! Oh, save us! Name him not in my presence, for to name a demon is to summon him!" Once again, he seized Attila, this time by the hem of his ragged tunic. Attila eyed him with something approaching disgust, and let him rant. "There is a she demon of similar name, worshipped in Syria with the foulest and most depraved rites known to man or beast, in the Groves of Ashta—Oh, but I dare not speak her name. Her eyes burn like the fires of Gehenna, and on her front she has an hundred breasts."

"Astur is the name of the god of my people," said the boy coldly, "and if you insult him you insult me and my people and the thirty generations of my ancestors who sprang from his seed."

"Boy, thou dost not understand!" howled Holy John. "Thy ancestors burn in Hell, every one of them, even as we dally on this accursed mountainside. And thou thyself art in mortal danger of burning likewise."

Attila spoke very slowly, his eyes never leaving Holy John's contorted face. "You are telling me," he said, "that my mother, who died when I was still an infant at her breast, now burns forever in your eternal Christian Hell?"

"Oh, most assuredly," wailed Holy John. "Her very flesh, and those very breasts that gave you suck, her soft and perfumed womanly hair, her lissom limbs and her shapely womanly buttocks are kissed by the Hellish flames, and all, all consumed daily in the irremediable torments of the damned."

The boy had already retrieved his scabbard and drawn his sword. "Leave me now," he said quietly.

"That I shall not!" cried Holy John. "The Lord God of Hosts Himself hath led me here this day, to make a glorious conquest of thy soul! And conquer it for Christ I shall, ere the sun hath—"

Attila put the point of his sword to the wrinkled and sagging wattles of the old man's throat. "I said, *leave.*"

"I fear thee not, thou demoniac sinner," cried Holy John, trembling nevertheless with something that resembled fear. "I fear not them that can destroy the body, but only them that can destroy the soul!"

"Then you are a fool," said the boy. "Even the smallest child among my people could tell you that the body and soul are not two separate things, nor can the soul be taken out of the body like a plum stone out of a plum. Rather the soul and the body are one, like, like"—he searched for an image—"like the sun and the sunset it makes."

Holy John stared at the boy and began to moan, a deep wail of lamentation rising from his belly.

The boy pricked the point of his sword a little farther into the sagging throat. "Now go," he said. And with a faint smile he added, "And may Our Father, Astur, have mercy on your soul."

Mention of the demonic name worked where the sword had not. With a howl Holy John turned and fled from the glade, his hands to his ears and his long and filthy skirts flapping round his skinny, mottled legs.

It began to rain. The boy broke camp, mounted up, and rode from the glade.

Even then, Holy John had not altogether finished with him. From the shelter of the trees, from where he had been spying on the boy, he called after him, "You ride under the wings of demons, boy!"

Attila did not turn round. Instead he bowed his head, muttered, "Then let it be," and rode on into the rain.

He rode up into the mountains, among the tall pines, their resinous scent fresh on the wind and the damp air. High on an exposed ridge he rode into his first flurry of snow. The flakes settled and then quickly melted on his forearms and on his horse's mane.

At night he built a rough shelter of pine branches and huddled in his single blanket, sick with longing. He ached with cold and loneliness. But even when he fell asleep his teeth remained clenched. For he scorned even his own sorrow.

He set horsehair snares for rabbits, watching out for their twilight runs at evening. He boiled up birdlime from grass grains and holly leaves, and he smeared the lime on the higher branches of trees to trap birds. Each one when roasted over the fire was little more than a mouthful; he ate them bones and all. He had better success with a wickerwork fish trap he made from hazel twigs, and he gorged on baked river fish till he could eat no more.

As the year deepened in its colors into autumn, he found enough wild fruit, seeds, and nuts to sustain him. He knew how to bite away the nourishing skin of rosehips without digging deeper into the irritant hairs in the center. He knew how to bake a pinecone just long enough for it to crack open and give up the tasty kernels within. And he certainly knew how to skin and gut a rabbit, and roast it on a spit of alderwood. He grew lean with a faraway look, but he knew he would survive.

But there came an evening when he could find nothing to eat. He had fished in a lake all day with pegged-out lines and baited hooks of hawthorn, without success, and his belly felt light with sadness and emptiness. He sat his horse on a rocky outcrop and looked down into a neat little valley below, and saw the torches and rushlights of a village burning. He even thought he could hear the sound of laughter and coarsevoiced song. He slipped from his horse and led it down into the valley.

10

THE VILLAGE

It was no more than a circle of wooden huts round a well, with a big hay barn to one side and an ancient timber longhouse to another. His ears had heard aright: there was laughter and song, and they came from the longhouse.

He tethered his horse in the shadows at the edge of the wood, and crept over to the longhouse. Pulling himself up on an upended chopping block, he craned to see through the open window.

Inside a feast of abundance met his eyes. His stomach felt more pitifully hollow than ever, and his mouth flooded with forlorn expectation. Within the building sat the entire population of the village, as many as a hundred peasants with rubicund faces, laughing and singing, drinking and gorging themselves in celebration, by the light of a score of rush torches. It was too late for the harvest celebrations, surely; but in the country districts, it was well known that an excuse was found for a drunken celebration at least once a week, especially as the year sank into the gloomier months of winter.

Clay wine pitchers were being passed around, and flat osier baskets piled high with rolls of coarse but wholesome bread. Two great pigs, fattened up beautifully on the acorns that they had foraged in the oak woods in the hills for the past few weeks, were turning golden brown and shiny with fat on the blackened iron spits. The face of the gasping turnspit at their side was almost as golden brown and greasy as they, but he was grinning from ear to ear at the thought of all that delicious roast pork to come, the flesh juicy and slightly nutty to the taste.

Huge bowls of clay or olive wood bore mounds of steaming winter vegetables, roast parsnips and turnips, roast chestnuts, winter kale, bowls of lentils cooked with soft goat's cheese, various kinds of cured hams and sausages, roast and boiled partridge and pigeon from the woods, and after that apples, pears, apricots, and plums in abundance, their skins shining plumply in the torchlight.

Suddenly the barn door beside him flew open, and the boy froze. There appeared a plump, middle-aged woman, wheezing out in the cold night air, her face glowing with good food and rather too much wine. Oblivious of the boy standing as still as a statue on the chopping block, she leaned one hand against the barn wall, squatted down, hitched up her voluminous skirts, and began to pee noisily. When she had finished, she wiped herself with the hem of her skirts, and heaved herself upright. Only when she turned round did she see the boy frozen there, and give a little gasp of fright.

"Jove bless us and save us, I thought you was a robber or something." She peered at him more closely. "What you doing out on a raw night like tonight?" She pushed his shoulder and turned him to face her. "Looking hungrily in at our feast like a wolf off the hills, are you? Or maybe eyeing our young daughters—though you hardly look old enough for that kind of caper." And she gave a great belly laugh.

Attila had already decided he would neither fight nor flee, but wait and see what happened. And sure enough, after a moment's thought, the woman said, "Well, you best come in and have some of ours, anyhow.

Wouldn't do to have a lonely traveler turned away from our door on a night like this. We'd soon be hearing the drums of You-Know-Who in the hills."

And with that mysterious deprecation, she laid her plump hands on his shoulders and propelled him inside.

The assembled company looked curiously, some even suspiciously, at this newcomer with his hair tied up in a barbaric topknot on the crown of his head, his slanted, glittering yellow eyes that gave away nothing, and his scarred and tattooed cheeks the color of the night sky. Several of them speculated about his origins, right under his nose.

"He's from the hills," said one, "from the south. Full of belly and empty of head, they say."

"No, he's no Sabine," scoffed another. "He's from the east, from the marshes. Look at his fingernails. He's a fish eater, morning, noon, and night."

Attila himself said nothing, and no one thought to ask him directly.

Another speculated that he might be from farther south still. From Sicily, even.

"Sicily?" cried the first. "Look at him, Sicily, indeed! What did he do, *swim* here?"

And after that, no one seemed to mind much where he came from, as long as he accepted their endless profferrings of meat, and bread, and wine, and more meat, and more wine. . . .

The woman who had brought him in from the cold sat him between herself and a girl she said was her daughter, a well-fed, rosy-cheeked girl of about seventeen or eighteen. Not only was she better fed than the wretched starvelings in the city but, like all the people here, she was also purer skinned and brighter eyed. Her light brown hair was drawn back from her brow with a ribbon of plain white wool, and she wore a simple white woolen tunic belted round the middle. The front of the tunic was deeply slashed, showing her plump young breasts and the shadowy cleavage between. The boy kept his eyes shyly fixed upon the food in front of him.

"I know, she does show them off doesn't she?" cried the girl's mother, seeing his discomfiture with great amusement.

"Mother!" said the girl.

Beyond this girl sat another, rather thin and pale, with dark shadows under her eyes. She said nothing, but Attila felt her gaze upon him, and once or twice he glanced along at her. Eventually he smiled, and she smiled back. Then she looked shy again and turned away.

"Fresh meat, y'see," leered the old man across the table with the spittled mouth and the unshaven chin. "All the girls'll be after you this e'en. Nice bit of fresh meat in the village. Who'd want an old smoke sausage like me, when there's a nice bit of fresh meat going begging!"

The woman squeezed Attila's thigh under the table, and said, "How old are you, boy?"

"Fourteen. Fifteen this snowfall."

"I know what you're thinking, you little wanton," she scolded, leaning across and slapping her daughter on the back of her hand. "Old enough, I warrant." She grinned at the boy and squeezed his cheeks. "Look at you, all ragged and drawn—thin as a winter gnat you are. You need some good old local hospitality, dearie, you do. A bit of meat inside you, and some good few cups of wine. I know I likes a bit of meat inside *me* whenever I can get it. And maybe a bit of the other kind of hospitality too and all later on!" She rocked back and forth on her bench with laughter.

"You ever been kissed, then?" asked the girl.

The boy looked down at his plate. "Yes," he said defensively.

"Aw, bless," said the girl. "And you know what the Saturnalia is for, don't you?"

He didn't. But he was about to find out.

The great double doors at the end of the longhouse creaked open and, to deafening cheers and hallooes from the assembled villagers, in came a procession of men and women bearing a train of crudely carved but unmistakable images. First came a rather stately matron carrying a statue of Priapus sporting a huge jutting phallus, carved from olive wood and seemingly oiled specially for the occasion. Priapus, the little grinning god of fertility, stood on a bed of winter berries, elderberries and hips and haws, and his proud phallus was lovingly decorated with wreaths of broom and ivy. Several of the women leaned forward to kiss it as it passed by. Next came a tall, dark-skinned man bearing a primitive but rather touching statue of the mother goddess, Cybele, seated and in long robes, suckling her infant son, whom she cradled on her knee. Many people reached out to touch the magical statue. There followed more villagers with long poles garlanded, or hooked with lanterns, singing and cheering as they walked round and round the long tables, while everyone else fell in behind them. Children ran and squealed and scurried in every direction, breathless and laughing with excitement.

One red-faced man leaped up on the table and raised his wooden goblet to the rafters. "To fertile fields and fat old pigs for another sunny year!" he cried, and he tossed back his goblet, draining a full *sextarius* of warm red wine in a few mighty gulps. All joined in the toast at the tops of their voices.

The boy watched and took everything in, his slanted yellow eyes missing nothing, although with some astonishment. Among his own people, as among all lean, ascetic nomad peoples, matters of fertility were kept much more veiled. But among settled peasants and farmers who work on the land, fertility and the copulative act went easily together, and were regarded as essential to the fecundity of the earth. They saw the animals copulate freely, the only outcome of which was a happy one, the birth of new lambs or calves; and they saw no reason to conduct themselves otherwise. For a woman to give herself to a man, husband or no, was seen as an act of pure generosity—indeed, it was regarded as positively unhealthy among these folk not to engage in intercourse at regular intervals.

No wonder the unworldly and nature-fearing Christians of the city condemned all those who did not follow their god as *pagani*, which meant simply "country dwellers." The people who dwelt in the fertile southern valleys of the empire had long been most resistant to that gaunt, grim-visaged, sin-obsessed desert-religion from the east; and long would remain so. Here, where greenery and the ancient gods still throve, fertility and the breeding powers of Nature were still worshipped above all else.

More wine flowed from freshly unstopped barrels, and the village musicians began to puff away on their reed pipes, or saw away at their coarse-toned three-stringed lutes, and people began to dance and sing. They sang *"Bacche, Bacche venies!"* and *"In taberno quando sumus,"* and many other folk-songs of love and wine and the earth, which they had sung in these valleys before the grand poets in Rome ever put pen to paper:

Si puer cum puellula
Moraretur in cellula
Felix coniunctio!
Amore sucrescente,
Pariter e medio
Avulso procul tedio,
Fit ludus ineffabilis
Membris, lacertis, labiis!

If a boy and little girl
Tarry in a little room,
Happy is their copulation!
Love arises with elation,
Weariness flees far away
When they hide in bed to play,
And their nameless game begins,
Of sighs and whispers, lips and limbs!

"O mercy, mercy!" cried the old man with the spittled mouth and the unshaven chin, jigging around in the dance with the rest. "You take me back to my young sapling days, and I'm all of a frustration that my member will not perform as it did once, in the swelling springtime of my lust."

At which everyone told him to pipe down, and said they didn't want to hear about his member, or the swelling springtime of his lust. Someone poured a full goblet of red wine over his white locks, pronouncing that he was now anointed and blessed by Priapus himself. Whether the charm worked was unclear, but the wine trickled over his face and down his furrowed cheeks, and the ancient dancer licked it happily enough from his beard.

"This time next year we'll have a carving of a crucified man on the table," cried another wag.

"You must be joking!" many voices objected.

"A jolly feast it'd be with *that* in the middle of it," called another.

"No drinking, no fucking, no farting," roared another. "Thank Lord Jove I'm not a craven Christian."

Attila felt his hand taken warmly in another and squeezed. It was the rosy-cheeked daughter, pulling him away from the crowd.

"Come on, then," she whispered. "There's a nice little hut just round the corner."

The thin, pale girl watched them silently as they went. But the mother winked at them. "You treat him gently now, dearie," she beamed.

The night air was chill and the sky was clear, the stars shining coldly down from where their fires burned eternally in the heavens. Attila felt his chest tighten with cold and fear, but his hand in the girl's hand was warm as she led him over to a small straw-thatched hut near a cottage. His heart was thumping so loudly he thought she must be able to hear. She pulled open the rickety, cobwebbed door and drew him inside. He pulled the door closed behind them, but through the open window came enough pale moonlight for them to see each other's faces: his drawn and nervous, but with jaw set firm at the prospect of this new and frightening journey; and her eyes sparkling with delight at the prospect of a new conquest.

"I should know your name," he said.

She shook her head. "No names. And you tell me no names neither."

"Why not?"

"Because," she said, and sighed. "Because I know you'll be gone in the morning. So what's the point?" She smiled a little sadly. "Now then . . ."

She pushed him down and knelt with him in the hay, and leaning forward she put her mouth to his and they kissed. It was very silent. After a little while she slipped her tongue between his lips. Attila had been kissed before, of course, in greeting—even, revoltingly, by Eumolpus when they were first introduced—and on the lips as well, as was the custom in the Roman court. That was one Roman custom that no barbarian nation, and certainly not the Huns, would ever adopt.

But this was a different kind of kiss, thrillingly close and intimate, and he immediately felt a surge and warming of his blood. He kissed the girl breathlessly in return, their tongues running over each other, entwining, their mouths opening to each other, their hands reaching out to stroke cheeks and hair. . . .

"My, you are the greedy little one, aren't you?" she whispered. He could see her white teeth in the moonlight as she smiled. She lay back in the hay and pulled her shift up to her waist. She opened her thighs to him, and ran her middle finger, the *index lascivius* as physicians have named it (although perhaps rather lascivious of them to have done so) down between her ripe lips.

"Come on then, my darling," she said softly. "And here, too," she said, pulling her tunic down off her slim shoulders and exposing her breasts, "touch me here too, here, put your mouth to my breast, kiss me there, and with your tongue, oh my darling, oh. . . ."

Her sighs and gasps filled the air of the little hut; the boy was silent and enrapt, the girl whispering all the time as she guided him and stroked his tousled hair. "Oh I love that, I do love that, here, kiss them, take them in your mouth, gently, yes lick them like that, suckle them, oh that is so sweet, do they taste sweet to you, oh my darling, that feels so sweet, and there, oh yes, inside me, touch me there, oh sweet gods, oh I love you, my darling, I do love you. . . ."

And as she sighed and gasped, she reached down and pulled up the boy's tunic, and felt for his hard cock, and said nice things about how he might be small for his age but *that* wasn't, that wouldn't shame a grown man, that wouldn't. She spread her thighs wide and guided him inside her and closed her thighs tightly round his waist, and together they made excited young love for a short while, before the boy shuddered between her legs and pressed his cheek against hers and hugged her tightly and tensed and gasped and then slowly relaxed in her arms, his face pressed against her breasts. A few moments later he was asleep.

She looked down and stroked his tousled hair. "Typical," she whispered.

"And how was that, you little monkey?" cried the girl's mother, grabbing him round the waist. "You been outside with my daughter, I know you have, rifling through her treasures like a little bandit. I knew you for a little robber the moment I saw you outside. And I know what you've been up to, smile like that, like puss with the milk. Like a hedgehog at a young cow's udders, look at you, almost licking your lips you are."

"Mother, don't embarrass him," said the girl.

"Embarrass him? He knows well enough what he's been up to," she laughed. "And I know what he's been up to, too, eh? Boy that age, I bet you'd be up for another feather-bed jig later on, eh, my sweetheart? How's about something a little more grownup later on tonight, hey? A bit of a lying-down dance with her old ma, eh? A bit of moaning at the ceiling and groaning at the moon?"

"Mother!" cried the girl in outrage.

And then the bawdy peasant woman was away, whirling among the dancers with flushed cheeks and saucy eyes, her clay cup of wine held high in the smoky air.

Attila and the girl sat down at the table again, both hungry after their exertions. Under the table he took the girl's hand and squeezed it tight. Save me, he thought. The girl squeezed back and leaned over and whispered in his ear, her slim hot hand resting on the back of his neck, "You sleep in my bed tonight, don't you worry."

There was more formal dancing, with lines of men and women advancing toward each other, exchanging kisses in the center of the hall and retreating again, with giggles and mock bashfulness, eyes shyly averted even from those who had shared their beds the night before.

Then with still greater dignity, and with all the happy solemnity of the old pagan spirit, the little wreathed olive wood Priapus was taken up, and the whole village processed outside to the edge of the woods, where there stood a simple stone shrine. Within, lit by two precious beeswax candles, stood a naked statue of the Great Mother, smiling distantly, with benevolence and power, upon her simple devotees. Both men and women took it in turns to kiss the phallus of Priapus, before the little god was laid reverently between the Great Mother's thighs. A white woolen veil was drawn over the pair, and they were left in discreet privacy for the night, to couple and so to ensure that the Earth herself should be born again in the spring.

No sooner had the villagers stepped back from the shrine, and bowed their heads one last time to their beloved deities, than there came a hoarse cry through the night air, from the hills above. The frenzied words cascaded down upon them, in a voice as cracked and dry as the wind in dead leaves.

The girl leaned close to Attila, so that her soft hair tickled his cheek deliciously, and whispered, "It's a local madman called Holy John."

The boy nodded. "We've met," he said.

"Idolators! Fornicators!" cried Holy John. "May Christ have mercy upon all your Christless and unshriven souls! For ye dwell in the very mouth of Hell, and are mired in the very mire of the devil's own bowels in all your lusts and filthy fornications."

The people looked at each other and guffawed merrily. Some even began to dance, as if his words were a kind of irresistible music.

"Holy John," they cried, raising their foaming mugs of wine as if in salutation. "Holy John, come down from the mountain. Welcome to our Feast of the Great Mother, Holy John."

There was a scuffling in the woods above, and the old man appeared, standing on a jutting rock, looking more wild eyed than ever, Attila thought. He wore a long, begrimed habit of coarse brown stuff, his gray beard was matted, and his thin lips worked in a fury. Even from this distance, the boy thought he could smell the old man's rank odor: many hermits took literally the injunction of St. Jerome: that those who have washed in the blood of Christ have no need to wash again.

"Woe unto you, O Israel, for your filthiness is in your skirts. And, as the prophet Ezekiel saith, you have committed harlotries, and have lusted after your paramours, whose members are like the members of donkeys, and whose emissions are like the emissions of stallions."

"Where? Where?" cried one of the women in the crowd. "I could do with some of that!"

"Wherefore I say unto you—"

But already Holy John upon his rock was being besieged, first by loud obscene cries, so that his cracked and ancient voice was drowned, and then in person, by the girl's mother, who to the approving roar of the onlookers hauled her considerable bulk up onto the rock below Holy John, and tried to lift his skirts.

"Away from me, thou Scarlet Woman!" cried Holy John, trying frantically to hold down his habit which she had hauled up over his scrawny, scabbed old knees, and he continued to preach with what dignity he could muster. "Avaunt thee, O thou Jezebel, without sense or shame!"

The crowd was in uproar, until eventually the two of them, hermit and peasant woman, came shuffling in a close-knit but inelegant dance to the edge of the rock and fell in a heap into the crowd below. Some of the sturdier younger men tried to catch them as best they could. No harm was done, and soon Holy John was staggering to his feet again. He retrieved his staff in a fury, and was about to stride off to a safe distance at the edge of the forest when his blazing eyes fell on the face of Attila who stood nearby, watching with great interest.

Holy John seemed horror struck. His bony forefinger pointed, trembling, at the startled boy. "Behold, behold, for the End of Years is upon you!" he cried.

The crowd fell silent, curious and a little taken aback by the sudden note of fear in the hermit's voice.

"For is it not written, in the Book of Daniel, that the king's daughter of the south shall come to the king of the north, to make an agreement? Aye, and has this not happened in our time, with the daughter of the late Emperor Theodosius, whom they call the Princess Galla Placidia, wedded now to the King of the Goths?"

The crowd stirred and looked uncertain. Such news meant little to them, but a prophecy fulfilled meant much. Attila looked struck by the news: he took a gasp of air, scowling in a fury at some private vision before him.

"Aye, and is it not written, in the same Prophecy of Daniel, that at the End of Years, a Prince of Terror shall come from the North, and shall utterly destroy you? For he shall come like a whirlwind, with chariots and with many horsemen, and shall overthrow the kingdoms of all the world. And he shall do according to his will, and shall magnify himself above all gods, and shall speak marvelous things even against the God of gods; for he shall magnify himself above all." Holy John's voice rose to a demented shriek, and his finger trembled even more violently in the boy's face. "And upon his face are the marks of his violence. See, see: he comes. He comes!"

At which the boy, to the stunned surprise of the assembled villagers, lashed out and struck the holy man a terrific blow across his face. Holy John staggered backward, but he did not fall. He leaned, gasping, on his staff a little while, blood trickling from his mouth and over his beard. Then he turned and stumbled away until he reached the shadowy edge of the forest. In the gloom they could hardly see him, and wished to see him no more. But still they heard his ancient, dried-out voice, taunting them.

"Oh, ye are the children of very daemons. Ye are all in the devil's own mouth, and shall be damned perpetually. And your gods and goddesses are the devils out of Hell, one with Moloch and Ishtar and Ashtaroth, whom I shall not name before the Most High God, but Great Whores all, whose only worship is itself a whoring and a fornicating and a revelling in the filthiness of women and of. . . ."

But at this the mood turned ugly. The people of the village were merrily impervious to the insults that Holy John or his fellow Christians hurled at them personally, but could not bear such attacks upon their most treasured mysteries, least of all on the night of the Feast of the Great Mother, and within the hearing of the goddess herself. No matter how festive their mood, they would not countenance Holy John coming down from the mountain and calling their beloved Great Mother, who gave them life and fed them all, a whore. Some of the younger men ran toward Holy John with a mind to give him a beating and a lesson. The old man evidently decided that, on this occasion at least, the one true and vengeful Lord God of Israel could not be relied upon to pluck him out and miraculously save him from this sinful crowd of idolators and fornicators, as He had once saved the Prophet Daniel in the lions' den. He swirled round and, with a surprising turn of speed for a man of his years, dashed away into the woods and was lost to sight.

The girl and Attila walked slowly back toward the village, side by side.

"Why did he say that to you?" she asked. "About the End of Years and everything?"

He shrugged. "I don't know."

She glanced sideways at him. "Where *are* you from, anyway?"

There was a pause, and then he said, "From the north." He grinned wolfishly at her in the darkness. "A Prince of Terror from the North."

She eyed him skeptically, and took his hand again. "Come on then, my Prince of Terror. Time for another conquest."

What he hadn't realized was that, in these poorer parts, although the girl had her own pallet to sleep on, her entire family slept in a single room, up above the animals. Fortunately, perhaps, her entire family consisted of only her mother and her younger sister, the thin, pale, watchful girl with the dark-shadowed eyes. The father had died some years back of a wasting fever.

So that when he and his new love were just reaching the heights of transport, he looked over to see both her sister and her mother lying close by, watching with smiles on their faces, and even whispering to each other about what was going on.

"Mother!" cried the girl, covering them both with a sheet.

"We can still hear you, even so!" cried her mother.

Despite the proximity of the other two females, however, the boy and girl had only an hour or two of fitful sleep that night, and both looked flushed and tired in the morning.

Before the boy took his leave, the girl and her mother gave him a cloth-wrapped bundle of fresh bread, smoked sausage, dried apricots and figs. There was no sign of the younger sister.

"There's a horse tethered at the edge of the wood, round to the west," said the boy. "About half a mile away."

"Whose horse?" said the mother suspiciously.

"Mine, of course," he said. "Only I don't want it anymore. You have it."

"How far away did you st —did you get it from?"

"A long way away," said the boy. "Don't worry, it's fine. It's a good horse."

"Well, the Goddess bless you," said the woman, still a little uncertain. "What'll you do for the journey?"

"Oh, I'll soon st —I mean, find another."

The woman tutted and muttered a protective oath. The girl just smiled. Her Prince of Terror, her tattered outlaw.

The sun was rising in the east, the morning star its herald still visible, and the cockerels were still crowing, when the boy left them waving after him at the cottage door.

The younger sister was waiting for him in the woods beside the path leading north into the hills. The low eastern sun slanted in through the trees, pouring coppery light over the ground padded with fallen pine needles.

She leaned back against a tree. Not a word was spoken between them. How frail she looked compared with her buxom sister, gazing up at him with her large, pensive eyes. When she raised her arms for him to take off her shift, she started to cough painfully. Her breasts were small and tender, her hair long and lank but sweet smelling, for she had brushed it with rosemary water that morning, before dawn, for him.

She lifted her long hair in her slim hands and trailed it round the back of his neck, smiling shyly. They kissed. Her smile was wan and far-away. She touched his scarred cheeks. They kissed again. A little patch of her long dark hair was gray, just above her ear, as gray as an old woman's. He touched it gently. She tried to push him away but he stroked her hair again, with its strange gray mark.

At last she whispered, "My sister is more beautiful."

But he shook his head and kissed her again.

She looked into his eyes, the gold-flecked, slanted eyes of this strange, alien boy with the blue tattooed cheeks. She saw his desire for her, and at that her own desire burned, too. She leaned back against the sun-warmed tree trunk, wondering with a thrill at her own shamelessness, and slowly drew up her skirt, her eyes downcast.

Afterward, as she walked down the path to the village, she looked back over her shoulder. He took a step after her, quite unconsciously. In that moment, even his deep, deep longing for home was overcome by his longing for this thin, pale girl with her large, sad eyes. It was as much as he could do to stop himself running after her, and, and. . . . With the other girl he had felt a hot, mind-numbing surge of his blood, but with this girl he felt it in his heart—and how it ached, so painful and so sweet. She smiled and waved to him, and he waved back. She turned away and walked on down to the village.

He looked after her for a long time, even when she had vanished from sight. He wanted to run after her and protect her from other men, and monsters, and demons, witches, and storms, and whatever else might ever come to threaten her gentle flesh. He wanted wolves and bears to appear from the forest, so that he could run after her and protect her, draw his sword and kill them all in front of her, even if he should die himself in doing so. It would be such a sweet death.

Eventually, he turned back and began to ascend the long path to the north.

When he at last emerged from the woods on to the free, grassy, wind-blown hills, his heart leaped furiously within him, and his heated blood surged again. He flung his arms wide to catch the burly, buffeting wind, and he bellowed over the pale, wintry valley below that he wanted to conquer the whole world, and have every woman in it. Then he ran madly on until the air grew chill and seared his lungs, and drove his blood more and more madly through his veins, laughing and roaring as he ran higher and higher into the mountains.

Early one morning, not long after Attila had left the village, a troop of soldiers rode in from the Palatine fort near Ravenna. They were led by an officer with a face so scarred and lopsided that he made the children cry and run from him. Even the ragged dogs of the village yelped and hid under carts or in the shelter of cottage doorways.

He called his troop to a halt in the center of the village, beside the thatch-roofed well. The people emerged from their humble dwellings spontaneously at this new arrival, murmuring among themselves. He said not a word but only held his hand up. His fingers were heavy with signet rings. The people fell silent. His horse stepped sideways and its breath trumpeted into the frosty air. The officer looked around and then spoke.

"We are here on the orders of General Heraclian. You have entertained a fugitive from Roman law in this village. A boy of some fourteen summers, with barbarian tattoos on his cheeks and his back. Where is he?"

The people tried not to look at each other, but some failed. The officer saw everything. He turned to his burly decurion and nodded. The decurion vaulted from his horse, strode over to the nearest hut, and emerged a few moments later with a flaming brand taken from an open fire.

"I will not ask a second time," said the officer. "Answer me."

The plump-faced miller said, "We know of no such boy, Your Honor. We are only simple—"

The officer nodded to two more of his men. "Bind him."

They dismounted and seized the miller's arms, wrenched them behind him, and tied them tightly with coarse rope. The miller, strong man though he was, could not suppress a muted howl at the agony he felt.

The other villagers eyed each other in open fear, but none of them could bear to betray one who had so recently been their guest. Every custom and law of hospitality rebelled against it. Inwardly, even now, they braced themselves for the inevitable punishment they would suffer for their insolent silence. They had had dealings with the enforcers of Roman law before, when they came round each season to collect the village's meager but hard-felt contribution to the imperial exchequer. Every taxation left them a little poorer, a little more bitter. Nothing they paid in tax ever came back to them, in kind, in protection, in security. They saw nothing for their money. Only their quiet, unknown valley kept them safe from the depredations of the wider world. Except when the representatives of the Roman state came to visit.

The officer read the situation with cruel exactness. He kicked his horse and rode over to one of the barns, lifting a spear from the grasp of one of his troopers as he passed. In the doorway of a barn crouched a furry, tatty-eared little dog, his brown eyes never leaving the lieutenant for a moment. But even so he was not quick enough. As the officer rode by, with an icy nonchalance that appalled even the most tough-minded of the villagers, he jabbed the point of his spear downward and impaled the dog on the end, then wheeled and rode back toward the center of the village square, the poor creature howling with its last breath as he came.

The officer rested the spear with its horrible load on the edge of the well, blood dripping slowly from the dog's body and darkly staining the stone lip of the well.

"No!" cried one or two of the villagers, stepping forward, unable to believe that anyone could be so savage.

The officer said, "The boy?"

They stopped in their tracks, and hung their heads in anger and shame, and said nothing.

The officer looked back at the dark mouth of the well. And then he drew back his arm, and scraped the blood-soaked corpse of the dog from the end of his spear. The clotted mass of fur and blood rested for a moment on the lip of the well, and then rolled and tumbled over. A moment later they heard a heavy splash, and the whole village gave a low, collective moan.

The officer turned to his decurion, who still carried the flaming brand. "Fire the hay barn," he said evenly.

At this the girl's mother waddled forward in a fury, unable to contain herself. She screamed at the officer that he was a disgusting pig of a man, and a disgrace to humankind, and that surely the gods and the goddesses who looked down, would—She was cut short by a swinging back-handed blow, the officer's heavily ringed fist sending her spinning to the ground.

"Mother!" cried the girl, running forward.

"I'm all right, m'dear," she mumbled, struggling up from the dust, her mouth bleeding profusely. "Unlike this disgusting pig of a man will be soon enough, God willing."

"Sssh, mother, please," pleaded the girl.

The officer ignored her.

The woman was helped away by her daughter. "Well," she said, "that tooth he's knocked out was giving me grief anyhow. Hurt like crazy in me poor old skull, it did."

No one else had the courage, or the foolhardiness, to protest openly, much as they might admire their neighbor for her sharp-tongued bravery. But in their hearts—those hearts as sturdy and enduring as the hearts of peasants everywhere—the more they saw their liberty abused and their property destroyed, the more silently, woodenly rebellious they became. At the outset, one or two of them might have considered telling soldiers which path the barbarian boy had taken into the mountains, in exchange for a quiet life. But now not one of them would dream of it. Their water might be polluted, their precious winter fodder for their cattle might be burning before their eyes, and the great hay barn, which had taken the whole village two weeks of hard labor to build, might be reduced to ash. But not one of them now would cooperate with these wretched, bullying minions of the state.

The soldiers did not stay to watch the barn burn to the ground. Once the flames had taken inextinguishable hold, they regarded their work as well done.

The officer looked over the cowed but undefeated villagers. "We will be back tomorrow," he said. "And then you will tell us what we want to know."

The villagers huddled together more closely than ever that night, but not a voice was raised in dissent. They would take whatever was meted out to them, and they would say nothing. Nothing would break them.

Some say that the peasants and country people have no sense of honor, and care only for brute survival. They say that a peasant will do anything, say anything, swear any oath or betray any friendship, to save himself and his family and his few precious animals. And it is true, perhaps, that honor is a virtue that only the rich can afford. A poor country girl in the city is quickly obliged to choose between her honor and her life. But in place of honor, the peasant nurtures a passion less overt, but every bit as fierce and intractable: a loathing for being told what to do.

General Heraclian's soldiers did not return the next day. Nor the day after that. Their promise to do so had been only an idle threat, intended to terrorize recalcitrant villagers and remind them of their lowly status in the heaven-appointed scheme of things. The troop had already moved on after the barbarian boy, taking up fresh trails where they could. The villagers set about rebuilding their barn, draining and cleaning their well, gathering and drying what further winter fodder they could from the surrounding land that kept them. They would not see the soldiers again until the spring and the next levy of taxes. Meanwhile they could live in poverty and peace.

11

COMPANIONS ON THE ROAD

Attila remained happily unaware that the soldiers of Rome followed so closely on his trail. He even managed to push to the back of his mind the bewildering news that Galla Placidia had married the King of the Goths; and that the Eternal City would not be destroyed after all, but would triumph yet again, to subdue, civilize, and finally Romanize her Gothic conquerors themselves. But at least now the Huns would know who their enemies were: everyone.

Despite the complications and treacheries of the wider world, as the boy saw them in the fierce simplicity of his adolescent heart, still that heart sang within him with youthful lust and longing, and sometimes he sang aloud as he walked the dusty goat paths of Italy toward home.

One bright morning he was walking along a stony path with cliffs rising high to his right, and steep pine-clad slopes falling away to his left, through which he had just climbed, along a winding, zigzag path. He had stopped for breath and was staring up into the eternal blue sky. He thought he could hear something—the sound of horses' hooves approaching. He wondered if he ought to get off the path to be safe, but he lingered, peering a little longer, to see if he could glimpse who it was, coming through the sparse pines below.

His blood froze with horror. On the bend in the path immediately beneath him, a full cavalry troop of Roman horsemen, Palatine guards in their ominous black armor, was walking steadily up the hill toward him. The leader kept his eyes steadily, almost lazily on the ground beside his horse, taking in every slightest sign that the boy's light feet had made. Immediately behind the tracker rode the officer of the troop in his black plumed helmet, his terrifying visage deeply scarred and half collapsed from where an enemy blade had severed his cranial nerves.

Attila whirled round in uncharacteristic panic. He knew now, deep in his heart, that they meant to kill him. This time they would not bind him with ropes and drag him back to the emperor or his sister for imprisonment again. This time they would stretch him over the nearest rock and hack his head from his body.

He thought as he ran. The horsemen would be round the corner in moments, and the instant they saw him they would gallop forward and bring him down with their spears, and he would be done for. Dashing down into the woods would take him nearer them. The only alternative was the cliff to his right, but that was a crumbling golden limestone wall of forty feet or more—unscalable, surely?

There was no more time to hesitate. Silent as a deer stepping through woodland, he crept into the pines and moved along, only a few paces above the horsemen. He heard one of them say how close they were to him now, how fresh the trail marks were. He stopped breathing for a moment. Then he moved deeper into the forest alongside the path, hoping to find refuge in the green gloom of the pines. He was so intent on watching the cavalry that he almost forgot to look ahead. When he did he saw only woodland ahead of him, but he felt in his blood that something wicked was coming steadily toward him. He could hardly bear to look, wanting to tear his eyes away. And when he did, he nearly cried out in terror. Before him on the narrow woodland path, walking silently toward him with eyes fixed, were more of the soldiers in black armor, on foot, their swords drawn, their faces terrifyingly expressionless. They might have been the ghosts of soldiers rather than men of flesh and blood.

Gasping with fright, his blood hammering, the boy flung himself off the path and into the trees, scrambling uphill to the stony track above. As he burst out onto it the cavalry troop rounded the corner and saw him. It must have been the officer's voice, harsh and authoritative, that called out to him. But he was already scrabbling at the cliff face. A shard of dust-dry limestone came away in his frantically grasping hands, and he could hear the sound of the horsemen trotting easily toward him. They were almost upon him. One of them was already slicing his thick sword blade through the air.

With a cry Attila ducked lithely under the horse's neck, swerved and ran on a little farther. To his right he saw a crevice in the cliff, a tiny valley carved by millennia of water running from the hills above, a single scrawny juniper bush guarding the entrance. He scrambled into the crevice, dragged himself behind the juniper bush, and gazed up: the damp, steep crevice ran all the way up the cliff. But it was impossible to ascend. The limestone was slick as oiled skin where the water cascaded down, and crumbling dry where it did not. Behind him he could hear the men dismounting and the officer telling them to get on in there and bring him out. He whipped round in desperation. His hand fell on the pommel of his sword. If he must die here, trapped like a hunted animal in a crevice in the rocks, he would at least try to take one of them with him.

Something touched his cheek. He whipped round again, and found to his astonishment that it was a thin rope, knotted at regular intervals for grip. The soldiers were just the other side of the sentinel juniper bush, hacking at its branches to get through. Without questioning this miracle, the boy clutched the rope as a drowning man would clutch a spar of wood, and crawled up it in a trice. He came to a narrow ledge about fifteen feet above the ground, and rolled free onto it. Looking down, he saw the soldiers at the foot of the rope, gazing up in amazement. One began to climb up after him, but now he had a chance—just the one chance, just one slender advantage. He tore his sword free from his scabbard and slashed at the rope at the edge of the ledge. In two swift strokes it was severed, and the soldier tumbled back down to the ground, angry but uninjured. Immediately there were yells for their comrades to bring more rope and some spearhafts. They would not be long in pursuing.

Lying flat on his belly for fear of sly arrows, Attila looked around the narrow ledge, still too dazed with terror to think rationally about the presence of the rope. The back of the ledge was damp and dark, overshadowed by the huge overhang of the cliff above. He wriggled toward it. It was as black as pitch. He hated confined spaces. It was his secret terror. For a second, he felt he would rather die than have to squeeze himself into so confined a space. But he gritted his teeth, and even grunted at himself in fury, and pushed himself in under the overhang. The narrow horizontal gap in the rock was just enough for him to wriggle through, and then he was inside the cliff itself, rolling downward several feet to a halt. He had no idea where he was, for the narrow slit in the rock admitted no light. His terrified gasps told him, however, that he was in a cave or a chamber of some size, for they echoed back at him from all sides.

Against the dim light of the slit in the rock he saw the silhouettes of soldiers who had shinned up to the ledge and were working out where he had gone. He felt sure none of them would be able to crawl through after him, so with a mix of fear, courage, and pulsing hatred he crawled back up the slope to the crack in the rock like a lizard, hands and feet moving alternately, his sword blade gripped between his teeth. As he reached the crevice, and drew the sword blade from his teeth, a soldier's face appeared just outside and peered in unseeing. Attila drew back his sword and thrust it forward through the crevice, straight into the soldier's face. No scorpion under a rock ever gave a more terrible sting. The soldier howled with agony, clutching his hands to his face, which spurted gore between his splayed fingers, and tumbled backward. A few moments later, a muffled thump told the boy that he had rolled off the ledge to the ground below. Attila heard distant shouts and roars of anger, and he bared his teeth like a wolf in the darkness. Then he turned and crawled back down the slope to his unseen cave.

After some time, the sounds of the soldiers died away. But Attila was no fool. He would not emerge from that cave for at least a day.

He found by touch a place on the wall where water trickled down from the rock above, and he put his tongue to it and drank what he could. The water tasted green and slimy, but it would do. It would keep him alive a little longer. He would survive. He would always survive.

He crouched all day in the cave, his arms wrapped tightly round his knees. When night came, even the sliver of daylight through the crevice vanished, and he was in utter darkness. His fear of enclosed spaces came back to him with full force, and he imagined the most terrible of things. He imagined a deep, distant rumbling of rock, and then the overhang shifting, just a few inches, and his escape route being sealed forever. He would sit in absolute darkness, unable to see or move, and scream until he died.

But he gritted his teeth and willed himself to sit out the night. If he returned to the crevice and the upper air, the soldiers would be waiting, and they would drag him out like a rat from a hole, and crowd around to drive their swords into him with all their anger and frustration. He screwed his eyes shut so that at least he had the light of the red and green stars that played upon his eyeballs, and he waited.

He awoke from troubled dreams when he heard a scuttling in the darkness. A bat, he told himself. But it was bigger than a bat. It was more of a shuffling. He prayed that it was not a cave bear. He prayed to Astur his father in the eternal blue sky that there was not another entrance to the cave, and that a monstrous cave bear had not returned home, its dark fur glistening with blood.

He drew his sword and stared into the darkness, but it was like trying to see through tar. He couldn't make out so much as his hand in front of his face. He had the horrible feeling that someone—some *thing*—was at this very moment squatting malevolently, immediately in front of him, its face only inches from his own, its black eyes boring into his, its long fangs dripping. He even dared to sniff the air a little, hoping against hope. . . . He smelt no foul carnivorous breath, nothing but damp cave air. Yet still he could hear the snuffling noise, and it was coming closer.

He thought of his people's stories about foul creatures which lived in darkness and crept out at night to crawl through the trees, or fly through the night air with their outstretched bats' wings. They alighted under the eaves of lonely cottages to sniff the air, crawling inside to fix their sharp fangs into the soft flesh and to drink the blood of babies, leaving them only a black and withered dried-out husk in their cot, to be found by their screaming mothers in the morning. Perhaps the sound was one of those ghastly vampires, flesh moon white and translucent, eyes like jelly, scuttling home to sleep with a bellyful of babies' blood. He pressed himself against the wall and held his sword more tightly. You could not kill a vampire, they said. Metal would pass through it as it would pass through mist. And when they had sucked your blood, you became one of them.

He heard a weird, high-pitched cry that was almost a scream, and he could have sworn, though it was impossible in the night, that it was the high, lonely cry of a sparrow hawk. Or maybe a vampire . . .

But it was no vampire who spoke from the darkness beyond. It was the voice of, he guessed, a young boy.

"Pelagia!" the voice whispered. "Are you all right?"

Attila kept silent. There was no other noise.

"Pelagia!"

There was another pause, and then beyond the entrance of the cave there came a soft scraping. Suddenly against the blackness there flared a small yellow flame, and by its dim light, Attila saw a slim, grimy hand reach in, followed by the body of a young boy, two or three years his junior, gripping a spear in his other hand. He set the flickering lamp on a stone ledge and looked around. The instant he saw Attila he crouched lower and aimed his spear straight at his belly.

"If you have touched her," he hissed. "If you have harmed her in *any way.* . . ."

"Who?" whispered Attila, bewildered, but keeping his sword up in readiness all the same.

The boy glanced across the cave, and there, by the dim light of the little lamp, Attila saw for the first time that there was a roll of blankets against the wall opposite.

The boy said no more but scuttled over to the blankets and drew back the edge very gently. Attila realized to his astonishment that he had shared the cave all night with a young girl, and had never known a thing. The poor waif must have been terrified, yet he had never heard her breathe, let alone scream. She was only about six or seven, and her face was pale and drawn. The boy leaned down, kissed her forehead and whispered a prayer of thanks. The girl turned her head where she lay and looked across at Attila, her eyes huge in her thin face, her lips pale and bloodless.

"He killed a man," she whispered. "A soldier. Over there."

"That was the blood on the ledge?" said the boy jumpily. "That was your doing?"

Attila nodded. "I didn't know anyone else was in here. I was hiding."

"Well, so are we. You an escaped slave as well?"

Attila suppressed the lofty contempt that he felt at this slur on his ancestry. "No," he said with as much evenness as he could muster. "I'm a . . . from the north. I was taken as a prisoner of war. I'm going back to my people."

"Beyond the Great River? You mean, beyond the empire?"

Attila nodded.

The boy stared at him. Like his sister, he had wide, staring, hare-like eyes, although he looked healthy enough. Skinny and undernourished, maybe, nervy and excitable, but well enough for a runaway slave.

He said, "Pelagia and me—I'm Orestes, by the way—we ran away."

"They were horrid," whispered Pelagia. "And fat. And the mistress of the house used to stick pins in us if we didn't work hard enough, or if we spilled anything."

Orestes nodded rapidly. "Actual pins. In our arms, or in the backs of our hands. So we ran away."

Attila smiled. "Well, that's three of us."

Orestes stared at Attila a while longer, then he said, "Can we come with you?"

"Not really. I go much faster than you. Anyway," he added, a little brutally, "your sister's not well."

"How do you know she's my sister?"

"You look the same."

The boy nodded again. "Yeah, well, she is my sister. She'll be all right." He leaned over her: she seemed to be asleep again, her breathing fast and shallow. "You'll see."

"You didn't come across any soldiers out there?"

Orestes shook his head.

Attila grunted. "Well, soon as it's dawn I'm off. I wish you luck."

"There's another way out of the cave if you need it. Just be safe. Down there." He pointed.

"Well why didn't you tell me before?" he said with some anger.

The boy stared wide eyed at him for a little while longer, then lay down to sleep beside his sister.

Attila had only been walking a mile or so, in the gray light of dawn, when he heard footsteps behind him. He hid up and waited, and soon there came in sight the boy Orestes, hand in hand with his sister. Their faces were bright in the chilly early air, their cheeks flushed. Pelagia's were too flushed, red with hectic spots.

Attila waited for them, then stepped out. "I told you," he said.

"Have you got any food?" asked Orestes. "We're really hungry, Pelagia especially."

Attila looked at the girl, and then back at the boy. Reluctantly he reached into his leather bag and handed them some stale bread. "It's all I've got," he said.

They broke it in two and began to eat. The girl chewed slowly and painfully, but she ate it all.

"Thanks," said Orestes.

"It was nothing," said Attila sourly. He walked on.

The two children walked on behind him.

After awhile, he turned back and said, "That noise you made, outside the cave, like a sparrow hawk. That was you, wasn't it?"

The boy nodded proudly. "We use it as a signal. I'll teach you if you like."

Attila struggled with his pride a while, and then said grudgingly, "It was a pretty good imitation. Go on, then."

"All right," said the boy. "You use a blade of grass. You take it between your thumbs and . . ."

They made slower progress now there were three of them, but they managed to steal more food and rest up on warm days in the woods or the hills. The Greek slave boy talked endlessly, until Attila had to ask him to shut up. Pelagia seemed to grow in strength again. She even began to put on a little weight.

"You're good at stealing," she told him when he returned one night from yet another lonely farmhouse with a flask of thin wine, some bread, salt pork, dried beans, and even a purloined wood pigeon, ready roasted.

"It's my greatest talent," he said.

"You could be a proper thief when you grow up."

"Thanks," he said.

"I'm going to be in a circus," said the little girl. "And ride on a bear.

I saw it once, in a circus. We were only allowed to sit right at the top, so we were a long way from the arena, but I saw a woman riding on a bear. She was very beautiful, and she had long blonde hair and her robes were orangey and gold, like a queen's." She tore off a big chunk of pigeon. "Then they put some people to death and everybody cheered, but that was boring, and we were too far away to see much, anyway. And when we got home the mistress stuck pins in our arms because we were late." She swallowed the chunk of pigeon meat without chewing properly, and nearly choked. Attila banged her on the back. "Bless you," she said when she had composed herself again, wiping her watery eyes. "We will serve you when you get home. Are you rich?"

"Fabulously," said Attila.

"Fabulously," she repeated. "Fabulously rich." She liked that word.

He said, "In fact, I am a prince. My father's house is built of pure gold, and even my slaves are dressed in robes of silk."

She nodded. "Do you have bears?"

Little girls are *weird,* thought Attila. "Hundreds," he said. "We ride them everywhere, like other people ride horses."

Pelagia nodded again. "That's settled, then. We will be your servants when we get to your kingdom."

12

REST ON HER LIGHTLY,
EARTH AND DEW

They came down from the mountains and crossed the plains of the Po in the frosty start of the new year. Attila dreaded leading them up into the towering white peaks of the Julian Alps at such a season, but they must move on. They had made it so far because there were so many refugees on the roads, so many alarms and rumors sweeping the country, so many tales of the Goths, and even the dreadful Vandals, still on the warpath, and the emperor going mad in his marsh-bound palace.

No one had stopped to question three ragged children on the road along with all the others. Yet. But it only needed one soldier to block their path with his spear, to demand of the oldest boy why he kept his face covered, and to rip the rags away and see his bright, tattooed cheeks, and his slanted, leonine eyes. It was well known what punishment was meted out to runaway slaves, no matter what their age might be. First, the letters F U G would be branded with a red-hot iron on their foreheads, for *fugitivus*. Then the real punishments would begin. . . .

They must press on. They would not be safe until they had crossed the snowy peaks of the Julian Alps and the mountains of Noricum, and come down into the Pannonian plain, and finally crossed the wide brown waters of the swollen winter Danube to freedom.

They passed by Verona, and keeping near to the flat coast passed by east of Patavum. At last they halted by the roadside, weak with hunger and weariness, and a cold wind blew in from the lagoons to the east, and from the mountains of Illyria beyond. The three children shook with hunger and fatigue, and the little girl was racked with coughing, as if her very ribs would break. Orestes had asked again and again if they couldn't steal some horses, but Attila replied that they would draw too much attention to themselves that way, now that they were out on the more populated plains of the Po. They must walk on, like all the other thousands of nameless fugitives on the roads of Northern Italy. But they could not walk on. They were exhausted.

As they rested, a great gilt carriage, flanked by numerous bodyguards, came down the dusty road, heading for the famous city of Aquileia on the shores of the Adriatic Sea. It drew up alongside the huddled children. Inside sat a handsome, clean-shaven man with gold signet rings flashing on his fingers. He stared at them for a little while, and a smile gradually crept over his face. Pelagia, at least, smiled back, and then had another fit of coughing. The man touched his hand to his mouth, and began to question the children from within his carriage. At first the two boys were wary and suspicious, and only wished that he would leave them alone. But after a little while he won their confidence, and even Attila, usually so acutely sensitive to danger, was taken in; perhaps his senses were dulled by hunger and exhaustion. After a few minutes, the children were persuaded and taken with the wealthy man and his train into Aquileia.

A few wealthy men, a very few, might put themselves out in a charitable way for a trio of travel-sore little guttersnipes, none too sweet smelling, and coarse in their manners and address. But the great majority of such men, suddenly overcome by an apparent excess of charitable feelings which they have signaly failed to display hitherto, will have another, rather less amiable motive behind the benevolent mask of their charity. So it was with this man, the richest citizen in Aquileia, a merchant and dealer in everything from horses to ships, from cinnamon to silk, from pepper to papyrus to perfumed beeswax candles. Surprisingly, perhaps, given what transpired later that day and on into the night, in his private bathhouses at his villa in Aquileia, guarded at every entrance by his expressionless, highly paid bodyguards; surprisingly, given what he called his "Tiberian theatricals," which the three children were forced to enact, sometimes at the point of a dagger, for his purring delectation; surprisingly, this good citizen was also a family man. Indeed, he was the head and *paterfamilias* of the Neriani, a clan who had dominated the finances and politics of that wealthy trading city on the shores of the Adriatic for generations, and would continue to do so for a generation more—until a whirlwind came out of the east, and visited Aquileia with a punishment as terrible as any city has suffered in history.

No one ever understood the motive for that atrocious punishment, a punishment Carthaginian in its finality. It might have been better understood if those who were baffled by it had seen that rich merchant on the road to Aquileia, taking the two poor vagabond boys and the little girl into his carriage, and flattering them with promises, soothing them with candied sweetmeats and little goblets of honeyed wine.

After Aquileia, bound and blindfolded, the three children were galloped out of the city gates in the middle of the night, and dumped some miles away beside a remote farmtrack. There they were left to die—for it was extremely unlikely that they would find the strength and will to crawl along the track until they could find at least the edge of a stone sharp enough to fray the vicious cords that cut into their wrists. But strength and will they did find, under the furious urgings of the eldest. Once free, they stumbled some way in the starless darkness, and finally collapsed together in a half-ruined sty, to dream their dreams or their nightmares until dawn.

None of them spoke that night, nor all the following day. None of them ever talked about Aquileia again. Orestes and Pelagia trudged wearily on up the track to the north, and the cool, clean air of the mountains across the plains of the Po. There they would find crystal-clear streams to wash in. But Attila looked down at his wrists, at the blood still oozing through the abused and broken skin where the flaxen cords had cut in. Then he turned and looked back at Aquileia, reclining richly in the bright winter sun: the Bride of the Sea, the Queen of the Adriatic. And he swore in his heart that one day he would return and that his return would be the stuff of that city's nightmares. His heart was set as hard as stone. One day . . .

The two boys recovered in time, at least in their flesh. But Pelagia did not.

They had gained the foothills of the Julian Alps, and washed that day in a freezing but clear mountain stream. In the cold frosty night Attila awoke to the sound of Pelagia's rasping cough. Orestes was already awake beside her, his face drawn with worry.

"It's too cold for her," he said. "It's her lungs. We need shelter."

"Tomorrow night, maybe," said Attila. "There are no lights in this valley for miles. There's no choice."

Orestes watched his sister cough and gasp for breath. After a little while, he drew off his own blanket and laid it over her. Then he curled up against her and closed his eyes and began to shiver.

Attila watched a while longer. Then he drew off his own blanket and got up and went over and laid it over her likewise. He lay down on the other side of her, and closed his eyes, and began to shiver.

Some nights they begged successfully for shelter, or the suspicious country people allowed them at least to sleep in their barns, and gave them a bowl of vegetable pottage at dawn. Some days Pelagia seemed better. And some days not. One morning she awoke and coughed so violently that flecks of blood flew from her mouth and spotted her hands and arms, and she wept with fear. Her brother cradled her to his chest and said that she would get better soon. When spring came and when it got warmer, she would feel better. It was just a winter cold. She looked at him with her huge, orphan eyes and said nothing.

Not long afterward, Attila awoke to the early dawn and saw Orestes sitting beside his sister, his knees drawn up to his chest and his arms hugged tightly round them. Attila called to him, but Orestes didn't stir. He called again, and finally the Greek slave boy looked up. His face was streaked with tears.

They dug a shallow trench as best they could, and laid Pelagia in it wrapped in a blanket. They found sprigs of rowan and gorse to cover her, and laid rue and the red berries of bryony around her gentle head, and heaped the earth over her. Orestes wept uncontrollably. Attila went into the woods and found a flat piece of bark. He handed it to Orestes with his pocket knife and went away again.

A few minutes later the slaveboy was ready to leave. Attila went over to the small grave of sad dimensions, and read the lettering on the bark: *"Pelagia, much beloved, sleeps with her parents now."*

Attila showed Orestes another piece of bark that he had painstakingly carved with the point of his sword. In one corner was a rough outline of a bear, and below it was an old epitaph on a young slave girl, which his Greek pedagogue had made him learn by heart and which now came back to him in all its simple, heart-wrenching force:

> *Rest on her lightly, earth and dew,*
> *She put so little weight on you.*

Orestes wiped the tears from his eyes and nodded. Attila went over and laid the inscription at the other end of the grave. He bowed his head and said a prayer to his father Astur, the Father of All. Then he went back and stood beside Orestes and waited until he was ready. They walked on together into the mountains.

13

THE DREAMERS OF DREAMS

The two boys walked for many days, climbing higher and higher into the towering Julian Alps. The weather so far was mercifully cool and clear, the air sharp and aromatic with the pines. They spoke little.

Late one afternoon, as the sun was going down in the west, they found themselves forced to descend rather than climb, because of the unassailable steepness of the surrounding mountains. They followed a narrow track which led down into a deep, dark valley where the evening mist was already beginning to settle. They muttered prayers and supplications to their gods under their breath, for each boy felt in his bones that this valley breathed the air of other worlds.

They came to the edge of a dark river which sang none of a river's usual song of mirth and life as it ran, but flowed on in black, inky silence through the heart of the valley, muted and full of foreboding. The river's edge was lined with the mournful, lamenting shapes of willow and aspen, and the mist gathered thick on the water. The boys stepped uneasily through dense growths of small, stunted oak and hawthorn, thickly hung with mosses and lichens that muffled the very air they breathed. Among the rocks grew maidenhair fern, and the pools were thick with marsh horsetail. Not a breath of wind was felt in that dank valley, and no birds sang. They felt that no human being had ever walked here before them.

At last, without a word being spoken, for fear of what terrible guardians of that unholy place their voices might awaken, they settled under the low branches of a tree for shelter, and wrapped their blankets tightly round them. Neither looked at the other, and both felt a profound desolation in their souls. The chilling mist folded in about them and they could see no more than a few feet in front of their faces. They longed to be away again, far away from this demon-haunted valley, to breathe the free, clear air of the mountaintops, and to see before them the long way to the North. But they knew they must first creep through this dread place, silent and un-noticed if they could, for someone, something, was watching them.

Attila was drifting off into fearful but exhausted sleep when at his side Orestes started up.

"What was that?" hissed Orestes, his hare eyes staring.

Attila awoke fully and closed his fingers round his sword hilt. "What?"

"Through the trees. Over there."

But they could see nothing except the eerie shapes of the trees through the wreaths of freezing mist. They looked a little longer, then Attila said, "It was nothing. Go to sleep."

They settled down again and each pretended to be asleep. But both lay wide awake, their limbs trembling, and not only for cold.

The air around them stirred and whispered,

We are the Music Makers,
And we are the Dreamers of Dreams.

The boys shot up and stared wildly around.

Attila, knowing they had been discovered, and feeling that familiar surge of contempt for any injury or death that might come—since come it must, one day—cried out into the all-enveloping mist, "Who are you? What do you want?"

Orestes shrank to hear his companion yell out into the night so fearlessly, but Attila was emboldened by the hot surge of his angry and indignant spirit. He leaped to his feet, brandishing his bright, unsheathed sword and slicing it through the invulnerable mist and darkness.

"Who are you? Come on out and show yourselves!" He held his sword out before him, the muscles in his arms as tense as the blade itself. "Come on!"

The trees around them seemed to pause for a moment, contemplating this small, fierce boy in their midst. Then something happened to the mist between the trees. It drew apart, like a veil, and the gloom and closeness of that haunted valley, which had weighed upon the boys so heavily, lifted a little. There even seemed to be a source of light shining down upon them from above, stronger than any moon could be. They saw a figure standing among the trees a little, way off, and were not afraid.

Orestes immediately thought it was Jesus, come to save them from the surrounding demons of the mist. Attila thought it was perhaps the ghost of his dead mother. But the figure in its long white robe came nearer, and they saw that it was a young girl, her hair braided like that of a priestess.

She came closer still and stopped before them. "She plays in a sunlit field," she said softly, her pale gray eyes never leaving the eyes of Orestes.

"Wha—what?" he stammered.

She reached out and laid her hand on his head, and pushed him down with some force. Orestes knelt at her feet, and the girl said, "Rome bore her, Aquileia destroyed her, Aquileia will be destroyed. But now we see her. She plays in a field of buttercups. And now her mother comes to her and finds her, and they run down to a clear stream. She has made a necklace of daisies for her mother. See how her mother is laughing. And there is a cow, we see a brown cow with glossy flanks, and Pelagia pats its damp nose and laughs."

Attila saw with wonder that tears were coursing down Orestes' cheeks.

"She is happy now," said the girl. "So happy."

A breath of wind blew around them for a moment, and the mist cleared. A gleam of pale sunshine came through from the skies above, for night had passed—in a matter of minutes, it seemed—and the sunshine fell on the kneeling boy, haloing him in the pale gold of dawn light.

There was a long silence. At last the girl took her hand away from Orestes' forehead and slowly he stirred, as if awakening from a long sleep.

The girl turned and walked away into the mist-shrouded trees.

"Wait!" cried Attila.

She walked on.

"Come on," he yelled, grabbing Orestes by the arm and hauling him roughly to his feet.

The two of them stumbled after her into the mist. As they ran, barely able to see the trees before them, they heard the soft voice again, but now it sounded like a mysterious chorus of voices chanting in unison:

We are the Music Makers,
And we are the Dreamers of Dreams,
Wandering by lone sea breakers,
And sitting by desolate streams;
World losers and world forsakers,
On whom the pale moon gleams:
Yet we are the movers and shakers
Of the world forever, it seems.

At last they emerged from the dense mist of the woods, and ran out into a sunlit glade beneath a black, overhanging cliff that towered above their heads. There was the dark opening of a cave at the base of the cliff, and beside it grew a tree which, in the sudden break of early morning sunshine, looked as if its boughs were golden. Attila ran headfirst into the tree before he could stop, and snapped off one of its delicate lower branches with the force of his onward rush. The girl, who had paused in the mouth of the cave, glanced back over her shoulder. When she saw what he had done, the trace of an enigmatic smile crossed her face.

"Well," she said, as if something had been confirmed for her. Then she looked across at the panting Greek boy. "Thus far and no farther for you, greatest friend and greatest betrayer."

Orestes scowled. "What do you mean, 'betrayer?'" he said.

"Greatest friend unto death, and greatest betrayer thereafter." She stretched out her arm toward him. "O little father of the last and least, sleep now."

Without fuss or drama, Orestes trotted over to the edge of the glade where the sunlight caught the edge of the trees, lay down, and instantly fell asleep.

The girl looked at Attila, and the smile vanished from her face. "This is for you alone," she said. She turned and walked into the cave.

At first Attila could just make out the dim white shape of the girl ahead of him, as silent and flowing as a ghost through a graveyard. But very soon it was so dark that he could not even see that much. He simply kept walking, as if into a void, trusting that it was his destiny to do so.

"Follow on, Attila, follow on," chanted the girl mockingly from somewhere ahead, deep in the darkness of the mountains. "For surely you will never follow another again! O leader, O conqueror, O great lord and king!"

The boy did not reply, but followed as bidden.

The walls of rock around him echoed to voices, the girl's voice and manifold voices chanting in the same tone and time. They hailed him, the voices echoing from the dank walls of the mountains, in a tone that he feared, for there was both mockery and supreme knowledge in those chanting voices combined.

"All hail, Attila, son of Mundzuk, Lord of All and None!"

"O Lord of the World from the rising to the setting of the sun!"

"The Eagle and the Serpent fought, and fell in Italy!"

"O Lord of the World from the desert to the shores of the Western Sea!"

The voices grew louder, echoing bewilderingly from every direction as he stumbled on, gritting his teeth in grim defiance, sometimes stumbling against the walls of the passageway and grazing his arms and legs against the cruel and jagged rocks, speckled with mica. His head spun with the words that tumbled in the dank air around him, but he was determined, as determined as ever, not to surrender to fear or force, or ever to halt or turn back.

"In the time of the Seven Sleepers, Lord of All!" cried the voices in deafening unison.

"In the time of the shaking of the City of Gold, Lord of All!"

"In the time of the Last Battle, Lord of All!"

Abruptly the clamor of the voices died, and he saw ahead of him a cave, lit with flickering torches and with a low fire burning in the center, and a single voice whispered in the air around him. The voice was soft and pitying and maternal, and his heart was torn by its sound, for something told him that it was the voice of his mother.

"O Attila," whispered the woman's voice, "O Little Father of Nothing."

The boy emerged shaken into the torchlit cave and found the young girl standing opposite him with both arms outstretched.

She stepped across the fire to him and closed his eyelids with her thumbs. Then she leaned close to him and spat once upon each eyelid. She took up a handful of ash from the edge of the fire, and blew it in his face. When he opened his eyes he was blind. He cried out in fear, but she only told him to sit.

"Seeing eyes be blind, that blind eyes may see!" she said harshly.

Trembling with fear, but still determined neither to weep nor to flee, he sat awkwardly down on the hard stone ground. The air was filled with words, and his blinded vision was filled with images. Images of battle, of cities burning, and the thunderous sound of horses' hooves on the plains. He started in shock when he heard the girl's voice, for now it sounded as ancient and hoarse as if it came from the ancient Sibyl herself. As ancient as Tithonus, who asked for eternal life but not eternal youth, and was granted it, until he grew so old and tiny and withered that he was no more than a chirruping cricket in the grass.

"I have more memories than a thousand years," croaked the voice.

Even in the depths of the mountain, a soft whisper of wind seemed to sigh back among the rocks.

The ancient voice in the cave said,

Four will fight for the end of the world,
One with an empire,
One with a sword,
Two will be saved and one will be heard,
One with a son
And one with a word.

Although dizzy with fear and disorientation, Attila nevertheless felt a thrill of excitement run down his spine. He had a dim sense that he had heard these words before, though he could not remember where, and he found himself thinking of Aeneas's journey to the underworld, which he had once studied wearily under the stern eye of his Greek pedagogue. Now he had the uncanny and terrifying sensation that Virgil's great work was not merely poetry but history, and that the story had gone into reverse, falling backward into chaos and the fiery abyss—and that he was part of it all. . . .

In perfect consonance with his thoughts, the cracked voice in the cave spoke again, saying, "They will call you Anti-Christus, the Scourge of God, but they do not understand. You are not Anti-Christ. You are Anti-Aeneas!" She cackled madly, and told the boy to open his eyes. He did so, feeling the sticky mess of spittle and ash parting over his eyelids. And then his eyes flared wide with horror, as he saw the ancient thing that sat before him in that unhallowed cave.

It was a haggard crone, toothless, blind, and unimaginably old. Her ancient, clawed hands trembled in the firelight, and rheum ran from her blind white eyes and stained the furrows of her parchment cheeks like snail trails. She wore tattered robes as gray as ash. She spat into her withered palms, and her spittle was as thick and black as tar. She looked up at him, and her watery old eyes gleamed sightlessly. "To build a new city you must first destroy the old!" she cried. "But keep the stones perhaps for your foundations!" She paused and when she spoke again her voice was more grave and rasping. "But remember this, and this above all.

> By a King of Kings from Palestine
> Two empires were sown,
> By a King of Terror from the east
> Two empires were o'erthrown. . . .

She leaned forward, and scooped up some ash from the edge of the fireside. Through the dancing flames, her mouth made a toothless, lipless O.

"Only youth is beautiful," she croaked, more softly. "But old age is sometimes wise."

She threw the ash back into the fire, and the cave filled with black smoke. Attila coughed and choked and scrambled to his feet, searching blindly for the exit. But it was useless. When the air cleared again and the torchlight gleamed once more through the dust, he saw only a young girl sitting cross-legged against the wall opposite, her head bowed, as if she were sleeping. Her hands rested tranquilly upon her knees, and they were the smooth, soft, delicate hands of a young girl!

He snatched a torch from the wall, and turned and ran back along the passageway to the upper air.

There was bright sunlight in the glade, and Orestes lay sleeping as peacefully as a little child. Attila shook him and he rubbed his eyes and stared around. When he remembered, a shadow passed over his face, but no more.

He said to Attila, "Your face is a mess. You need a wash."

Attila looked away.

"Is she . . . has she gone? And the voices?"

Attila nodded. "They've gone."

Orestes tore up some grass. "What did you hear from them?"

"Everything. And nothing."

Orestes got to his feet.

Attila said, "We should move on."

As the two boys walked down the valley in the bright winter sunlight, the voices came to them again, sighing through the trembling aspen leaves by the dark and silent river:

We are the Music Makers,
And we are the Dreamers of Dreams,
Wandering by lone sea breakers,
And sitting by desolate streams;
World losers and world forsakers,
On whom the pale moon gleams:
Yet we are the movers and shakers
Of the world forever, it seems.

We, in the ages lying
In the buried past of the earth,
Built Nineveh with our sighing,
And Babel itself with our mirth;
And o'erthrew them with prophesying
To the old of the new world's worth;
For each age is a dream that is dying,
Or one that is coming to birth.

The boys said nothing to each other, as if neither of them had heard. They bowed their heads and walked on.

At last they ascended out of the haunted valley, and began to climb a steep, rocky slope, into the high mountain passes. The slope caught the full force of the winter sun, and was hot even at this time of year, the air rising off the rocks and into the deep blue sky above. Attila paused for breath and gazed into the Eternal Blue Sky, the home of Astur his father. And there hung a lammergeier: lamb stealer, bone breaker, greatest of all the European vultures, almost motionless on the thermals that arose from the sun-heated mountainside. His great wings outspread twelve feet or more, and his head turned slightly from side to side as he surveyed the world beneath him with his bright, fierce, fearless, all-conquering eyes. That god of the sky. That god-made Lord of the World, from the rising to the setting of the sun.

O Little Father of Nothing . . .

"Come on," called Orestes from ahead.

What did it all mean? What did the gods *want?* Other than to be entertained, perhaps, by the sorrows and deaths of men?

Attila lowered his gaze and looked ahead at his friend, and walked on.

14

THE LAST OF THE LEAVES

On a gusty autumn day, Lucius led Tugha Bàn ashore at Noviomagnus, and went to the customs house. A few minutes later he returned and paid the captain in full for his passage. The captain grunted, bit the coins and slipped them into his leather purse. He wished the horse lover well. The horse lover wished him likewise and vanished into the crowds on the quayside.

He rode west down to Dumnonia. The roads were still good, and he felt no fear of bandits. Here, on the far fringes beyond the empire, all seemed peaceful. Britain was returning to being no more than a fogbound little island off the shoulder of Europe, forgotten and at peace. Lucius grinned to himself. It suited him well.

The weather was mellow and there was soft autumn sunlight on the brambles and gleaming on the ripe clusters of blackberries and elderberries as he rode down the narrow lanes toward his own beloved valley, stretching down to the glittering silver sea. Tugha Bàn whinnied with delight, and her flanks rippled and quivered, as she smelt the familiar earth where she had been foaled. The soft autumn wind whispered through the oak woods and the hazel stands and answered her whinnying with its own wordless rapture.

At last he came to his long wooden house, and she appeared in the doorway in her plaid apron, and everything slipped from his grasp, every stern control and strong reserve. He practically fell from his horse, in most ungainly and unsoldierly fashion, and by the time he had found his feet she had flown across the farmyard, faster than it was possible for any woman to move. But her feet did not need to touch the ground. She flew like a homing swallow through the air. Then they were in each other's arms, and it would have been impossible for even the strongest team of horses to pull them apart.

It was many long minutes before the sounds they made to each other made any sense or formed into words, and many of these were repetitive sounds, murmuring echoes: each other's name, repeated over and over again, as if to confirm the miracle of their being there together; and the soft Celtic word *"cariad,"* whispered time and time again between their kisses.

"Ciddwmtarth, cariad . . ."

"Seirian, cariad . . ."

At last they stood back from each other, unable to let go of each other's hands, but able at least to look into each other's eyes without their own eyes blurring, or needing to cling to each other again.

Over her shoulder he saw a little girl with big dark eyes and a mop of dark curls, peeping out of the doorway shyly at him. It was Ailsa. He went to pick her up, but she ran from him. He laughed and turned back to Seirian, and froze to the spot. Her expression . . .

"What is it?" he demanded. And then "Where is Cadoc?"

She crumpled into his arms again, but this time there was no joy or peace in it at all.

They sat late into the night by the light of one flickering tallow candle, their hands entwined, and their hearts finding some comfort in the steady, childish breathing of Ailsa nearby in her wooden bunk.

The candle flickered dangerously, and they dreaded it. They dreaded it going out in front of them, and both prayed in their hearts that it should keep burning forever. Seirian felt the guilt within her, weighing her down with a great gray weight inside. And Lucius felt repeated surges of red anger, which he shoved back down indignantly: ridiculous and shameful anger, as if his wife were, somehow to blame for what had happened. They tried to talk, in stumbling, broken sentences.

"I did write," he said, "but . . ."

"The *cursus* is finished," she said. "Not even Isca gets letters now, they say."

"But you knew I'd come back."

She nodded. "I always knew. I'd have known if anything had happened to you."

He felt stung and angry afresh. Why had he not felt what had happened to Cadoc? But that was the difference between men and women, he thought. Women were linked by silver threads, more fine than spiders' silk, to all those they truly loved. Men had no such threads; or if they had, the threads withered and fell away with indifference; or men broke them irritably, feeling their responsible weight as something far heavier and more restrictive and punishing than the light gossamer silk that women felt. To women, those threads were as sweet a burden as a baby in the womb.

"About two months ago," she said, "you were very ill. I trembled all night, and in the morning my back was covered in weals."

He nodded. The night he had been beaten in the cells of the Imperial Palace. But he would tell her nothing of that. "I am well now," he said.

"And will you go away again?"

"I will have to go away again," he said.

She nodded and looked down and tears fell to her apron.

"But at last I will be back," he said. "*We* will be back."

She nodded. "And we will wait for you both."

They slept in each other's arms all night, clinging together in silent desperation, and feeling the dark space between them that was their vanished son. An aching void which could not be ignored or filled.

Lucius arose before dawn and climbed the hill behind the cottage. Mercury, herald of the sun, hung like a tiny lamp in the eastern sky, and he knew that Britain was not simply a peaceful, isolated, fogbound, and forgotten island off the shoulder of Europe. For history and the world would keep breaking in; and there wasn't a tribe in all the world, not even in the remotest mountains of Scythia, which did not know the weapons of war.

Tugha Bàn stood peacefully asleep in the paddock behind the cottage, a gray ghost. Lucius felt an overwhelming sense of all the other lives that had been lived in this valley, all the other joys and tragedies of the families who had farmed this land and loved these hills and woods. And of all the people, all the parents and children to come, in the next hundreds and even thousands of years, with their new languages and their strange gods. His mind reeled at the thought. So many people, so many stories, and none of them would leave behind more than a scratch upon the earth of Dumnonia, a six-foot scratch in the rich red earth. And that, too, would soon be grown over and forgotten.

His mind came back to the present, and the all-consuming now that must be lived in and embraced for everything it was. Every moment was miraculous, a wise man had once said to him, no matter how terrible. Life itself was a miracle. The sun showed a gold rim over the horizon, its light coursing along the tops of the oak trees on the ridge like molten gold, and he raised his face to its distant heat and prayed for help. He prayed to the unknown rulers of the universe for help in this time of sorrow and direst need.

When help came, it came not as a radiant young god in a chariot of the sun, riding down from the heavens; nor as a white-robed goddess, stepping silently through the trees toward him in her golden sandals. It came in the form of a mere mortal: a battered old man in a moth-eaten Phrygian cap, who marched doggedly up over the crest of the hill from the north, with a twisted old yew staff rapping along the flint-strewn chalk track as he walked.

Lucius stared, his prayer barely out of his mouth. "It can't be," he whispered.

The figure came closer. An old, old man with a long gray beard, but nevertheless walking vigorously now that he was on the downward slope, with long, rangy strides, as fitted his frame, which was a lean and sinewy six feet or more. Apart from the knobbly yew stick he clutched in his right hand, he went unarmed. But even his walk had an unmistakable stamp of authority and purpose. And then he raised up his face when still afar off, and Lucius thought he even saw the twinkle in those deep-set, hawklike eyes.

"Gamaliel," he whispered.

The old man saw Lucius and smiled. They clasped each other's arms.

"Lucius," said Gamaliel.

"Old friend," said Lucius.

Gamaliel smiled, but Lucius was too overwrought to do more than stare, and cling.

Seirian appeared. The old man embraced her and kissed her, and held her back from him and gazed at her from under his bushy gray eyebrows.

"Ah Seirian, Seirian, fair maid in a million," he sighed. "If only I were a few centuries younger. . . ."

"You leave my wife alone," said Lucius.

Gamaliel leaned forward and gave her another kiss on the cheek and then stood tall again. "I'm more than a little peckish," he said. "Do you have any oats simmering away? You know how I like my porridge."

Seirian stoked up the fire in the hearth and set milk and water to simmer, stirring in fine oatmeal when it began to steam. They sat with steaming bowls of porridge on their laps, the porridge running with thick yellow cream, and ate in companionable silence. The winter birds twittered in the bare branches outside, hopping from twig to twig and coming down into the yard to peck for scattered meal.

Eventually they set their bowls aside, and Lucius and Seirian between them told Gamaliel as much as they could.

He nodded. "We will find him. We must."

"But how?" asked Lucius. "Where do we begin?"

Gamaliel, typically, did not answer the question directly. "We begin where we begin. But we will find him. I feel it in my water." He looked especially grave. "I read it in the patterns of my porridge."

Lucius couldn't help grinning. Gamaliel the wise man, older than the green hills of Dumnonia. Gamaliel the hooded and cloaked wanderer of the wilderness, the great traveler and sea voyager, who had been as far as the fabled Empire of China and back, so they said. Gamaliel, who had lived for a thousand years or more, and talked calmly and inscrutably of how he had known Julius Caesar, and how the great dictator used to cheat at backgammon; or spoke of Socrates' rather unpleasant personal habits, as if he had known him personally; and even of Alexander the Great, and how he had been his tutor, "and a far more useful one to him than that old Stagirian pedant Aristotle. Do you know, he once tried to persuade me that if a camel mated with a panther it would produce a giraffe? Preposterous!"

Gamaliel the storyteller, riddle maker, joker, trickster, and holy fool, who wore his wisdom as lightly as his moth-eaten Phrygian cap.

"Now then," said Gamaliel, settling back. "I believe you have the last of the Sybilline Books."

Lucius gaped at him. He had almost forgotten the scrap of parchment that General Stilicho had given him. It seemed so long ago. "How in the Name of Light do you know that?"

"I know everything," said Gamaliel mildly. "Well, almost everything. Everything that is *worth* knowing, at any rate. Unlike that logic-chopping,

platitudinous dolt Aristotle of Stagira, with his ridiculous *genera* and his
probabilistic enthymemes—"

"Look, leave your dead Greek philosophers out of this, will you?"

Gamaiel harrumphed and crossed his arms. "Anyway," he said. "You
do have the last of the leaves, I trust?"

Lucius nodded. "But what has this to do with finding my son?"

"Everything," said Gamaliel. "Everything." He laid his hand on Seirian's arm and said gently, "Now, my dearest, tell me everything that '
happened."

She took a deep, brave breath and began.

She had been sitting on the beach with Ailsa, looking for seashells,
when the Saxons came. Cadoc was out in his beloved little coracle, the
tiny hazel frame covered with freshly tarred oxhide and rather grandly
named the *Seren Mâr,* the *Star of the Sea.* He was letting down freshly
baited lines and hauling in mackerel, as obliviously happy as only a busy
boy can be, when his mother shaded her eyes and looked to the clear
horizon, and saw a square sail bellying in the southerly wind. She watched
it for some time as it came closer, and when it was only a mile or two
offshore and closing fast she saw that the device on the sail was no eagle,
as she had thought, but a crudely stitched wolf in black.

In an instant she was on her feet with Ailsa in her arms, screaming to
Cadoc to come in. In her desperation and terror, it seemed to her that the
boy moved terribly slowly, reeling in his last line, looking back over his
shoulder in some alarm, but not enough, never enough. The young never
fear the world enough, and the old fear it too much.

Seirian had to make the most dreadful of choices: whether to take to
the hills and the woods at once, hand in hand with Ailsa, or to stand and
wait in agony while her eleven-year-old son rowed slowly in to shore, and
to risk all three of them being captured, or worse. She chose to flee with
Ailsa, praying to the gods that her sharp-witted son would make good his
escape. She was halfway up the west cliff toward the dense hazelwoods

when the Saxon pirates' ship crashed onto the beach, its cruelly beaked prow cutting into the shingle as a sword would cut through the edge of a poor man's shield.

Their first sport was to catch the young Celtic lad who was scrambling up the beach ahead of them, having stopped to tie his coracle to a keg post in case of summer storms. How the Saxons laughed. They slashed the oxhide of the coracle into ribbons with their great long swords as they ran past, and they caught the boy at the top of the beach, knocked him to the ground with their cowhide shields, and shoved him headfirst into a hessian sack. They tied him up in the sack like a trussed fowl, and left him screaming there on the beach, while they roared on into the village to see what they could find.

They found a woman at a quern and her daughter salting fish nearby, and they raped them both, but they killed only the mother. They took the daughter with them, bleeding, bound, and gagged. They killed a family in another longhouse up the valley, and slew all their cattle, but took one young heifer for meat aboard ship. They burned a couple more houses, and a Christian chapel—they hated Christians and their pious houses. That done, rather disconsolately, with only a single noisy heifer and a couple of slaves to show for all that effort, they made their way back to the beach and pushed off into the small waves of the Celtic Sea, tacking eastward for another raid farther up the coast of the white cliffs.

When at last Seirian had finished, Gamaliel let go of her hand and stood up. "Come," he said. "Seirian, my dearest, we should walk."

Lucius stood up, too.

Gamaliel shook his head. "You stay here."

"What do you mean?" said Lucius indignantly.

"When we are gone," said Gamaliel, "take the last of the leaves, and learn everything that is there. Learn it all."

"Learn it?" repeated Lucius. "What on earth for?"

"For the sake of the future," said Gamaliel. Then he smiled, at his most infuriating and enigmatic, and chanted in a low, soft voice,

For the time will come when the people will walk the fields like a setting dream,
And talk, as though the days were long, and the starlight deep.

Then he said more briskly, "After all, what was your father?"

"You know what my father was," said Lucius. "A son of the *druithynn*."

"Then learning verses runs in your blood," said Gamaliel. "Your father could have recited ten thousand verses, without so much as a pause for a mouthful of mead."

Lucius snorted.

"Learn it well," said Gamaliel, "every word, without fail. Now I am going for a lovely long walk with your pretty wife." And they vanished out of the door.

Lucius heard Seirian giggle at one of Gamaliel's jokes as they crossed the farmyard to the gate. It was the first time he had heard her giggle since his return.

Settling grumpily back on his stool, he pulled the tattered parchment from his leather wallet, and began to read.

Seirian and Gamaliel walked for a long time, down the valley to the sea, and along the fateful beach. Seirian drew to a halt and looked away across the gray sea, the cries of the wheeling gulls desolate in the autumn air. Gamaliel reached out his old hand and touched her bright young cheek.

"Be comforted," he murmured.

She turned to him, a little scornful. "How can I be?"

"Be comforted," he said again, more gently than ever. " 'Content' I did not say."

She looked out across the sea again. Then she turned and they walked on along the creaking shingle, up the west cliff into the woods, back along the ridge and down through the damp meadows. They spoke no more.

But that evening, by firelight, the three of them having eaten a good stew of lamb, hazelnuts, and winter vegetables, they talked again.

"You have learned it all?" demanded Gamaliel.

"Here," said Lucius, handing the parchment wearily to his old friend. "Test me if you like."

At which Gamaliel cried in a loud voice, "No! Do not offer them to me," and dashed the parchment away with a flying hand.

Lucius and Seirian looked at him in astonishment. It was rare to see him moved to anger.

"But—"

"They are not for me," said Gamaliel, a little more controlled. "You do not understand. Never show them to me. In fact . . ." He stood up and, with a deft flick of his yew staff, twitched the parchment from Lucius's hand into the fire.

"What the—?" cried Lucius, reaching out to retrieve it.

Gamaliel batted his arm down sharply with his staff, and ordered him to sit. "They are not needed now," he said simply.

They watched the ancient parchment curl up in the flames, the lettering flowing strangely in the heat, as if the words might somehow outlive the parchment they were written on. There was a faint odor of something . . . unhallowed, as if from the charnel house or the grave, and the parchment was burned and gone in a wisp of dense black smoke. Gamaliel plucked a bunch of wild marjoram from where it hung from a nail in the wall, and cast it onto the fire to freshen the air again.

"What was that," asked Lucius, "the breath of the grave, and the black smoke?"

But Gamaliel did not answer. He only said, "You are the last of the leaves now." He smiled a little and said to Seirian, "Woman, behold your husband: the Last of the Sibylline Books." More gravely, he said to Lucius, "One day you will pass them on to your son, as was the Celtic custom with holy things of old. For you and Cadoc are of the line of Bran, and the blood of the *druithynn* runs in your veins, as you say."

Lucius looked uncertain. "But you must tell me more, Gamaliel. I am all in a Kernow fog."

The old man smiled, and gazed into the fire. "Alas, I am not so wise as you think. Mysteries are many, and none so mysterious as man. As regards the Sibyl's prophecies . . . who can truly scry the future? Would the gods put such awful power into the feeble and treacherous hands of men? Is the future written in a book of heaven, unalterable and fated from the egg to the end? Do you not know in your heart that you can choose between the dark path and the Light?"

Seirian said to Lucius, "You know it."

Lucius looked down, as if obscurely ashamed.

"Then man has choice," Gamaliel continued, "and the future is unwritten, and prophecies are worthless doggerel. Even the parchment they're written on isn't fit for wiping an emperor's ass!"

Lucius grinned. "Then why bother with them?"

"Because men believe in prophecies. They hear their horoscopes avidly, they cling to their birthstones and their mythical forebears and their little, little lies. Our systems have their day, they have their day and cease to be. But during that day they surely have their power, to hurt or to heal. Therein lies their power."

Lucius nodded slowly.

"The world is changed," said Gamaliel, "and we with it." He smiled at them with sadness. "And to this gentle land, and even to this valley, the Saxons are coming."

Seirian spoke. "I know little of the Saxons. I know that their name means 'the People of the Sword.' I never saw a sword drawn in quiet valley till that day. And I know that now my every dream of them is a dream of blood."

"That is how they want to be seen—and dreamed of, too," said Gamaliel. He went on, in a low chant:

Nine days and nine nights,
Lord Odin hung
Nailed to the world tree,
A sacrifice to himself.

Then the sky cracked open,
The thunder spoke,
The dawn arose
And the longships set sail.

A sword people, an ax people,
An ice age, a wolf age,
And no quarter given
Between man and man.

"They are but one of many coming tribes," said Gamaliel. "Yes, they are a fierce and terrible people. In time, out of that fierceness something great and passionate may come, but now they are a People of the Sword, as you say, dear Seirian, and a People of Blood, and *saxa* is their word for their dreadful, biting long swords. They worship strange, dark gods, and the name of Christ is a torment to their ears. The sea is theirs, and in their narrow-beaked ships they traverse it by day and by night with a great hunger and with lust in their eyes. They laugh that they will sail across the uttermost ocean, to the mouth of Hell itself, which is like a great dark cave into which the sea flows in a black torrent. They jest without fear of the gods that they will sail into that infernal abyss itself and ransack even Hell for gold."

Despite the warmth of the fire, Seirian shivered.

"Then what must we do?" asked Lucius.

"The last of the Celtic kingdoms will fight against the pagan invaders," said Gamaliel. "And the fight will be glorious."

"Will Britain be extinguished in the end?"

"Every nation and empire will be extinguished in the end," said Gamaliel with a gentle sadness. "But not all will live on in legend as gloriously as the last of the Celtic kingdoms will live on." He looked into the fire. "It is as our soothsayers have said. It is as the Man of Myrddin has said. A hard age is coming for us all, and everywhere beyond the frontiers the tribes are stirring. The Saxons are a fierce people, yet no fiercer than the Sueves or the Goths or the Vandals, nor yet that other tribe that will come from farthest off. 'Storm from the east, O Storm that will not cease.'"

"What will become of us, Gamaliel?"

Gamaliel smiled. Often, when he was at his gloomiest, as if surprised by a cheerfulness which welled up from deep within and which no one else could feel or comprehend, his lined and ancient face would break into a mysterious smile, and he would say, as he said now, "All will be well, and all manner of things will be well."

"How can that be?"

"What the caterpillar calls the end of the world, the Master calls the butterfly, as I was told by a wise old man whom I met in the mountains between China and the deserts of Scythia."

"You talk in riddles, old friend."

"I talk in riddles because life is a riddle. Not a riddle to be solved, either, but one to be taken upon your shoulders, as you would take a heavy load, and to be carried on down the road, singing the praises of the world that God in his wisdom has made, untroubled in your heart." He stirred the fire with the battered end of his staff. "And, just so, we will bring your Cadoc back. For he is of the line of Bran, praise singer and hymn maker, and he was born for a purpose, which will not be served by his standing in chains in the slave markets of Colonia Agrippina."

Seirian winced at the cruel image and bowed her head. But Gamaliel would do nothing to lessen the truth of Cadoc's plight. He only said again, "We will bring him back."

"*Can* you bring him back?" asked Seirian, aggression and anger in her doubt.

Gamaliel said, "We shall see." He smiled gently at her and laid his dry old hand over hers. "In the heart of the darkest nighttime, we shall see."

"Riddler," said Lucius.

Gamaliel rested his other hand on Lucius's muscular forearm. "Old friend," he said.

The next morning, Seirian and Gamaliel stood watching Ailsa herding the chickens out into the yard, with Lucius up on the hill above, mending a fence by first light.

Seirian said to Gamaliel, "He does not talk."

Gamaliel sighed. "He is a soldier, not an orator. If you want to know his heart, mark his deeds, not his words. You know how little he wants to go back to the empire. He only wants to find his son—for himself, for Ailsa, and for you. Watch his heavy tread and his weariness as he walks the road out of the valley. Remember why he does it, and with what heaviness of heart he leaves you again. Do not doubt him."

"I do not doubt him!" exclaimed Seirian with sudden fierceness, her eyes flashing darkly. "I have never doubted him. There is not a breath of cowardice or faithlessness in him. It is that which makes me despair. A weaker man would give up, and stay home, and, and . . ."

"And you would live happily ever after?"

She looked down at the rough cobbles of the yard, and shook her head. "No. You are right. It is because he is going that I love him. If he stayed by our fireside and tended me, all smiles and kisses and sweet nothings, like some high-born noble lover, I would despise him a little." She smiled a little at the contrariness of the human heart.

"He is a good man," said Gamaliel. "Good is the opposite of weak, and it often enjoys little comfort and contentment in the world. Be patient, and watch over Ailsa like a mother hawk, as I know you will. And watch, too, for the dark shadows of the Saxon longships, for there is no knowing when they may come again. We will be back. Before too long, we will be back, with your son, and you will be a family once more."

Seirian brushed her tears angrily from her eyes and nodded briskly.

"I know. I know. Here," and she turned and slipped back into the cottage. Gamaliel followed her in, stooping low so as not to bump his head, as he had often done before. She retrieved a cloth package from the bread oven beside the hearth and thrust it into his gnarled hands. "I made some honey cakes."

"Ah, the far-famed honey cakes of Seirian, daughter of Maradoc!" cried Gamaliel, raising them above his head. "How can we come to harm with such talismans of great power in our pockets? Surely even the gods look down and smell their savor rising unto heaven, and toss aside their bowls of ambrosia and their cups of nectar, and wish themselves mortal men upon the earth, that they might taste the joys of the blessed honey cakes of Seirian, daughter of Maradoc!"

"Enough, enough, you old fool!" cried Seirian, and she bundled the old man out of doors into the sunshine.

Ailsa had finished herding the chickens to her satisfaction, and she came over to him and stopped in front of the tall old man and squinted up. "Cadoc showed me the flowers, and he always caught fish," she said, "lots of fish. He was very clever."

"He still is very clever," said the old man gently.

Aisla stared up at him. "Now when we have breakfast he's not there. . . . You will find him again, won't you?"

He laid his hand on her mop of curls. "Have no fear, little one. Your brother will be here again soon."

They left the next morning at dawn. Seirian and Lucius clung to each other wordlessly and with such desperate longing that Gamaliel had to turn away in his sorrow for them. He felt his hand plucked by a smaller hand, and he looked down into Ailsa's bright brown eyes.

"Are you going, too?" she asked.

"Yes, little one, I am going, too."

"Your hands are all dry and wrinkly. Are you a captain of a ship?"

"Not exactly, no."

"But I like your hands anyway," she added hurriedly.

"Thank you, my dear."

"And you're too old to fight any bad men."

"That is true."

"So what *do* you do?"

Gamaliel smiled. "I wonder that myself sometimes," he murmured. "Well, I will keep your father company on the long voyage to find your brother."

"But you don't know where he is."

"We don't know *exactly*."

"So how will you find him?"

"By looking."

Ailsa thought for awhile. "Sometimes I find things by looking. I found my hoop in the pig house the day before yesterday, and *I* never put it down there, and the pigs don't play hoop. They'd be too fat and it'd get stuck round their middles." She frowned. "And sometimes I can't find things and give up, and then they come to me anyway. It's odd, isn't it? Does that happen to you?"

"Ah," said Gamaliel, "all the time."

"Hm," said Ailsa. Then she ran off to play.

Lucius and Seirian came over hand in hand, and she kissed Gamaliel, and he said quiet words to her, and she nodded and smiled with an effort. Then all three of them held hands in a triangle.

Gamaliel said to Seirian, "The Comforter be with you. May He guard your fields by day, may She sit at your fireside by night."

Seirian replied, "May the road rise up to meet you, may the sun make his face to shine upon you, may God be the third traveler who walks by your side as you go."

Lucius and Seirian said nothing to each other, and Gamaliel knew why. The deepest things cannot be caught in words.

Ailsa came running back and pushed into the triangle indignantly, so they had to make it a square. She closed her eyes and prayed, "May Daddy and the old man not have to go to bed without any supper ever, or be killed or eaten by sea monsters, or anything else." She thought, and added, "Or even just get their arms and legs bitten off, and have to come home in a wheelbarrow."

At which they all solemnly said, "Amen," and the little group broke up.

Lucius and Gamaliel took up their leather packs, and Gamaliel took his yew staff in his hand.

Ailsa ran to Lucius and threw her arms round his legs. "You didn't come back for very long," she said. "I didn't even remember you when you came back."

Lucius kept his voice steady. "I am only going away one more time, and I will come back with your brother."

The little girl beamed with delight. Seirian lifted her into her arms, and they watched from the rickety wooden gateway as the two men, the tall, gray-eyed, broad-shouldered younger man, and the other, lean, rangy, and as old as the hills, walked on together up the lane toward the ridge road and the east.

15

THE SEA WOLVES

Along the coast at the little port of Saetonis, they persuaded a local merchant and his crew to ship them across the Celtic sea toward Belgica.

When they left the coast of Dumnonia in the *Gwydda Ariana—The Silver Goose*—it was bright sunshine, and with the wind behind them and only slightly abeam, they were making a good hundred miles a day. They would be at the coast of Belgica by nightfall.

In the afternoon the wind dropped to the south, as suddenly as if someone had closed a door against a draft, and from the crow's nest—which is to say an old barrel roughly roped to the mainmast—came the cry of fog ahead. They drifted on until they could see the fog banks from the deck: great dense shapes that lay unmoving across the flat and windless sea, ominous and forlorn.

They sailed on a little with what wind they could find, the trickling of the bow wave eerie in the surrounding silence as they approached the fog banks that lay across the channel, obscuring the white cliffs of the

Gaulish coast from view. The sea, which had up to now been a typical channel sea of short, choppy waves, fell as calm as a village pond, and the dumpy little vessel began to roll placidly to port and starboard, her sail flapping futilely in the listless sea.

The captain, a grizzled old veteran with two gold earrings and a left eye damaged by a swinging crossbeam, scowled into the fog bank and gave no orders.

"Why aren't we setting oars?" demanded Lucius.

The captain didn't respond for a long while. When he did, he growled, "I don't like this."

"It's only fog. How many more miles to the coast?"

"Another twenty, maybe."

"Well, can't we break out the oars? We'll be there in a few hours, wind or no wind."

The captain still didn't look at Lucius. He spat over the gunwale, and said, "The Saxons. They love a fog."

After some hesitation the captain gave the order to put out the oars, and they rowed on into the fog. The silence was unnerving, the only sound the slow dip and sweep of the oars in the water below. They passed through thinner patches, and Lucius could see the poor watchman in the crow's nest, high above the deck. When they hit another fog bank, he vanished from sight as entirely as a bird in the clouds.

At last the fog thinned and dissolved behind them, and then the rain came down. Gamaliel and Lucius sheltered in the cabin, the sailcloth drawn tight across the stanchions and the raindrops drumming down furiously. The wind, at least, got up again, from the west now. The captain gave orders for the sail to be unfurled and they plunged onward through the beating rain. No other vessel, hostile or not, would see them through such a curtain of water.

In the late afternoon the rain slowed and stopped and the sun broke through. The watcher in the crow's nest stripped off his clothes and hung them on the sides of the barrel to dry. He began to scan the horizon.

Nothing. Though to the east there was still cloud low on the horizon, and . . .

He was hauling his clothes back on when a speck of color caught his eye on the eastern horizon. He straightened and stared. Ten miles off or more. No, less. It was nearer than the horizon. He hadn't spotted it soon enough; his eye had grown lazy. Bright sail and dark hull, and closing on them straight. Dreading his captain's wrath, he leaned over the side of the barrel and called down, "Sail off the port quarter, sir."

The captain glared. "How far?"

"Six miles, sir. And closing."

"If you were sleeping on watch, sailor," roared the captain, losing his temper with impressive abruptness, "I'll have the cat across your back quicker than you can spit."

"Not asleep, sir. No, sir."

Lucius and Gamaliel appeared on deck again. Lucius gazed out across the sea. At deck level the distant ship was still on the horizon.

"What is it?" he asked.

The captain hawked and spat. "Trouble. It's always fuckin' trouble."

Their sail was bellying in the full wind. The captain gave the order to turn to port, and it luffed and shimmered.

"Jupiter's balls," growled the captain.

"Purple sail," called the lookout.

"Time was," growled the captain to his two landlubbers, "purple sail meant a Roman sail. Now it could mean fuckin' anything. Rich ladies wear flaxen wigs like whores, ships go under purple sail, and the emperor in Rome wears yellow fuckin' panties, for all I know."

Lucius nearly reprimanded the foul-mouthed old curmudgeon, but he hesitated. What had the emperor's dignity to do with his concerns now? Besides, every captain was an emperor aboard his own ship. That much even a landlubber knew.

"Steersmen!" roared the captain, stumping back along the deck. "Three points to port and hold her steady. Haul in the starboard sheet."

The two huge steersmen, their arm muscles bulging with the strain of turning the ship under full sail, strained at their steering oars, the broad leather support belts round their waists creaking with the effort. A group of sailors hauled in the starboard sheets, and the bulky merchant-man swung slowly, painfully slowly, to port. The captain barked further orders, and at last the *Gwydda Ariana* was sailing almost at right angles to the wind. She could turn no closer.

Ahead, the watch saw the purple sail swing round, too—to starboard. It swung much faster. The dark hull, he could see now, was low and lean. The two ships were running parallel, to the north. He touched the bone-handled dagger at his side.

Lucius asked, "What's so fashionable about purple sails these days?"

"Don't show up against the sea like white," snapped the captain. "Purple lets a pirate get in close."

"You can't be sure it's a pirate."

"Yeah, and I can't be sure my mummy ever fucked my daddy, neither. But I'd be prepared to lay a bet on it." He swiveled away. "Deckhands, break out the starboard oars. On the fuckin' double!"

The six remaining crewmen obeyed, resting the oars in the six crude holes at either beam, only a few inches above the deck. Instead of rowing benches, such as a warship or quinquireme would boast, this old bucket had only cleats pegged to the deck for bracing. The scraggy-looking sailors braced their bare feet against the cleats and began to heave at the oars.

The ship swung onto a course farther from the approaching ship— and the approaching ship did the same. The captain cursed again.

"We're heading for . . . ?" asked Lucius.

"The gates of Hades," he growled.

"You swear too much," said a low, steady voice behind him. "And my friend here asked you a question. I think you should have the courtesy to give him a plain answer, unadorned by redundant copulative allusions, and explain to him whither we are bound."

The captain turned in some surprise, and saw the old man with the priestly beard and the certain look in his eye. To Lucius he said grumpily, "We're bound back for the coast of Britain, around Portus Lemanis, if we can make it before our friendly visitors get—"

He was interrupted by a sudden lurch of the boat as the sail ceased drawing and began to flap violently in a wind that was now coming from just forward of the port beam.

The captain roared orders for his men to put out the port side oars, and there was a mad scramble to do his bidding. He might be a tough old bird who hadn't smiled in twenty years, but they'd faced hard times before, and he'd always got them through.

"Furl sail!" he roared out. "Steersmen, hold her west of north!"

The wind now blew in their faces. The buntlines snapped taut and the sail shrank into bundles of canvas along the yard. The *Gwydda Ariana* lost headway immediately, beginning to roll as she started to move across what had been a following sea. Waves slopped over the bow, the ship wallowed in the trough and nosed slowly forward, as she steered more and more to windward.

"Row! Row you gutless yellow-livered sea-spawned bastards! Row like you've got a knife at your throat and the devil at your back. Remember every tale you ever heard of the tricks of the Saxon pirates, my boys, and row till you bust your guts and spew up blood. Heave at those sweeps, my boys. Push and heave. Tired muscles will mend in a day, but a cut throat takes a little while longer. Ha!"

The captain lined up the rest of the crew to take over at regular intervals as each oarsman tired. "If you see a man puke or drop, knock him out the way and take his oar. By the time your wind's broken we'll have another man for you."

Lucius and Gamaliel eyed each other. The foulmouthed old goat was almost enjoying this, all the more alive in the face of death.

The two men took their place in the prow, and waited.

"What was wrong with the sail?" wondered Lucius. "We're hardly moving now."

The captain was behind them again, glaring over his sweating oarsmen with his hands bunched into fists behind his back. Lucius and Gamaliel jumped as he growled his answer.

"That's a fast ship," he said. "They'd catch us no trouble under sail."

"And we're quicker under oar?"

The captain grinned a black-toothed grin. "No fuckin' chance, mate. They're faster than us on the oar, too. But the question is: can they be bothered? Any fool can unfurl a sail and sit back farting in the sun. But rowing bow to wind takes some determination. All that's in it for them is the off chance of some loot. What's in it for us is our sorry little lives." He swiped his arm under his nose and snorted. "So who d'you think's going to row harder?"

"Well," said Gamaliel, nodding toward the purple sail, "it looks as if they're going to do their utmost."

The captain sucked in a hiss of air over his teeth. For there was the pursuing ship, its big purple sail now shrinking against its yard. At the same time there came flashes of bright light as its crew broke out the oars and began to swing them through the waves in unison. And now her bow, her cruel, sharp-beaked warship bow, was swinging lightly round and coming straight for them.

They rowed on, harder, harder, but it was useless. The distance between them and the warship shrank to three miles, two, one, half a mile. . . . On the deck of the *Gwydda Ariana,* the broken-winded rowers lay choking in pools of their own vomit while their replacements heaved and sweated in their stead, their muscles burning cords and the soles of their feet splitting against the cleats in their furious press and strain. But strain heroically as they might, there was no escaping the speed of the lean, dark warship.

"Lay off, men," called the captain at last, his voice sounding as weary as they looked.

It was done. They were finished. The *Gwydda Ariana* wallowed to a sluggish halt in the troughs and waited.

A hundred yards off, and they could see the Saxon crew easing up on their short oars, hefting their great ashen spears in their fists and setting on their plain steel velite helmets. Their warship was beautifully crafted, even Lucius had to admit, predatory, fast, and sleek, with a close-packed eighteen oars each side. No wonder the *Gwydda Ariana* had been so easily outrun. This ship might outrun even the fastest two-banked Liburnian warship in the Mediterranean.

Some forty Saxons crowded silently to the stern. They held themselves erect and expressionless. This was fate. The gods were with them. In their beliefs, none of these fierce Germanic warriors ever had even the room for doubt. Things were as they were. You lived, you fought, you died. All that mattered was to be strong.

Their captain was a blustering, red-faced, barrel-chested giant with a bearskin wrap round his beefy shoulders. His eyes were a sharp, keen blue, and a triumphant smile played on his lips.

The lean, cruel-visaged bowsprit eased alongside, a slanted eye painted either side of the beaked prow like that of the silent sea monster it was intended to represent. The Saxon longship sat lower in the water than the bulky merchant vessel, cutting barely a wave through the glassy sea.

As they hove to and came alongside, the Saxons at least pulled in their vicious-looking iron-bound cathead: that deadly beam which projected sideways from the prow of a warship, and which could sweep close alongside any boat that was its prey and smash every oar to pieces as it passed.

The Saxon captain called out a word or two, and the sharp-beaked *corvus,* or "raven," slammed down from the back of the longship, its iron-toothed underside biting into the deck of the merchant vessel.

The men lined up and began to cross, led by their burly captain swinging a hand ax, when they suddenly stopped in bewilderment. Gamaliel was blocking their path, his yew staff rooted firmly in the planking of the *corvus.* Only a fraction of a second before, they could have sworn they had seen the old man in the bow of the boat, but now here he was, his eyes boring into them with an intensity that made even these hardened sea wolves falter. He thumped his staff down on the wooden planks.

"Do not step aboard this ship," he said quietly. "Raise the *corvus* again, go back, and sail on."

Lucius stepped up beside him, his hand on the pommel of his sword, but Gamaliel ignored him.

The captain gave a roar of laughter, but already there was a strange uncertainty in his eyes. "You're in no position to give orders, old man. Now step out of the way or I'll have you beheaded over the gunwale and your graybeard old head jammed on our bowsprit for decoration."

His men laughed, too. But their hearty laughter was drowned by the roar of Gamaliel's voice, of such a volume that the laughter thinned out and died. Holding his staff out before him, the old man bellowed, *"Then you are bound for Hell!"*

The captain reeled back, enraged both by the old man's words and, even more, by the unsettling, indefinable aura of power that emanated from him. It should have been the easiest thing in the world simply to step up and lop the old fool's head off with a single swing of his ax. And yet, and yet . . . he knew that he could not do it, and his heart burned with rage at this unaccustomed feeling of powerlessness.

He shouted back, hearing even as he did so the weakness and irresolution of his voice compared to the bewildering storm blast of the old man's roar.

"Vex me not with your talk of Christian punishments, old man. I would not so much as wipe my ass with the teachings of the Christians and their yellow-livered morality of slaves."

With that the Saxon began to advance, and something terrible happened. Gamaliel also advanced, taking a step toward him; and Lucius, close behind the old man, heard his footfall on the narrow planking. But it was not the light, tremulous footfall of an old man. It was more ominous than that, and far, far heavier than it should have been. The gangplank shivered under its weight.

Lucius craned to look at Gamaliel, but only for a fraction of a second before he had to glance away again. Something in the old man had changed, which the soldier could barely comprehend and hardly wanted to. His blood ran cold. Even on the sea air, he thought he could smell the odor of rank, carnivorous breath. Below the ship, the tall shadow of Gamaliel was cast across the water, broken and rippling on the waves. To Lucius's horrified eyes, it looked less like the outline of a man than that of a monstrous, rearing bear. . . .

He stumbled back from the hulking, brooding shape that blocked the *corvus,* and his gaze fell on the Saxons opposite. He had never seen such expressions of blind fear, as they faced whatever it was that looked out at them from underneath the shadowy cowl of what had been Gamaliel. Their limbs rigid with terror, they started falling back, knocking into each other in their haste to retreat. Lucius, still unable to look directly at the massive shape before him, saw its shadow on the surface of the sea shrink back to resemble Gamaliel's again, and he heard his voice once more, strong and calm.

"Now, tell me: what of the Celtic slaves that were taken from the coast of Dumnonia in the summer? Whither were they bound?"

The Saxon warlord was babbling with terror, forcing his way back onto his ship between his desperate men.

"To Colonia Agrippina! All that batch went to Colonia Agrippina. You still get good prices on the Rhine." Then he turned back to his men and with a panic-stricken cry ordered them to raise the *corvus* and hoist the sail. He gave no hint of direction, but there was no need. His men understood. Anywhere, anywhere away from this haunted and unholy vessel.

Without another word the Saxon sea wolves winched back the *corvus,* pushed off from the side of the merchant ship, and set their course nor'easterly with full sail. Not a man aboard dared look back. And at no point later that day, or in any of the days to come, did any of the Saxons dare to mention the subject of the weird old man again. For their hearts chilled within them at the memory of him, and the eyes of their minds were filled with images of terror.

The *Gwydda Ariana* sailed east for the many mouths and sandbanks of the Rhine. Toward evening the last of the fog banks finally lifted and the wind picked up again from the southwest, and they made good speed.

Lucius sat in the prow of the boat, pretending to whet his sword blade, but his strokes were listless and ineffectual. Gamaliel sat near him. After awhile, seeing the terrible weight upon the young man's shoulders, he said quietly to him, "In the world you shall have much tribulation. But be comforted: I have overcome the world."

Lucius stared at him wordlessly.

"She is well," said Gamaliel softly. "She and the child will be well."

Lucius started. "How did you know what I was thinking about?"

"I wasn't born yesterday," Gamaliel smiled. "Besides, if I had a wife such as yours, I'd be thinking about her all the time, too."

"Were you ever married, Gamaliel?"

"Well, there was a young Athenian girl once . . . but her father disapproved of me. I was working as a nocturnal water carrier at the time, studying philosophy by day at the Lyceum. Not the sort of husband he had in mind for his beloved daughter."

Lucius smiled vaguely. Here was his old, absentminded friend Gamaliel again. And yet, and yet . . .

At last he dared to ask, "Gamaliel, what happened back there with the Saxon pirates?"

He knew he'd not get a straight answer, of course. And he didn't.

"Ah," said Gamaliel. "These powers pass through me, but they are not my powers. They only pass through me, like the wind through the leaves."

"Stop riddling. Whose powers?"

"The one thousand and one names of the autumn wind in the leaves," said Gamaliel. "Now stop pretending to sharpen that sword and go to bed. We'll be at the mouth of the Rhine by sunrise tomorrow."

The *Gwydda Ariana* set them down at a damp wooden trading station on the marshy banks of the Rhine delta, and soon after that they found a riverboat to take them south.

They sailed upriver, through the great trading city of Lugdunum Batavorum, and into Colonia Agrippina. There they questioned every slave dealer they could find, and their hearts sank at the news. Many of the Celtic slaves from this summer's raiding season had been bought by Frankish warriors newly enriched from their raids into Belgica and Gaul. But some of the Franks had been waylaid in their turn by war bands marauding in from the east. By eastern horsemen, on shaggy little steppe ponies . . .

Gamaliel sat all night gazing into the fire, while Lucius slept fitfully, restless with despair.

At dawn, the old man raised his head and said, "We go east."

They sailed on up the great Rhine river, through the grim frontier cities of Vangiones and Argentoratum, and on south. At last they disembarked upon the eastern shore, and crossed through the Alemanni's wild country, which they called the Black Forest. Many were the dangers they faced and the hardships they endured there, among the dark pines and in the sullen, smoky villages. But they set their faces grimly and went on, and came at last to the banks of the Danube, where they took ship again for the east: a river barge taking Moselle wine down to Sirmium and the road to Epidaurus. At every encounter they questioned closely those they met, and most thought them mad to be trying to find a single slave somewhere in, or even beyond, the greatest empire known to man. But occasionally, just occasionally, they caught glimpses, heard echoes, and their hearts told them to press on.

"We should never abandon hope," said Gamaliel.

"Even though hope has long since abandoned us?" said Lucius sourly.

Gamaliel looked at him with a flash of anger in his eyes, and Lucius bowed his head, a little ashamed. Gamaliel often repeated the words of Christ, that despair was the greatest sin of all; but he had no need to repeat them now. Lucius remembered those strange and startling words, and said no more about abandoning hope.

"I am not greatly interested in the finer points of philosophy and theology, as you know," said Lucius. "So-called wise men drowning in the swamp of their own words, words, words."

Gamaliel sighed. "I came to that conclusion myself a while back," he said. "I think it was when all Athens got excited over the logical paradox of the *Pseudomenos—The Liar.*"

Lucius looked blank.

"Quite," said Gamaliel. "That is to say: if I say, 'I am lying,' then if I *am* lying, I am telling the truth. And if I am telling the truth, I can't be lying. And yet if it *is* the truth, it must be true that I am lying. And yet again, if I am—"

"Stop, for pity's sake. My head's hurting."

"Well, you see my point."

Lucius wasn't sure he did, but he said nothing. He was used to the old vagabond's ways, as rambling and discursive as his wanderings over the wide earth; and with their own kind of foolish, ungovernable wisdom, somewhere underneath the patched old cloak and the moth-eaten Phrygian cap.

"My old friend Chrysippus," Gamaliel went on, "not a bad philosopher in his way—a Stoic, you know, and pupil of Cleanedhes—wrote *six books* on the matter of the *Pseudomenos.* And another, Philetas, wasted himself to death with anxiety over it. I think it was then that I began to feel skeptical about the . . . the purely *intellectual* approach to life. There was much to be said for the more pragmatic wisdom of my old friend Crates. A sensitive young student of his, one Metrocles, once—there is no polite way of putting this—once *broke wind* thunderously in the agora one day, to the general mirth and ridicule of hundreds of his fellow citizens. They could be very cruel in their humor, those Athenians. They even began to suggest that he might have to quit Athens altogether in his shame, and nicknamed him μετροκλης μετοικος."

Gamaliel chortled to himself, a little shamefacedly.

Lucius looked unimpressed.

"Never mind," said the old man. "It's a Greek pun."

The soldier shrugged. "It's all Greek to me. But—not wishing to be rude or anything—but does this story have a *point,* at any point?"

"Ah, yes, well. You see. Now. So there's Metrocles, covered in shame at having—emitted such a stercoraceous effluvium in this unfortunate manner. *Fundamentally* embarrassed, you might say!" Again, Gamaliel chuckled. "So Crates, to show how ridiculous it is for any man to be ashamed of what is, after all, a perfectly natural bodily function, promptly devoured five pounds of lupins—which, as you know, are powerfully flatulofacient, if not downright poisonous—and went about eructating at all the greatest men of Athens for the next week. Metrocles saw the point, and ceased to feel any shame."

"Hm." Lucius still wasn't quite sure that he saw the point.

"Anyway," resumed Gamaliel. "Philosophy aside, you were wondering . . . what?"

"I was thinking about what you said about Hell: that a man may still be redeemed by good deeds, even a man such as that murderous Saxon there."

Gamaliel too grew serious. "How could eternal punishment treat with justice?" he said gently. "I knew one of those theologians you speak of once—a man better than most, in fact. A neat little Egyptian; Origen, he was called. He is principally remembered now for having emasculated himself with a knife, the better to serve Christ."

"Idiot," said Lucius.

Gamaliel ignored this untheological interjection. "He took the teachings of the Son of Man a little too literally, perhaps. But far more interesting was his own teaching on Hell. He said that eventually, all would be forgiven. He said that even the Devil himself would one day repent, and his shriven soul be admitted to the mansions of heaven."

"Well." Lucius gouged his knife into the wooden bulwark of the boat. "I learn something new every day."

"Keep your eyes open and your heart humble," said Gamaliel, "and you will learn a thousand new things every day."

One morning, as they passed Augusta Vindelicorum on the southern shore, Gamaliel found Lucius staring down into the brown and turbid waters of the great river. When he raised his eyes, Gamaliel saw that they were bright with tears. The old man laid a hand on his shoulder to comfort him, but Lucius only shook his head and smiled and said he was not sure if he had dreamed it or not, but he thought he had heard a boy on the farther bank of the river whistling a certain tune. It was the same tune that Cadoc used to whistle every morning, as he pottered around in the yard at home, scattering meal for the chickens, or as he sauntered through the woods and fields of Dumnonia, hand in hand with his sister.

Lucius looked up at Gamaliel. "Is it possible?" he said. "That we are following even the trail of a song?"

"Anything is possible," said Gamaliel, "except for a one-armed man to touch his elbow." He slapped Lucius jovially on the back. "Perhaps it has been laid down for us, even to follow a boy's whistle."

Led thus by strange and unexpected clues, they followed the river east. To starboard lay the empire, and to port stretched the tribal lands of the north: the contested and warlike lands of the Hermunduri and Marcommanni, the Langobardi and Cattameni, and still other tribes whose names were yet unknown. They passed through the frontier towns of Lauriacum, Vindobona, and Carnuntum, their mighty legionary fortresses rising sheer from the banks of the southern side, and they came to the great bend in the river where it turns south into Illyria, with the wild lands of Sarmatian Jazyges and then vast and unmapped Scythia beyond. There they disembarked, having heard another clue which seemed to Lucius both tantalizing and terrible but barely seemed to surprise Gamaliel at all.

"These things happen," he said equably.

In a smoky wineshop full of drunken frontier soldiery, they had heard a blind Scythian beggar singing a haunting tune. They questioned him, and found out his name, and heard that he had been blinded by his own people for spying on the king's concubines when they were bathing. He had been driven out into the wilderness to die like an animal, but had found a refuge of sorts here in the borderland between Scythia and Rome, singing cracked tunes in taverns and brothels for coppers.

Gamaliel and Lucius looked at each other over their cups of foul wine, and Lucius said he had had dealings with some of that tribe before.

Gamaliel nodded. "So have I."

They tightened their belts, hitched up their packs, and set off across the grassy plains of Scythia, for the famed black tents of the most dreaded tribe of all.

16

THE LAST FRONTIER

Throughout the heart of the bitter winter, Attila and Orestes struggled on through the towering white mountains of Noricum, lips chapped and bleeding, snowflakes on their eyelashes, their hands and feet bound with no more than rags. Whenever they found wild berries or trapped game, they divided every mouthful precisely between them, so that even if they were both slowly starving, they would at least starve at an equal rate. Every night, crawling into whatever shelter they could find or improvise—usually no more than a rough bivouac of silver fir branches—they unwrapped the sodden cloths from each other's feet, and rubbed life back into them. Then they slept side by side, shivering through the night. In the freezing dawn, their bodies were as stiff and unbiddable as old men's. They said nothing, but each dreaded waking one morning to find the other dead. They both prayed that if one should die, the gods would take the other, too, in the same instant, to the sunlit lands beyond the dark river.

One morning, as they brushed past under the low branches of a fir wood, there came a soft, slithering sound from above, and an entire shelf of snow was dumped on Orestes' head and shoulders. When he had pushed back his hood, and wiped the stinging snow from his eyes, Attila was grinning at him.

"What are you grinning at, you idiot?" he gasped.

"It's melting," said Attila, still grinning. "It's thawing."

When Orestes understood what he was saying—that they had made it—they threw their arms round each other, and howled in triumph at the bare blue sky above, while more snow slithered from the branches of the silver fir above and fell upon them both. A cloak of soft white snow over their heads and about their shoulders, equally and without distinction.

Soon they came down into the thinner snow covering of the lower slopes, which in the summer would be the higher pastures for the sleek brown cows of that country. They even found the first raw shoots of greenery, and chewed the sprigs of yarrow and salad burnet that peeped from the long-hidden grasses. But though they no longer had to fight the bitter cold at every step, there were more villages now, more people to be avoided, more dogs set barking as they passed by in silence and darkness.

After some days they passed along the ridge of hills to the north of the great lake of Balaton, and that evening they came down to its tranquil shores. Attila fixed up a wooden pole with some barbs cut from bone, and went gaffing for trout in the shallows. They baked the trout on hot stones and gorged until they could eat no more.

Later that night, as he did every night, Orestes went a little way away among the trees, knelt down, leaned his forehead against a cold, mossy trunk, and prayed for the soul of his departed sister. Then he returned to the campfire, his face alight and glowing, both radiant and calm, as if he had received comfort and solace even from the cold and glittering silence of the sky.

They came to the gates of the city of Aquincum, and the bored *vigiles,* the night watchmen, allowed them entry without a word. Two ragamuffins from the country come to sell their paltry, stolen wares, or maybe themselves, who knew?

The boys, of course, had come to Aquincum not to sell but to steal. They were nearly free, but still they had the great barrier of the Danube to cross. For that they hoped they could steal a boat or a raft, or perhaps stow away aboard a merchantman bound for one of the log-wood trading stations on the other side. And for that they needed to get down to the quayside.

Aquincum was a grim little frontier town of timber and mud, with the stone frontier fort of the legion rising at one corner, near the river. The narrow streets stank of the shambles where the animals were driven in and slaughtered, of open drains, of the pigs crowded together in filthy backyards, and of the charcoal furnaces of begrimed and weary-looking coppersmiths working late.

Approaching down the cobbled street was a group of drunks. So close to their longed-for goal, the boys had grown careless. Attila especially, feeling his princely blood stirring as he got closer to his homeland, and thinking of the astonished delight that would receive him amid the tents of his people, had grown proud and reckless. So when one of the drunks bumped into him, deliberately or not, he reacted as no fugitive and secret traveler should. For he had been in this situation before.

"Hey, you fat oaf," he shouted, "watch yourself!"

Suddenly the group of drunks didn't seem so drunk. Rather more orderly, though the wine on their breath still stank, the five of them halted.

"What did you say?" demanded one.

Orestes, standing a little way behind, glimpsed a flash of something beneath the man's coarse woolen cloak. Something like steel, something like plate armor . . .

Before he could stop himself, he cried out, "Attila!"

Whatever fumes of wine had slowed the men's minds and made unsteady their steps, vanished in an instant.

The man wheeled on Orestes. "*What* did you call him?"

Orestes began to back away, his face a torment of fear and guilt. "My master, my master," he groaned softly, "come away. Run away. . . ."

But the older boy's hand was already reaching inside his ragged cloak, and he knew that everything they had travailed and suffered for, over so many weeks and months, would end now, in a damp and dismal backstreet of Aquincum.

The drunks were clearly no drunks at all, but a squad of tough frontier troops who had merely thrown back a few goblets of wine to help their supper go down. Furthermore, they were led by a keen-witted *optio* who actually read the despatches from legionary headquarters in Sirmium, and knew that the whole of this stretch of the river was under orders to be on the lookout for a fugitive Hun boy with distinctive blue tattoos and scars on his cheeks. A prince of the royal house of King Uldin, and a most valuable hostage. A boy called—

Attila's sword was only half out of his scabbard when the *optio* placed two meaty hands on his shoulders and slammed him back against the wall of the gloomy street.

"You, boy," he rasped, "your name?"

Attila said nothing, his slanted yellow eyes glittering.

The *optio* was about to rip the felt cap from the boy's head, when he seemed to give a slight lurch backward.

"Sir?" asked one his men, moving toward him.

The *optio* fell backward into his soldier's arms, staring wildly up at the sky, black blood gushing from his gaping, wordless mouth and over his stubbled chin.

And then Attila, the bloody sword still in his hand, was running down the street, dragging an open-mouthed Orestes after him. The soldiers' wild shouts echoed from the high walls of the dank little street, and their hobnailed sandals rang on the cobbles as they pounded after them.

The boys twisted and turned through the narrow backstreets and shadowy courtyards of the town, trying to find their way to freedom, which had seemed so close.

"If we're caught," panted Orestes, "you will . . . won't you?" He drew his hand across his throat. "I'm not—"

"Save your breath," said Attila harshly.

They pressed into the shadows of a wall behind some columns as the soldiers clattered past, their lungs aflame as they held their breath tight. Once the soldiers had gone, their breath exploded outward and Orestes collapsed to his knees.

"On your feet," hissed Attila.

"Can't," wheezed Orestes. "Just another—"

"What happens to runaway slaves?" demanded Attila cruelly. "Hands off? Eyes out?"

Orestes shook his head. "Please," he whispered.

Attila grabbed his arm and hauled. "Then *on your feet,* soldier. We're nearly there."

"Where?"

"The quayside."

"How do you know which way?"

Attila eyed him in the darkness. "Because land slopes *down* to a river, mutton brain. Now let's go."

They ran on, downhill through the streets wherever possible, until at last they could hear water lapping against wooden barques and wharves, and smell the damp, pervading smell of the mile-wide river. Rats scurried in the darkness. The boys slid out between two huge wooden wharves and saw the gleam of the Danube. On their side, occasional lights and torches burned from the churches and wealthier houses of the city, but on the eastern bank and beyond . . . nothing. Not a light showed from the black plains out there. Overhead, the uninterrupted, silvery shimmering of the Milky Way, the brilliant winter stars of Orion's belt, and gleaming Sirius, the Dog Star, bringer of storms, rising and burning more brightly than any earthly light.

"There," breathed Attila. *"There."*

They slipped down to the quayside and saw not a soul about. A cat mewed on one of the tethered grain barges where it had been ratting, and eyed them pitifully and crept away. They approached the barge. It might be big enough for them to hide aboard somewhere, under some filthy and neglected canvas, or even inside a stinking coil of sodden rope.

There came the sound of horses' hooves in the night, and they froze. Torchlight gradually spread along the ground from round the corners, and at last, at either end of the quay, they saw troops of frontier cavalry, as many as forty or fifty men. Attila, still clutching Orestes' arm, made to run for the wooden quayside and hurl them both into the river. But a pair of cavalrymen spurred instantly into a gallop, and one hurled a Batavian net over the boys. They stumbled and fell, struggling as helplessly as flies in a web.

They were dragged to their feet and struck sharply across the face for good measure.

The commanding officer, evidently senior, with cropped white hair and a brutal, unflinching stare, ripped Attila's cap from his head and ran his stubby fingers over the welts of the boy's tattooed cheeks.

"So," he said. "Attila. You have come a long way."

The boy spat in his face. The officer instantly struck him, so hard that his head spun round and he reeled back. But he did not fall. The officer was surprised. Such a blow would have felled most grown men. When Attila's head had cleared enough for him to see again, he stepped back in front of the officer and stared him in the eye.

Wiping the spittle from his face, the officer nodded at Orestes. "And who's he?"

Attila shrugged. "No idea. Just some hanger-on. Pain in the ass."

Orestes said nothing, but as he was dragged away by two guards his eyes never left the sullen, unsmiling figure of Attila.

"Give him a good kicking and throw him out of the city gates," said the officer. He paid no farther attention to Orestes. All his attention was on Attila, and all his thoughts were of imperial gratitude, of speedy promotion, of donatives of silver and gold and finest Samian ware. . . .

"Manacle him hand and foot," he said at last, "and bring him to the fort. No more beating—I want some answers from him. This one knows more than he lets on."

Orestes lay gasping in the mud for some time, he didn't know how long. When he tried to stir, he ached all over. His arms and shoulders felt bruised to the bone, and one flank hurt deeply every time he took in a lungful of air. His buttocks almost cramped with pain, his legs, his feet. . . . Even the roots of his hair still stung, where he had been wrenched about by the guffawing soldiers.

Worse than all this, his heart ached with loss. Attila had been everything to him. He had never felt so utterly alone in his life.

At last he crawled to his feet and walked slowly away from the city, to the open fields alongside the river. The river was so wide, so dark. He could never swim it. He limped on through the night until he came to a creek. And there among the reeds and the nodding bulrushes, miraculously, tied up to a half-rotting landing stage, was an ancient wooden boat with a single wooden oar lying in it, gently sliding to and fro in the wash from the river. They needn't have bothered with Aquincum.

Orestes crept down to the creek, and a surprised moorhen erupted from the reeds and beat away across the dark river, setting his heart thumping anew with fright. He stepped painfully into the boat. It was taking in water slowly, an inch or two swilling muddily in the bottom, and it stank of old fish. It would be no easy matter to move and steer the boat with a single oar, and maybe bail, too, with only his cupped hands, across a mile of the great flowing river. But it was a boat, for all that, and a boat meant freedom.

He squatted in the bottom of the boat, the muddy water oozing over his bandaged toes, clutched the end of the flatboard oar, and brooded. That stinging denial of Attila's, was, he knew, his salvation. That was why he sat here now, on the verge of reaching freedom in the ungoverned lands on the farther shore. While the tattooed boy who called himself a prince was incarcerated in a locked and bolted dungeon reeking of ordure, somewhere back in the city, being "questioned" by his unsmiling captors.

Orestes looked up at the clear winter stars. Did they care what happened to him or the other boy? Did they care what he did next? Did it matter if they cared or not? When he looked down the stars still shimmered at him inescapably from the surface of the black water. They would not leave him alone.

At last he sighed, laid the oar down against the side of the boat, and stepped painfully back out onto the slimy bank of the creek. He crept up through the reeds and the galingale, and limped slowly back toward the city.

Attila was manacled hand and foot, as the burly white-haired officer had ordered, and half dragged, half carried up a narrow, spiraling stone staircase to a small upper room with a single, strongly barred window. There he was set down upon a stool, and two guards stood by him with spears set firmly in front of his darting eyes.

After a few minutes, fresh from his dinner, the white-haired officer came strolling in and ordered the door to be shut behind him. He was still mopping his mouth with a linen napkin, and his demeanor was more relaxed now that he had a bellyful of food and wine.

"Just wait till my people hear how I have been treated," hissed Attila, before the officer could say a word. "Just wait till my grandfather Uldin hears. He will not endure such an insult to his blood."

The officer raised an eyebrow. "Who says he will ever hear of it? You are escaping no further now. Your next stop, and your place of residence for a long, long time to come, will be the imperial court at Ravenna."

"Never," said Attila. "I will die first."

"Spoken like a man," said the officer. Despite himself, he was beginning to admire, or at least enjoy, the lad's sheer, naked ferocity. As one might enjoy the spectacle of a wolf fight in the arena.

"Neverthless," he went on, "that is where you are bound—and with the agreement of your people, don't forget. You are a hostage. It is all a perfectly civilized arrangement."

"Civilization," spat the boy. "I've been there before. Give me anywhere else but civilization."

The boy and the man eyed each other in silence for awhile. Then the boy looked away.

The officer said, "I have never been far beyond the river. Just the occasional punitive expedition when the Alamanni or the Marcomanni have got uppity. Tell me about your country beyond."

My country? thought Attila. How would you understand my country? You *Roman,* with your mind as straight and unwavering as a road? How to describe to you, you oaf, my beloved country?

He took a deep breath, pulled at his cruel wrist manacles, and settled his hands in his lap. He said, "My country is a land without boundaries or frontiers or armies. Every man there is a warrior. Every woman is the mother of warriors. Cross the gray Danube and you are in my country, and you may ride for weeks and months and never leave it. There is nothing there but the green, green grassland of the steppe, feather grass and hare's-tail grass as far as the eye can see. As far as the eagle flies, a hundred days' riding eastward into the rising sun, it is still the green grassland of my country."

"You have an active imagination, boy."

Attila ignored him. He could no longer see him, or even the dank walls of the dungeon around him. He could see only what he described.

"In March," he said, "the grasslands flash young and green like the kingfisher's breast on the Dnieper. In April they are purple with saxifrage and vetch, and in May they are yellow, like a brimstone's wings. There, many days' riding beyond the steppes, which are a thousand times the size of your empire, with never a fence or a barrier or a plot of land that is owned or fenced in, nothing to stop you galloping all day and all night, as far as you want, as if you and your horse were flying. . . . There, there is a freedom such as no Roman has ever known."

The officer stood very still. The two guards did not move. They listened.

"Beyond the steppes, there rise the white mountains, where the souls of the holy men are fed when they go to dream and commune with the ancestors. Beyond the black waters of Lake Baikal, and the Snow Mountains, and the Blue Mountains, are at last the Altai Mountains, the soul and navel of the world, where all men must go who would be wise or powerful. The high Altai are seen for many days' riding, high over the plains and the eastern deserts. They are the home of all magicians, all shamans and holy men, and all who hold converse with the Eternal Blue Sky since time began. They say that even your god Christ walked there, in the time before his time of sacrifice."

He fell silent. It was blasphemy that he had spoken. He would say no more, for even to talk of the Altai was treachery to any who did not know.

After a long pause, the officer said quietly, "And I always heard that the Huns had no poetry."

"The Huns have poetry," said Attila indignantly, "but they entrust it not to paper but to memory. All that is holiest and most dangerous is entrusted to memory alone."

The officer was silent again for awhile. Then he nodded to the two guards and they opened the door. With a somber tread he walked from the room, and left the boy to his dreams of his unknown country.

Attila lay on his side on the lumpy straw pallet, comfort impossible with his arms wrenched behind him and his wrists manacled. They had said he would be unmanacled tomorrow. But tomorrow was tomorrow.

He could see the bright winter stars through the bars of iron: green and twinkling Vega low on the horizon, and Arcturus, and brilliant Capella. And then he heard the high, distant cry of a sparrow hawk. It came from far below, near the ground, which was wrong, and in the middle of the night, which was even more wrong. A sparrow hawk's cry, like that of all birds of prey, was a cry of power and triumph, as it wheeled high in the sky in the bright day, and surveyed all the earth below it as its kingdom. He tensed and strained his ears, and after awhile the cry came again. Not a real sparrow hawk: it couldn't be. It was a boy with a shiny blade of grass trembling between his taut thumbs. . . .

He had no grass to answer with, and anyway his hands were not free. Unable to contain the beating of his heart and the hot surge of his blood, he cried out in a loud voice, the cry echoing round the little cell and bringing the guards running. They shot the bolts and flung open the door and roughly demanded what he was up to. He said he must have been having a nightmare. They eyed him suspiciously and then left again, double-bolting the heavy door behind them.

He waited patiently on his straw pallet for the cry to come again. *Patience is a nomad.* But he heard nothing. Instead, something fell like a shadow across the stars beyond the window. He thought at first that it was a night-flying bird come to roost on the narrow shelf of stone outside the bars, but it was gone in an instant. Then it came again, and fell with a barely audible thud on the ledge. He got up and hobbled painfully to the tiny window. There on the ledge was the end of a knotted rope. He didn't stop to consider, but hurled himself at the bars, reaching his head forward to try and grab the rope with his teeth. He could not reach it. He tried again, flinging himself at the bars with bared teeth, but it was hopeless. The knot trembled on the very verge of the ledge, and fell away and was gone. He sank back in despair.

Again and again the rope end flew through the night air toward the little barred window, and again and again it fell away uselessly. Attila stopped even waiting for it to come. And then at last, thrown in a wider arc than usual, it sailed cleanly, miraculously, through the bars and fell back against the inner wall. Attila was on his feet immediately, grabbing the knot and holding on to it for all he was worth. There was a tug, and he tugged back. Then a much stronger weight, and he gasped with pain as his pinioned arms were wrenched upward with the force. He sank to the ground and still clutching the rope he laid his whole weight upon it and braced his feet against the wall. He hoped and prayed it would be enough.

Twice the rope began to slip and his arm muscles screamed in pain, but he held on. The rope trembled in his grasp like a fishing line. And then a shadow blocked the stars through the window, and a piping, boyish voice whispered his name.

He struggled up. "Orestes?"

The shadow nodded.

"You came back."

"Yes."

The shadow against the stars was perched precariously on the tiny ledge, squatting like a goblin. One hand clutched one of the bars; the other held a thick length of wood.

"You need a crowbar, you muttonhead," said Attila. "You can't move iron with wood."

"People don't just leave crowbars lying around, you know," hissed Orestes, indignantly. "It was all I could find."

He set the thick log between two bars and began to lean his weight back against it, his body stretched almost horizontally out from the wall of the fort, thirty feet or more above the ground. Nothing. He collapsed back against the bars.

"Here," said Attila, "try this end one."

Orestes changed his grip and tried again, and this time it shifted slightly. The mortar setting gave in a little cloud of dust, and the bar fell on its side.

"Now use that bar on the others," said Attila.

"I know, I know," said Orestes.

He had managed to break off two more bars when they heard soldiers unbolting the door.

"Quick, the other bar!" cried Orestes.

Attila twisted painfully and managed to pass it up. The first door bolt was shot. Orestes stood the bar upright in its place as the second bolt was shot.

"Get down!" hissed Attila, and he flung himself back onto his pallet and closed his eyes.

The door swung open and the soldiers looked in. They saw the little runaway hooligan asleep, sleeping like a baby. At the window, two boyish hands clutched the bars and a knotted rope, but the soldiers saw nothing. The door was closed and bolted again.

One more bar was wrenched free, and then Orestes could just slither in to the cell. He took the rope from Attila and tied it to the one remaining bar.

"Will that hold?" asked Attila.

"It'll have to. Here, kneel down."

"My ankles first, you fool. No one ever runs away on their hands."

With a harsh twist of the bar in his ankle manacles, Attila's feet were free. Then Orestes did the same for his wrists.

He grimaced and rubbed his bruised flesh. "Right. Time we left."

It was the loose bar left carelessly on the window ledge that did it. Attila got down safely, but Orestes swung a little too much in his descent. The rope grazed over the ledge, nudged the loose bar and set it rolling across the the stone. It dropped with a loud, echoing clang—inside the cell.

In a trice the soldiers were back at the door and shooting the bolts. The door was flung open, and they stood open mouthed at the sight of the empty pallet and the window with four bars missing. Then they sprang into action: they ran to the last standing bar, and slashed the rope knotted round it.

Orestes fell fifteen feet. Attila heard his bones break. He heard the crack quite clearly in the still night air, and he heard his friend scream.

"Run!" cried Orestes. "To the river—run!"

But Attila grabbed him and hauled him to his feet. He looped Orestes' left arm over his own shoulders, and together, hobbling, not running, they made for the shelter of the reeds down by the silent river.

Behind them they could hear the creaking of the wooden gates of the fort. The soldiers were coming after them.

"Leave me," gasped Orestes as he stumbled at Attila's side. "Run!"

The older boy ignored him. He did not look back—he might stumble and trip. He dragged Orestes on down through the meadows beyond the town to the misty riverside. He could hear horses close by as they harrumphed their astonishment and displeasure at being pulled from the stables and galloped so hard at this peculiar hour of the night.

They came to an orchard and ran panting into its shadows. The branches were bare, and last year's sere and yellow leaves strewed the ground; the grass was long and damp. They fell against a tree trunk and let their lungs suck in the cold night air as quietly as they could. They could hear the shouts of men through the trees.

Orestes' leg throbbed with its new, twisted form, but it did not yet give him agony. Despite the broken bone jutting out like a malignant lump under the skin, the terror and excitement of their flight somehow dulled the pain. For now.

"We must go on," said Attila. "Follow me."

Beyond the orchard was a stony cart track, and then the dense reeds along the river's edge. Cavalrymen from the fort were spreading out all along the track, blocking all approaches to the river.

The two boys crouched at the edge of the orchard and peered out through the long grass. There was no moon, but even the winter stars seemed cruelly bright.

"We're trapped," moaned Orestes. "And the boat's just there, near that broken-down old landing stage."

Attila stared at him.

"Just there," said Orestes, indicating the place with a jerk of his head. "I found it."

"You found a boat?" said Attila. "And you still came back for me?"

Orestes shrugged, embarrrassed.

Attila gazed across the misty river. Once they were back on the windy plains, he thought, there would be no manacles for either of them. Nor would he permit his friend to be hobbled, as most of the Huns' slaves were: the tendons in the heels were cut to stop them running away. But this Greek boy—he would be treated differently.

He slipped away and came back a few moments later with a stout-looking stick which he handed to Orestes.

"When you can," he whispered, "run for the boat."

"Run?"

"Well, hobble or whatever."

"But they'll see me. Where will you be?"

"In the river."

"Can't they follow you in? Can't they swim?"

"Are you joking?" said Attila. "Some of those Batavian cavalry units can swim a horse across a river in full armor. But . . ." He looked around desperately. "Well, whatever." And he was gone.

He made his way along the edge of the orchard, and then down a filthy-smelling drainage ditch that ran to the river. The soldiers in their winter cloaks were still spread out along the frosty cart track, looking uncertain, their orders vague. Somewhere the white-haired officer was riding around in a rage, but the chain of command seemed chaotic.

Attila drew in a deep breath, leaped from the ditch and ran.

He ran straight between two startled horsemen and on into the reeds, slowing horribly as his feet were sucked down into the oozing mud. He hallooed as he stumbled on.

The horsemen shouted and galloped after him, but they, too, were slowed down in the thick reeds and the clinging, viscous mud. The boy felt a rope whistle past his ear and fall with a sigh into the reeds. He grinned and struggled on, knee deep in mud. No one could throw a rope as well as a Hun.

He felt gravel under his feet, and the reeds thinned out, and he hurled himself forward into the freezing river.

Orestes watched as the horsemen on the track all made for the place where Attila had dived in. They gathered in a useless knot, leaving the track unguarded. He hobbled to his feet, clutching the stout stick in both hands, his broken leg dragging behind him. Clenching his teeth to keep his agony silent, he hauled himself over the cart track like the sorriest cripple in the empire, and on into the reeds beyond. He wasn't seen.

Dragging himself through the ooze of the mud was harder. With his whole weight on only one foot he sank deeper with every step, and the stick sank deeper still. He cursed his bad luck for having fallen from the wall. But he dragged himself onward, his lungs aflame as if he had just run five miles. Every muscle in his body ached. Even his neck ached terribly—he couldn't understand why—but he went on.

Upriver, there was no sign of the Hun boy but for a stream of bubbles on the surface. No more than a diving otter might make in the black, starlit waters.

At last Orestes got to the boat and hauled it down to deeper water. He pushed off, utterly exhausted, with the single oar and with the stick on each side. Then, almost collapsed in the bow of the boat, which was dangerously low in the water, he began to paddle, a stroke each side of the bow, like a barbarian in a dug out on the Rhine.

He didn't know what he was supposed to do next. His head spun, his limbs burned, his eyes were almost blind with sweat and dizziness. He heard shouts from the bank, and heavy splashes, and knew he had been spotted, and that the cavalrymen were dismounting and diving in, or ordering their own boats upriver, or even plunging in on horseback like true Batavians, as the Hun boy had said.

Then he was aware of another sound, and looking blearily down he saw two hands appear on the gunwale of the boat, then two arms and a soggy topknot, and then a round head with yellow, glittering eyes. With a great gasp and heave, as if he still had as much energy and strength left in him as ever, Attila was up over the side of the rocking boat and into the back.

"Give me the oar!" he shouted, grabbing it from the startled Orestes, and he began to paddle furiously, one side then the other.

Dark shapes bobbed on the river upstream: the heads of men and horses. Downstream, near the fort, showed the black hulls of the legion's river fleet. But they were too slow. The boys were already in midstream and crossing fast.

Attila knew it. "Here" he said, tossing the oar to Orestes, who took it with weariness but without complaint. To Orestes' astonishment, Attila got to his feet, and began dancing like a lunatic in the stern of the dangerously unstable little boat. He shook his fists and tossed his angry head at the speechless soldiers staring from the bank and the river.

"You fucking assholes! You thick, Roman bastards!" he screamed. "You useless fucking scum-sucking motherfucking sad-assed abortions of men! You haven't got a hope in Hell of catching us, you steaming sacks of mule shit! Come and get us if you can, you fucking Roman wankers! Astur piss on you all!" He stopped jigging for a moment and turned, raised his tunic and bared his buttocks at them. Still there came no sound from the soldiers or their open-mouthed officers.

He resumed his taunting. "You couldn't run a bath, you couldn't invade a fucking Corinthian brothel, you feckless big-nosed cunts! You dog-breathed turds of the Devil! You try swimming after us and you'll sink to the bottom like lead weights, shit brains! Come on, try and get us! Come on! Assholes!"

He whirled to face Orestes, grinning with insane delight, his eyes aflame with a burning, furious madness. In the darkness, Orestes couldn't see the soldiers' faces, but he saw that their dim shapes had stopped dead in the shallows, still mounted. He could imagine their expressions.

Attila turned back again. "Losers! Abortions! Scumsuckers! Pigfuckers! You're all going to rot in Hell! Rome's going to fall! We'll be back, and there'll be nothing left of your rotting fucking empire but a heap of blood and rubble!" He wiped spittle from his mouth on his ragged sleeve. "And fuck your emperor, and his sister, too! Fuck him right up his scrawny chicken ass!"

Almost choking with lunatic laughter, he sank down in the stern of the boat. He leaned his head back, raised his fists at the stars and cried one last time, "Fucker-r-r-s!"

At dawn, a company of the Palatine guard arrived at Aquincum.

"You have the Hun boy held captive," rasped their commander, a lieutenant with half his face collapsed and shapeless from injury. "Where is he?"

"Dismount and salute when you address your superior officer!" roared the colonel, red with rage.

In answer, the Palatine lieutenant simply held out a sheet of parchment with the imperial seal on it. The colonel lost his confidence at that moment.

"The Hun boy," repeated the lieutenant.

"He . . . he's escaped," said the colonel.

The Palatine looked at him in disbelief. "Escaped? From a frontier fort?"

"He had an accomplice. What do you want him for, anyway?"

"No business of yours."

The colonel looked away over the river, quite calm now, in the face of his impending punishment at the edge of the sword. "He has gone away across the Danube, back to his people."

The Palatine looked over the river likewise and said sourly, "So. I suppose we will never hear from him again."

The colonel replied, "Oh, you will hear from him again."

The Palatine remembered what they said about dying men's prophecies, and under his gleaming black armor he shivered.

PART III

INTO THE WILDERNESS

1

THE DEATH OF THE HEART

After three bitter days of struggling across the wide Pannonian plain, the fugitives came to a safe place to rest. Attila found a medicine woman who set Orestes' broken leg, scolded him roundly, and told him not to move a muscle for at least two weeks. After that he must walk only with a stick, and put as little weight as possible upon his injured leg for at least another moon.

It was early spring by the time they journeyed again, and came to that great range of mountains which in the Gothic tongue are called the *Harvaða,* in the Hun the *Kharvadh,* and in the Latin the *Carpathians.* They crossed the high passes of those wild mountains in flower-bright springtime, and came down at last onto the limitless steppes of Scythia in March, when the grasses, as Attila had said, flashed young and green like the kingfisher's breast on the Dnieper.

They walked for many days across the steppes, silent and intoxicated with their vast emptiness, their beauty and their immemorial loneliness. One morning they came near to one of the slow, winding rivers of that country, and they heard a woman singing by the riverside as she washed clothes and dried them on the rocks. She sang her nomad songs in the tongue of the Huns, and Attila knew that he was nearly home:

My beloved, how proudly he rides,
Proudly, like the wind;
Soon he will be gone,
Like the wind, like the wind.

My beloved, how proudly she dances,
She dances like the wind;
Soon she will be gone,
Like the wind, like the wind.

See, the tribe is moving on,
Flattening the grass like the wind;
Soon we will be gone,
Like the wind, like the wind.

The woman started in fear when they called to her, but when she saw it was only two grubby, travel-stained boys she relaxed and listened to them. She saw that one boy was of the people, with his tattooed cheeks and his fierce topknot tossing in the wind. He went naked to the waist, like the warriors of the tribe, and even though he was barely out of boyhood she could not help but admire the sinewy, muscular strength of his arms and chest. She lowered her eyes when she replied to him, as she would to her husband or a man of the tribe, for the boy had a strange authority. Then she pointed across the river to the shallow valley beyond, where the black tents were encamped.

The boys said thank you and walked on.

As they neared the rim of the valley, they saw a boy walking through the long grasses, his head bowed as if in sorrow, moving slowly, noticing little. A few paces behind him walked his slave.

Attila called, "Who are you?"

He stopped and looked up. This boy who walked by himself, as if burdened with the sorrow of the world, stood a full head taller than Attila. His eyes were a clear blue, his features very fine, his nose straight and classically Roman. His limbs were long and well knit, his brow high and noble. Only his hair still retained a certain boyishness in its thatched brown tangle. Otherwise he looked and acted far older than his years.

When he spoke, his Hunnish was perfect. "Who are you?" he asked calmly.

Attila faltered, and then with some reluctance answered, "I am Attila, son of Mundzuk."

The boy nodded. "I am Aëtius, son of Gaudentius."

On the same day that Attila was born—such is the ironic humor of the gods—under the same proud, blazing summer sun in Leo, another boy was born, in Durostorum in Silestria, a frontier province of Pannonia. He was christened Aëtius. His father was one Gaudentius, master general of the cavalry on the Pannonian frontier.

In the black tent of Mundzuk, that night, the father crouching still anxiously over the perspiring, smiling mother and the tiny baby at her breast, an old woman moved her hand slowly over the tiny, wrinkled baby and said, "He is made for war."

In the master general's fine military palace in Durostorum, while the straight-backed father paced the colonnade outside, and in an inner room the mother clutched the tiny newborn baby to her breast, an ancient *haruspex* pushed the midwife impatiently aside, gazed keenly down upon the little form and then into the crushed oak leaves she held in the palm of her hand, and said, "He is made for war."

Attila and Orestes began their descent into the valley.

"Your father, Mundzuk," called the Roman boy from above.

Attila stopped. "What?" he said.

The Roman boy hesitated, then shook his head. "Nothing," he said.

Attila walked steadily on into the camp of the Huns. Orestes walked behind, his hare eyes darting among the tents, his lips working nervously. He, too, had heard of the Huns. He trusted his friend implicitly, but what of the rest of the tribe?

The Huns did not build walls to defend themselves, and when they were not at war with their neighbors they hardly set a night guard over their camp. There was a magnificent carelessness in their lack of fear, which struck only greater fear into the hearts of their enemies.

One day a Byzantine ambassador had asked them why they built no defensive walls.

Uldin stepped up uncomfortably close to him, put his face into the face of the startled Greek, and said, "Our walls are made of men, and spears, and swords."

Now women sat outside some of those undefended tents, stirring black pots on smoky turf fires. Many had the same deep blue tattoos on their cheeks as Attila. They regarded the newcomers inscrutably as they walked by. None said a word.

Beyond the tents they could hear the whinny and snicker of the corralled horses, the Huns' most valued possession. Somewhere among them was a white mare, her mane long and her tail almost down to the ground. Chagëlghan, his horse, his beloved mare . . .

At last the boys came to the principal tent in the encampment, an imposing pavilion stretched across three massive tent poles, the awning fringed with tassels. Two posts stood at either side of the great tent, and from them hung feathers and ribbons, mummified birds of prey, and flensed and polished human skulls.

Orestes swallowed. He wanted to say something, if only his friend's name. But he couldn't speak. His mouth was as dry as the steppe in the August sun.

A single man stood in the entrance to the tent, but he was a man bigger than Orestes had ever seen. Not in height, in breadth. His torso was as massive as that of an ox, his legs were like tree trunks, squat and thick and seeming to bow slightly under the weight of his hugely muscled body. But they said that all Huns had bow legs. It came from sitting on their horses all day. They even slept on their horses, it was said.

The man crossed his arms over his chest, and his huge biceps bulged the more. His mouth was clamped tight shut under his thin, drooping mustache, and his narrow eyes never left the approaching boys. They stopped in front of him.

"We wish to see the king," said Attila.

The man did not move.

"Step aside."

The man did not move.

"Bulgü, I said, *step aside.*"

The man-mountain started and looked more closely at the boy. Then, to Orestes' astonishment, he lumbered to his left, the ground shaking beneath his felt-booted feet.

The boys went in.

The tent was long and deep, like the hall of one of the Germanic tribes, only of felt, not of wood. For nothing is built to last in the world of the Huns; everything passes away, like the wind, like the wind.

At the head of the tent was a raised dais, and there on an elaborately carved throne sat the king. He had heard of the boys' approach and hastily taken up position to receive them. His beloved grandson . . .

Attila cried, "Uldin!" and ran to him.

As he ran, in the dimness of the tent, something terrible happened. The king's face changed. The face of his grandfather, old King Uldin, changed. It was no longer the wrinkled, grim but honest old face of his grandfather but a younger face, heavily bearded—far more heavily bearded than was usual among the Huns. The eyes were narrow, the nose snub and red, but the mouth, most revealing of features, was almost hidden beneath the dark, bushy beard.

As the boy reeled to a halt before the crude wooden throne, the mouth revealed itself in a broad smile. The teeth within revealed themselves, too: yellow gravestones overlapping and collapsing, and the smile never reached the narrow, watchful eyes.

"Attila," rumbled the king.

"Ruga!" gasped Attila.

"Astur and all the gods in heaven be praised," said Ruga. "You have returned."

Attila gaped and said nothing.

"Our Roman allies informed us that you had . . . taken your own path, though you were an important hostage in the court of the emperor."

"You would ha—my grandfather would have had me escape, had he known. . . . My father. Where is my father?"

The narrow eyes looked coldly back at him.

"Where is my father, Lord Mundzuk?"

"Do not raise your voice to me, boy," said Ruga quietly, but with insidious menace.

Behind him, Attila heard the tent flap pulled aside, and a heavy presence step within: Bulgü. Orestes still stood trembling at the back of the tent. This was not how it was supposed to go, and the quick-witted Greek boy knew it immediately.

"My father, Lord Mundzuk," repeated Attila, keeping his voice calm and respectful with the greatest of effort, "son of King Uldin."

Abruptly, and with the terrible, unreasoning violence that made him so feared, Ruga leaned forward on his throne and roared, "On your knees before my throne, boy, or I'll have you whipped and bloodied at the back of an oxcart from here to the Takla Makan!"

Shaken even in his sturdy young soul, Attila sank to his knees.

Ruga rumbled on, "Stand before me and demand answers of me, would you? Your manners have deserted you in the courts of Rome, it seems." He settled back in his throne and narrowed his eyes again. He stroked his tangled beard.

"Lord Mundzuk, son of Uldin. Yes. I, too, am a son of Uldin, and the brother of Lord Mundzuk."

Attila waited in agony, though in his heart he knew what was to come.

"The great King Uldin," said Ruga, "died only lately, in his bed, his women at his side, and full of years. Only days later, Mundzuk was killed in an accident while out hunting. A single arrow. . . ." Ruga shrugged. "The will of the gods. And who are we to question it?"

The boy bowed his head. His father, the all-knowing, all-powerful god of his boyhood world. The noble Mundzuk, beloved of women, admired by men. His reign over his people would have been great and long. And Attila had not even said farewell to him before his long and bitter journey, had not had his dying blessing on his head. . . .

"He is buried in a fine grave mound," said Ruga, "a morning's ride to the east."

Attila did not move; he could not. His eyes were tight shut so that the tears could not flow.

"Go now."

At last the boy got to his feet and turned all in a single movement, so that Ruga should not see the tears springing from his eyes. As he approached the door of the tent, Ruga called after him, "The Romans maltreated you, you say?"

The boy stopped. Without turning, he replied, "They tried to kill me."

"You lie!" roared Ruga, aflame with anger again, springing from his throne and pacing down the tent. He was a big man, but swift. "They would not dare so to insult their allies the Hun people."

Then Attila turned, and although his face was streaming with tears his eyes were steady on the narrow eyes of his uncle. He said, "I do not lie. They tried to kill me. They tried to make it appear I was killed by the people of Alaric the Goth, so that you would turn against the Goths, the enemies of Rome, who are now their allies."

Ruga stared at him and shook his head as if to clear the fog of bewilderment from his brain. He knew the boy spoke the truth. It burned from his eyes with a light no liar could summon.

"Those Romans," he muttered at last. "They think like vipers."

"They kill like vipers, too."

Ruga looked at Attila again and saw him as if for the first time. He saw a certain quickness and strength, and of a sudden he admired him as well as fearing and resenting his return.

He laid his big hand on the boy's shoulder. "Go," he said. "Get some new clothes, see the women. And then go to the grave mound of your father."

Attila turned and left, Orestes trotting anxiously after him.

Ruga beckoned to Bulgü. "Bring me Chanat," he said.

A few moments later a tall, lean Hun stepped into the tent, naked to the waist, his hair long and oiled, his mustache black and resplendent across his high-colored face. He showed no surprise or dismay at the command of his king. He bowed, and left the tent, and went to the great wooden corral to find his horse.

Heavy gray clouds rolled down from the north, and a bitter wind swept before them, as the boy rode out on his white mare, Chagëlghan, to find the grave mound of his father. He rode with his head bowed, and even the mare's head hung low. The wind whipped around them, and then it began to rain. They rode east.

The vast and treeless steppe was obscured by hanging curtains of rain. The grass was flattened by the gusting wind from the north, and horse and boy both turned their faces away for respite and shelter. After some hours' riding the rain abated, and a watery sun came out. Still far away across the steppe, the boy saw a break in the endless flat horizon, and it was the mound where his father lay buried.

He came to the mound and dismounted and sat cross-legged on the top. He raised his face to the last of the raindrops falling from the Eternal Blue Sky, and held his hands out wide, and he wept for a long time.

It took him all afternoon to ride back to the camp, and it was dusk by the time he returned. He went down to the river's edge to wash away the dust and sorrow that clung to him. The riverbank was steep, but he slipped carelessly from his horse in his grief and exhaustion, and almost fell into the deep water. It was cold and he gasped and came back to life again. He stripped off his clothes, tossed them up onto the bank and sank under the water. When he came up again for air, the world was dark and silent around him, and he could hear nothing but the soft paddling of the sandpipers making their springtime nests even in the last moments of twilight. Making their nests, raising their young.

He began to shiver with cold and grief again, and started to scramble back up the bank. But it was steep and slippery, and his wet body made it more slippery and muddier still, and he slithered back helplessly into the water. He looked up, and there was the Roman boy, Aëtius, at the top of the bank, looking down at him without expression, his horse standing close behind him. Attila's eyes flashed with anger, but Aëtius seemed impervious to it. He knelt down and held out his hand. After some hesitation Attila reached out and grabbed it, and Aëtius hauled him up the bank; he was strong. He picked up Attila's clothes and handed them to him. Attila pulled them on: cross-laced leather breeches, a coarse woolen shirt, and a fur jerkin belted round the waist. They said no word to each other. Then Attila went over and got onto his horse as best he could, with his cold, stiff, trembling limbs.

The Roman boy mounted, too, on his taller bay mare, and they sat for awhile and looked across the darkening steppe.

At last Aëtius said quietly, "My father died the summer before last. I have never seen his grave."

They looked at each other in silence for a moment. Then Aëtius wheeled his horse round alongside Attila's and they rode back into camp side by side.

For a week more Attila was permitted to mourn the death of his father, then it was time for the ceremony. He had known that it would come soon. . . .

He was grooming Chagëlghan with a bristle brush when one of the warriors came cantering over. He reined in and waited for Prince Attila to speak first.

Attila jerked his head in inquiry.

"It is time," said the warrior. "Your uncle the king and the holy men have decreed it."

The boy nodded. He patted Chagëlghan on her flanks, and whispered into her flicking ears one last time.

It was time for the ceremony of manhood and the *Kalpa Ölümsuk:* the Death of the Heart.

It reminded Aëtius of a Roman triumph, the way the people formed up alongside the wide ceremonial way to the Stone, while the boy processed between them. But the singing of the harsh, pentatonic songs and the wailing and keening of the women was anything but Roman. And the grim-faced priests of the tribe who followed behind, the front of their heads shaven and then pasted with blood-red paint, naked to the waist, wearing belted kilts hung with feathers and animal skulls, reminded him in no way of the well-born patricians who served as priests in the Christian churches of Rome.

Attila led Chagëlghan close behind him, and his expression betrayed nothing. Any emotion except rage was unfit for a man.

Aëtius had asked what the ceremony entailed, but none would tell him. It was his own slave boy, the brown-eyed, soft-voiced Cadoc, who said something to him about it.

"For many people, to become a man you must know your heart. But for the Huns, to become a man you must kill your heart. You must kill the one thing in the world that you love most."

Now Aëtius pushed through the crowd of chanting and ululating tribespeople, and watched in dawning horror as Attila drew his treasured mare to a halt before the great gray Stone at the end of the processional way. For the last time he patted her smooth white flanks. The crowd fell silent. There was a terrible tension in the cool spring air, and a somber silence as once more they witnessed this ceremony that turned a boy into a man.

Attila kept his eyes downcast. His horse stood patiently by. At last he reached up and drew the long, curved sword from the scabbard that hung at his back. Without a moment's hesitation, all in the same swift movement, he brought the bright clean blade down upon Chagëlghan's patiently bending neck. Her front legs gave way and she stumbled to her knees, her big velvet eyes looking stricken and pained, not understanding. The boy brought the sword down again with all his might and with a terrible cry. The deep wound he had cut into the mare's neck went far deeper this time, and her spinal chord was severed. She sank down into the dust and oblivion. The boy cut down once more, and again, and again, crying words no one could understand, until at last the head was completely severed from the slashed and ragged neck. He tossed the bloody sword upon the Stone, and knelt before it. The crowd erupted into wild cheering and ululation.

Two men of the tribe seized the kneeling boy and dragged him to his feet. They raised him up so that he sat on their shoulders, and half walked, half ran back down the processional way, the people strewing their path with bright spring flowers, and tossing coronets of woven grasses at the boy's bowed head.

Now he was again one of the tribe. Now he was truly of the people, a prince of the royal blood, and a proven man.

2

THE TENT OF THE WOMEN

That night there was great feasting in the tent of the people. The men drank and roared and sank their teeth into the roasted flesh of eight different kinds of animals, horses included. The women regarded the noisy excesses of their husbands with a certain tolerance, for once. Then there was potent koumiss, fermented from sweet mare's milk, which set them all dancing in the middle of the tent, and grabbing the captured dwarves they had enslaved and ordering them to dance. The boldest men made everyone laugh by tossing the dwarves to and fro like sacks of dried grass.

At the king's high table, along with other members of the royal family, sat a boy only a little older than Attila, but very different in demeanor. His name was Bleda, and he was Attila's elder brother by two years. He sat grinning stupidly to himself for much of the time, and ate so much that at one point he had to go outside to be sick. When he came in again, he fell upon his food as if he hadn't eaten for days. He and his younger brother seemed to have little to say to each other.

King Ruga did not dance, but he certainly roared and guzzled and drank immense quantities of koumiss. Attila sat obediently nearby, eating and drinking little. Once he looked up because he could feel eyes upon him, and he saw that the Roman boy, picking carefully at a leg of mutton on the bone, was watching him with a certain expression on his face. Suddenly the roaring in the tent was very far away, and Aëtius with his grave blue eyes was very near. Attila nodded slightly to him. Aëtius put a strip of roast mutton in his mouth, and nodded back equally slightly.

The feast went on.

Attila's cup was refilled from behind, and glancing back he saw that it was Orestes. The slave boy managed a smile. Attila tore off a strip from his own haunch of venison and passed it to the boy. Feeding slaves at a feast was strictly forbidden, but Attila didn't care. Orestes took it and guiltily popped it in his mouth. Then, trying not to look as if he was chewing, he moved on down behind the lords and warriors of the tribe, refilling their goblets as he went.

Attila took another sip of koumiss and his hunched shoulders relaxed a little. Not everything he loved was destroyed.

And then it was the moment that he dreaded almost as much as the Death of the Heart.

Ruga stood up and held his goblet aloft. He staggered a little into the man next to him, and was helpfully pushed upright again, and then he roared, "Today, my nephew Attila has become a man!"

Everyone cheered and shouted and some threw chunks of food by way of celebration. Bleda threw a gnawed deer bone along the high table, which would have struck Attila in the face if he hadn't ducked. His brother hooted with mirth.

"Today he has bloodied his sword at the Sacrificial Stone," cried Ruga. "Today he has shown himself a warrior who scorns even his own heart."

There was more, still louder acclamation.

"And tonight . . ." said Ruga, allowing for a dramatic pause, "tonight . . . he goes for the first time to the Tent of the Women."

At which the entire tent erupted into deafening applause.

Attila bent his head and took another, longer sip of koumiss. He could feel it warm in his throat and in his belly. It felt good. He took another. He felt he was going to need it.

There tumbled into the middle of the tent an extraordinary figure in a motley of fur and feathers, bright ribbons wound round his topknot and with a manic grin on his face. It was Little Bird, the mad, all-licensed shaman of the people. He whooped with laughter and clapped his hands, and sang a song about how the noble Prince Attila must go and make love in the tent of the women, for now he was a man.

"And you must get many sons, for there are not enough to go round," cried Little Bird.

Ruga glared and shifted in his seat, but the shaman went on.

"And there must be more babies born, for you know that there are many graves yet to fill, and we wouldn't want the earth growing hungry."

People laughed uncertainly at Little Bird's jokes, for they were always strange and disturbing. But then they drank more koumiss, and solaced themelves with drunkenness, and laughed more and more at the cruel jokes and songs. Little Bird laughed, too, though he never ate or drank a single drop.

The Tent of the Women was a great white circular yurt, with a central pole made from an entire fir tree. It stood at the center of the Compound of the Women, which was where the female captives and slaves were kept, jealously guarded. Hun wives, of course, lived with their husbands in their own tents, often having to share space with concubines and slave girls picked up in the wars. But the Compound of the Women belonged to the king alone, and it was in his gift to permit his family or guests to enjoy its pleasures.

Aside from the Tent of the Women, there lived Ruga's own personal concubines, whom none might touch or even look upon, jealously guarded day and night by castrated slaves. But so far, since the accession of the king, nearly a year ago, not a single one of his concubines, or his wives, had yet become pregnant. But it was not considered too wise to raise the matter.

The cool night cleared Attila's head a little, and he sucked air deep into his lungs. He could feel the meat and koumiss sitting heavily in his belly, but his blood coursed hotly around his body, and he felt that, though he would not go quite fearlessly into the Tent of the Women, nevertheless he would go in not visibly trembling.

The two huge, armed eunuchs who guarded the yurt grinned and made ribald comments as they unlaced the tent flaps and let him step inside.

It was dimly lit within, and a fire burned near the middle, the smoke stealing out through a hole in the roof. Round the central tent pole were spread huge mounds of animal furs, and on them lay some of the women. Others lay farther off round the sides of the tent, dozing or gossiping in low voices, filing their nails with sandstones, or combing and braiding each other's hair by lamplight. The air was dreamy with woodsmoke and hair oil and the light, soft aroma of women.

Two women arose and came over, both some years older than him. They smiled and held out their hands. One was a Circassian, perhaps, with pale blue eyes and very fair hair and complexion. The other was darker, surely from the empire, perhaps from the east. She wore heavy gold earrings and she touched him brazenly, her painted fingernails bright in the lamplight, her hands running down over his chest.

But most of the women were not like that. The Tent of the Women was no Roman bordello, and the air was heavy also with sadness and captivity. Many of the women lay and dreamed of their lost husbands and children, their vanished villages and their homelands far away. Many had come here by way of war and atrocity, and few came to caress their new master with brightly painted fingernails.

The boy moved away from the painted eastern girl and the Circassian, whose faces fell in dismay and scorn as he turned aside. He went round the tent in the shadows, and some of the women stirred and looked at him, and his confusion pulled inside him; his body hotly flushing at the thought that any—that *all* these women could be his for the taking. That was why so many men strove to be kings. But he knew none of them was here for any reason but by the sword.

At last his eyes settled upon a girl huddled in the corner, buried in woolen wraps drawn up round her shoulders and even over her mouth. Her long hair spread out over them and her eyes were lowered. Then she looked up, and he saw her large, haunted eyes in the gloom, her narrow face, and he thought back to another girl, many months ago. He reached out and touched her, and slowly she let the woolen wraps fall and got up from her couch.

Some of the other women had gathered round, cooing and giggling, and the eastern woman with the painted nails was already beckoning them toward a fur-covered couch. As if it was the custom for a man to take his pleasure here with any woman he chose, while the other women gathered round and praised him, their eyes shining with fake lasciviousness, driven only by their desperate desire to be moved from one tent to another: from the herdlike Tent of the Women to one of the private tents of the wives and concubines.

Attila, flushed though he was with koumiss, balked at the idea of such openness. He shook his head at the other women, took the girl's pale hand, led her away behind one of the hangings where they slept, and drew it across behind them.

The other women returned to their couches and waited. They would spend their whole lives waiting, until they were too old, when they would be sold as household slaves for less than the price of a horse's corpse.

Attila drew the girl's shift up over her head and looked at her for a long time. She looked steadily, silently back. At last he pushed her down onto the couch and began to kiss her. He paused for a moment, raising his head and looking down at her. Still a little overawed by the entire experience of the Tent of the Women, he began to mumble something about they didn't have to . . . everything, if she, and he was sorry. . . .

She reached up and pulled him down again. He was surprised and thrilled to feel her kissing him back with ardor. Then she placed her hands on his chest and pushed him aside hard.

"What?" he said bewildered, sitting up.

She laughed softly. "We don't have to . . . everything . . . I'm sorry. . . ." she mimicked cruelly.

She leaned over him and pulled at the lacing on the front of his shirt. "How do you know *I* don't want to as well?" she said, arching her eyebrows. Then she ripped his shirt off over his head, rolled on top of him and straddled his bare chest with her naked thighs. "I might enjoy it sometimes, too," she said.

The boy stared up at her open mouthed. Then her mouth closed on his, and he could think no more.

3

CHANAT

Nearly a month later, a single rider, naked to the waist, with his hair worn long and oiled and his mustache luxuriant, rode into the city of Ravenna. The guards blocked his path at first, but when he said who he was from they reluctantly allowed him to pass, albeit accompanied by an armed escort.

At last, deprived of his horse, thoroughly searched for weapons—he carried none—and obliged to don a white cloak over his sinewy shoulders for the sake of decency, he was allowed into the presence of the Emperor of Rome.

The emperor's sister was also present. A woman—seated on her own throne, as if the equal of a man! These *Romans,* thought the warrior with distaste.

He stood with his arms crossed over his chest, and instead of keeping his eyes respectfully bowed to the elaborate mosaic floor he dared to look the Divine Emperor Honorius in the face.

These *barbarians,* thought the emperor with distaste.

"*Asla konusma Khlatina,*" said the warrior. "*Sizmeli konusmat Ioung.*"

There was some uncourtly confusion while the palace chamberlains scuttled about looking for an interpreter who could understand the ugly language of the Huns. An awkward silence reigned meanwhile in the vast, dimly glittering Chamber of the Imperial Audience. The messenger's eyes never left the face of the emperor. It was intolerable. Honorius looked down into his lap. His sister stared coldly back at the Hun messenger. His bold, slanted eyes reminded her unpleasantly of the eyes of another, younger visitor from the steppes.

At last an interpreter was found, and arrived in the Chamber looking frankly terrified. He stood trembling, some steps behind the Hun warrior, and waited for him to speak again. When the warrior repeated his words, the poor man looked even more stricken at the unenviable prospect of having to translate such impertinent words to the frosty Imperial Throne.

"*Asla konusma Khlatina,*" repeated the warrior. "*Sizmeli konusmat Ioung.*"

The translator stammered, "He says, 'I do not speak Latin. You must speak Hun.'"

"We had already surmised his ignorance of the learned tongues," cut in Galla Placidia.

The emperor glanced nervously at his sister, and then turned to the messenger and, via the interpreter, offered his greetings.

"Likewise," said his sister, "our greetings to your king, the noble Ruga."

The warrior did not offer greetings in return. There was a further silence, further moments of excruciating embarrasment, for all, it seemed, except the warrior himself.

At last Princess Galla said to the interpreter, "Do you think you could trouble him to inform us why we are so blessed with his gracious presence, on this particular day? I can't imagine that he has ridden all this way from God knows what lawless outer darkness, just to tell us that he knows no Latin."

Looking shakier than ever, the interpreter prompted the Hun.

The warrior remained inscrutable. At last he said, "My name is Chanat, the son of Subotai."

Galla arched her eyebrows. "I'm afraid I have not had the pleasure of your father's acquaintance."

Chanat ignored her sarcasm. "I come with a message from my king."

The emperor quivered a little. His sister's lips tightened, becoming more bloodless than ever, but she said nothing.

"One moon since," said Chanat, "the king's nephew, Attila, son of Mundzuk, returned home to the camp of the Huns, beyond the Kharvad Mountains."

There was silence.

"He told us that he had escaped from being a hostage in this land, that you Romans had plotted to kill him."

"He lies!" cried Galla Placidia.

Reluctantly, Chanat supposed that, if the woman addressed him, he must address her. These Romans . . . "He is a prince of the royal blood," he said calmly. "He does not lie."

For a long while the icy eyes of Galla and the slanted eyes of the Hun warrior met across the vast, brittle space of the Audience Chamber. It was Galla who, at last, looked away.

"In all the moons and years and generations henceforth," resumed the warrior, addressing Honorius, "the Hun nation will never ally with Rome again."

The emperor looked up from his lap, where he had been watching his sweaty fingers writhe around each other in perplexity. "You are going to come and attack us?"

Galla winced with irritation.

Chanat remained motionless. "What I have said, I have said."

Honorius looked down at his writhing fingers again, thinking how horribly they looked like maggots, and then he cried shrilly, "I could have you killed!"

Galla was about to signal to one of her chamberlains to come and escort them away, for the audience was clearly at an end, when the warrior spoke again.

"Nothing you could do to me," he said, smiling broadly, as if at a joke, "would be so terrible as what my lord and king would do to me if I failed him."

Honorius stared at this terrifying barbarian for a little while longer, his small round mouth agape. Then, with a high-pitched shriek, he sprang from his throne and ran off down the steps toward the rooms behind, clutching his skirts up round his bony shanks as he went. His sister stood and hurried after him.

The moment they were gone, Chanat ripped apart the delicate brooch that held the white silk cloak around his shoulders. The cloak slithered from his golden, lean-muscled torso and fell with a whisper to the floor. He turned and trod it underfoot and walked out of the Chamber of the Imperial Audience.

At the gates of the city, his horse was returned to him. He checked the reins, and found that not one of the decorative gold coins was missing. He complimented the guards on their honesty in perfect Latin, vaulted onto his horse, and rode away across the causeway over the flat Ravenna marshlands toward home.

Attila and Aëtius hunted together more and more, along with their slaves, Orestes and Cadoc, until they began to be referred to among the people simply as "the Four Boys."

They competed endlessly in games of wrestling and swordplay, spear and noose throwing, or the ancient Hun game involving furious galloping after an inflated pig's bladder which they called a *piilü*. They came to worship Chanat, the greatest and most fearless warrior among all the people, but he told them to admire not strength but wisdom.

"Wisdom," snorted Attila. "Give me strength any time."

Chanat shook his head. Then he began to speak; strangely, he spoke of Little Bird, though Attila had not mentioned the mad shaman.

Nearby Aëtius stopped to listen, his deep blue eyes grave in his fine-featured face. He, too, wondered about Little Bird, this high-born Roman boy, raised on the solemn teachings of Seneca and Epictetus as much as the doctrines of the Holy Catholic Church, and all their fine words about the wisdom of Providence, and the ultimate goodness of the world. In his heart the words and songs of Little Bird frightened him more than any other.

"There are many reputed to be wise in this world," began Chanat slowly, "but we among the people know that Little Bird alone in all his madness is wise. He is wise because he is god maddened. He alone has walked with the gods in counsel. He sat for nine winters and nine summers on a mountaintop in the holy Altai Mountains, and he ate nothing but a grain of rice a day. For water he sucked the snowflakes that landed on his lips. And for nine long years he never once opened his eyes upon the sensate world, but walked only with the gods, with the unknown powers behind the curtain of the world. When he came back, he came back not with a message of comfort."

They waited for his words.

"He came back from them, those beings with hawk heads and eagle eyes, who cast shadows on the earth bigger than mountains, those makers of the bear's claw and the boar's tusk—such things delight them. Since then, Little Bird only dances, or sings nonsense songs, or talks with his only friend, the wind. He delightedly mocks any who speak wise, grave words about the justice of the heavens, or the high duty and destiny of men. For, he says, we men are only the idle jokes of God."

Aëtius was afraid of Little Bird; or at least of the words that Little Bird madly spoke and sang. And he knew that his friend Attila was afraid, too.

4

THE FOUR BOYS

Attila was preparing to ride out one morning with Orestes, each of them astride one of the squat, large-headed little Hun horses, when Aëtius and his dark-eyed slave boy came riding back into camp.

"You've been hunting already?"

The Roman boy pulled a duck from his shoulder bag.

Attila sneered. "A day's ride, and we'll be in boar country. There's a wooded valley to the northeast. We'll stay the night and hunt tomorrow. But"—he reached over and flicked the quiver that hung from the Roman boy's shoulder—"you'll need more than your little boy's bow and arrows."

Aëtius glanced down and saw the heavy spear slung along the belly of Attila's horse. He rode off without another word, and a few minutes later reappeared, riding out of the camp with a long ashen spear, a thick iron crossbar just below the long, pointed head: a boar spear, to stop the animal's furious charge. For it wasn't unknown for a boar to receive an ordinary spear in its side and yet push its way onward, screaming, right up the shaft to rip open the horse's belly with its six-inch tusks, even in its bloody death throes.

Attila narrowed his eyes as the Roman approached, his silent, faithful little slave behind him.

"Come on, then," he said to Orestes. "He'll have to catch us up."

Driving his heels hard into his little pony, he set off at a gallop across the bright green grasslands of the unfenced and endless steppes.

By the end of an unremitting day's ride, when they reached the edge of the wooded valley, all four boys were exhausted, though none would show it. They said little as they made camp in the shadows of the trees, dragging up firewood and building themselves a comforting orange glow.

"You, boy," said Attila to Aëtius' slave, "bring more firewood up to last the night."

The boy trotted off to do his bidding.

Attila nodded. "He's good."

"He's very good," said Aëtius.

"What people?"

"He's a Celt—British."

"Ah. Good fighters once."

"Good fighters still."

"And he understands Hunnish."

"He speaks and understands Hunnish, Latin, Celtic, Saxon, Gaulish, and some Gothic."

"Educated, for a slave."

"He wasn't always a slave."

The boys stared into the fire for awhile, wondering how else they could compete. Then Attila said, "Here, have some of this." He passed over a leather flask.

"What is it?" asked Aëtius suspiciously.

"Kind of fermented sheep's milk."

"Not koumiss again?"

Attila shook his head. "No, it doesn't get you drunk. It's just sheep's milk that's gone sour, sort of. It keeps well in hot weather."

Aëtius put the neck of the flagon cautiously to his lips and tasted. An instant later he held the flagon aside and spat his mouthful of the stuff straight into the sizzling fire.

Attila roared with laughter and took the flagon back.

Aëtius wiped his lips, an expression of revulsion on his face. "What in *Hades* was that?"

Attila grinned broadly. "We call it *yogkhurt.*"

"*Yogkhurt?*" repeated Aëtius, even more gutturally.

Attila nodded.

Aëtius shook his head. "Sounds as bad as it tastes."

The next day they went looking for boar. They picked up a spoor very soon—telltale hoofprints of two main toes, with two barely visible either side—but lost the track in the dense undergrowth where their horses couldn't go. Later they found what looked like a wallow beside a fallen tree trunk. Attila dismounted and gave a low whistle, crouching beside the tree trunk, running his fingertips over the bark.

"What is it?"

"These grooves. They're deep." He grinned. "It's a big one."

They rode on.

"It'll be lying up somewhere," Attila called back. "We'll have to flush it out."

"I can smell something," said Cadoc.

Attila turned and stared at the slave boy. "You have boar in your country, as well as perpetual rain?"

The boy nodded. "Many boar. In the autumn, up in the beech woods, we—"

The boar came screaming out of nowhere. It flashed across Attila's mind, even as he glimpsed the great, bristling curve of its back as it charged snorting toward them, that it must be a mother and they had stumbled on her close to her litter. No ferocity in nature like the ferocity of a mother protecting her young. But then he registered the boar's size, the length of its tusks—eight inches? nine?—and his ears registered the thunderous galloping of its small hooves across the clearing, carrying its massive weight of four hundred pounds or more—

His ears were filled with a more dreadful sound, of a horse screaming. He was lying facedown on the forest floor, his mouth full of a mulch of last year's leaves. His horse was writhing in agony across his legs, as the huge boar worked furiously away on the other side, opening up the horse's belly with lightning-quick slashes of its terrible tusks.

The three other boys dismounted in an instant, and Aëtius scrabbled desperately to drag his spear from its sling. At any moment the boar might tire of tearing the horse's guts from its stomach and turn its beady little eyes and monstrous tusks on them. Or on the other boy, trapped and helpless beneath his dying horse. If the boar trotted round and began to work on him, he would be dead in seconds.

The boar stopped, and there was silence in the glade but for the thrashing of the dying horse. The boar raised its massive head. Aëtius thought it might weigh four hundred and fifty, even five hundred pounds. It was the biggest boar he had ever seen; bigger than any in the arena, in the forests of Silestria, anywhere. The stench of it filled the forest glade with a thick, dark musk, and its cruel off-white tusks, gleaming through the dripping blood and the tendrils of torn intestine from the disembowelled horse—nine inches long was perhaps an underestimate.

The boar stared at them for a little while longer, its flanks heaving furiously as it got its breath back, unhurried and unafraid. Then it sensed movement beside it, and suddenly was afraid again, and hot with rage. It turned to gore the horse. But it wasn't the horse, it was something else.

Snuffing the air, the boar galloped round to where Attila lay trapped and twisted, lying there helpless in last year's leaves, and moved furiously toward the fallen boy with lowered tusks.

The Celtic slave boy moved as fast as a forest animal. He slithered in the horse's spilled guts, scrambled over the mound of its open belly and thrust his sword into the boar's flank, just as the first swipe of its tusks opened up a deep cut across Attila's back. The blade went in less than an inch, but it was enough. The boar turned on him, screaming with fury, and drove straight at him. But Cadoc slipped back over the dead horse and the enraged boar drove its tusks uselessly into dead flesh again. Then it felt a far deeper, more terrible wound along its back, penetrating deeply into its tough old bristling hide. It whipped round on its neat little hooves and saw Aëtius. The Roman boy pulled the spear free again and braced his back against an ancient beech tree. The butt of his boar spear was braced deep among the roots, for a boar that size would knock a man and spear aside like gossamer if they were not rooted in the ground like the roots of an oak.

Out of the corner of his eye, Aëtius saw the Celtic slave boy about to scramble over the horse again and try to attack the boar from behind.

"No, Cadoc!" he cried. "Let him come to me."

The boar eyed Aëtius a moment longer, its ears deaf to their human cries, filled only with the furious pound of blood in its brain. Then it charged.

The thick ashen spear snapped in two like a twig with the force of that five-hundred-pound weight, and Aëtius threw himself aside only just in time. But in its mad unheeding charge, the great boar had also driven its own chest deeply onto the spearhead, which was buried up to the crossbar in its lungs and killing it. The boar reeled back, squealing, and fell to one side, slashing at its invisible tormentors, bright pneumonic blood frothing and spraying furiously from its champing jaws. It struggled to its feet again, but then its hind legs collapsed, its forefeet still planted unyielding in the soft forest floor.

Aëtius crawled to his feet, dazed and shaking, and saw two boys—the two slave boys, both acquainted with the lash and chain of their masters—creep toward the dying boar from either side, small blades in their hands. Aëtius shouted "No!" to them, for the boar was dying anyway, and yet, even in its last moments, it might turn that massive, bristling head and slash a man open from navel to throat. But the two slave boys for once ignored the command of the master, and moved in closer, carefully avoiding that slowly swinging, bloody head. As one, they pounced forward and drove their blades into the creature's body, Cadoc's blade going deep into its tough, muscled neck, and Orestes' slipping between its ribs. Still the boar swung its head, butting Cadoc and tossing him back into the leaf litter as if with mild irritation, but making no contact with its terrible tusks. Its mad ferocity was draining away now with its blood. It lay down in the leaves, and gave another heave of its blood-soaked flanks, and then after a long while another. And then it died.

Aëtius steeled himself and tried to shut his nose against the stomach-turning reek of the disembowelled horse. He grasped it by its hind legs, ready to drag it off the fallen boy, and shouted orders to the slaves to take hold likewise. But from the other side he heard a cry, and there was Attila. He had hauled himself free, and although he clutched the back of one thigh, where he felt he had twisted a tendon, and he could sense the back of his shirt soaked where the boar's tusk had ripped through the skin of his back, nevertheless he was only slightly hurt, and too full of the furious thrill of the danger to feel real pain yet.

In that instant the mood of the four boys changed, and they were suddenly dancing around in the forest glade as four equals, slapping one another's hands and punching the air, whooping like the most barbarous tribesmen in all of Scythia. They hopped and hollered round the huge, bloody mound of the slain boar, and seized their swords and their broken spears again and stabbed at it ceremonially as they circled. They shouted defiance at the boar's ferocious soul, and even at the unknown gods who made such a creature of blood and horror and set it on the earth with a smile to be a terror and a torment to all men. They smeared themselves and one another with boar's blood, and then a primordial paste of boar's blood and moist forest earth, and howled at the high blue sky glimpsed through the waving light green leaves of the springtime canopy. Four different languages chaotically mingled, Greek and Celtic, Latin and Hun, but all crying the same angry defiance, the same bloodstained defiant triumph over life and death.

At last they fell exhausted to the forest floor and gradually regained their breath, their composure, and their awareness of difference and hierarchy. As their hot blood cooled, and their taut-strung limbs relaxed, they even said prayers, each of them. They prayed to the spirit of the boar, begging forgiveness, and to those nameless spirits behind the curtain of the world who made the boar, who bent and formed its curved spine in their iron hands, set with black bristles, who made its thundering hooves, and shaped its terrible ivory tusks.

Attila ordered the two slaveboys to make a fire, and began to slash the boar's flanks, pulling away the thick hide to reveal the dark pink flesh, the meaty haunches of its powerful hind legs. They spitted the meat on green-wood twigs and roasted them over the fire. Despite the boar's vast size, the four ravenous boys still made considerable inroads into its carcass, before they sank back into the leaves, unable to eat a mouthful more, and fell asleep.

When they awoke it was growing dark. They warmed themselves by building up the fire, by roasting yet more meat, although none of them felt they could eat another thing, and by taking turns to hack at the boar's massive neck. With only their lightweight swords it was hard work, and each boy hacked himself to the point of sweating exhaustion.

"But we can't leave it here," said Orestes. "They'll never believe us."

It was strange that he, like Cadoc, now presumed to speak his opinions before the masters asked for them. But an ease had settled over the four that would not have been possible in court or camp.

Attila nodded. "All that meat's going to waste, anyhow. But we have to take the head back."

After nearly an hour of hacking and slicing through hide, sinew, muscle and bone, at last the mighty head fell free of the neck. There was some discussion about how to get it back, for the head alone must have weighed nearly two hundred pounds. At last it was decided to build a rough travois of strong hazel sticks, drag the boar's head onto it, make it secure with more hazel twigs hooped over the top, and haul the travois back to the camp of the Huns, changing ponies every hour or so.

"We'll be the heroes of the people," said Orestes excitedly.

"The envy of every man there," said Cadoc.

"And the dream of every woman," chuckled Attila.

The other three all looked more or less embarrassed.

Attila grinned. "What, *none* of you have ever done it? To a woman?"

The two slave boys flushed deeply. Aëtius shook his head.

Attila settled back and grinned. "Well, well." It was good to feel powerful. He liked that feeling. After awhile he said, "So you miss home?"

Aëtius looked up and saw he was talking to him.

"You pine for Rome?"

Aëtius pulled a face. "I miss Italy," he said. "Rome is—"

"Rome's a cesspit," said Attila.

"And you escaped it."

"I escaped it," said Attila. "No offense, but . . . your soldiers are useless. Mostly."

The two boys eyed each other a little warily, then Attila laughed. Aëtius didn't.

"And you," said Attila, rolling onto one elbow and waving regally at the two slave boys. "You two. You'll go free and laden with gold the moment we get back to camp."

They stared.

Orestes stammered, "But—but I've nowhere else to go."

Attila said seriously now, "You want to stay, Greek boy? Stay with the dreadful Huns, who eat raw meat and never have baths and refuse to bow to the meek dying and rising god of the Christians?"

Orestes looked down.

"Then stay you will," said Attila. "But slave no more."

Aëtius was sitting cross-legged opposite Attila, watchful and wary as ever. He thought how like a king the boy already sounded, grandiloquently dispensing judgments and freedom and gold to left and to right with regal carelessness and magnificence.

"And you," said Attila, turning to Cadoc, "you'll go free, too. You almost saved my life."

"I *did* save your life," blurted Cadoc indignantly.

For a moment Attila stared at the dark-eyed slaveboy, and Aëtius wondered if he might not erupt in fury at this impertinence, like his fiery uncle. But then he laughed, and they all relaxed. None of them wanted to see Attila lose his temper.

"Very well," he said. "You *did* save my life. And my uncle will lade you with so much gold in gratitude that you won't even be able to walk out of the camp!"

It took two ponies to drag the leaden weight of the boar's head on its hazel-wood travois. Two of the boys rode, and two of them walked, swapping places every hour or so. The three others tried to insist that Attila, at least, should ride, with his torn thigh muscle and his cut back, but he insisted on walking his fair share like the rest of them.

It was an arduous progress, and it was late the following night when they made it back into the camp of the Huns, so only the few warriors on night watch greeted their return.

But the next morning when people awoke and came blearily out of their tents, there in the middle of the camp, set on the back of a high-wheeled wagon to exaggerate its size still further, was a monstrous boar's head, as big as any man or woman of the people had ever seen. Beneath the wagon lay four exhausted, grimy, travel-stained boys, huddled together under a heap of coarse woolen horse blankets, fast asleep.

The people gathered around in open-mouthed amazement, some of the bolder reaching out to touch the boar's great muzzle, or even tap its white fangs with their knuckles where its bloody jaws hung open. And they began to murmur among themselves.

The boys awoke to the sound, and crawled out from under the wagon and stood and stared. When they realized what was taking place, they began to grin and accept the many slaps on the arm or back, and agree that, yes, it was a terrific, and incredibly dangerous, feat that they had managed. They had slain the Monstrous Boar of the Northern Woods, and dragged it, or at least its severed head, all the way home to show the people with their own disbelieving eyes.

Two burly men of the tribe plucked Attila into the air, set him on their shoulders, and began to parade him around, while the women sang and ululated in praise of his great feat of arms. Other men had killed boar, they sang, but Attila had killed the King of the Boar. The sun shone bright from the bold eyes of Prince Attila. Surely there was no warrior in the land like Prince Attila.

Some of the women called out bawdy comments, saying that they would be happy to have a son by him anytime, if he cared to visit their tent one night. . . . Attila grinned and waved and lapped it up, his injured thigh and back forgotten for the moment. Meanwhile, the other three tried not to look too resentful: their contribution to the death of the boar was wholly ignored in favor of the people's prince. Then the parade suddenly came to a halt, the singing died away, and an ominous silence settled heavily upon the crowd.

There stood King Ruga, flanked by his personal guard. He did not sing and ululate at his nephew's great achievement. He did not hail him as the killer of the King of the Boar, or declare that the sun shone bright from his bold eyes. He stood grimly before him, folded his beefy arms across his chest, set his face grimly, and said nothing.

Attila slid down from the men's shoulders, wincing as he took his weight on his torn thigh muscle again, and stood before him.

"We slew a boar," he said, waving at it as casually as he could.

Ruga nodded. "So I see."

"And the slave boys and the Roman boy, they slew it, too. In fact, they saved my life. The debt of the Royal Blood of Uldin is upon their heads, and I have given them their freedom."

Ruga was silent for a long while. Then he repeated slowly, softly, "You have given them their freedom?"

Attila nodded, hesitantly, his eyes falling away from the king. "That is to say. . . ." His voice weakened and tailed off. He knew he had made a mistake.

The voice of Ruga roared out across the circle, and the very sides of the surrounding black tents shivered under the blast, and as he roared he strode toward the suddenly cowering boy. "It is not *yours* to give a slave his freedom! It is in the gift of the king!" With a gigantic backhanded swipe of his fist he knocked Attila into the dust. "Unless you think that you are an equal of the king, now? Is that it, boy?" He planted his felt-booted foot hard on the boy's chest, knocking the wind from his lungs, and roared again, "Is that it? Boar slayer? Upstart? Malformed whelp from your mother's womb?"

All Attila's ardent spirit died under the righteous wrath of his uncle, and he turned his face into the dust and did not reply.

Suddenly Ruga looked across at the Roman boy, and the people were baffled. A few had glimpsed what Aëtius had done, as had the hawk-eyed, bearded king. Almost despite himself, Aëtius had taken a step forward when he saw Attila knocked to the ground, and his hand had reached for his sword.

Little Bird, with his bird-bright eyes, had seen, and seemed to think it funny. "White boy draw a sward, father! White boy draw a sward!"

"Peace, madman," growled Ruga, brushing the capering fool aside. "You talk of nothing."

"Everything is nothing," said Little Bird sulkily, and sat in the dust.

Ruga turned his lowering gaze back to Aëtius. "Approach me with your weapon, would you, boy?" he rumbled.

Aëtius faltered and stopped, but he did not step back. And he said, so quietly that only the very closest could hear, "Do not hurt him."

"Do you give me orders, boy? The days when the Huns took orders from the Romans are long gone. Aye, and if I were to mete out just punishment to you, for the sins that your people committed in their maltreatment of this boy, this prince of the royal blood—for all his impudence—I would have you stripped of your skin in a trice, and your bleeding carcasses dumped on the anthills of the steppes to be picked clean down to its meager bones! A pretty death for such a high-born boy, eh? Eh? Answer me, boy."

But Aëtius said no more. He took a single step back, dropped hands at his sides, and lowered his eyes to the ground.

The people looked warily on, anxious lest the king's wrath should turn against them, too. He was only one man, and they were thousands, and tens of thousands, yet the will of Ruga, like the will of all the kings of the Huns, and perhaps all kings among men, was as real and powerful as an iron rod on your back, and none but the very strongest might oppose it.

Ruga stepped back from Attila and looked angrily around at his people. None met his gaze.

At last he gestured at his prostrate nephew, and said to his guards, "Take him and his dear Roman boyfriend, too, and lash them to the wagon out on the plains. The two slaves—and they are slaves still—they shall serve in *my* tent henceforth, And woe betide you," he called across to the wide-eyed Orestes and Cadoc, "if you should spill so much as a drop of koumiss when you refill my royal goblet, do you hear?"

Ruga turned on his heel and strode back to his great adorned pavilion, and the chastened people shuffled slowly away. The two slaves crept uncertainly after the king.

And the two boys, Roman and Hun together, were led out by a group of spearmen, and walked for three miles across the baking steppe, until they came to a high flatbed wagon, the grass grown long about its solid wooden wheels. There they stripped the boys naked, and lashed them flat on their backs across the bed of the cart, even their necks and heads tied so tightly that they could not turn away from the sun. And they left them there, to burn and then freeze for a day and a night.

"Well," said Attila companionably, when the guards had ridden away back to camp and they had only the whispering wind and the burning sun for company.

"Well," said Aëtius.

"Here we are."

"Indeed."

"Are you thirsty?"

"Of course I'm thirsty. Have you got any water?"

There was a pause. Then for some reason, from the fear before and now the long pain of the day and the night that lay ahead of them, they began to laugh. They laughed hysterically, until the tears ran over their cheeks.

Attila said, "Stop, stop, we need to conserve our water," but they only laughed the more.

Eventually the laughter died on their lips, and the tears dried on their cheeks, and they fell silent.

The sun burned down. They screwed their eyes shut, but the red and orange sun cooked through their lids. Their lips began to dry and crack, and their cheeks and foreheads to burn.

"Keep your mouth closed," said Attila. "Breathe through your nose."

"I know, I know," said Aëtius.

"We'll survive this."

"Damn right we will."

Toward dusk they heard a sound in the long grass, not far away. For a moment they hoped it might be the guards, come back to release them, Ruga having relented of his harshness. But no, Ruga never relented of his harshness.

"What is it?" croaked Aëtius, his throat as rough as the skin of a shark.

Attila snuffed the air, and his insides gave a lurch of fear. "Golden jackal," he whispered. "Pack of them."

The Roman cursed, the first time Attila had ever heard him do so, then said, "Can they get up?"

Attila tried to shake his head, but of course he couldn't. "Don't think so," he said. "Make a loud noise if they do."

As dusk settled over the vast and lonely plains, the two boys lay in taut silence, hearing and smelling the rank hot smell of the golden jackals as they snuffled round the wheels of the cart, raising their damp noses into the air and sniffing the warm, salty aroma of sunburned human flesh.

Although unable to raise or turn their cruelly bound heads, the boys knew that the jackals were just below them, their slender, powerful jaws drooling, slavering into the long grass. And both boys imagined the same thing: the feel of those sharp white teeth as the creatures tore at their stomachs, pulled the skin aside, and delved their long muzzles into their innards, devouring their rich, bloody livers and spleens as they lay there, still alive. Or the jackals nuzzling lower, and feeding on their sunburned, exposed . . .

Whether it was simply a warm gust of air, or whether it was truly a jackal, its forefeet up on the side of the wagon beside his head, its hot canine breath wafting over his face, Attila would never know. But with sudden urgency he said, "Now—*shout*!"

The boys broke into a frenzied shouting, as loud as their blistered and sun-parched throats could manage. When they stopped shouting they could still hear the distant whimpering and bickering of the jackal pack, far off now and curving away into the feather grass.

But they would be back.

Throughout many more hours of dusk and night, Attila and Aëtius lay
side by side, driving the jackals away with their panicked, grating voices
raised to shouts. It would be only a matter of time before the jackals realized that shouting was all they could do, and then . . . But the jackals
never did realize.

Flies and mosquitoes came out and bit them from head to toe. Moths
fluttered up from the long grass and sipped the crusted saltwater that lay
on their skins. Toward dawn both boys were shivering so badly in the
chilly steppe land night, that their chattering teeth sounded like the call
of two giant cicadas in the day.

But they had survived. Dawn was coming up, surely—and soon the
warriors would come to unbind them, and sling them semi conscious
across the croups of their horses and ride them back into camp.

As the first pale gray of the dawn light washed up over the steppes from
the east, Attila lay in a pained, wretched half dream, and he thought he
dreamed of a voice he knew, saying, "Don't tell me—you're in trouble
again."

In his dream, he opened his eyes, and looked up at the swimming,
familiar face above him, and croaked, "Don't tell me you traveled all this
way, just to see *me*."

Then the face was grinning, upside down over him so that it looked
all wrong, and a sharp blade was cutting the ropes that bound him, and
the blood was flooding back with agonizing needles into his bloodless
hands and feet and flowing hotly under the skin of his scalp.

Aëtius was cut free, too, and after some minutes of gasping and rubbing
their wrists, the boys were offered water in leather flagons. They tried to
guzzle it down, but the flagons were snatched back after only a mouthful
each. Only then did they sit painfully up, and stare at their rescuers.

"Is it really you?" said Attila at last.

"It really is," he nodded.

"And you didn't come here just to see me."

He shook his head. "No, I came here to see my boy. And to take him home."

"Your boy?" Slowly it dawned on him. "The slave? The Celtic boy?"

He nodded.

"But," blurted Attila, "but he saved my life!"

Lucius grimaced. "Like father, like son," he said laconically.

5

THE LOST AND THE SAVED

When the boys' limbs at last felt mobile, they climbed down stiffly from the cart, and Lucius chucked them each a tunic to put on.

"I know some of you barbarians fight stark naked," he said, "but . . ."

"I'm no barbarian," said Aëtius haughtily and in perfect Italianate Latin, far more correctly accented that Lucius's own, with its soft, Celtic burr.

Attila grinned and pulled his tunic on over his head.

"And you are . . . ?" asked Lucius.

"Aëtius, son of the late Gaudentius, master general of cavalry on the Pannonian frontier."

Lucius was taken aback. "I knew something of your father. He was reputed a good commander."

"He was," said Aëtius stiffly.

"Well," said Lucius. "And you are a hostage of peace here with the Huns? They are keeping you well, clearly."

Attila snapped, "Rather better than the Romans keep *their* hostages, I think."

Lucius was silent.

"And who's he?" said Attila, jerking his head at Lucius's silent companion.

"Cievell Lugana," said the old man with the long gray beard. His eyes twinkled at the boy, not unkindly. "At least, that is what I am called today."

Attila eyed him curiously, then shrugged and turned toward the camp. "Your son," he said. "And there's another slave. They're in the great pavilion of the king. At least, they'll be sleeping round the back. Take them both—take Orestes, too, my slave."

Aëtius looked sharply at Attila, but Attila looked back calmly. "It is better for him," he said. "It will not be easy for me here henceforth."

Lucius considered for awhile and then said, "We'll see."

They left their horses tethered lightly to the wagon, and they crept in silence and darkness toward the camp of the Huns.

Cadoc was dreaming, huddled under a flea-bitten horse blanket at the back of the king's pavilion.

The old man who called himself Gamaliel, or Cievell Lugana, and by many other names, smiled over him and murmured, "Time to wake up, song maker, bird catcher, Dreamer of Dreams, of the line of Bran, with the words of the world on your lips. . . ."

Lucius knelt and shook Cadoc awake, and the boy opened his eyes wide, and flung his arms round his father's neck. And they both wept, even as the father held his hand clamped over the boy's mouth for silence.

When the little group of six emerged round the front of the king's pavilion, there were torches burning, for the dawn light was still dim and cold and gray. They were surrounded by a hundred warriors or more, arrows knocked to their bowstrings, arrowheads gleaming coldly in the torchlight. For though the camp of the Huns might stand without walls, no group of armed strangers could creep in under darkness and not be noticed by the keen-eyed spearmen on watch.

For the second time in a day and a night, Attila faced his uncle in defiance, but this time he was one of six and he had more to fight for than merely his own pride. Lucius had come on an unimaginable journey this far to take back his abducted son, and he would not let him go home empty handed.

There was a breathless silence across the camp of the Huns, and over the natural arena formed by the ranks of watching tribes people, spell bound at this moment of terrible drama. All eyes switched back and forth between the small figure of the boy Attila and the hulking, bear-skinned figure of his uncle, King Ruga. The crackling battle of wills taking place between them was almost visible in the air in its intensity.

"Uncle . . ." began the boy at last.

"You have led armed strangers into my kingdom," said Ruga. "You have shown them the way into my camp. You have brought them to the felt walls of my pavilion with their swords drawn. You would see me slain in my sleep like a beast, Attila?"

Attila tried to protest, but Ruga spoke over him. "You have betrayed the people, O my nephew and my blood. You have opposed my word, and you have shamed and humiliated me before all the warriors of the tribe."

The boy never flinched, though by the law of the tribe any man there could have drawn a knife at any moment and slain him where he stood, for he was a pronounced traitor. But he did not stir.

Then King Ruga did a very strange thing. Slowly and, some who watched might have said, with profound sadness, he walked over to the boy, who remained unmoved and seemingly unafraid. The burly, full-bearded warrior-king reached out and laid his hands on the boy's shoulders. He looked down at him with an expression that appeared to mingle anger, pride, sorrow, and the deepest affection. And then he said, in a soft, deep, rumbling voice that few who strained to listen could hear, "Your brother Bleda is a fool, Attila."

The boy looked up then.

Ruga held his shoulders more tightly. "I would have made you my heir," he whispered. He blinked his bleary eyes and said even more softly. "I would have given you everything. I would have given you my kingdom and my nation, and dominion over the steppe lands from the Holy Mountains to the shores of the Roman River. For never will I have sons of my own, nor know another to match your matchless spirit. And now, instead, I should order you put to death. . . ."

Ruga turned away, and his broad, fur-clad shouders seemed to slump, like the curved, weakened shoulders of an old man.

"Let them go," he said. "Let them all go—except Prince Attila."

Just then, when it seemed that the ordeal was over and the grim sentence was passed, a blur of a figure came tumbling over in the dust toward the king, and sprang to his feet in the center of the circle. It was Little Bird, and all his attention was on Gamaliel.

"Why, father, do not set free this old fool here with the long gray beard!" he cried. "For he knows too much, too much. He is come to torment me, to torment all of us, with his wise and grave old sayings, about how the gods are just. His words are like flies which bother my weary ears."

Ruga turned back and stared in dim puzzlement at this encounter between his fool and the one among the strangers whom he had marked least.

"If the gods are just, old fool," went on Little Bird, capering round the still and silent figure of Gamaliel, "they are also unjust. You forget, you forget, you grow old and muddle headed in your wise and serious dotage. Do the gods weep to see the man on his cruel cross, with the Christians kneeling adoringly at his feet? They weep and they mourn, and then they turn round and bare their asses and fart in his bleeding face."

Gamaliel only looked on, grave and unblinking, at the dancing, mocking Little Bird, and said never a word.

"If God is a creator, He is also a destroyer. If God is a God of love, He is also a God of hate. You know it is true, old beardy fool, which is why you say nothing and cling to your flyblown old words of comfort and lies. Comfort and lies is all you dispense, old fool, like a quack of a doctor in the marketplace, selling flavored mare's piss for a panacea." Little Bird spun round on the spot and pointed at Attila. "Will the gods reach down and save the broken-hearted exile-boy sent away all unjustly under the grinning sky?"

"Mind your words, fool," growled Ruga, but Little Bird paid him no heed.

"They will not, and you know it. The exile-boy will ride broken hearted away, and the gods will not reach down and save him, not until my mother gives birth to piglets, and the moon falls down from heaven. You know it is true, old beardy fool, and I speak the way of the gods. It is time you paid another visit to the Old Man of the Mountains, old wanderer, old fool. Your wits are grown flyblown and mouldy as a month-dead mule."

Little Bird pointed unexpectedly at Cadoc, standing timidly near his father. "You are wise, dark-eyed boy. For he there loves his little sword, and he there loves his city, and he there holds the fate of the world in his scrotum, but you there hold the fate of the world on your lips. And words make the world, they do, for words are the movers and shakers of the world forever."

Attila and Orestes shivered at these last words, but Ruga stepped forward and cried, "Enough!" This untouchable shaman and fool, Little Bird, drove his mind to a spinning distraction sometimes.

"It is never enough, my father!" cried Little Bird, skipping across to where Ruga stood, and kneeling in exaggerated obedience. "Never enough!" With that he curled up in the dust at the king's feet, and appeared to fall fast asleep.

Ruga reiterated his commands, and not even Lucius or Gamaliel dared to argue with them. The king's violent and uncertain temper was plain to see, even at his most bowed and sorrowful.

The five—Lucius and Gamaliel, Aëtius, Cadoc and Orestes—were escorted from the camp by spearmen. They stopped and looked back once. Their eyes met the eyes of the Hun prince, and everything was said in that wordless exchange. And then they were gone.

The prince should have been put to death. The whole tribe knew it, and yet the whole tribe knew why he was not. They had seen the way their king had looked on him. They had seen a bitter, remorseful affection, even love, in the harsh king's eyes, which they had never seen before. And they knew that Ruga would never give the order for the prince to be put to death.

Later that day Attila was given a horse to ride and provisions for seven days. He was held down by two strong men while one of the priests leaned over him with a bronze knife, and cut three deep slashes in his forehead. The boy gritted his teeth and strained against the men's grip, but he made no sound.

Then he was helped up, trembling, onto the horse. The priest washed his hands clean of the blood-guilt in a bowl of water. He sprinkled some of the water in the direction of the mounted boy, and proclaimed the sentence before all the assembled tribe.

"For thirty summers and thirty winters you will ride out alone, wherever you choose. But you will not come into the country of the Black Huns, neither into the country of the White Huns. For they are your people, whom you have betrayed. You will ride alone and none shall own you. If you try to return into the country of your People, whom you have betrayed, every man's hand shall be against you, and every man's sword arm shall be raised upon you, and every woman's and every child's cry shall betray your presence. To mark your exile, you have been cut upon the forehead with the tripartite mark of the traitor. Now ride forth, with none for company but your own sin-stained soul."

And the boy rode out into exile.

None was permitted to look out after him, or even speak of him again. For the people, their prince had ceased to exist.

Yet speak of him they did. At the wooden water trough later that day, the women said among themselves, "He will return." One old woman looked out across the steppes to the east, and crinkled her eyes, and saw in her mind an image of that strange, fearless boy riding away across the endless grasslands, the hooves of his horse stirring up the dust of the plains as he rode. She nodded and said again, "He will return."

After riding all morning eastward, the brokenhearted exile came to the grave mound of his father. And there on the grave mound sat Little Bird, cross-legged, rocking back and forth, his topknot swaying comically as he conversed with his only friend, the wind.

The boy sat his horse and said nothing.

It was death for any of the tribe so much as to look at the cursed exile, let alone speak to him. But Little Bird was different and under the protection of the gods. He spoke to Nameless-Under-a-Curse as blithely as he would speak to anyone.

"Give directions to Little Bird," he sang. "Give directions to a seed head of feather grass on the wind. The result is much the same."

Little Bird talked always as if about himself, but really he talked about the people. He talked of tragedy with a laugh, and he spoke mournfully of the most ludicrous and trivial things. He rode into camp facing backward on his horse, he dressed as a woman, he danced and clapped his hands at children's funerals. He said that it was all one: that the gods bled when mankind bled, but they laughed when they bled, too.

Now he seemed to think the exile of Attila was amusing in the extreme. He joyfully sang one of his little songs:

Under the earth I go
On an oak leaf I stand
I ride on a filly that never was foaled
And I hold the dead in my hand.

The boy heeled his horse and began to walk wearily on.

"One day, when you were a baby, baby piglet. . . ." Little Bird called after him.

Attila hesitated, sighed, then drew in his horse. "What?"

Little Bird grinned tormentingly. "One day, when you were a boy—do you not remember? You and your brother, Bleda with the Brain like a Grass Grain, went out to play in the woods. We were camped near the marshes of the Dnieper in those days. Do you not recall, little father?"

Attila shook his head.

"And in the woods, you met an old woman," went on Little Bird lilt-ingly, "you met an old woman with a wart on the end of her nose, a wart the size of a molehill. But that, I admit, is by the by. And maybe I'm making it up altogether. Maybe I'm making it *all* up altogether."

The boy waited patiently. His horse shook its head free of flies and waited likewise.

"Anyway. The woman smiled her ghastly smile—and a bat flew out of her mouth as she smiled! And she creaked and croaked and pointed her pointy old finger, and she told you and your ass-brained brother that the first of you to run back and hug your mother—your mother was still alive in those far-off days, little father, and very beautiful and lovesome she was, too—"

The boy did not flinch.

"—that the first of you to run and hug your mummy would be king of the world. Now, if some droopy nosed old beldame, and with droopier milk sacks by far, I fear—if such a noisome old dame, as I say, were one day to accost *me* in a bat-haunted forest and tell me to run and hug my mother, I might think twice before doing her peculiar bidding. But not you, O innocent, boyish little chap that you were in those days, nor your galumphing, ass-brained brother. So you both set off running, in your quest to become kings of the world. And your galumphing, ass-brained brother gets to your mother first, where she is sitting so beautiful on a rug in the sunshine and carding sheep's wool, or whatever it is that women do all day. And much startled was she to get a hug all out of the blue that way from Bleda her ass-brained son. But you, O noble princeling, were way behind, for you had fallen flat on your face. Or perhaps your not so ass-brained-as-he-looks elder brother had tripped you up as you ran? For *I* never said that the world was a just and joyful place, little father. At all events—in falling—in falling, you seized two great handfuls of dust. And you stood and shouted to your brother that you had seized your mother earth. He looked back, did Prince Bone-Headed Bleda the Dim, and he saw your little joke, and oh! how he did scowl!"

Little Bird paused and regarded the boy on the horse with eyes which twinkled with strange, otherworldly amusement. "Well," he said at last. "What do you make of that tale, little father?"

Attila's eyes lowered slowly toward the ground as he heard the madman's words. Then he slowly reined his horse around, and began to ride on.

"O King of the World!" Little Bird cried, throwing a single blade of feather grass like a spear futilely after him. "O Princeling! O Little Father of Nothing!"

As to the five, they took their separate ways.

Orestes vanished one night, soon after they had left the camp of the Huns, long before they crossed back over the Kharvad Mountains, and they never saw or heard from him again.

After fond farewells, Gamaliel went south toward Byzantium, where he said he had pressing business.

Aëtius they said farewell to at the gates of a Danube fort, and he was taken from thence back to Rome.

Lucius and Cadoc, father and son, made the long, long journey home to Britain.

As to their homecoming, and the joy that was there in the eyes of Seirian, wife and mother, and in the upturned face of curly haired Ailsa—it would take a pen greater than mine to do that scene justice.

But I do not suppose that there has been such pure happiness often in the history of mankind.

There was only one more encounter before the exiled prince left the land of the Huns forever.

Two more days to the east, on the horizon he saw a figure sitting on a horse. The figure did not stir. A full hour later, he pulled up alongside.

"Stolen?" he said, indicating the horse.

The other boy nodded.

Attila examined it. "Rubbish choice. It's half spavined already."

The boy grinned.

Attila grinned, too.

Master and slave rode on into the eastern steppe lands together.

Once back in Rome, Aëtius was adopted by a high-ranking, self-regarding but not unkindly senatorial family. In the autumn he was given a personal pedagogue, for it was felt that his manners and education must have fallen behind dreadfully during his time with the unwashed Huns.

The boy regarded the pedagogue with a certain aloof scorn. "Greek?"

The pedagogue nodded.

"Ever traveled beyond the Alps? Ever fought in battle? Ever—"

"Aëtius," interrupted his adoptive father, "that is enough."

"No, master," said the pedagogue mildly. "It is true that I am neither a traveler nor a soldier. But not all men are born for the same tasks."

Aëtius considered for a moment, and thought it a fair enough answer. "What is your name?"

"Priscus," said the pedagogue. "Priscus of Panium."

EPILOGUE

And there, lest I begin to sound as self-important and disingenuous as Caesar in his dubious *Gallic Wars,* let me cease referring to myself in the third person.

Upon Aëtius's return to Rome from the camp of the Huns, yes, it was I who for two short but rich years was his pedagogue. At sixteen he left home to join the army. But for those two years I shaped and formed him, as I had others, though only five years his senior. And I watched over his progress for fully the next forty years.

As an old man I have come to write the life and times of the most remarkable pupil I ever taught, the most remarkable man I ever knew. Or rather, the life and times of Aëtius and Attila. For you cannot write about one without the other. They were sun and moon, they were night and day, they were as destined and inseparable as lovers, as Troilus and Cressida, as Dido and Aeneas. Nothing could separate them, yet nothing in the end could bring them together, either: for the great tide of history, or perhaps the will of the unknown gods, was set against them.

And a more tragic tale of two great men I do not think there has ever been.

LIST OF THE PRINCIPAL PLACE NAMES MENTIONED IN THE TEXT, WITH THEIR MODERN EQUIVALENTS

Modern equivalents marked with an asterisk are approximations only.

Aquileia—a little town still bears the name, on the Laguna di Grado. No Roman remains are visible.

Aquincum—Budapest

Argentoratum—Strasbourg

Augusta Vindelicorum—Augsburg

Baiae—Baia

Balaton, L—Lake Balaton

Beneventum—Benevento

Bononia—Bologna

Britain—England and Wales

Caledonia—Scotland

Campania—the countryside around Capua, known to the Romans as *Campania Felix*—Happy Campania, on account of its natural beauty, gentle climate, and extraordinary fertility, which often allowed three crops a year.

Cannae—Canne della Battaglia

Cappadocia—Central Turkey

Capua—Capua Vetere

Carnuntum—Hainburg*

Caudium—San Martino*

Chersonesus—Sebastopol

Cisalpine Gaul—Lombardy*

Colonia Agrippina—Cologne

Consentia—Cosenza

Cumae—Cuma

Dacia—Romania*

Dubris—Dover

Dumnonia—Devon

Durostorum—Silistra, Romanian-Bulgarian border

Epidaurus—Dubrovnik

Euboea—Evvoia

Euxine Sea—the Black Sea

Falerii—Civita Castellana

Falernus Ager—a district of northern Campania, and origin of the magnificent Falernian wine

Florentia—Florence

Gades—Cadiz

Gallia Narbonensis—that quarter of Gaul commanded from Narbo Martis, or modern Narbonne. Roughly, the Languedoc/Roussillon area.

Gaul—France

Gessoriacum—Boulogne

Harvatha Mountains—the Gothic name for the Carpathians (see "Kharvad")

Illyria—Bosnia/Serbia*

Isca Dumnoniorum—Isca of the Dumnonii, i.e. Exeter

Isca Silurum—Isca of the Silures, i.e. Caerleon

Isle of Môn—Anglesey

Kernow—Cornwall

Kharvad Mountains—the Hun name for the Carpathians (see "Harvatha")

Lauriacum—Enns*

Londinium—London

Lucrine Lake—near Baia. Oysters were first farmed here, by the enterprising Sergius Orata, in the first century BC. He had already made a fortune inventing the domestic shower. See Pliny, *Natural History.*

Lugdunum Batavorum—Lugdunum of the Batavians, i.e. Leiden

Lutetia—Paris

Margus—Pozarevac, Serbia

Mauritania—Morocco and Northern Algeria*. *Not* to be confused with present-day Mauritania to the south, virtually unknown to the Roman world.

Mediolanum—Milan

Neapolis—Naples

Noricum—Austria*

Noviomagnus—Chichester

Numidia—Tunisia*

Ophiusa—a Greek name meaning "abounding in snakes," common throughout the Eastern Mediterranean. Rhodes and Cyprus were each known colloquially as "Ophiusa"—"Snake Island." Scythian Ophiusa, a Greek trading station on the Euxine, is today's Odessa, in the Ukraine.

Panium—a humble and unremarked little town in Thrace

Pannonia—Hungary*

Patavium—Padua

Portus Lemanis—Port Lympne, Kent. One of the haunting lost cities of Roman Britain; once a bustling international port with a huge natural harbor, now no more than a few broken walls on a green hillside.

Puteoli—Pozzuoli

Sarmatia—see Scythia

Sarmatian Jazyges—the flat, rich, much-coveted pastureland of the Hungarian Plain, that lies between the Danube and the Tisza.

Scythia—Russia, Ukraine, Kazakhstan, and all points east*

Silestria—Northern Bulgaria*

Siluria—South Wales

Sirmium—Sremska Mitrovica, Yugoslavia

Tanais, R—the River Don, in the Ukraine

Tergestus—Trieste

Teutoburg Forest—Much of present-day Germany. Scholarly consensus now is that the legions of Varus were destroyed near to Osnabrück, north west of the hills still called the Teutoburger Wald.

Tibur—Tivoli

Toletum—Toledo

Trasimene, L—Trasimeno, Lago. The massacre took place between the two villages known to this day as Ossaia and Sanguineto—"the place of bones" and "the place of blood." Any visitor there will soon understand the brilliance of Hannibal's huge-scale ambush and use of landscape.

Vangiones—Worms

Vindobona—Vienna

ACKNOWLEDGEMENTS

Thanks to Jon Wood and Genevieve Pegg at Orion for enthusiasm, encouragement, and patience throughout; to Patrick Walsh of Conville and Walsh, my incomparable agent; to Anthony Cheetham for the original impetus for this trilogy; to Marcella Edwards for all her support; to the wonderful staff of numerous libraries, especially Chelsea, Kentish Town, the London Library, and the Highgate Literary and Scientific Institution; to several people for a quiet place to work, including Mark and Yseult in Somerset, Michael and Trisha in Ashdon, and my parents in Eynsham. And for a not-so-quiet place to work, Anita's, the only Internet café in the entire department of Intibucà, Honduras, where under slightly unusual circumstances, much of this novel was revised: thanks, Anita. The "sibylline verses" that appear on pages 288 and 293 were first set down in English by the Victorian poet, Arthur O'Shaughnessy; the translations on pages 46–48 are my own, from a eulogy of Claudian to the Emperor Honorius which is, alas, quite genuine.